COSMIC CONTACT

Also by James A. Cusumano

Fiction

The Fallen: As Above, So Below

Twin Terror: Good Seed, Bad Seed

The Dialogue: A Journey to Universal Truth

I Can See Clearly: Rise of a Supernatural Hero
(Book One of The Luc Ponti Chronicles)

Seagull's Revenge: Beyond Fear
(Book Two of The Luc Ponti Chronicles)

Nonfiction

Freedom from Mid-East Oil
(with coauthors Jerry B. Brown and Rinaldo S. Brutoco)

Cosmic Consciousness:
A Journey to Well-being, Happiness, and Success

BALANCE: The Business-Life Connection

Life Is Beautiful: 12 Universal Rules

JAMES A. CUSUMANO

COSMIC CONTACT

THE NEXT EARTH
A NEW BEGINNING

THE LUC PONTI CHRONICLES
– BOOK THREE –

Waterside Productions
Cardiff-by-the-Sea, California

Printed in the United States of America
First Printing, 2023

ISBN-13: 978-1-958848-68-5 (print edition)
ISBN-13: 978-1-958848-69-2 (e-book edition)

Waterside Productions
2055 Oxford Avenue
Cardiff-by-the-Sea, CA 92007
www.waterside.com

For
Cosmic Consciousness

The source of all love, compassion,
understanding, forgiveness, truth,
intelligence, and wisdom . . .

CONTENTS

PART IV COMMUNION

PART V EXTRATERRESTRIALS

PART VI THE NEXT EARTH

"When the mind has settled, we are established in our essential nature, which is unbounded Consciousness. Our essential nature is usually overshadowed by the activity of the mind."
—PATANJALI

AUTHOR'S NOTE

If you have not read Books One and/or Two . . .

As with most authors, I hope that my novels reach as many readers as possible. However, if you don't intend to read Books One and Two and have decided to just read Book Three, you can get a good sense of Luc Ponti's and the SPI Team's evolutionary path by reading the synopses in Appendix III, complete with "spoilers" and more. Of course, you won't get a sense of the personal growth and subtleties of the protagonists, or be privy to a number of action scenes; however, there is enough substance in these summaries to provide the necessary background to understand the thrust of Book Three.

I'M AN ARDENT BELIEVER in the power of positive thinking. Used in the right way, with proper follow-through, it can help manifest many things in your life. In fact, it has brought about most of what I've sought over the years.

However, when what you seek depends on a major change in the thinking and behavior of billions of people, it can be a much more challenging affair. And so it is with global topics such as climate change, the elimination of nuclear arsenals, universal acceptance of diverse cultures, and several more complex issues that brilliant men and women have toiled over for time immemorial. Many of us would like to simply wish these concerns away.

In *Cosmic Contact*, we come face-to-face with one of these existential issues—and it's for real: climate change. As with Books One and Two, I've taken the license to weave together fact and fiction. The facts are based on good science and meshed with fiction—sometimes with *science* fiction—which means that it's often conjecture and not yet proven as scientific fact. By proceeding in this way, sometimes I employed the "possible," did my best to lend credence to the "implausible" becoming possible, and avoided the "impossible"—those actions that violate the laws of classical and quantum physics, or Einstein's special and general relativity.[1]

I have two objectives in this approach: First, I'd like to provide you, the reader, with entertainment based on a fusion of espionage, politics, science, technology, and what some might call the paranormal. And second, I'd like to present one vision of where humanity is headed over the next several decades in its battle with anthropogenic climate change; the short- and long-term global impact that is likely to occur; and in a final analysis, what changes could be made to ameliorate the drama that has already begun to unfold and is primed to accelerate. Unlike previous climate-induced extinction events over the last billion years, this time our human species is a primary contributor.

It's my conclusion that the unfortunate endpoints can no longer be prevented, but hopefully, with enough political and societal will, they can be minimized by creating reasonable means for adaptation to a new and sustainable "state of the world." I'd like to believe that there's still some hope for a reasonable future for humanity—actually, for all Earthbound species.

I like the quote attributed to Roman emperor Marcus Aurelius: "Live each day as though it were your last, without frenzy, without apathy, and without pretense." In doing just that, it has been my experience that you can appreciate the power of gratitude for life itself and what it has given you. Then, nothing—not even the smallest of comforts—will be taken for granted, and your focus will be on those things that are truly important to you.

Jim Cusumano
www.JimTheAlchymist.com
April 14, 2023

---

[1] In Books One and Two of this trilogy, Thay, the Buddhist-monk member of the Super Paranormal Intelligence (SPI) Team, spent quite some time instructing the other members of the team on the physics of consciousness so that they could optimize the use of their superpowers and achieve highly improbable tasks. He called this science *spiritual physics*—no theological or religious connections intended. There is a review of Thay's teachings in Appendix I.

Part I

A WORLD ADRIFT

BEYOND BELIEF

"Life can only be understood backwards;
but it must be lived forwards."
— SØREN KIERKEGAARD

JANUARY 2030—WHAT IN THE WORLD?

"What were they thinking? How in God's name, or anybody's name, for
that matter, could they have done this to us?"

There's likely not a young person alive today who hasn't angrily ver-
balized these comments more times than can be counted in one form
or another, directed at the generations that came before them. Yes, the
future can be a disappointment, but what do you do when you're told
that there may be no future? This potential existential crisis has oc-
cupied the thinking of the SPI Team for some time, and it is finally
beginning to dawn on many of the inhabitants of planet Earth—unfortunately, much later than it should have. . . .

EVERY FOUR YEARS, the National Intelligence Council, which represents all 18 US intelligence agencies, publishes the results of a detailed analysis in a document called Global Trends. A comprehensive
work by analysts within the intelligence community, with extensive
input from experts in various disciplines from around the world, it's
an assessment of where their best data and intel suggest the world is

3

headed over the next two decades. Although not a precise forecast, it has often been correct.

In 2008, for example, although the world had not experienced similar physical and emotional devastation since 1918, the report presciently warned of the possible emergence of a perilous pandemic, originating during the next two decades within East Asia, and rapidly spreading throughout every corner of the world. No place on Earth would be untouched, except perhaps a few isolated places in the Arctic and Antarctica.

The 2020 report[2] found the predicted pandemic, COVID-19, to be the most significant, singular global disruption since World War II, with medical, political, and security implications that would reverberate throughout the world for many years to come, and indeed, have and will continue to do so. True to form, this pandemic was a preamble to a far darker picture of what began to unfold with increasing ferocity during the past decade.

It's important to recognize that viruses first appeared on Earth about 1.5 billion years ago. They have since become quite "intelligent," having had lots of time to "learn" about the process of viral evolution. It's why there have been numerous deadly virus pandemics since then, and this will continue to be the case until the end of all life on Earth some 7.5 billion years from now, when our sun morphs into its red giant phase and expands beyond Earth's current orbit and swallows it.

The 2020 intelligence report accurately foresaw a more contested world divided by forces and violence resulting from the potential impact of accelerating climate change, aging populations, financial crises, and new technologies. This strong polarity among people, institutions, and governments correctly anticipated a deep divide—rather than the unification of people around the world—thereby straining societies and generating shocks that could be catastrophic, and planting the seeds for long-lasting damage to humanity.

The report accurately concluded that the gap between addressing critical national and global challenges such as climate change, and the ineffectiveness of the institutions charged with addressing these challenges, would continue to grow, so that state, national, and global politics would likely become more volatile and contentious. No region

---

[2] https://www.dni.gov/files/ODNI/documents/assessments/GlobalTrends_2040.pdf.

would be immune, nor would there be any effective strategies implemented to deal with these critical issues.

At the international level, the intelligence agencies also correctly anticipated a world increasingly shaped by pressures applied by an insecure, yet strongly egocentric Russia—that is, Vladimir Putin—which wanted more respect from the major powers. Hence, the outbreak of "Vladimir Putin's War," initiated in Ukraine on February 20, 2014, and accelerated by Russia's invasion of that country on February 24, 2022. The agencies also focused on China's challenge to the United States and the Western-led international system, thereby increasing the risk of conflict.

In support of this outcome, we now see large segments of the global population having become intensely suspect of private institutions and governments that are perceived as either unwilling, or worse—unable—to address their needs. A majority of people have continued to gravitate to like-minded groups in their desire for community and security. They include ethnic, religious, and cultural identities as well as groupings around interests and causes, such as the right to carry arms and freedom of the individual—regardless of whether these groups have the correct or best answers or not. They provide potential recruits with a common mantra: *I like what you say. I think like you do. Everyone better get on board with us—or else—no matter what!*

At the same time, as populations have become increasingly empowered and demand much more, governments have come under even greater pressure from new, overwhelming challenges and diminishing resources. This widening gap has created greater political volatility; the continued erosion of both trust and democracy; and expanded roles for alternative providers of governance, irrespective of whether they propose reasonable solutions or not. When swallowed in fear and disillusion, it's often the lure and captivation of difference, as in: *Anything's better than what we've got now! Let's try something new!*

Accelerating shifts in military power, demographics, economic growth, environmental conditions, and technology—as well as hardening divisions over new governance models—have increased competition between Russia and China on the one hand, and on the other, a Western coalition led by the United States.

At the state level in the US, relationships between societal groups and their governments in every region of the American continent have faced persistent strain and tension because of a growing mismatch between what the public believes it needs or expects and what the government can or is willing to deliver.

The 2020 *Global Trends* report outlined several possible global scenarios focused on what the intelligence community labeled as *Competitive Coexistence, Separate Silos, Tragedy and Mobilization*, and the *World Adrift*, in which the international rules and institutions were largely ignored by major powers such as Russia and China, as well as regional players and non-state actors. As summarized at the time in a *New York Times* editorial:[3]

> The gloom, however, should not come as a surprise. Most of what *Global Trends* provides are reminders of the dangers we know and the warnings we've heard. We *know* that the world was ill prepared for the coronavirus and that the pandemic was grievously mishandled in most parts of the world, including the United States. We *know* the Arctic caps are melting at a perilous rate, raising sea levels, and threatening dire consequences the world over. We *know* that for all the grand benefits of the internet, digital technology has also unleashed lies, conspiracies and distrust, fragmenting societies and poisoning political discourse. We *know* from the past four years what polarized and self-serving rule is like. We *know* that China is on the rise, and that it is essential to find a manageable balance between containment and cooperation.

The age of misinformation, distrust, and dissatisfaction is upon us. Trying any governance or technology but the status quo has increased and widened the gap between clear thinking and "anything goes."

All of these points increased the "trust gap" between an informed public that believes in the possibilities of government solutions and the ever-increasing level of the wider public with deep skepticism of government and public institutions and a rapidly growing predilection for wild conspiracy theories.

---

[3] *Why Our Spies Say the Future Is Bleak*, April 16, 2021, Section A, p. 22, of the New York edition of the *New York Times*.

The one issue that was woefully underestimated by the 2020 *Global Trends* report was the rapidly emerging potential of a climate apocalypse to eradicate the human race. Yes, eradicate!

In the decade since 2020, the world has experienced a 25 percent increase in atmospheric-warming CO_2 from 410 ppm to more than 500 ppm, with no possibility by the century's end of meeting the 2021 Intergovernmental Panel on Climate Change (IPCC) target of maintaining the rise in global temperature to a maximum of 1.5°C above the preIndustrial readings of the 18th century.

In fact, during each of the last six years, beginning in 2024, a rise of 1.5°C was measured for several weeks. How much higher the temperature will increase beyond the IPCC target depends on whether ineffective global strategies to reduce climate change do a rapid 180 to those that can make a huge difference. Because of action paralysis caused by too many strongly embraced dissonant ideologies in large segments of the global population, this doesn't even look like a remote possibility.

Scientists had warned that superstorms, especially tornadoes, while perhaps not increasing in frequency, were definitely increasing in destructive power due to global warming. Warming seas pumped higher levels of energy into the atmosphere, which directly feeds the force of tornadoes.

On Tuesday, June 30, 2025, an F5 tornado slammed into Oklahoma City and caused thousands of deaths and massive devastation—400-mile-per-hour winds propelled vehicles thousands of feet, and brick homes were swept completely from their foundations. As unbelievable as it may seem, there were still some right-wing climate-change deniers who maintained that this was an act of God bringing vengeance on those damn "Democrat infidels"!

On Wednesday, March 15, 2028—*The Ides of March*—an F4 tornado ripped through Chicago causing more than 500 deaths, massive home destruction, and major structural damage to numerous skyscrapers, estimated at a cost of hundreds of billions of dollars. The message was beginning to hit home.

But it wasn't only tornadoes. Over the last decade, severe category 5–plus super typhoons of unbelievable power rampaged all over Asia. For example, in 2027, a super typhoon slammed into the Philippines causing massive destruction, and deaths in the tens of thousands. Between typhoons and rising sea levels, the surface landmass of this ravaged country has decreased by 15 percent. And so it was in even greater extremes with small low-lying countries like Mauritius and the Maldives, rapidly on their way to complete extinction.

Each year since 2020, the world has experienced record-temperature lows and highs, rapidly rising seas, violent storms, rampant precipitation and devastating floods caused by explosive cyclogenesis, also known as "bomb cyclones"—as never before experienced.

Some countries are so distressed by the reality and direction of Earth's climate change that they're trying to make up for lost time and their inaction by pursuing major geoengineering solutions—for example, launching massive stratospheric solar sails, or sending micro-droplets of sulfuric acid into the upper atmosphere—both meant to reflect back some of the sun's rays. These technologies are completely untested and could have dire unforeseen consequences, not only on their country, but on the world as well—another example of the lack of intercountry cooperation in dealing with a dire global issue. Trust seems to be an admirable virtue of the distant past.

An unexpected negative "catalyst"—methane gas—has contributed to the rapidly rising ocean and air temperatures, which continue to foster climate change much greater than any of the scenarios predicted by the best computer models. It's known as the Methane Accelerator Effect,[4] and until recently, little effort has been expended to understand and eliminate or minimize its impact.

Huge amounts of methane, formed by the degradation of biomass over many millennia, exist in two major sources: permafrost and deep-sea clathrates. Together, they contain hundreds of times greater amounts of methane than all that is available from the earth's total fossil-fuel reserves.

The biggest contributor is Russia. Permafrost covers more than 65 percent of all Russian landmass, and global warming is causing it to melt increasingly quickly, releasing methane gas into the atmosphere.

---

[4]Rinaldo S. Brutoco, *Perspectives: The "Methane Accelerator"—Climate Change Is Moving Past the Tipping Point,* https://worldbusiness.org/perspectives-the-methane-accelerator/.

The thawing of extensive and deep permafrost on the East Siberian Arctic shelf has become a huge issue with no solution in sight. In some places, due to lightning strikes, the ground has caught fire, thereby accelerating the rate of methane release, and converting some of it to CO_2, both climate-changing gases rapidly rising into the atmosphere.

Methane clathrate is a solid similar to ice, formed when water and methane gas come into mutual contact at the high pressures and low temperatures deep within the ocean. Warming ocean temperatures are driving the release of trapped ancient methane gas from deep-sea clathrates.

With a lifetime of more than 100 years after its release and subsequent conversion to CO_2, methane is 25 times more potent than CO_2 in warming the atmosphere. It was *the* driver for two previous mass extinctions on Earth—not CO_2. The Paleocene–Eocene Thermal Maximum (PETM) occurred around 55.5 million years ago and raised Earth's global atmospheric temperature by a deadly 5–8°C. The Permian–Triassic (P–T) extinction event occurred approximately 251.9 million years ago. It was Earth's most severe event of this kind, and nearly every living thing on our planet perished. The causes of this extinction are thought to have been elevated temperatures and widespread acidification of the oceans and their loss of oxygen due to the release of large amounts of CO_2 and methane caused by volcanic activity in Siberia.

Another critical, unforeseen issue to occur over the last decade— likely facilitated by the Methane Accelerator Effect—has been the rapid melting of the ice sheets underneath Antarctica, which continues to release huge volumes of biotically formed CO_2. This was caused by climate change impacting the great Antarctic Circumpolar Current— the largest oceanic current in the world, which flows clockwise, west to east, around the Antarctic continent; and continues to lift CO_2-saturated water from two miles beneath the ocean, releasing it into the atmosphere.

This current has been nearly solely responsible for shrinking and fracturing the huge Antarctic Pine Island and Thwaites Ice Shelves at an accelerating rate. The Thwaites glacier is an immense island of ice, the size of Florida and well over a mile deep. Sea levels are rising at rates faster than ever seen before and are predicted to increase by more than a meter within the next two years.

Storm surges have flooded large parts of Manhattan and many other large cities located on the sea. Unprecedented flooding and destruction has occurred in Mumbai, Guangzhou, Shanghai, Miami, Ho Chi Minh City, Kolkata, Osaka-Kobe, and Alexandria. Many of the low-lying areas on the US coast, such as Florida, Louisiana, and Texas, have been inundated. New Orleans is nearly nonexistent. Bangladesh, among many other large coastal countries in Southeast Asia, is disappearing. The death toll, property devastation, financial crises, and human migration are beyond comprehension.

Many have asked, unfortunately in hindsight: "If we knew, why didn't we do something sooner?" Perhaps *New York Times* film critic Manohar Dargis had the answer when she said a decade ago, "We're too numb, dumb, powerless, and indifferent . . . too busy fighting trivial battles."[5]

With no change in the global status quo in sight, the US intelligence agencies firmly and convincingly estimated that there are at best, 100 to 300 years before the accelerating effects of climate change will result in humanity's annihilation—primarily through massive destruction resulting from intense climate events, civil war, and possibly nuclear extinction. As experienced historically, sometimes due to unforeseen occurrences and circumstances, these kinds of estimates have been wrong before—the worst could come sooner rather than later. Faced with a high probability of the tragic demise of our species, the US government turned to the one thing it can control—its technical agencies. It tasked NASA with a top-secret program: *Project Phoenix*.

Technically uninformed government leaders were quickly counseled by their best scientific advisers that the unprecedented and incredibly challenging goals of Project Phoenix were well beyond the science and engineering base of classical and quantum physics. Where then to turn?

---

[5] https://www.nytimes.com/2021/12/23/movies/dont-look-up-review.html.

Major John Dallant, now director of both the CIA and the NSA, knew of only one possible hope of achieving what would be the most difficult and risky project ever pursued by any scientific community. It had been an eye-opener for him when he'd seen this strategy work successfully a decade ago to achieve what everyone thought was an impossible mission—the takedown of the brilliant but violent Russian operative, Seagull, in Novosibirsk. Access to the power of what Dallant had learned to be spiritual physics would be an absolute necessity for Project Phoenix to even approach success. He knew very well that there was only one source of that expertise on Earth.

Chapter One

THE CELEBRATION

"Only those who dare to fail greatly can ever achieve greatly."
— Robert F. Kennedy

Sunday, April 14, 2030—Washington, DC

It was Bella's 25th birthday, and she was reluctantly on her way to an intimate party with her closest friends, organized by our pal Eric, as well as me, her fiancé, Luc Ponti, at 2941, one of her favorite restaurants in the DC area. Bella had always been uncomfortable with any kind of celebration that focused solely on her.

The restaurant, located in Falls Church, Virginia, was a 30-minute drive from Union Station in DC. I had taken her there about a year ago when unexpectedly to both Bella and myself, I'd asked her to marry me. It was a spontaneous and magical moment for both of us, having been best friends for nearly all of our lives—and much more than that since our junior year at Palo Alto High School. This moment was long in the making.

The nonstop Amtrak train from Baltimore—where Bella lived and worked at Johns Hopkins University as an associate professor of astrobiology—to Union Station was only a 45-minute trip, but it gave Bella some precious moments alone to think about the formidable challenges she feared were in front of her, and that would also affect those she cared about most. She had become increasingly troubled by the pernicious path the world was on.

Eric and I would not accept a no-party get-together. As I'd put it, "After all, my dearest Gravitas [Bella's SPI Team moniker], it's been a quarter of a century, and look at all you've done!"

She'd replied, "Yeah, right, Emperius [my team name], but what about the future—*our* future?" An understandable concern considering the struggles we'd be faced with.

Our SPI Team had thought we could coast for some time after the Seagull debacle nearly a decade ago. But that wasn't to be. Since then, we had inherited increasingly difficult assignments from our "dear friend" Major John Dallant, now a primary influencer in Washington as head of both the CIA and NSA, one of the last administrative changes the president had made before she was kidnapped by right-wing terrorists and then rescued by the SPI Team a week later from a deserted horse ranch in the badlands of Utah, exercising nearly all of our superpowers to do so. It happened so quickly that the world had been completely unaware until the president was safely rescued and the terrorists were apprehended. Good ol' positively inclined Electer (Eric's team name) was fond of saying, "At least this keeps us in practice!"

It certainly wasn't a sedentary life for us. Over the past decade, we'd prevented a series of major terrorist attacks in Chicago, Dubai, Paris, Berlin, and Beijing—the latter staged by the Islamic State (ISIS) in response to what the Chinese had been doing to their Muslim population. Ironically, because of our team's success, China now had a slightly improved view of the US—and surprisingly, was treating their Muslim citizens somewhat better.

But these undertakings could not compare with what was finally globally recognized as happening to planet Earth—even though it had been known and well documented by reliable scientists for more decades than anyone dared to count.

For years, too many public corporations had been driven by their shareholders to better their quarterly performance, and similarly, too many political leaders were consumed by their hunger for the votes necessary for reelection. High levels of office provided power and wealth, two metrics that were drivers for what some leaders perceived as the *only* measure of success—even if it came at a huge cost to others—like their constituents. Too few of these leaders were galvanized and inspired by an admirable sense of Life Purpose to make a positive difference in the lives of those they led and who depended on them.

But time had run out, and this continued to bother Bella's psyche during her waking and nonwaking hours. *Why has humanity foolishly ignored the serious realities for which it is totally responsible, and thoughtlessly by default decided to destroy itself and all other species on the planet as well?*

These kind of thoughts increasingly concerned Bella. As she peered mindlessly out the window to the Maryland landscape streaming by at 135 miles per hour, another frequent mental loop kept repeating: *Why did I spend eight good years of my life in my prime getting an MD and then a PhD in astrobiology only to face the consequences of ever-approaching existential crises from increasingly likely nuclear events, global toxic leadership, and climate change, among too many other possibilities to name? What will the future of life be like on this miserable planet?*

Ironically, Bella's doctoral thesis had been titled *Catalysis: A Critical Force for the Creation of Carbon-Based Life.* Using molecularly designed inorganic and enzymatic catalysts, which Bella cleverly demonstrated could easily have formed eons ago under a broad range of Earth's environmental conditions at that time, she was successful in synthesizing what are believed to be among the first living species to appear on Earth about 3.5 billion years ago—*cyanobacteria*—the blue-green scum that appears in many stagnant ponds. About 2.5 billion years ago, they evolved to a point where they learned to "eat" hydrogen from water and excreted oxygen creating Earth's oxygen-rich atmosphere. It was Nobel Prize material, if there was even a future for such an award.

And her most profound thought: *After nearly a quarter of a century together since we were children in grammar school, Luc and I are finally engaged to be married—but for what? Can we really have children in the face of what's coming? I've heard that many young men are now getting vasectomies.*

This negativity wasn't like Bella. It was simply a fear of future reality—a reality that no one seemed to want to change. She just had to stop thinking these frightening thoughts. They weren't constructive, and lately they'd been increasingly disturbing. Fortunately, she was temporarily distracted by her train pulling into the DC station.

Wearing a tailored, light-pink two-piece suit with matching strapped spike heels, Bella exited the train on time at 6:30 p.m. in Washington's Union Station, located at Massachusetts Avenue Northeast, near the Capitol Building and the National Mall. Opened in 1907, Union Station was a beautifully restored building with vaulted ceilings and arches, and adorned with 36 Roman legionnaire statues perched high above its striking barrel-shaped Main Hall. All eyes were on her, although she wasn't aware. She was immersed in her awe of the hall's decor.

After several moments admiring the station's impressive architecture, Bella abruptly changed the train of her thoughts. *Where's Luc? He was supposed to meet me here.*

She hurried out of the entrance and spotted my 1957 red Chevy convertible, my part-time passion and hobby—a nearly 75-year-old, modified, restored antique. It had originally boasted a 256-cubic-inch (4,340 cc) V8 "turbo-fire" engine, producing 162 horsepower. Strict environmental laws put in place years ago by President Biden and then continually expanded by subsequent administrations weren't exactly compatible with the car's exhaust output; and besides, given that I was a committed environmentalist, I'd made the decision to make a big change.

Working part-time with Eric for several months, we'd converted my Chevy to a totally electric car using the latest Tesla technology—in fact, using an entire Tesla chassis. With its instantaneously responsive electric engine, it could outrun any car made in 1957—including a Corvette—and most of those on the road today.

Eric had even designed a "sound system" synced with the depression of the accelerator pedal. It funneled a loud performance sound of glasspack mufflers through the faux dual-exhaust tailpipes. Glasspacks muffle high-frequency sound, retaining loud, bubbly, deep exhaust tones. It might be totally electric, but it sounds exactly like the souped-up muscle cars from the 1950s.

It was much too peppy for Bella, and I was not beyond sharing frequent moments of acceleration to demonstrate my vehicle's—or perhaps my own—testosterone-driven prowess.

Bella took a deep breath and made a conscious effort to push out of her mind the deeply concerning thoughts that had plagued her for most of her train ride.

I raced up to Bella and hugged her, planting a kiss on both her cheeks and then a direct hit on her soft lips. Almost regaining my breath, I smiled and exclaimed, "God, you look amazing! Sorry I left Boston a little late. And then the traffic here was a bear."

"Not a problem, dear Emperius. Where's Eric? I thought he came up from Manhattan and was working with you at the lab this past week."

"He has been, but showed up two days late. The dean at Columbia had a surprise for him, which kept him in New York longer than he'd planned." I stopped and didn't say another word.

Bella asked, "Really? What now?"

I was going to let Eric share the news, but I couldn't resist. "He's been promoted to associate professor with full tenure and joint positions in the physics and engineering departments! Now, ain't that a cool piece of news?"

"Wow, that's fantastic! I can't wait to congratulate him."

Eric had earned a well-deserved reputation as one of the most creative and productive professors in the physics department. With his focus on engineering physics, he was collaborating with me at MIT to combine novel engineering concepts with my theoretical work on gravity control by modifying the bending of space-time—very far-out stuff.

I was excited to tell Bella even more, but I'd been sworn to secrecy by Eric not to utter a word. "Eric's got another surprise for you, but he wants to share it with you himself. In fact, he left Boston yesterday to get it all set up for you."

"Luc Ponti, that's not fair. Why did you even mention it? Now I have to wait to see Eric. Come on, at least give me a hint. You know how I am. It'll drive me crazy until I see him."

"Sorry, Gravitas, no can do. But look, let's get in the car and head over to 2941. In this traffic, it'll probably take 40 minutes. He must be there by now."

Bella let me have it. *"Si, tu pequeño dolor en el culo!"*[6]

I flashed one of my devious smiles and responded, "Si!"

With my lead foot, we made it to the restaurant in an amazing 30 minutes. Bella was happy I'd installed safety belts. They hadn't existed in commercial vehicles back in 1957. It was 1968 before they were

---

[6]Spanish for "Right, you little pain in the ass!"

mandated in US automobiles, thanks to the efforts of consumer activists like Ralph Nader.

Bella's comment as I opened the door for her was, "You know, 40 minutes, as you anticipated, would have been totally fine with me."

I responded, "But now we have an extra ten minutes to party."

Bella came back with one of her scrunched-up "Yeah, right" faces.

The restaurant had received lots of accolades over the years. Nestled in the heart of Falls Church, it was surrounded by lush landscaping, koi ponds, waterfalls, and a lakeside view.

As we entered the large reception area, Bella was once again impressed by the architecture—30-foot floor-to-ceiling windows, and breathtaking views of the outdoor grounds. Her focus was momentarily broken by birthday greetings from the maître d', but especially by Eric, who was nearly running down the hall to greet her.

"Happy birthday, Bella! Have we got a great program in store for you!"

What could she say? "I'm sure you do, Eric. I can't wait!" Bella smiled and added, "And by the way, congrats on your promotion and tenure. Now the three of us have guaranteed jobs!"

"Thanks, but forget about me. Tonight's all about *you*, right, Luc?"

"Right."

Eric, with his usual enthusiasm, said, "Okay, follow me to the fabulous Koi Room."

Bella was confused. "The Koi Room? Doesn't that seat about 50 people for dinner? You said there would only be a few of us for this party, right?"

I responded, "You're right. But don't worry, we didn't invite more people than I had mentioned to you on the phone. We wanted to go big on decorations, and we love the ambience of the Koi Room."

"Okay, guys, as long as it's just us."

Since it was still light outside, as we entered the Koi Room, we couldn't miss the beautiful scenery, the lake view and waterfall, as well as the amazing decorations throughout.

"Wow! Who did the decorations?" Bella asked.

Eric confessed, "We didn't even try. The restaurant manager put us in touch with a talented event group from DC who did it for us."

Next, Bella's eyes wandered through the dense decor and the beautifully set round table, carefully arranged for six people. And there she spotted someone she'd never seen before: a tall, beautiful, gray-eyed African American woman. Smiling, the woman walked over and stood in front of Bella and next to Eric.

As she extended her hand to Bella, Eric proudly announced, "This is my second surprise for the night. Bella, say hello to my *dearest*, Brianna Williams."

Bella was excited and happy at the same time. "Wow! This is some surprise! Hi, Brianna, I'm so glad to meet you!" She turned to Eric. "You're unbelievable. Why didn't you tell me sooner?"

"I wanted it to be a surprise for your birthday."

Bella answered, "Well, it's a wonderful surprise. I can't wait to learn more about you, Brianna."

Brianna smiled and said, "And I about you as well." She knew that Eric, Bella, and I did some "consulting" for the US intelligence agencies, and that we whimsically referred to ourselves as the SPI Team, but she had no idea what we had actually been doing for the agencies, for the US, and often for the world.

I couldn't contain myself. I flashed a huge smile and said, "You've probably noticed that the table is set for six people."

Bella replied, "Luc Ponti, you little rascal, who are those two places for?"

"Well, one of them, of course, is for Thay, and the other is for a surprise guest." At that moment, as planned, in walked Thay with a young, tall, handsome, muscular Asian man.

Thay was the first to speak. "Namaste, everyone. I know all of you, including lovely Brianna, whom I had the pleasure of meeting earlier this evening. And this, my dearest of friends, is my son from Japan, Pham Tuan Jr." He didn't say another word. He just stood there smiling in his usual mystical Buddhist manner. *A monk with a son?*

Except for me, everyone's jaw dropped as far as their facial anatomy would allow. Then, having previously received Thay's permission, I proceeded to share a deeply personal story that Thay had related to me years ago during the Seagull incident, when I had sought his counsel concerning my then-confused feelings for Bella.

Everyone listened with rapt attention and an increasing sense of compassion as I explained how during Thay's schooling at the monastery in Nepal, he'd met, and quite unexpectedly fell in love with, Amisha, a strikingly beautiful 18-year-old Balinese girl. Amisha had been hired by her uncle, the abbot at the monastery, to help during the summer before she went off to college to study biological anthropology.

Working in the Himalayas gave her an opportunity to pursue one of her passions—high-altitude mountain climbing. Thay had already been doing lots of climbing in the Himalayas, so it was natural that he and Amisha would become close friends. And that they did, and eventually, it went much deeper.

In September, when Amisha returned to her home in Bali, she discovered that she was pregnant. She immediately deferred her scholarship to Universitas Indonesia for two years in order to be with her newborn son, Pham Tuan Jr., during those first years, a critical parenting time for an infant. Subsequently, her mother took over while Amisha completed her studies, although she returned home as often as possible, and always for the summer. Only her unusual personal fortitude and a close, loving relationship with her mom enabled her to refrain from contacting Thay as she weathered the challenges of being a single parent as well as a full-time college student.

Unfortunately, shortly before graduation, Amisha was informed that she had an aggressive form of stage IV breast cancer. She died a few months after graduation, but not before she made her mother promise on her deathbed not to get in touch with Thay until he'd completed his studies at Harvard. Before she left the monastery, Amisha and Thay had made a pact not to contact each other until both had finished their academic pursuits. If their deep feelings were still there, they would then decide how to move forward together—or not. The former, clearly, would require Thay to forgo his calling.

It was also an incredibly difficult six years for Thay as he proceeded to complete his BS degree in a double major of theology and physics, and then a master's degree in theoretical physics. He decided to turn down offers from several top universities to obtain his PhD. He couldn't bear another three years without Amisha in his life.

The day he completed his studies, Thay tried to contact Amisha, only to discover from her aunt in Bali that she'd given birth to their son and had died just after graduation from college. Thay was devastated and wanted to see his son. He learned that the boy had been placed in the care of Amisha's mother. A longtime widow and a native of Japan, she had no other responsibilities in Bali, so she'd returned to Japan to be close to her family and to raise Pham there.

Abiding by her promise to Amisha, she planned to contact Thay after he finished his studies, but that wasn't to be—she died several months before that occurred. Pham was raised by his grandmother's family in Inawashiro, a small village north of Tokyo in Fukushima Prefecture, where the boy developed a passion for the martial arts—especially judo—and eventually became a high-ranking practitioner, competitor, and master-teacher.

Thay had spent much of the last decade working with a Japanese search agent trying desperately to find his son. After so many years, success finally came when Pham registered to renew his passport, which was necessary for him to travel to several other nations to compete in international judo competitions.

When I finished speaking, the group stared at Thay and Pham with heartfelt compassion and awe. Bella walked over, hugged Thay, and softly said, "Thay, Pham, I'm so sorry for both of you—the suffering you must have endured during those years apart!"

Thay, with both arms extended, held Bella warmly by her shoulders, looked deep into her eyes, smiled, and replied, "Bella, there's no need to be sorry. I found my son, and he is beautiful and remarkable—just like his mom. I have received the most wonderful gift any father could ask for."

Then Pham spoke. "Bella, I am elated to have finally found my father and his US family, of which you are an important member. So I, like him, have no sorrow, only gratefulness to be with him and to be accepted as a member of his family here with you, Luc, Eric, and Brianna."

Bella replied, "Thank you, Pham. Both you and Brianna just being here with our team is a birthday present beyond all I could expect. From now on, Pham and Brianna, you're definitely part of our family."

I immediately jumped in to change the tone and direction of the discussion. "Okay, guys and gals, let's not get too emotional on me. We have lots to celebrate, a great dinner, and a couple of presentations."

Bella interjected, "Luc Ponti, whaddya mean, presentations?"

"You'll see. Be patient. They're a surprise!"

Bella smiled and said, "I don't know how many more surprises I can handle tonight!"

Eric came to the rescue. "I'm sure you'll manage. Just wait!"

With that, the servers brought in glasses filled with champagne, and several toasts were made before we all sat down to enjoy the chef's four-course tasting menu. First course: Nantucket Bay scallops with Satsuma mandarin, coconut nage, finger limes, chili, and Thai-basil oil; second course: bluefin tuna with foie gras torchon, kosho-persimmon, and ginger sauce; third course: guinea hen au vin, a Burgundy braised leg with lardon, button mushrooms, turnips, and pomme Dauphine; fourth course: rum cake with huckleberry jam, puffed quinoa, and vanilla Chantilly. Each course was accompanied by an appropriate wine. It was a dinner fit for royals.

I had asked the chef to bring out the food slowly so there would be time for lots of leisurely conversation. And so there was—the round table was perfect for everyone to participate in each discussion.

Bella asked Eric how he'd met Brianna and was excited to know more about her background. Brianna explained that she'd grown up in Harlem with an older brother and a younger sister; her mother was an elementary-school teacher, and her father was a postal worker. At an early age, she showed special talent as a gymnast, and with her personal dedication and some financial support from the Children's Aid Charity in Harlem, Brianna was able to pursue her passion as a gymnast all through high school and become a star athlete.

Eric couldn't help but brag about Brianna, as he was so proud of her. He noted that she'd won numerous national competitions and was the first woman after world-famous Simone Biles to successfully demonstrate the incredibly challenging triple-double in a competition. Known in gymnastics-speak as a triple-twisting, double-tuck, Salto backwards, it's often referred to as "the hardest gymnastic move in the world." As a result of Brianna's success, she was asked to join the US Women's Gymnastics Team and train for the Olympics. But that wasn't to be. Brianna decided to make a difficult personal decision.

She had a longtime parallel passion for science, one that could sustain her for the rest of her life and perhaps allow her to make important contributions to humanity. From her readings and experience during her science courses in high school, she'd become convinced that the world was headed in a dangerous direction because of rampant environmental pollution, and particularly climate change.

She couldn't understand why companies and governments around the world couldn't see the potential impact that was coming our way—and much sooner than many would expect. Brianna wanted to do something about this but couldn't pursue gymnastics and simultaneously manage full-time studies in the necessary sciences and mathematics at a university. Much to the disappointment of her coaches and fellow athletes, she withdrew from gymnastics.

Brianna received a full scholarship to a Harlem "neighbor"—Columbia University—where she majored as an undergraduate in mathematics and chemistry, and then remained at the school for her doctorate in atmospheric physics with Professor James Hansen, the scientist best known for his 1988 congressional testimony on climate change, which helped raise awareness about the dangers of global warming—but apparently, not enough. Brianna had twice read Hansen's book, *Storms of My Grandchildren: The Truth about the Coming Climate Catastrophe and Our Last Chance to Save Humanity*, and was devastated by what Hansen predicted about the future of planet Earth. She resolved to find some way to help those who wanted to address what had become *the* foremost existential issue for our civilization.

As for Pham, he possessed the balanced ego of an accomplished Japanese athlete, and his father proudly spoke about his son and his accomplishments. Perhaps it was a genetic demon—just as with Amisha, Pham's grandmother had died of breast cancer when he was ten years old. She had taught him both Balinese and Japanese. Pham's uncle, who lived in Inawashiro and was a retired officer from the Japan Maritime Self-Defense Force, better known as the Japanese Navy, taught him English, which Pham mastered to a greater degree by reading numerous American classics.

When Pham was a young boy, and because of his serious interest in judo, his uncle introduced him to Sensei Akihiro, an elderly man who had been a high-level judo master and had retired to a small dojo in Inawashiro close to where Pham lived. All through school, he worked with Pham, and after graduation from high school, at Sensei Akihiro's recommendation, Pham moved to Tokyo, where for several years he studied at the Kodokan Judo Institute. He became one of the most accomplished spiritual martial-arts practitioners in Japan.

The tenor of the dinner conversation was energetic and positive, with Eric cracking one joke after another until I quieted him down as I announced my present for Bella, which was a slide presentation filled with photos all the way back from when we were in junior high up through our adventures as part of the SPI Team. It started with our takedown of CIA executive Tamara Carlin, a unique and dangerous Russian double agent, who had been well along a path that if successfully executed, would have endangered the security of the US as well as the entire world. As a result of the secret nature of the information behind these photos and the presence of Brianna and Pham, no deep discussion on their subject matter took place among Eric, Bella, and me.

But the final slide was the best of all, and it brought tears to Bella's eyes. It had been taken by the maître d' of the 2941 restaurant when I proposed to Bella on one knee, asking her to be my lifelong soulmate.

Bella looked at me with tears in her eyes. "Luc, what a beautiful presentation—I'll never forget it. And, yes, as I told you then, I will be your soulmate for the rest of our lives—and beyond! It's all I could think about on the train ride here. But if I'm honest, I also pondered a thought that preoccupies me way too much lately: How can we have children in a world that seems to be spiraling out of control and descending into a black hole?"

I got up from my chair, stood behind Bella, and put my arms around her as she sat there teary-eyed, staring at the last photo on the wall. "Not to worry, Gravitas. We'll find a way."

Bella smiled, and the group applauded. I kissed her on her cheek and went back to my seat.

Good ol' Eric was determined to keep things light. He said, "I agree with Luc. You'll find a way. As I see it, you'll have two great kids—a boy and a girl. Thay will be godfather to the first, and I'll be godfather to the second. No problem—it's all arranged!"

Brianna laughed and quickly responded, "That's one of the many things I love about you, Eric. You always have a long-term strategy!"

Eric replied, "Well, B, gotta think ahead, ya know?"

Everyone started laughing.

Changing directions, Eric said, "Now I'd like to give Bella *my* present."

Bella smiled and said, "Eric, that's sweet of you, but your friendship alone is a beautiful gift."

Eric got up from the table and walked over to the front of the room. "Oh, but dear Gravitas, you'll love this one. I think most of you know that I'm a big fan of doo-wop music from the 1950s. Since you, Bella, and Luc literally brought me back from the dead when we first met, and forever changed my life for the better, I thought it would be appropriate if I offered both of you the benefit of my favorite doo-wop song, *Life Is But A Dream*, by the fabulous Willie Winfield and the Harptones. Imagine that Luc is singing the lyrics to you—except *I'll* do the singing, since we all know he has a terrible voice!"

Everyone, including me, was laughing as Eric picked up the microphone and pushed a button on a portable karaoke sound system—and sang.

None of us had ever heard Eric sing before. Only a few seconds had passed when it became perfectly clear that his voice and range were amazing, and the lyrics were so apropos to Bella and me as a couple. He couldn't have picked a better song—starting and ending with the same lyrical request from me to Bella: *Will you take part in my life, my love? That is my dream.*

Everyone stood up, clapped, and cheered as Eric hit the last note for "dream" in a perfect falsetto. Bella had tears running down her cheeks. She ran over to Eric and hugged him. "Thank you, Electer!"

Eric returned to his seat as Brianna exclaimed, "Eric, I never knew you had such a great voice—and what a beautiful song—so appropriate for Luc and Bella!"

Eric kissed her on the cheek and quietly answered, "Thank you."

When the applause died down, Brianna noted, "You know, Bella, everyone here gave you a special and personal gift—Luc with his presentation; Eric with his favorite song; Thay by bringing his son all the way from Japan . . . so I'd like to offer you something personal as well."

Brianna got up from the table and walked slowly to the far end of the room. She was sporting a black-leather miniskirt, black tights, and a silver silk blouse. She removed her high heels, so it was pretty clear she was going to do a gymnastic demo for Bella. Everyone waited expectantly.

Brianna closed her eyes, took one deep breath, and then ran unbelievably fast—like a cheetah pursuing its prey—three-quarters of the way to the opposite wall, and jumped higher than anyone would expect Newton's Law of Gravity to allow. As she elevated toward the ceiling, fortunately located 30 feet above the floor, she completed two somersaults and two full twists before landing deftly on her feet. Except for the run, the move looked deceptively like slo-mo.

Everyone stood up and cheered and clapped enthusiastically. Brianna exclaimed, "Thank you! That move is known as the Silivas, named after a good friend of mine, Romanian Olympic gymnastic champion Daniela Silivas. I would have done the triple double, but although this room is big, it's not big enough for me to get the speed I would have needed. I didn't plan on this, so I'm glad I decided to wear tights under this miniskirt!

Eric went over and gave Brianna a gracious hug and a kiss, as I called for everyone's attention. "Hey, guys and gals, it's getting late; and Thay, Eric, Bella, and I have a meeting tomorrow with Major Dallant at his office in DC. Brianna, can I suggest that you meet up with Pham at his hotel in the morning and maybe give him a small tour of the Capitol. We should be done with our meeting by noon, or shortly thereafter. Then we can have a nice lunch together. I'll make reservations for us at 2:00 p.m. at the Peacock Café on Prospect Northwest in Georgetown."

"I'd be happy to do that, Luc," Brianna said.

And so it was that everything ended on a high note, and Bella was now in a much better headspace. But there would be many challenges ahead for her and our SPI Team. She certainly knew that, but just for tonight, she wanted to bathe in the positive afterglow of the evening's festivities.

Chapter Two

NO CHOICE

*"It's in your moments of decision that your
destiny is shaped."*
—Tony Robbins

Monday, April 15, 2030—Washington, DC

Thay and our SPI Team arrived at CIA headquarters in Langley, Virginia, at 8:45 a.m. Our names were on the visitors' roster, but it still required further effort on our part to provide the security officers with additional personal information before our 9:00 a.m. meeting.

A pleasant, conservatively attired young lady in her 20s, wearing professorial, rimless eyeglasses, came to meet us, introduced herself as Kathy, and quietly accompanied us to Major Dallant's office on the sixth floor. After being promoted to his current position, he had decided to remain in the CIA building, occupying former CIA director Anthony Stephano's office, who'd been chosen by the president to fill the position of head of Homeland Security.

As our group approached Major Dallant's office, I quietly—though obviously not quietly enough—remarked to Bella, "I remember this office. It's former director Stephano's old office."

The astute young lady, overhearing my whispered comment, said, "Oh, you've been here before?"

Having visited only during one of my out-of-body experiences, or OBEs, when dealing with the Tamara Carlin affair, I responded with a weak smile and muttered, "Kinda."

Kathy looked at me inquisitively but apparently decided not to follow up on my curious response. Fortunately, she was distracted at that moment, as she opened the door to the major's office and there he stood, offering an unusually low-keyed southern greeting. "Morning, y'all. Come right in. Let's go to the conference room next to my office, but before we do, anyone for coffee, tea, or water?"

Everyone, except Eric, opted for water—he wanted black coffee, at which point Kathy said, "Major, there's bottled water, both still and sparkling, hot coffee and tea, and Danish pastries in the conference room on the console table. Anything else?"

"No, that's fine, Kathy. We're good."

"Super. I hope you all have a great day!" She directed one more somewhat puzzled glance at me, and then she was gone in a flash.

All sweet-toothed Eric heard was "coffee and pastries," and he was all smiles. He grabbed two pecan-filled croissants and a large cup of black coffee as we all sat down along one side of the conference table. Major Dallant sat opposite us beneath a projection screen on the wall behind him. I was thinking that the major probably had a lot to say. And he did.

Dallant opened the discussion. "I appreciate your meeting with me this morning, and by the way, Bella, happy birthday."

Bella was surprised and asked, "Now how did *you* know that?"

I answered for the major. "Dear Gravitas, need you ask—I mean, he *is* the director of the CIA and NSA."

The major smiled as Bella softly agreed with my comment. "Right."

He continued. "This morning's discussion is top-secret. I want to make you aware of probably the most important mission our intelligence community has ever embarked on, and I'm going to tell you right up front, I don't think we can succeed without your help."

I thought, *Where have I heard that before?* and grinned at the major. Dallant returned my smile and went on with his presentation. "I'll start with some background and won't go into too much scientific detail, first and foremost because I don't have the technical background to do so, but primarily since y'all are scientists, and probably with the exception of Thay—sorry, Thay—you are knowledgeable about our country's commitments in the astro-sciences, in particular our numerous launches of satellites and remote telescope facilities for deep-space exploration—"

Eric had to interrupt. "I wouldn't be so sure about your exception. We continue to have lots of discussions with Thay on the stellar-physics research we're doing for NASA, and he has helped immensely."

Major Dallant acknowledged that fact. "Yes, I know, and I'm pleased that he's involved, because as we did in our mission ten years ago in dealing with Seagull, I believe we will need his help again."

Thay just smiled as the major remarked, "Thank you, Eric. And sorry, Thay. My comment wasn't intended to demean your knowledge and experience in astrophysics, but simply to emphasize our need for what I'm convinced the SPI Team can bring to this problem."

Thay smiled again. "No offense taken, Major."

"Thanks. So let's get right to it. As you'll see, I'm going to be talking primarily about our ability to discover Earthlike, life-supporting exoplanets."[7]

I thought, *An interesting topic, but why all the concern about its criticality? But knowing the major, I bet there's much more behind the obvious.*

Major Dallant continued. "Please look at the slides on the wall behind me." With that, he pushed a button on the mouse sitting in front of him next to his laptop, and a slide appeared on the wall.

"As you can see, this is the Kepler telescope, which was launched in 2009." Referring to the telescope with a feminine pronoun, Dallant noted, "When she ran out of fuel in 2018, she was immediately retired. However, even I can say that during her nine years of life, Kepler did a most amazing job. She observed 530,500 stars and discovered more than 4,000 exoplanet candidates."

Eric remarked, "Impressive for an older lady."

Bella immediately corrected him. "Careful with your language, Electer!"

"Gotcha, Gravitas!"

Major Dallant moved to the next slide. "This, of course, is the Transiting Exoplanet Survey Satellite, or TESS, launched in 2018, which added a few hundred more exoplanet candidates to those found

---

[7] *Exoplanets* refer to planets that are "beyond our sun," orbiting a different star.

by Kepler. Next slide. And this is the amazing $10 billion James Webb Space Telescope, or JWST, launched on Christmas Day of 2021. It, too, has added several thousand more exoplanets, as did the Nancy Grace Roman telescope, launched in 2027."

Bella commented, "That's impressive. And speaking of women scientists, dear Eric, I'd like to point out that it was the late Nancy Grace Roman in her role as NASA's chief of astronomy who was a major force in spearheading NASA's commitment and strategies with respect to discovering exoplanets."

Eric smirked just slightly and said, "Duly noted."

Bella continued, "But, Major, what about the JWST?"

"That's where I'm going next, Bella. You see—and I'll explain why in a moment—we have an urgent need to find an exoplanet that we're more than 95 percent confident can support human life, and JWST can't do that to our required degree of confidence."

Thay, who had just been listening so far, inquired, "And why is that? Will it be too challenging for that telescope?"

Major Dallant quickly responded, "I'm going to answer your question, Thay, but you'll need a little more background information first."

The major put up a new slide, and on it were images of the mirrors for the Hubble and JWST telescopes. "As you can see, the JWST has a primary mirror of 6.6 meters in diameter, which is almost three times as large as the 2.4-meter Hubble mirror. But even at its size, the JWST does not have the light-gathering resolution power to identify an exoplanet with as high an accuracy as an Earthlike planet with more than a 95 percent probability of being human-friendly."

I had to comment. "Right. Which is why we have invested over $30 billion in the Large UV/Optical/IR/Surveyor, or LUVOIR, telescope, which is behind its launch date, but hopefully will be launched this year. It has a 15.1-meter primary mirror and should be able to do all the things you're asking for, Major."

He agreed, as he added an image of the LUVOIR mirror—which dwarfs those of Hubble and JWST—to the slide on the wall. He pointed out, "As I understand it, the light-gathering power of the mirror is directly proportional to the square of its radius, and if you do a little arithmetic, you'll find that JWST has seven times the light-gathering power of the Hubble telescope, and LUVOIR has 40 times the light-gathering power of Hubble. Now, I don't know much about astronomical telescopes, but I do know that light-gathering power is the factor that makes all of the difference in getting excellent resolution. Which is why we are anxious to get LUVOIR in position at a point in space you astrophysicists call Lagrange Point 2."

Bella, a talented astrobiologist, but not extensively familiar with the details of celestial mechanics, asked, "Okay, I give up, what is Lagrange Point 2?"

I offered, "I can help you out with that. Lagrange points are stable positions near large bodies in orbit. When two large bodies are in orbit around each other, there are specific places that a third body can occupy without it experiencing major gravitational disturbances. It's a special solvable case for the challenging three-body problem in celestial mechanics. Lagrange points can be found in the orbits of the Earth and the sun and for the moon and the Earth.

"Located 1.5 million kilometers directly behind the Earth as viewed from the sun, Lagrange Point 2, or LP2, is an ideal position for astronomy because a telescope at that point is close enough to readily communicate with Earth; it can keep the sun, Earth, and moon behind the telescope for solar power; and with appropriate optical shielding from the sun's rays, it provides a clear view of deep space and possible exoplanets. By the way, for the Earth-Moon system, there are five Lagrange Points that are of interest, but LP2 has the most stable operability for what we want to do."

Eric added, "Now that is so cool, but since our inimitable leader, Emperius, is of Italian descent, allow me to share another point." Eric didn't give Luc or anyone else an opportunity to comment. He continued, "The Lagrange Points are named after Giuseppe Luigi Lagrange, an 18th-century Italian mathematician, who made significant contributions to classical and celestial mechanics."

I interjected, "Thanks, Eric, but I thought Lagrange was French."

"Nope! He was born in Torino. But he dumped his lovely Italian wife, moved to France, married a French sweetie, and was naturalized as a French citizen—an Italian traitor!"

I responded, "Figures, a northern Italian. We Sicilians would never do that!"

Everyone chuckled.

Major Dallant stepped in. "Interesting historical anecdote, Eric. And thanks, Luc, for explaining Lagrange Points. Now I understand them as well. But we need to move on. Time is of the essence, and you have not yet heard the bad news."

That got everyone's attention. The major continued. "Our detailed analysis over the last five years presents a frightening picture for the inhabitants of our planet. We've been entangled so deeply in nonconstructive political forces in our country and in other countries as well, that it has been virtually impossible to build a broad intercountry strategy to address the impending dire challenges and consequences of climate change.

"Y'all have seen the severe tragedies that have occurred globally over the past two decades—endless huge and destructive forest fires, catastrophic flooding along coastlines, horrendous storms and tornadoes never before encountered anywhere—and it's getting progressively worse. We have long since passed a critical tipping point, and we're now on a path of no return."

Bella remarked, "You've got my attention. This is one of the global issues that's been eating away at me for some time—probably the worst of those in front of us."

Major Dallant responded, "You're so right. Let me share with you what we see from our analysis and future projections. Our intelligence agencies, supported by some of the best engineering and scientific minds in the world, see only two scenarios. The first is staying with the status quo, which will yield some marginal improvements against climate change. That, unfortunately, is basically what the world has been doing for the last 40 years, and you can see where it has gotten us.

"The second is to recognize that unless the world gets its act together, which doesn't look promising, we've reached a point where much of humanity will be progressively destroyed at an ever-increasing rate until there are few, if any, of us left to help preserve the human species."

Everyone at the table was in quiet shock. No one said a word. So Major Dallant continued.

"Faced with a high probability of the tragic demise of the human race, the US government has turned to the one thing it can control— its technical agencies. It has tasked NASA with a top-secret program— Project Phoenix—within two years, to identify at least one exoplanet,

31

which can support human life, and within the following five years to develop a means to initiate a workable process to begin the transfer of large of numbers of selected passengers safely and continually to that planet for as long into the future as conditions here on Earth will permit.

"It's been estimated that there are, at best, another 200 to 300 years before the effects of climate change result in humanity's annihilation—primarily through climate-caused destruction, civil war, and possibly nuclear-extinction events. But our estimates have been wrong before—the worst could come sooner rather than later."

Bella certainly had her concerns, but she'd never considered this kind of dreadful picture—and so soon. She had to interject. "Major, you're painting an incredibly frightening picture. How confident are you about these conclusions?"

"Bella, I wish we were wrong. But the answer to your question is that we are highly confident that this is the course we are on."

Eric asked, "What about those bases we're now establishing on the moon and Mars? Don't they fit into this picture?"

Major Dallant said, "Not really. Not in the near term, but perhaps in the longer term, they can play a role. The presence of large numbers of people on those challenging and inhospitable destinations is quite a ways into the future. We need another Earthlike planet, and we needed it yesterday!"

I had to put in my two cents. "Look, Major, for the moment, let's suppose we accept your conclusions. But as for the time frame to accomplish what you're asking—I see that as impossible. It would require a series of miracles."

Thay added his take. "Nothing is impossible under the right circumstances. And you know what I think about miracles.[8] Let's listen to the rest of the major's presentation, if he has more to present. And then let's open it up for debate."

---

[8] Thay often quotes Paramahansa Yogananda from his book *Autobiography of a Yogi*, chapter 30, p. 375, Self-Realization Fellowship, Los Angeles, CA 2007: "A miracle is commonly considered to be an effect or event without law, or beyond law. But all events in our precisely adjusted universe are lawfully wrought and lawfully explicable. The so-called miraculous powers of a great master are a natural accompaniment to his exact understanding of subtle laws that operate in inner *Cosmos Consciousness*. Nothing may truly be said to be a miracle except in the profound sense that everything is a miracle. That each of us is encased in an intricately organized body, and set upon Earth whirling through space among the stars—is anything more commonplace? Or more miraculous?"

"I do have more." Major Dallant gathered his thoughts for a moment and then continued. "Our technically unskilled government leaders were quickly counseled by scientists at NASA and elsewhere that this unprecedented and most challenging undertaking had two obvious issues—at least to them—that had to be addressed.

"First, the most promising exoplanets might be 100 to 1,000 light-years away, or more. So, let's assume a midpoint of 500 light-years from Earth. That means in our physical observation, limited by the speed of light, we would be looking at that exoplanet as it existed 500 years ago. But what is it like now? And second, even if we wanted to communicate with any existing intelligent life on that planet, and we sent a message, it would be limited by the speed of light, so our message would take 500 years to travel there. And their message, if there is a 'their,' would take another 500 years to travel back to us—a thousand years just to exchange hellos!"

Bella concluded, "Unfortunately, doesn't that mean the whole project doesn't make any sense?"

Major Dallant, who knew that this question would be coming, answered Bella. "Not necessarily, which is why I wanted to meet with the SPI Team."

Eric was puzzled. "I don't get it. Why's that?"

The major responded, "Because, Eric, as I have been counseled by some of our top physicists here at the CIA and elsewhere, your and Luc's theoretical research is specifically focused on the warping of space-time to control gravity, and you both have joined the ranks of the top astrophysicists in this field, including the likes of Matt Visser, Frank Tipler, and Nobel laureate Kip Thorne at Cal Tech.

"As I understand it, your research is at the leading edge and could be the answer to solving the obvious issue we just put on the table. Furthermore, I've been cautioned that the physics that underpins warping space-time in a way that would solve our problems likely goes well beyond classical, quantum, and general relativity physics—perhaps, to spiritual physics, which the SPI Team and Thay pursued so successfully in dealing with Seagull ten years ago.

"To be more specific, we think if you could engineer the construction of a wormhole with an entrance located somewhere in the vicinity of Earth, maybe at LP2, and an exit at the coordinates of the chosen exoplanet, this would enable nearly instantaneous and direct communication with any intelligent life that might exist on the planet."

Unfortunately, I couldn't contain myself. I stood up and waved my arms erratically in the air. "Major, are you kidding me? This is pure science fiction! No one has ever created a large wormhole—and for lots of good scientific reasons that Eric and I have addressed in our publications." I tried to quell my emotions and sat down.

The major responded, "I know, I know, Luc, but there are a number of bright and respected scientists around the world—and you know who they are—who have published data that indicate that, yes, it's a significant challenge, but it's a real possibility. The creation of a wormhole does not violate any fundamental laws of known physics."

I guess, hoping to give me a chance to calm down and gather my thoughts, Bella asked, "Science fiction—right! I read about this kinda thing before in sci-fi books, but if it were possible, I mean wormholes, warp-drive, or whatever you wanna call it, how would it work, and why would it solve the problem of communication with an intelligent alien race many light-years away?"

I jumped right in. "The explanation is simple. It's the execution that's the problem. Here's the explanation. First of all, it is correct that wormholes are predicted and permitted by the fundamental equations of Einstein's theory of general relativity. In fact, Einstein and a coworker, Nathan Rosen, published a paper in 1935 on what were initially called Einstein-Rosen bridges—huge light-year distances between two locations in the universe, made amazingly short by bending space-time. They were eventually christened 'wormholes' by the late Princeton cosmologist John Archibald Wheeler.

"And here's a simple, but realistic, model. Think of a long, narrow strip of paper, say a meter long. Now place a small dot at both ends of the strip. Draw a line between the two dots. Let's say one dot represents Earth and the other represents an exoplanet 500 light-years away. One light-year represents 5.8 trillion miles, so our exoplanet is at a distance 500 times that figure from Earth—about 2,900 trillion, or 2.9 quadrillion miles, away. The one-meter line between the dots represents that distance. With our current and most advanced space-travel technologies, it might just as well be an infinite distance.

"Even traveling with a spaceship capable of going 100,000 miles per hour, which is more than twice the maximum speed we can currently achieve, it would take about 3.3 million years to travel that distance! Essentially not worthy of discussion.

"Now take that paper strip and fold it in half so that the dots are immediately adjacent and on top of each other. In creating a wormhole by warping space-time between Earth and a distant planet, there would be a funnel-like entrance at each dot, connected to each other by a short, narrow tube—the wormhole.

"For the specific case of our communication with an exoplanet, let's say 100 light-years away, as a consequence of bending space-time between Earth and the exoplanet—in this instance, a 100-light-year distance on that strip of paper—think of one funnel entrance located at Earth at that first dot. The funnel is attached to a short wormhole that terminates at the exoplanet, represented by the second dot, where there is a similar funnel. Travel of an electromagnetic communication signal entering one funnel would arrive at the end of the other funnel essentially instantaneously.

"There are several reasons why this would be an unstable system, and astrophysicists have proposed theoretical means to deal with them, but no one has ever succeeded. The most significant issue is that the moment any 'normal' positive energy or mass enters the wormhole, its walls would immediately collapse, and the only means to avoid this collapse is by the presence of 'nonnormal' negative energy or mass—so-called exotic matter. Essentially, since gravity throughout the cosmos is a positive force field, you need a form of negative gravity to keep the walls from collapsing. Crazy, right?"

Major Dallant said, "Thank you, Luc, for your forthright critique and also for the simple model. Now I understand the issues, but I'm getting in over my head on the science, so I need to go to the last reason why you have to immediately jump on board to see what can be done."

I interrupted him before he could start. "Major, I don't see why we need to approach this at light speed. We should wait until LUVOIR is launched, later this year, and then proceed in an orderly manner to find a few exoplanets that meet your criteria, hopefully closer to Earth so that we can get a more accurate picture of what's currently happening on the surface. From what I've read about the project, LUVOIR will have incredible resolution.

"In fact, you probably recall the famous 'Pale Blue Dot' photograph of Earth? It was taken on Valentine's Day, February 14, 1990, at a distance of 3.7 billion miles from Earth as the Voyager One space probe was leaving our solar system. In the photograph, Earth appears as a tiny blue dot against the vastness of space, among bands of sunlight reflected by the camera on the probe.

"Voyager One had completed its mission, and at the request of Carl Sagan, NASA turned its camera around and took one last photograph of Earth. LUVOIR will have this same resolution, but amazingly, for planets that are more than 100,000 times that distance from Earth! With its advanced coronagraph, spectrometer, and camera, it will do even better than what you're asking."

The major responded, "You're absolutely correct about LUVOIR's potential, but waiting is not a viable option—and here's why. About 15 years ago, one of our top scientists at NASA, for whatever reason, went over to the other side and became a Russian mole. We only found out a year ago, when he and his Bulgarian wife absconded to Russia. It turns out that her father had been a high-level KGB agent during the Soviet regime. During her husband's stay with NASA, they funneled huge amounts of top-secret data and intel concerning our space program to the Russians.

"The Russians, having both their and our data, created a program when LUVOIR was in the planning stage to do what we were targeting, except they went bigger, faster, and much, much riskier. Instead of a 15.1-meter primary mirror, they created one that is 20 meters in diameter; and instead of sending the telescope to LP2 and remotely opening all systems for operation, as we plan on doing, they sent a number of astronauts into space and constructed the space probe in situ at LP2. It was much faster and less costly than our approach, but as I said, very risky—they lost four of their best astronauts and ten engineers.

"But they completed the project in 2027 and named it Gargarin, in honor of Yuri Gargarin, a Russian astronaut and the first person to journey into outer space. They studied more than 4,000 exoplanet candidates and found a number that likely have an Earthlike, habitable environment. As best our intel was able to uncover, one is a planet that is definitely, as we say, in the 'Goldilocks Zone,' meaning just right for us human beings, animals, and plant life. However, all we can determine is that the exoplanet is about 100 light-years away, but we have no idea where that is in our universe.

"But, with their system, the Russians were able to get highly accurate data that demonstrates a favorable atmosphere and temperature and, very important, the presence of large amounts of water.

"LUVOIR will be able to do the same, perhaps even better, since we've made improvements on our 'stolen' data. Our system has the three critical elements necessary to zero in precisely and accurately on the planet's atmosphere and surface: a powerful coronagraph screen to block light from the planet's star; inside the coronagraph, we have an advanced imaging camera to detect small, rocky planets like Earth; and an extremely sensitive spectrograph, functioning at a broad range of wavelengths, to identify elements like oxygen, bio-formed methane, carbon dioxide, and a host of organic molecules that might exist in the planet's atmosphere or on its surface. The Russians have similar elements, but not nearly as advanced as our final system.

"Our assets in Russia have done an excellent job of retrieving and supplying us with many of the details as to where the Russians are at this moment—except for the coordinates of the exoplanet they have zeroed in on. We've tried several times to identify the planet, but unfortunately, so far, to no avail. There is just too much space up there."

Eric asked, "So what is it you want from us?"

The major was quick to respond. "I want to give the four of you all of the information we have, and I want Bella to look at the atmospheric and surface chemistry data and determine if life, as we know it, is possible on that planet. By the way, the Russians' multi-wavelength spectral data have detected large amounts of the chlorophyll molecule. That, I'm told, says something about oxygen and carbon dioxide, and the presence of life as we know it.

"And I'd like Luc and Eric to consider what it would take to bend space-time and create a wormhole between Earth and that exoplanet so that we could send a transmission through it and have instantaneous communication with any intelligent life that might exist on the planet."

Bella smiled and said, "Oh, I see. That's all? And you want it by when?"

I also had a comment for the major. "Even if we *could* create a small wormhole for the passage of a communication signal, making one large enough for spaceship travel is a whole different ball of wax!"

Major Dallant admitted, "I understand, but let's take this one step at a time. I know this looks like I'm asking for a bunch of miracles, but I keep thinking of Thay's comments over the years that there's no such thing as a miracle, only our inability to understand the science to make things happen. And from what we know, the existence of wormholes does not appear to violate any fundamental laws of physics.

"I know the SPI Team and Thay are the best people in this crazy world to work the magic of spiritual physics. There isn't a morning I wake up that I don't think about what you pulled off ten years ago in Novosibirsk, under the guidance of Thay and focusing on the tenets of spiritual physics—to be specific, what you refer to as the *Manifestation Sequence*. In all my experience, I had never seen anything like it."

Thay shared his thoughts. "What Major Dallant has presented today and asked of us is an unbelievable challenge. Before we make any rapid, rash judgments, I suggest that the major give us ten days to study and discuss the data he will provide, the challenges we see, and then we meet afterward and show our presentation to him to see if the unbelievable can be made believable. During that time, I will also lead you into several deep-dive meditations to raise your levels of consciousness and stimulate your creativity so that you can access whatever is needed from the Akashic Field to do our best to help the major, our country, and the world. I have one technical idea for us to ponder, but it would be dangerous and risky. We can discuss it when we meet later this week as a team. What do you say?"

We all answered affirmatively, although somewhat reluctantly.

The major was grateful for Thay's input. He asked, "Any more questions before we adjourn?"

I had one—an important one. "There's something I've been thinking about since Bella's party last evening. "I would like to ask Bella, Eric, Thay, and you if it would be acceptable to add two additional 'super people' to the SPI Team."

Major Dallant shot back, "I thought you'd never ask, Luc, and yes, they're fine with me if they're committed to joining the team and pursuing the challenges in front of us."

He caught me by surprise. "Whaddaya mean—'yes'? You don't even know who I'm talking about?"

"Sure, I do. It's Brianna and Pham Jr."

Bella was amazed. "How do you know about them?"

"It's my job. They're excellent choices, and if they want to come on board, we've already vetted them, and they can immediately have top-secret clearance. We could use Brianna's knowledge and exper7ise on atmospheric physics as applied to both Earth and the exoplanet.

"If there are no further questions, I have one last piece of information I was leaving for the end of our meeting, as I didn't want to distract your focus." Major Dallant took a deep breath. "The lead Russian scientist, the one who has made the most significant contributions to the Russian project and is leading their efforts, is an astrophysicist at Cambridge University: Sophia Stepanova."

I couldn't contain myself. "No! This is crazy! How could that be? Ten years later and that damned Seagull fiasco is still following us!"

Dallant continued. "And by the way, she has given the exoplanet a name—*Zoi*, Greek for 'life,' as I understand it."

As we got up to leave Major Dallant's office, Bella rolled her eyes and had the last word. "Unbelievable."

MAJOR DALLANT HAD ARRANGED for a limo to take us to the Peacock Café to meet up with Brianna and Pham for lunch. Although it was a beautiful April day and lunch outside under the restaurant's striking blue awning would have been a delight, I had decided that inside, away from the roadside, would be a quieter and more private venue for our discussions. I wanted to disclose to Brianna and Pham what we really did for the CIA and NSA and ask if they would be inclined to join the SPI Team in the same "part-time capacity" as Eric, Bella, and me. Yeah, right—part-time!

As was the case with the three of us, Brianna was committed to her climate research at Columbia—she had four grad students and two postdocs working with her. As for Pham, he was intent on making his new home in California near Thay and wanted to open a dojo to focus on his passion for the martial arts. I was convinced that both of them would bring strong complementary skills to our team.

We were several minutes late arriving at the restaurant. As we entered, I could see Brianna and Pham sitting in the far corner across from the bar at a table that had been set up for the six of us. The subdued lighting made it difficult to see much detail, especially with dilated pupils after exposure to the bright sunlight outside. As we got closer, I saw the damage.

I exclaimed, "Oh my God, Pham! What in the world happened to your face?" He had a sizable black-and-blue mark on his cheek, just below his eye.

Before he could answer, Brianna did it for him. "You should see the other guys!"

In his usual calm, controlled voice, Thay asked, "Pham what happened?"

He responded, "Brianna and I were leaving the Lincoln Memorial. I wanted to see the Martin Luther King Jr. Memorial next, and even though it was just a short walk away, I convinced Brianna to take a shortcut through a wooded area next to the Korean War Veterans Memorial. That was my *first* mistake.

"We ran into three guys sharing a bottle of some kind of whiskey and smoking marijuana. They were belligerent and really out of it. They kept saying, 'Now lookie here at the yellow dude and his black mama. Aren't they a colorful duo?'

"We tried to ignore them, but one of them—a tall heavy-set guy—came over and tried to grab Brianna's arm. I pulled his arm away, and he quickly swung at my face with his other arm. I blocked his punch, but only lightly. I didn't want to do what I could have done. It would have injured him. That was my *second* mistake. It was clear that he and the other two guys, who were now running over to join the brawl, were not going to let us leave peacefully—if at all."

Brianna finished the story. "All I can say is that in a matter of a few seconds, there were three guys lying on the ground, moaning in pain, trying to regain their breath. We immediately left for the Martin Luther King Jr. Memorial. Pham kept apologizing to me for putting these wiseasses where they belonged—flat-faced on the ground."

Pham directed his comment to Thay. "Sorry, Dad. I didn't mean to hurt them, but I had no choice."

Thay said, "Not to worry, Pham. You did the right thing in an imperfect world."

Eric added, "Hey, good buddy, I owe you one—for protecting Brianna!"

Bella asked, "Brianna, Pham, are you sure you guys are okay?"

Pham answered, "We're fine, just hungry. Right, Brianna?"

"Right!" she responded.

I was glad to see that they were fully recovered. I suggested that we all be seated, as there were some things I wanted to discuss. We did just that, and after we ordered lunch, I told Brianna and Pham that we had something confidential we wanted to talk with them about. At that point, Eric, Bella, and I shared a summary of our personal histories and what we'd been doing for Major Dallant, off and on, for the last decade. I think that Pham and Brianna were both more entertained than shocked by our stories, although there were quite a few "Oh my Gods."

But most important, they agreed to join the SPI Team and do whatever they could to help—whenever and wherever—as long as they could continue to pursue their personal passions as well. Both apologized that they didn't have superpowers to contribute—especially OBEs. Thay told them not to be so sure of that. I wasn't certain what he meant, but I knew I'd eventually find out.

We agreed to have several discussions via teleconferences connecting our respective locations during the week to see if it was possible for us to help Major Dallant, and if so, just how we would do so. It would be an uphill battle for this one, but I guess you could say that they've all been that way.

Part II

MENTAL AND PHYSICAL CONSTRUCTION

Chapter Three

CAN IT BE DONE?

"Start by doing what's necessary. Then do what's possible.
And suddenly you are doing the impossible."
— FRANCIS OF ASSISI

MONDAY, APRIL 22, 2030—PALO ALTO, CALIFORNIA

For some reason I could never understand, Thay was quite comfortable not being a formal member of the SPI Team. Instead, he preferred to be known as our counselor, or *consigliere*, although he was always ready to do whatever was necessary to help in any way. Maybe it was because Francis Ford Coppola's first *Godfather* film was his all-time favorite movie, and one of the major characters functioned as Don Corleone's consigliere. In any case, Thay and our SPI Team, now with five members since Pham and Brianna had agreed to join us, had engaged in several intense videoconferences over the past several days, and we were now about to share our conclusions with Major Dallant.

Thay and Pham stationed themselves at our office in Palo Alto Square and connected with Eric and Brianna in New York City, Bella in Baltimore, and with me in Cambridge. As soon as our videos were on-screen and working well, I connected us to Major Dallant in DC. After a few minutes of small talk, he suggested that we start our discussion.

I shared an introductory thought with him. "Major, I don't mind telling you that we've had some interesting, though intense, debates concerning the material you sent us. Based on it and our analysis, we've come to some preliminary conclusions as to what we believe might be possible, given what you're asking us to do."

To be sure that Major Dallant had a clear picture of the challenge he'd given us, Bella added, "Some of those debates I'd say were downright arguments, a few without resolution—we simply agreed to disagree."

The major was in a humorous mood. He commented, "I'm not surprised. Just like in that old Clint Eastwood spaghetti western, *The Good, the Bad and the Ugly*—throw it at me! Let's see what sticks."

I started. "I'll do my best to cut through all of the material you sent us and summarize only our most important conclusions. First, it's clear that the Russians did a thorough job of hacking into NASA and our most important space telescopes, and by combining our work with their own, they had everything they needed to dwindle down thousands of identified exoplanet candidates to a few with a high probability of human habitable life on them. And based on their focused analysis, we agree that statistically, with greater than 95 percent probability, Zoi is in the Goldilocks Zone, which would support life as we know it—at least this was the case a century ago. Remember, since it's about a hundred light-years from Earth, the transit time for communication is limited by the speed of light. Bella will explain how the Russians came to their conclusion that life exists on Zoi."

With that, Bella took over. "The breakthrough that led to this finding is that Sophia Stepanova and her team appear to have developed a highly advanced polarimetry technology."

Major Dallant asked, puzzled, "Polarimetry technology?"

Bella answered, "That's right. Similar in principle to the technology used in your sunglasses to reduce the glare of sunlight, except a whole lot more sensitive and with amazing resolution. Furthermore, their polarimetry appears to have incredible resolution over a broad range of wavelengths, ultraviolet through visible, and both near- and far-infrared. Let me explain some of the key points that make this a critical technology for what you want us to do."

Major Dallant nodded. "Go ahead, Bella, I'm with you, at least for now."

She smiled and continued. "Astronomers have long known that starlight reflected off of a cosmic body like an orbiting planet contains a huge amount of information about the surface and atmosphere of the planet. The challenge has been that the important information is contained in only the polarized light component, which often is 1 or 2 percent of all the light reflected from the planet, so it's necessary to somehow separate it from the massive amount of nonpolarized light."

Bella was on a roll. She loved this stuff. "Think of light as an electromagnetic wave, moving through space with its electric component vibrating like an up-and-down sine wave, and its magnetic component doing the same thing, but at a right angle to the electric component. Most of the light we encounter like that from the sun, or from a light bulb, is unpolarized—meaning that the wave is vibrating in many directions.

"Polarized light, however, vibrates in only certain well-defined directions. It just so happens that starlight reflecting off of a star's orbiting planet is polarized, and the way in which it's polarized says a lot about what's on its surface and in its atmosphere. It can even provide information about living things on the planet—but you need a superpowerful, high-resolution polarimeter to see this component of the starlight reflected from the planet."

Major Dallant asked, "Living things, really?"

Bella answered, "Yes. Let me explain. It depends on a special molecular property called *chirality*. The word comes from the Greek, meaning 'hand' or 'handedness.' Many molecules can be left- or right-handed. To demonstrate . . . your hands are chiral. They're mirror images of each other, but you cannot perfectly superimpose one of them on top of the other with both palms facing in the same direction.

"Similarly, two molecules can have the exact same chemical formula, and like your hands, they are mirror images, but because of differences in the spatial position of the atoms in each of the molecules—like the fingers on both of your hands—they cannot be perfectly superimposed on each other. The chemists call them *enantiomers*. One is known as the L-enantiomer, and the other, the D-enantiomer. Each of them changes polarized light in a different way, which can be measured accurately in a polarimeter. And each enantiomer often exhibits huge differences in its chemistry and overall reactivity.

Eric asked, "So why is that important?"

"I'll tell you why it's so important. As an example, back in the late 1950s and early 1960s, a 50-50 mixture of L- and D-thalidomide called Contergan was introduced in Germany as an over-the-counter drug for treating morning sickness in pregnant women. As it turned out, the D-form was very effective, but the L-form was a potent teratogen, which caused a few thousand deaths and more than 10,000 tragic birth defects before it was pulled from the market.

"But here is a more pleasant example: The molecule D-carvone is a flavoring agent. It smells and tastes like spearmint leaves, while the other enantiomer, L-carvone, smells and tastes like caraway seeds. As I said, we can use polarimetry to identify these molecules because they change polarized light in opposite ways. The D-enantiomer rotates polarized light clockwise in a circle, while the L-enantiomer rotates it counterclockwise. This can be observed clearly in a polarimeter."

Eric excitedly interjected, "Ah, now I get it, 'D' is for right-handed polarization, and 'L' is for left-handed polarization—probably from the Latin *dextro*, meaning 'right'; and *levo*, meaning 'sinister' or 'left.'"

Bella smiled and responded, "Right you are, Electer. No pun intended. But getting back to a key point, much of life on Earth is based on molecules made from left-handed L-amino acids. And there's something unique about the way life—plants in particular—modify polarized light. For example, the reflected light from clouds and oceans on a planet is linearly polarized—that is to say, the light waves vibrate in a line in the direction in which they're traveling. Plants, on the other hand, create circular polarization—the reflected light off the plant's surface rotates in a plane at right angles to the direction of travel. Whether the rotation of polarization is clockwise, D, or counterclockwise, L, depends on the chirality, or handedness, of the molecule from which the light is reflected.

"And if you have a sufficiently sensitive polarimeter, you can measure these differences. Furthermore, if you carry out these measurements in conjunction with a supersensitive spectrometer that analyzes the light waves at various wavelengths and identifies constituent atoms on the planet's surface and in its atmosphere, you have the best of both worlds. Because of molecular polarity and changes in polarity, with a high-resolution polarimeter, it's possible to identify surface water, clouds, wind speed, and even the wave height on the surface of oceans in an alien world."

Major Dallant commented, "Amazing! You can do all that with light from a small blip a hundred light-years away?"

Bella's response was direct and accurate. "*We* can't, but Sophia Stepanova can. I analyzed all of her data, both the polarimetry and the spectrographic readings. It's beyond amazing! From their Gargarian station at LP2, she has used their polarimeter and spectrometer—both aimed directly at Earth, 1.5 million kilometers away—to obtain numerous polarimetry and spectra scans, which are accurate calibration signatures of what an alien exoplanet that supports life would look like. That's how she identified the presence of green plant life containing chlorophyll.

"There are two conclusions, probably a result of the data she stole from us as well as data the Russians obtained for Zoi. First, they have the most advanced space polarimeters and spectrometers I know of; and second, Zoi has the right name. There is abundant life on that planet—at least there was a hundred years ago. I can't vouch for what is there now."

Major Dallant's responded assertively, "Excellent work, Bella! Now where do we go next, Luc?"

I told him, "For starters, let's put Zoi's distance from Earth in perspective, since it has everything to do with our going forward with this mission. Currently, our maximum flight speed for astronaut-carrying rockets in outer space is about 25,000 miles per hour. Let's assume that we can double that to 50,000 miles per hour. If you do the calculation for a hundred light-years, it will take about 1.4 million years to reach Zoi from Earth via conventional space travel! So you see, this is not a *starter*. It's a *nonstarter* unless we can move into warp speed; have access to a large, stable wormhole; or come up with some other sci-fi solution."

I could see that Major Dallant was disappointed with the substance, and especially with the tone, of my comment. Actually, so was I. I guess it was just a measure of my frustration after our team meetings last week. Then things started to go in a better, or at least more constructive, direction.

Our dear consigliere, Thay, reminded me, "Luc, to do the impossible, we must first look at the possible, right?"

"I guess so, but what *is* that?"

Thay responded, "I will put a *Gedanken* experiment on the table, and maybe it will move us in that direction." He was talking about a thought experiment in which a hypothesis, theory, or principle is laid out for the purpose of thinking through its consequences.

He said, "I think we can forget about warp speed. That's only for diehard *Star Trek* fans. Furthermore, we're not going to put people on spaceships, even if they can hit 50,000 miles per hour, for the reason you concluded based on your calculations. And I agree that creating a wormhole big enough for the rapid traverse of a spaceship from Earth to Zoi does *seem* like it's in the realm of the impossible—at least for now. However, if we were to succeed at what I'm about to propose, we could come back to this kind of space travel. But let's start with what might be possible, first.

"So, let's look at a special case for a wormhole, one that only requires an entrance and exit of quite a small diameter—especially if our first task is to communicate through it with any intelligent beings who might exist on Zoi. We only need a wormhole with a modest-sized diameter—maybe just 10 to 20 centimeters."

Eric quickly inquired, "But, Thay, even if we could create a narrow-diameter wormhole, where are we gonna get the exotic matter to keep it from collapsing the minute we put a communication signal through it? Physicists today don't even know what exotic matter looks like, except to say that it must have a negative energy field. So tell me, how would we keep the wormhole from collapsing?"

Thay's answer was, "With the help of a very special woman."

We didn't know whether to laugh or be serious. Our comments were more than frivolous. First mine: "You're kidding, right?"

"No, I'm not," Thay answered adamantly.

Then Eric: "Let's hear it for feminine power!"

Then Bella and Brianna in unison: "Hear, hear!"

Then Pham: "Now I know why I joined this team—this is crazy, but it's fun!"

We were all weary and giddy from our analysis, having looked under every rock we could think of with little success.

Thay responded to our wild-ass digs: "I'm *dead* serious." He stopped for a moment. "However, I retract the adjective."

Much more optimistic than the rest of us, Major Dallant intervened. "Let's hear what Thay has to say. And please, let's stay open-minded."

"Thanks, Major," Thay said. "That woman is Bella . . . and before you interject, let me tell you why." Thay stopped for a few seconds, and Bella's eyes nearly popped out of their sockets. He continued. "Most of what Bella has done in her active role as Gravitas has involved using her gravity-pulse superpower to knock things down—like people. Remember what happened to Tamara Carlin in DC, or to the Russian spy who tried to kill Bella's mother with Seagull's weapon?"

Almost in unison, Eric, Bella, and I answered, "Yes."

Thay continued. "And there were also times when she demonstrated the ability to attract things to her. Luc, do you recall your visit to Bella in the hospital when she'd just come out of a coma after that hit-and-run attempt on her life?"

"I sure do. It was one of the highs in my life after a terrible low."

Thay explained, "I remember you telling me that Bella had no trouble rapidly pulling her iPhone from far across the room into her hands. Am I right?"

Bella confirmed, "Absolutely. I still do it on occasion when I'm too lazy to get up."

Thay went on. "Well, here's a brief on the science. Although I'll be the first to admit I don't understand how Bella creates her gravity pulses, I'm quite confident that her superpower somehow enables her to connect directly with the laws of spiritual physics and seamlessly mesh them with those of classical physics. I'm also sure that she doesn't understand *how* she does it. She just *does* it. It's like riding a bike. You don't ever think about your balance or what to do to turn and stop. Once you know how to do it, you just do it.

"However, the part I *do* understand is based on the laws of classical physics. When Bella wants to attract something to her—like her phone in the hospital—that's a normal case of two-body gravitational attraction—Bella and the phone. She somehow—unbeknownst to me and even to Bella—creates a gravitational force field, and that unquestionably has a *positive* energy density that bends space-time in a way that connects her phone with her hands.

"However, to use gravity in reverse—antigravity—namely as a repulsive force field, requires a *negative* energy density. My recollection from reading Kip Thorne's theoretical research on wormholes is that some form of negative-energy density is required to prevent a wormhole from collapsing when a positive mass like a person or spaceship—or a positive energy field such as photons in a radio transmission—enter the wormhole. Physicists speculate that creating this negative energy requires some unknown kind of 'exotic matter.' But no one knows how to make exotic matter, or even what it would look like.

"I have no idea how large of a negative force field Bella could create, but I've seen her knock a 200-pound man high into the air. I've seen her push a large car—examples of negative energy in action. I also know that her gravity superpower enables her to go from attraction to repulsion with a flick of a switch in her brain."

I couldn't withhold my question. "So where's all this leading, Thay?"

"Well, suppose I could help her reach a super-high level of consciousness by leading her in a very deep meditation. Perhaps she could power up her negative-energy antigravity to a point where she could help you and Eric create a stable mini-wormhole with openings between the spatial coordinates of the LP2 point and the surface of Zoi?"

Thay stopped, and Bella said, "You're kidding, right?"

"No, I'm not. And for a reason I'll mention in a moment, even if we decided to do this, it would have to be done with great care, as it may be of significant risk to you. I'm just opening it up for discussion to see where it leads."

I just had to ask. "Let's suppose this were even possible. Why would it be a risk for Bella?"

Thay explained, "Because I have no idea how much physical and mental energy would be required by her to create a sufficient level of negative energy."

Eric asked, "I don't mean to be a the-glass-is-half-empty kinda guy, but how do you propose we create the wormhole?"

Thay answered, "About ten years ago, there was a paper written by three physicists from the University of California, Santa Barbara, on creating a small wormhole by connecting two small black holes and keeping them opened by threading them with an infinite cosmic string.[9] Now forget the cosmic-string idea—we would use Bella's negative, repulsive energy field."

Eric asked, "And how, consigliere, would we create two small black holes?"

Thay replied, "This should be of interest to you, although it may raise some unpleasant memories. It involves the electrokinesis superpower that you and Luc have, which is how he 'killed' you the first time you two guys met. So that all of us understand what I'm talking about, I'll remind us of what happened that day."

Eric said, "I'm not really anxious for Brianna to hear this, but go ahead."

Thay continued. "I won't go into all of the gory details since it involved the rambunctious 'old' Eric, who, as we all know, no longer exists. That in itself is a long story!"

Eric couldn't resist. "Thanks, Thay. I appreciate it—I think!"

Thay went on. "In any case, more than a decade ago, Eric and one of his long-gone muscle-bound hoodlum friends were trying to steal Luc's and Bella's bikes at the Ravenswood Open Space Preserve in East Palo Alto. Luc and Bella caught them, and within moments, Eric's friend clamped Luc tightly in a stronghold, while Eric began to flirt with Bella."

Brianna was absolutely amazed. "No! Eric, that wasn't you, was it?"

"No, it wasn't the *real* me, and I can tell you the whole backstory some other time. It's long and complicated, but it has a happy ending."

Brianna looked distraught, so Bella offered, "Not to worry, Brianna, it *did* have a happy ending for all of us. Whatever Eric leaves out in his account to you, I'll fill you in."

Thay explained, "What Luc did in a moment of extreme anxiety and anger, an expression of his unconditional loving concern for Bella, was to use his high level of consciousness energy—a subtle force not recognized by conventional physics, only by spiritual physics—to generate separate from, yet close to his body, a microscopic black hole, quite similar to the much larger astronomical ones in deep space studied by you astrophysicists.

---

[9]Zicao Fu, Brianna Grado-White, Donald Marolf, *Transferrable Asymptotically Flat Wormholes with Short Transit Times*, https://arxiv.org/abs/1908.03273, November 12, 2019.

"He created it from what is known in quantum physics as the zero-point energy of the universe. We can discuss the physics, if you wish, some other time. What I can say at this time is that physicists would like to find a means to tap into the zero-point energy field, as it would offer the possibility of an infinite level of free energy to the planet. So far, all efforts to do so have failed. But Luc, and now Eric, because of their ability to access high levels of consciousness, can do this."

Pham exclaimed, "That's amazing. I wouldn't want to make you angry at me—you're well beyond any match for the martial arts!"

Thay continued his explanation. "Although Eric was electrocuted—and fortunately, resuscitated—Luc wasn't affected by the electric bolt of lightning because he never touched the microscopic black hole, which he created from zero-point energy in a space immediately adjacent to the surface of his hand, and directed it at Eric with a powerful consciousness force field that he clearly has the capability to generate, especially under stress.

"As that minuscule black hole flew toward Eric, it swallowed the atmosphere existing in its path, and ionized the oxygen and nitrogen components of air to much higher energy levels, similar to putting an electrical discharge through a gas such as neon, as is done to make neon signs, but to much higher energy levels, like a lightning bolt.

"As the atoms of the ionized nitrogen and oxygen degenerated or fell back to what is called their ground or normal state, they emitted high-energy photons—that is, light particles in the form of the high-voltage electrical discharge of lightning you experienced. When it hit Eric, it electrocuted him. He was lucky that Luc had created a small black hole. Otherwise, he might not be with us. He would have been fried to a crisp."

Major Dallant was astounded. "That's an incredible story, Thay. I had no idea that had ever happened. So your point is?"

"My point is that with a little further thought and study of the work by those astrophysicists at UC Santa Barbara, maybe we could find a way to do the following seemingly impossible steps. Eric and Luc would use their superpowers to create two small black holes—maybe 10 to 20 centimeters in diameter—and connect them to form a small wormhole that is stabilized by Bella's superpower to create negative gravity. The wormhole would be contained in a high-vacuum container.

"The device would then be launched by rocket to orbit LP2; and there, using the tandem and simultaneous superpowers of Bella, Eric, and Luc—in an elevated state of consciousness catalyzed by deep meditation—the exit spatial coordinates of the wormhole at LP2 would be connected with those for the surface of Zoi."

Everyone, including Major Dallant, was quiet, but I couldn't contain my thoughts. "Thay, this would take a barrel of miracles to pull off successfully, and I know what you think about the nonexistence of miracles! How do you expect us to do all this?"

Thay responded, "We'll take it one possible step at a time until, hopefully, we look back and see that we've done the impossible."

We continued our discussion with Major Dallant—but it was Thay's words on making the impossible possible that lingered with me for quite some time.

Chapter Four

THE CHAMBER

"The saddest aspect of life right now is that science gathers knowledge
faster than society gathers wisdom."
— Isaac Asimov

Sunday, September 1, 2030—Cambridge, Massachusetts

It had been nearly six months since we'd agreed to our "possible-creating-access-to-the-impossible" mission. Thank you, Thay! If that philosophical insight had come from anyone else, we wouldn't be on the serious path we were pursuing.

Because of the urgency and secrecy surrounding Project Phoenix, Major Dallant used his political influence to convince Columbia, Johns Hopkins, and MIT to grant Brianna, Bella, and me each a one-year sabbatical domiciled at MIT to "work on a critical, top-secret government mission." Fortunately, Thay and Pham were able to join us as well. The entire team was once again physically united.

Thay was granted a transfer from his position at the Palo Alto Buddhist temple to the Fo Guang Buddhist Temple in Boston. The temple has had an informal relationship with MIT dating back to the early 1990s, when several of their monks were invited to give talks on Humanistic Buddhism. They have also been involved over the years in studies at MIT funded by US intelligence agencies on the power of elevated consciousness to manifest unusual capabilities in human behavior—like OBEs for distance travel, mind reading, and clairvoy-ance—all spy stuff.

As a result of his impressive international reputation as a martial arts master, Pham had no trouble getting a teaching position at the Cambridge Tang Soo Do dojo. He had studied Tang Soo Do in Seoul and was enthusiastic about its philosophy. A Korean martial art, its origin dates back more than 2,000 years. It is taught strictly as an art rather than as a sport, and enables the body to gain enhanced capabili-ties in its faculties through intensive physical and mental training.

So, our team was again spatially reunited. MIT was generous enough to provide us with special research facilities in the Green Build-ing, or Building 54, as it's also known. Designed by MIT alum I. M. Pei, and funded by another alum, Cecil Howard Green, cofounder of Texas Instruments, it houses the Department of Earth, Atmospheric, and Planetary Sciences and is one of the tallest buildings in Cambridge. It was an appropriate location for what we had set out to accomplish.

Brianna kept us abreast of damaging events that were increasing globally and acknowledged to be caused by human-induced accelera-tion of climate change. In addition to the large number of tragic events that had occurred during the last decade in North America—and par-ticularly in the US—other leading world powers, especially Russia and China, were also suffering from the grave effects of climate attack. The temperature elevations in those countries was even greater than the global average.

For Russia, in 2020, the average annual temperature increased by 1.1°C compared with the two decades between 1980 and 2000. That didn't seem to get the Russians' attention, but a recent report projected a rise between 2.6 and 3.4°C by 2050. Even based on Russian data, that now seems impossible. It's more likely to be closer to 5°C by 2050, as supported by frequent cycles between terrible floods and droughts; and devastation of their wheat, barley, and oat crops. They are on the brink of a long-term famine. These data and an increasing number of tragic events throughout Russia had finally galvanized the Russian government to view global climate change as a serious existential cri-sis—not something that would occur in somebody else's backyard. Few people around the world would be left untouched by the increasing number of intense weather-driven outcomes.

There were devastating floods wherever the sea touched the Russian coast. St. Petersburg—the Venice of Russia—had recently experienced massive flooding from the Baltic Sea via the Neva River. A two-meter-high wall of sandbags surrounded the world-famous Hermitage Museum as precious art pieces were being removed and transferred elsewhere to higher ground. The museum would be closed for good, eventually becoming an architectural relic, submerged in a rapidly rising sea.

The temperature increase in China due to climate change is also projected to be above the global average. In 2020, the projections had shown an increase of average temperatures in China to rise 2.5°C by the 2050s and 5.2°C by the 2090s. As is the case for Russia, that's no longer accurate. Updated estimates show 4.5°C by 2050, and the horrendous number of 6.5°C by 2100! These are frightening outcomes when you consider that an estimated 43 million people in China live on land that could be well underwater by 2100 if the global average temperature rises by just 2°C, let alone 6.5°C.

During the past decade, massive and extensive flooding at the ports of Dalian on the Yellow Sea, Yingkou on Liaodong Bay, Jinzhou on the Bohai Sea, and Shanghai—the busiest port in the world—is a testament to what's ahead for China.

Last year, Brianna had consulted for the Chinese Consulate General in New York City, and in quiet moments over dinner after enough Baijiu had been consumed, a few of the diplomats and the ambassador asked her where she thought a safe place would be to live in the near future, in light of what had happened in China and elsewhere, and what's projected to happen over the next several decades.

The world was finally waking up to reality—human-induced climate change is here—it has been for decades—and it will get much worse. Very few places, if any, will escape its grip of devastation. It was no longer a case of "What can we do to prevent climate change?" but more a case of "What can we do to adapt safely and securely to what is currently happening and to what is about to happen?"

ERIC AND I HAD WORKED FEVERISHLY over the past several months to design and manufacture a cylindrical titanium alloy chamber, the inside of which would simulate and withstand the vacuum and temperature conditions of interstellar space.

The chamber was delivered last week. It is 1 meter in diameter and 5 meters long, with walls that are 8 centimeters thick—lots of expensive titanium. Along the entire length of the cylinder, there is a 20-centimeter-high, 8-centimeter-thick, tempered, fused-quartz window. It has the same curvature as the titanium chamber in which it fits perfectly flush. On the outside of the cylinder, a titanium shield can, if necessary, be remotely lowered to cover the quartz window and create total darkness within the interior of the chamber. This would isolate a stable wormhole from contact with stray electromagnetic radiation from the exterior environment, which could cause a violent explosion of the wormhole.

Two solid-gold properly insulated electrodes are fused through the titanium body to the inside of the cylinder, one located ten centimeters from each of the ends and on top of the cylinder. Both ends of the chamber are sealed in the shape of a hemispheric bubble. One end has an insulated gold electrode fused into the center of the hemisphere and is connected to the inside of the cylinder along its center axis. The other end of the cylinder has an entry hatch that can be opened, if and when necessary. There is a valved port in the center of the hatch for pumping down the chamber to an interstellar vacuum with a specially designed titanium sublimation pump.

The inside surface length of the cylinder has a network of special steel-alloy coils through which liquid helium can be run to create an interstellar temperature—about -269°C.

Our plan is for Eric and me to use our superpowers to tap into the zero-point energy field of the universe in order to create a high-density electrical current, and then direct that current onto the gold electrodes along the length of the titanium cylinder with the intent of producing two small black holes in line with each other.

According to calculations by our physicist friends at UC Santa Barbara, the two black holes should coalesce into a single wormhole, hopefully to a dimension large enough to precisely send an electromagnetic communication signal along its center axis. At the insulated gold electrode in the center of the spherical end of the cylinder is where Bella will input her antigravity field via the intense power she extracts from the zero-point energy field and hopefully convert it directly to negative energy—namely, an antigravity repulsion field to stabilize the walls of the wormhole.

Thay had been concerned that there would be a large energy release as a consequence of the fusion of the two black holes into a single wormhole. However, Eric's calculations indicated that the chamber should withstand the energy release—at least in theory!

Based on discussions with Thay, I was quite sure that Eric and I could each generate sufficient energy to create two small black holes. After all, I'd done it before on a slightly smaller scale when I inadvertently "killed" him during our first meeting under terrible circumstances I hoped I could eventually forget!

However, we still faced at least four critical challenges, two of which had possible positive outcomes supported by reliable theoretical calculations. The third and fourth were complete unknowns and frighteningly complicated, although for some reason, Thay thinks we can pull them off.

Our first challenge: Would the two black holes coalesce into a large enough wormhole before they collapsed? The second: Could Bella quickly extract sufficient energy from the zero-point energy field in the cosmos and convert it to a negative gravitational field that would stabilize the structure of the wormhole sufficiently to keep it from collapsing when we send a positive energy field—an electromagnetic field communication signal—through it?

Our challenges were getting exponentially bigger. Our third one: Once NASA safely rockets the titanium chamber containing the stabilized wormhole to its orbit position at LP2, could Eric, Bella, and I—working together at our lab in the MIT Green building here on Earth—bend space-time sufficiently from a distance of 1.5 million kilometers away and cause the wormhole to coil over on itself, forming a mini-wormhole connecting the two ends of the now bent-in-half large wormhole? One entrance of this mini-wormhole would have the coordinates of LP2, and the other, the coordinates of Zoi. We're talking a huge bend in space-time.

Which leaves challenge number four—*the biggie*! Calculations by Eric, Thay, and me confirmed that if the larger wormhole, which had coiled over on itself, was stable, then the mini-wormhole connecting its two ends would also be stable. To convince ourselves that this would be the case, we combined complex mathematical elements of anti-de Sitter Space (AdS) and Conformal Field Theory (CFT).[10] This had never been done before, so we consulted with several of NASA's theoretical physicists to check and recheck our calculations. They confirmed our results. We dearly hoped they were right. It would mean the difference as to whether or not there was an implosion when we sent a signal through the wormhole.

It was through the smaller conical wormhole that we would attempt to communicate with any existing intelligent life on Zoi. These four challenges were *all* we needed to meet in order to achieve instantaneous communication. And Thay doesn't believe in miracles!

Although Thay had been prepping us, it would be the first time Eric and I would attempt to bend such a large distance of space-time—basically converting positive zero-point energy to its negative counterpart. Bella—our dear Gravitas—of course, was the expert in that capability. Thay said he would give us a presentation that hopefully would assure us that we could succeed—even with the challenge of the 1.5-million-kilometer distance between Earth and LP2.

Eric was excited by the challenge, and Bella was optimistic and eager to succeed. I was skeptical, if not frightened, by the possible outcome—and I had to change that mindset, otherwise it would be negative karma for our mission. I wondered if turning pro in basketball after Princeton might have been a safer and less stressful job.

THAY HAD SPENT THE LAST MONTH training Bella for her task. Nearly every morning, they would leave Cambridge and drive south for 45 minutes to the Blue Hills Reservation, close to the quaint small town of Dedham and the Blue Hills skiing area. Fortunately, it was early fall, and the snowless ski resorts were closed. There were few tourists, which was great for the secluded work they needed to practice in the mountains.

Their routine was the same every day. It would start with Bella's one-hour deep meditation led by Thay. Next, he would have her shoot

---

[10]Ads/CFT duality is a prime example of the Holographic Principle, developed by physicists Leonard Susskind, Gerard 't Hooft, and Juan Maldacena in the 1990s. It is a complex mathematical theory used to study and describe black holes and the universe. Its mathematics show that all information, including time, that we perceive as our three-dimensional reality is actually stored on a two-dimensional surface—that is, everything we see in our subjective three-dimensional world is an illusion. Ads/CFT duality theory draws heavily on quantum entanglement, enabling complex three-dimensional systems to be reduced to two-dimensional space, making the analysis more tractable.

increasingly stronger antigravity pulses of a negative-energy force field at progressively larger boulders. At first they started with small rocks, but where she ended up was amazing, if not scary.

After four weeks, and sometimes five days a week, at this task, Bella was able to rapidly bend space-time and blast an approximate ten-ton boulder a distance of 500 meters at jet speed up a 30-degree incline to the top of a 250-meter-high hill. Thay told her that mental control would now be very important, and she would have to be careful when intending to shoot only a small pulse so that it wouldn't escalate to something much larger. This was the same discipline he'd taught Eric and me when using our electrokinetic, lightning-generating power.

IT WAS A DREARY RAINY MONDAY MORNING in Cambridge when the entire team gathered at our lab at MIT's Green Building. On the way to the lab, I was hoping that today's outcome would be a lot brighter than the weather. This would be our first try at creating two small black holes within the titanium chamber, and then hopefully seeing them coalesce into an acceptable-sized wormhole. What a small black hole and a wormhole would look like under our conditions, we had no idea.

And if we were lucky, since we would be shooting in the dark, would Bella be able to inject a firm level of stabilization into the wormhole, and how long would it last? The true test of that would be sending a positive-energy communication signal in the form of radio waves through the wormhole with no collapse of its walls.

To avoid sending the titanium chamber flying at jet speed across the room, Bella had to start her pulses at low intensity and slowly build up to maximum, all the while highly focused on only that single gold electrode. It would be a physically and mentally demanding task for her.

Pham and Brianna stood immediately behind Thay, Eric, and me as we all faced the plexiglass window to the isolation room. Its walls, ceiling, and floor were made of three-inch-thick, super-strength nickel-tantalum-tungsten alloy steel. The titanium chamber had been bolted on to a steel cradle, and the cradle in turn had been bolted to the floor of the isolation room about two feet behind the plexiglass window. Eric and I sat on high stools, facing our own 50-centimeter-high titanium lightning rod, which was immediately in front of us and wired through the thick wall of the isolation room to the gold electrodes on the top of the titanium chamber.

Thay started the proceedings. "Okay, Luc and Eric, I hope you both had a good night's sleep last night and are ready to deep-dive into our 30-minute meditation and then conjure up from the zero-point energy field of the universe a super-intense bolt of electrical energy. Eric, you will focus on the lightning rod in front of you that's connected through the wall of the isolation room to electrode number one on the left of the titanium chamber. Luc, you will focus on the lightning rod in front of you that's connected through the wall of the Isolation room to electrode number two on the right of the titanium chamber. Presumably, Eric, you've pumped down the chamber to interstellar conditions, which essentially means zero pressure."

Eric responded, "Right, it's been degassing for three days, and when I checked the pressure last evening and early this morning, it was 1.322×10^{-11} Pascals, the same as deep-space. Normal atmospheric pressure at sea level is 1.01325×10^5. That's a difference of about 10^{16}—or 10,000 trillion times! There's probably not more than a few air molecules left in the chamber."

I had to compliment him. "Eric, your engineering skills have really paid off, even with the insertion of that quartz observation window—no leaks!"

"Thanks, Luc, but our next step should be quite a challenge, and as they say, 'The proof of the pudding is in the eating.' Not that I hunger for a wormhole!"

Thay cut in. "Right, so let's get to it. First, turn off the main lighting in the isolation room, and turn on its infrared lighting system."

Pham asked, "And why is that necessary?"

Thay responded, "I'm assuming Luc and Eric will be successful in generating the two black holes. Black holes have gravitational fields so strong that even light cannot escape from them, and any visible light present is swallowed into the black hole. That creates a circular shadow—a shell of a black, featureless sphere called the *event horizon*. When they capture light or matter, they grow. We don't want them growing too large. The small amount of longer-wavelength, lower-energy infrared light in the isolation room will be enough to form a spherical shadow outline of the event horizon without causing the black holes to increase in size. That's how we'll see them and know we were successful in creating a wormhole."

Pham was more than impressed. "That's unbelievable—gravity so strong that it can suck up visible light!"

Thay continued. "It is. Okay, everyone, put on your night goggles, and let's turn the lights off in the lab and get ready to take our first big step!"

Eric turned off all of the lights. As requested, MIT had given us a lab with no windows, so everything was pitch-black; however, our sensitive night goggles provided some visibility due to the presence of the infrared light.

Then, Thay instructed Eric and me: "Assume your meditation posture, and let's begin. And when I bring you out of the meditation, I will count to three, after which you will both simultaneously conjure up an electric pulse the way we've been simulating for the past several weeks, except this time it won't be a simulation. Let it fly to your designated lightning rod on the titanium cylinder. Are you both with me?"

We answered in the affirmative, and with that, we were off into a deep-dive, 30-minute meditation. Next, Thay helped Bella into her meditation, which would last longer than ours. She would only come out of it when the two black holes had formed, coalesced into a single wormhole, and then had to be stabilized before it collapsed.

At the 30-minute mark, Thay brought Eric and me out of the meditation, and instantly on cue, we both released an immense electrical discharge to our designated lightning rod. As expected, because of the absence of air in the chamber, no visible lightning was generated, but the chamber appeared to vibrate in place; and then several seconds later, all was quiet and two approximate 20-centimeter-diameter, spherical shadows formed, one at each end of the titanium cylinder—the event horizons. We had actually succeeded in creating the first synthetic black holes on Earth. How about Thay and his "step-by-step possible as a means to the impossible"!

He smiled at our success and exclaimed, "We are most fortunate!"

I inquired, "Really? Why's that?"

"Because, if you look at the circular shadow defining the event horizon, it is visually spinning quite slowly. If it were spinning as rapidly as many of the black holes encountered in outer space, if they were to connect, as we hope they do, the energy released would be so large that it would make a mess of everything—including the titanium chamber—but hopefully not the explosion-proof room!"

I had to respond. "*Minchia!* Thanks for telling us . . . now!"

Thay said calmly, "I wasn't too concerned. As I studied those papers by the physicists at UC Santa Barbara, they strongly suggested that what we're seeing would be the outcome. You see, when 'normal' black holes, such as those created in the cosmos, merge, the huge rotational momentum energy from the rapid spin of those monsters has to go somewhere, and it ends up being split between gravitational waves emitted from the collision and the energy in the two black holes. Those waves can shake things up a bit, as you just saw in the vibration of the chamber and its cradle.

"But the real kicker is the energy that becomes part of the newly formed larger black hole. Researchers have calculated that the effect could accelerate it to speeds of hundreds of kilometers per second! But in our case, not to worry. As you saw, it was just some shaking of the titanium chamber and its cradle."

Eric added, "Luc's *minchia* is right on, Thay! On second thought, maybe it's better you hadn't mentioned all this until now! I'm not sure we would have gone ahead with it."

We continued to gaze at the two slowly spinning black holes. After a few minutes, the two event horizons began to move slowly toward each other, and then they fused into a single cylindrical structure that was clearly the beginning of our final wormhole. Again, there was some mild shaking of the titanium chamber and its cradle as the merging of the two black holes into a wormhole released a small amount of gravitational waves.

Thay immediately brought Bella out of her meditation. "Okay, Bella, you know what you have to do. Put on your night goggles, and please proceed carefully and slowly."

Bella acknowledged Thay's instructions. "Right," she said as she began to focus on her designated gold electrode in virtual contact with the single cylindrical wormhole that was forming inside the titanium chamber.

After five long minutes of total focus, having reached her physical and mental endpoint, Bella slouched in her chair and nearly fell over from total exhaustion. I immediately initiated an electromagnetic test signal aimed directly at the same electrode that Bella had focused on, sending it down the precise center of the wormhole. For the next 30 seconds, things went as planned. It appeared against all odds that we were going to succeed on our first try—but that wasn't to be the case.

Seconds later, there was a huge explosion, fortunately contained within the explosion-proof isolation room. The wormhole collapsed, and the energy of that transition was so strong that it blew out the quartz window on the titanium chamber and knocked it off its cradle and onto the floor. We were safe—but nearly back to square one.

When all appeared safe, we entered the isolation room. Fortunately, the titanium chamber looked okay, but it would require a new quartz window, which had been blown to smithereens. There wasn't a piece of quartz larger than a centimeter.

Brianna exclaimed to Thay, "This is terrible! Where do we go from here?"

He gave us a serious look that was very unlike him and then answered Brianna's question. "We are in uncharted spiritual-physics territory. I'm quite sure that the explosion was due to the energy released when the walls of the wormhole collapsed. Bella did a great job of propping up its walls—at least for several seconds—but it wasn't sufficient for total stabilization. It took more out of her physically and emotionally than I expected."

Bella had just opened her eyes, and chimed in, "You can say that again. I feel like I've been run over by a semitruck. Everything in my body, including my brain, aches."

I commented, "I'm really sorry, Bella. So, Thay, are there any other alternatives?"

He answered, "The only thing I can think of may be even more dangerous and risky for Bella than what she just did. So let's take a break, and tomorrow we can discuss our options, if there are any."

Bella responded, "Out of curiosity, when we meet, I'd like to know what that risky approach would be."

I looked at Bella. "No, you don't!"

Bella glared at me with one of her "Don't tell me what I want" expressions.

Quite a strong woman.

Chapter Five

THAY'S SECRET

"When things do not go your way, remember that every challenge, every adversity, contains within it the seeds of opportunity and growth."
— ROY T. BENNETT

TUESDAY, OCTOBER 15, 2030—CAMBRIDGE, MASSACHUSETTS

It was an unusually sunny extended summer day—72°F—in mid-October! Talk about global warming. Why not sunbathe at Mystic Lakes or Castle Island Beach, both a short drive from Cambridge? But that wasn't to be. As Thay had pointed out, we were smack-dab in the middle of a critical top-secret project, and we could all go to jail for discussing classified information on a public beach. I had to be content with sucking up those rays while driving to work in my '57 Chevy convertible with the top down.

And so it was. We were all back in the lab for a meeting to decide on our next steps after what had become known to our small group as the "Labor Day Weekend[11] Catastrophe." Once again, Major Dallant had pulled lots of strings to get our titanium chamber rapidly repaired. So, as far as we were concerned, we were going for "take two."

Thay opened the discussion. "I assume we can all agree that creating the two black holes at a reasonable size was a major success. And

---

[11]Labor Day occurs in the US on the first Monday of every September and is an annual celebration of the social and economic achievements of American workers.

as the scientists at UC Santa Barbara had predicted via their theory, with a little help from Luc and Eric, those two black holes coalesced into a twice-their-length, similar-diameter wormhole with entry and exit at its two endpoints—another success for which I'm grateful. Our challenge is stabilization of the wormhole to prevent it from collapsing with another catastrophic implosion."

Of course, we were all of one mind on those points—and getting that far was a major accomplishment. But then came the controversy.

Thay continued. "I've discussed our results with two theoretical astrophysicists at NASA who specialize in the theory of black holes and wormholes, and they both feel that there's no way Bella could pump in enough negative energy to prevent the wormhole from collapsing—at least according to the laws of known physics."

Pham asked, "Dad, do you agree with them?"

Without hesitation, Thay's quick response was, "No! At least if you look beyond the laws of known physics."

Eric asked, "Really? So what do you think?"

Thay went up to the whiteboard and said, "I don't believe there's any way Bella could pump in enough negative energy to prevent the wormhole from collapsing—that is, without further assistance. Let me explain.

"There are two possibilities that I see, and although they should work in principle, both are risky. Here's what I believe they are. He then wrote on the board: (1) OBE and (2) 4-phosphoryloxy-N,N-dimethyltryptamine."

Although all of us knew a lot about OBEs, we weren't sure what Thay had in mind. But number two had us staring at the board with bewildered expressions. Thay quickly continued before any of us could say a word.

"Let's put number one on the back burner for the time being. The reason for that is straightforward. It would involve an OBE to Zoi, and even if successful, it would not enable us to transport physical beings there, unless it had an advanced civilization that could educate us on how to create a large enough stable wormhole to do that—that is, if they were a friendly force and agreed with the idea. Also, as far as I know, no one has ever done an OBE off of planet Earth and returned to report on their findings. Although, I must admit, I don't know if anyone has ever tried."

Brianna asked, "Are you concerned that if someone did an OBE to, say, the moon, their consciousness might get stuck there, never to return to Earth?"

Thay's response was, "Maybe—I just don't know. Perhaps they could get stuck in the infinite field of Cosmic Consciousness or in another dimension and not be able to find their way back. I'm sure that there's a law in spiritual physics that governs that situation. We just don't know what that law is. If we seriously considered either strategy one or two, we would have to decide which one is riskier—and is it reasonable to try either of them?"

Minchia! With my mind spinning in and out of anxiety, I had to get to some kind of endpoint. I said, "Okay, Thay, I give up. If it's not an OBE, then what in the world is 4-phosphoryloxy-N,N-dimethyltryptamine, and what does it have to do with anything we're doin'?"

Before he could respond, Bella gave us the answer. "It's psilocybin. It's the main psychoactive hallucinogenic ingredient in 'magic mushrooms.' After ingestion, psilocybin is metabolically converted into the pharmacologically active form, known as psilocin. Psilocin, or as the chemists call it, 4-hydroxy-N,N-dimethyltryptamine, is a substituted tryptamine alkaloid and a potent serotonergic psychedelic substance. It prevents the uptake of serotonin neurotransmitters and is present in magic mushrooms together with its phosphorylated counterpart, psilocybin. In case you're not aware of it, psilocin and psilocybin are designated as Schedule I drugs under the Convention on Psychotropic Substances. They are illegal in most countries."

Eric was busting at the seams to speak up. "Well, that's a mouthful. But it's so cool! Thay wants us to become druggies and hallucinate our way to planet Zoi! But before he gets me off this ridiculous track and tells us the real reason for putting that complicated formula on the board, what's all of this bit about serotonin? Most antidepressants these days are called selective serotonin reuptake inhibitors, or SSRIs. So what's the connection?"

Brianna responded to Eric. "I can help you with that. According to what I can remember from organic chemistry, serotonin, or

5-hydroxytryptamine, is a monoamine neurotransmitter. Its biological function is complex and multifaceted, but it's known to affect your mood, cognition, learning, memory, and numerous physiological processes. But like you, Eric, I have no idea what all of this hallucinogenic stuff has to do with what we're faced with now."

Thay jumped in immediately. "Okay, folks, allow me to clarify." He looked at us as if he wasn't sure he wanted to proceed . . . but he did. "What I'm about to tell you will take a little bit of time, but you'll need this information to make the decision that we're faced with today. I learned about it from a brilliant elderly monk scholar named Gervesh while I was a student at the monastery in Nepal. Believe it or not, he was well over a hundred years of age. No one, including him, knew how old he was. And he was dying, so I volunteered to attend to him in my free time away from school. We became close friends and had lots of philosophical discussions. During those last days before he died, he went into guru mode and told me several amazing stories. The one I am about to disclose, he made me promise never to mention—to anyone. I will assume that his spirit will forgive me for this, as it may be the answer we need to do something of great value for humanity."

We were all mesmerized by Thay's words, as Pham cautioned his father. "Dad, you don't have to tell us. There must be another way that doesn't break your promise to your friend."

"I don't think so. I've thought about this for several days, and I believe that if Gervesh knew about our situation, he would offer his support."

I offered my input. "Perhaps, Thay, we could at least promise to keep your secret exclusively within our team."

"That would be deeply appreciated." Thay thought for a moment and then continued. "What Gervesh disclosed to me came from an ancient book you may have heard of—*The Egyptian Book of the Dead*. It's an ancient text of alchemy spells and magic formulas that was often placed in the tombs of Egyptian royalty and believed to protect and aid them in the hereafter.

"Over the centuries, numerous compilers and sorcerers modified the original text, often deleting and keeping for themselves the more powerful alchemical methods. The original text contained many great secrets, like the one I'm about to tell you. It was written about

2400 BCE, and according to Gervesh was hidden in the Great Pyramid of Giza, which was completed in 2600 BCE. Gervesh said that a lot of original information was removed over the millennia by well-meaning alchemists who considered it too dangerous to be in the hands of ordinary people.

"In the mid-19th century, Karl Richard Lepsius, a German Egyptologist, discovered the original text. He later traveled through the Himalayas and visited our monastery. He was so taken with the spiritual capabilities of our monks, especially Gervesh, that he donated the book to the monastery with the condition that it would be hidden and preserved in a safe place at the monastery, and only allowed to be read by those with highly evolved levels of consciousness and wisdom. Gervesh was among those few individuals."

Eric asked, "So where is it now? Was it ever found after his death?"

Thay responded, "No. Gervesh died before he disclosed its whereabouts."

I asked, "So what does all of this have to do with what we're trying to accomplish?"

Thay answered, "Before he died, Gervesh and I had numerous discussions about the power of deep meditation. He finally disclosed that he had studied the original ancient text in depth and that there were methods and formulas that, if followed carefully and precisely, could induce superhuman powers in ordinary individuals.

"There were several methods we discussed in great detail. One of them is pertinent to our current challenge. When a deep meditation is carried out by an experienced meditator after ingesting a certain amount of magic mushrooms, it's possible to create even greater powers in an individual—well beyond what you have or could imagine. He talked about people being able to fly freely in the air using just their thoughts for control—essentially, a form of antigravity. You could see something similar to this 30 years ago in the popular Ang Lee film *Crouching Tiger, Hidden Dragon*."

I asked, "Did you ever try anything Gervesh described from the ancient text, and if so, did it work?"

Thay hesitated. He was struggling with how to answer my question. "Yes, I did . . . and it worked exactly as Gervesh had explained.

But I would rather not discuss what I did at this time—perhaps at another time, when it's appropriate for all of us."

This was spooky. But I let it go, as did everyone else.

Then Thay said, "Perhaps you can see where this is going. If Bella, who is already gifted with significant antigravity powers, were to ingest the appropriate amount of psilocybin—preferably its rapidly acting metabolic counterpart, psilocin—in conjunction with her deep meditation, she might be able to generate enough energy to stabilize the wormhole. Essentially, it would be a way to temporarily attain the superpowers of a yogi—in the words of the ancient Wisdom Seekers, you would reach *Samadhi*.[12] However, as I mentioned at the beginning of our discussion, this would not be without great risk to Bella, and I'm not sure how it would work out."

I didn't hesitate. "No way! Bella is not even going to consider it!" I should have known better than to try to dominate Bella's feminine energy and decision-making powers.

She replied in a mild but controlled tone, "My dear Emperius, who are you to make personal decisions for me?"

"Come on, Bella, you must be kidding. I'm not gonna let you put your life in danger."

She asked with raised eyebrows, "Not even to help save the human race—something we've all done many times before?"

I could say no more. I closed my eyes tight—and worried like hell.

---

[12] Over the years, Thay had instructed the SPI Team on the means to use their minds to enhance their superpowers. When all thought is absent for 12 seconds, this is known as concentration. When trained to concentrate for 12 multiplied by 12 seconds—that is, 2 minutes and 24 seconds, the individual has achieved the first step in meditation. When the mind is then trained to concentrate with no thought for 12 mulitplied by 2 minutes and 24 seconds—that is, 28 minutes and 48 seconds, it has achieved what the ancient Hindu Wisdom Seekers called *Samadhi*. At this point, the meditator is capable of superpowers unexplainable by the laws of classical and quantum physics. The meditator has stepped into the realm of *spiritual physics*.

Chapter Six

THE TEST

"If you risk nothing, then you risk everything!"
— Geena Davis

Wednesday, October 23, 2030—Cambridge, Massachusetts

Bella was adamant. She was absolutely confident that she could help the team succeed in its mission. Nothing was going to deter her from using her powers to create a stabilized wormhole. The future of humanity was at stake.

After two days of intense discussions, we all finally agreed to support her in her efforts to stabilize the wormhole—that is, if we were again able to create one in our second attempt. If she succeeded, we had no idea how long the wormhole would remain stabilized, so Major Dallant made plans for immediate air transport of the titanium cylinder containing the wormhole to the Cape Canaveral Space Force Station in Florida, where it would be launched for its destination at LP2. Optimistic about success during our early efforts, we'd constructed a small explosion-proof container for safe transport of the titanium cylinder by truck and plane to Cape Canaveral—just in case it decided to go *poof!* on the way there.

If the wormhole remained stable at LP2, the next step would be for Bella, Eric, and me to attempt bending space-time to closely connect the entry coordinates of the wormhole at LP2 and its exit coordinates at our best guess for an exoplanet that might be Sophia's Zoi—and we would have to do this from Earth, a distance of nearly one million miles!

And, of course, assuming this all worked out the way we planned, we were counting on the conclusions from our gauge-duality[13] quantum-gravity calculations—that a small, conical wormhole would form, connecting the ends of the larger wormhole. It was through the smaller wormhole that we would direct our communication signal to the exoplanet. Right—nothing like technical challenges! But the rest of the team was still optimistic. I consider my occasional dicey conclusions as realism. When I expressed them to Thay, he just smiled—his message was clear.

Next, we would initiate radio communication from Earth and through the stabilized smaller wormhole to the exoplanet of choice. If we succeeded in bending space-time as planned but were unsuccessful in connecting with intelligent life on that particular exoplanet, unfortunately we would be faced with the prospect of modifying the initial space-time structure by moving the exit coordinates of the wormhole to those for the next exoplanet to which we wanted to send our communication. Talk about making the impossible possible!

Depending on how long the wormhole remained stabilized, we would continue this procedure throughout our list of possible Earth-like exoplanets, each time sending radio signals to the planet, hoping for a response from intelligent life. Even if we knew where the inhabited exoplanet was located, it would likely take some time to determine how to communicate with any alien beings who might live there. Those were our tasks at hand—that's all! Things weren't looking optimistic.

We continued to move ahead with frequent, deep meditations. Under Thay's tutelage, we were again following one of the primary laws of

---

[13]A conjecture proposed by Juan Maldacena of Princeton's Institute for Advanced Study. It is a relationship between certain quantum field theories and gravity theories. The idea is that a strongly coupled quantum system can generate complex quantum states that have an equivalent description in terms of a gravity theory (or a string theory) in a higher dimensional space.

spiritual physics: the Manifestation Sequence.[14]

As had happened several times before under Thay's counsel, we were planning on success in manifesting one of the most challenging—some would say, *impossible*—tasks before us. Thay requested that for the foreseeable future, we remove that word from our lexicon during our communications and discussions.

With help from our friends at CIA/NSA, Brianna managed to have 100 grams of psilocin secretly synthesized by one of her organic chemistry colleagues at Columbia. We'd decided to use the metabolite of psilocybin directly. It would be much faster-acting than waiting for psilocybin to be converted to psilocin in Bella's digestive system and subsequently dispersed into her bloodstream. Several clinical studies had been carried out in the past at Johns Hopkins University by a professor focused on the use of psilocybin to treat anxiety and depression, so Bella was able to get information on safe dosages and other relevant data.

For a 175-pound person, the amount of psilocybin for moderate-to-severe, unipolar or treatment-resistant major depression had been generally two doses of 25 milligrams each, usually seven days apart. Psilocybin's psychopharmaceutical effects typically became detectable 30 to 60 minutes after dosing, peaked two to three hours after dosing, and subsiding to negligible levels six hours after dosing, with no undesirable side effects. Based on Bella's discussions with the professor in charge of the study, Thay decided that Bella would take 40 milligrams of psilocin. We couldn't wait 30 to 60 minutes after dosing for the drug to take effect. Psilocin should have nearly instantaneous effects.

WE WERE READY TO PROCEED. Thay again led Eric and me into deep meditations, and then working in unison, we were able to repeat the synthesis within the titanium chamber, two opposing black holes of roughly similar dimensions. As before, they began a slow progression, moving toward each other to create a single wormhole.

---

[14]Manifestation Sequence: *Intention→Attention→Imagination→Belief→Detachment:* Properly practiced, this tool enables the manifestation of literally anything by directly accessing the wisdom of the Akashic Field, as long as the rules for manifestation are accurately adhered to. The Akashic Field is an infinite and eternal reservoir, located in an alternate cosmic dimension and comprising detailed information for every thought, action, or event that has ever occurred, or will occur in the future. To succeed at a task as difficult as ours requires frequent deep meditation. The most difficult step is *Detachment*—seeking success but detaching from your expectation of its achievement.

This time there were some major changes in procedure, since Bella's input had to be timed to take effect at just the right moment. Thay had given her the 40 milligrams of psilocin about 60 minutes before Eric and I did our thing. Thirty minutes into that process, we could tell from her comments that Bella was well into her psychedelic trip, but still cognizant of what was happening. Thay then led her into deep meditation, which he allowed to last for another 65 minutes. By then, the wormhole had been formed. He brought Bella out of meditation—she was smiling with intermittent giggling—and instructed her to do her focused access of negative antigravity energy from the zero-point energy field of the universe.

She hesitated for a few moments. We thought, *Oh my God, no way, she's too far gone into psychedelic la-la land!* Then she closed her eyes for the briefest moment, opened them with a serious focus on the wormhole, and we were off to the races. For the next five minutes, we could see the strain on her face. Suddenly, she started to shake—and so did the titanium cylinder containing the wormhole. Her shaking became severe. Her nose started to bleed, so I had to intervene.

"Thay, we've got to bring her out. She's falling apart."

"Not just yet. It would not only cause another explosion, but worse, it could be much more damaging to her."

"But, Thay . . ."

Suddenly, Bella closed her eyes and fell off her chair into a dreadful unconscious state.

Thay immediately pushed the button that closed the window on the titanium chamber. He switched on the room lights as he began to assess Bella's situation. "She's got a heartbeat, but it's very slow, and she's breathing.

Brianna nearly shouted, "Shouldn't we call for an ambulance?"

Thay responded, "There's no time for that. Luc, you'll need to help Bella with your hands-on healing powers."

As I'd done once before in the hospital when she was in a coma, I immediately began to stroke her forehead and speak to her in a low, steady voice. "Come on, Gravitas, you can do this. You're strong, and as far as I'm concerned, invincible. I want you to wake up—*please!*"

Eric started a whispering chant, "Gravitas, Gravitas, Gravitas . . . ," and he was soon joined by Brianna and Pham.

I was really scared, and I was starting to lose it. I continued massaging Bella's forehead and arms. "Gravitas, I need you in my life. Please wake up. What are you waiting for?"

Suddenly, Bella opened her eyes, gave just the slightest hint of smile, and said, "For you to say you love me like you did the last time we did this."

I picked her up from the floor and hugged her. "I love you!"

All of us had big smiles on our faces as I helped Bella up to her chair. We were so preoccupied with Bella that we'd forgotten about the wormhole—but Thay hadn't. He turned off the room lights as we all replaced our infrared googles. He then opened the window to the titanium chamber and exclaimed, "I believe we *may* have a stable wormhole!"

We were all unicorns and rainbows, jumping up and down. In our collective optimism, we'd missed Thay's use of the word *may*. He reminded us that we needed to send a radio signal through the center of the wormhole and be sure it didn't explode, as it had last time. *Minchia!*

As everyone held their breath or closed their eyes in meditative prayer, I did the test—no explosion! *Grazie Dio!*[15]

This time Thay said, "I believe we *have* a stable wormhole."

There it was, right before us. The long wormhole had bent precisely in half, creating a tightly formed structure that looked like a totally symmetrical letter *U*. As anticipated, a small micro-wormhole had formed, connecting the bottom of one end of the *U* with the top section of the other end of the *U*. Not a miracle, but a perfect example of the progression of *impossible* to *possible* to *probable* to *success*. *Way to go, Bella! Thank you, Gervesh!*

Thay continued with some urgency. "Luc, you'll have to immediately contact Major Dallant and have that special vehicle here ASAP for transport to Andrews Air Force Base. There's a plane waiting for the package for its delivery to NASA."

"Will do."

Eric asked Bella, "So what was it like to be on cloud nine?"

She replied, "Someday I'll give you the details, but for now, all I can say is that it was scary and exciting at the same time—one of the

---

[15] *Grazie Dio!* is Italian for "Thank God!"

most pleasurable experiences of my life—although when you look at the whole picture, I wouldn't want to do it too often, at least not with psilocin. I saw my life as I had never seen it before."

Thay noted, "With practice, you could do it without the drug, but it will require *lots* of practice. Speaking of practice, if Major Dallant's men pick up the wormhole this afternoon, it will likely be on a fueled rocket in the morning, and be ready for immediate jettison to LP2."

I asked, "How long will it take to get there? The James Webb telescope took about four weeks. But with the rocket system NASA has supplied and taking a much more direct route, which was not possible with the Webb telescope, it should be there in three weeks and be ready to send communications through the wormhole a few days later—that is, if what NASA is now calling *Moreno Stabilization* continues to hold.[16]

Eric had to comment. "Wow, Gravitas, you have an astrophysical process named after you, and you're not even an astrophysicist!"

"Thanks, Electer," Bella replied. "I'm not sure if that's a compliment or a critique of astrobiologists."

"No, I intended it as a compliment—really! I mean, let's face it, it looks like it will take a woman to save humanity."

I stepped in. "Hey, folks, we have a three-week hiatus to resume our own research before we can begin communication through the wormhole at LP2 to our exoplanet of choice—hopefully, it turns out to be Zoi. Whaddya say we celebrate our success so far at the MIT faculty club on Memorial Drive. If it weren't raining so hard, I'd suggest we walk, but let's just take our cars. I can fit Brianna, Bella, and Thay in my Chevy. Eric, can you take Pham in your pickup?"

"Absolutely!"

And with that, we all set out to celebrate our success so far in making the impossible . . . possible.

---

[16]Bella's full name—Isabella Moreno.

Chapter Seven

PHAM'S
TRANSITION

*"In order to change the world, you have to get your
head together first."*
—Jimi Hendrix

WEDNESDAY, OCTOBER 23, 2030—CAMBRIDGE, MASSACHUSETTS

We'd been at the faculty club for nearly 30 minutes, but Eric and Pham had not yet arrived, which made no sense at all. The lab was just a few minutes away from the faculty club by foot or by car. I was about to call them when my phone rang. It was Eric.

"Hey, good buddy, where the heck are you guys?"

Eric was breathing heavily, and his voice sounded terribly troubled. "Luc, we had a serious accident near the corner of Ambrose and Amherst. A truck slammed into us broadside on the passenger side. I'm okay, saved by the airbag. Just a sprained wrist. But Pham wasn't so lucky. The airbag system was turned off on his side. He's unconscious. His head was hit pretty hard. Lots of blood. I'm in an ambulance with him speeding to Mass General."

"Eric, sit tight. We're on our way to the hospital." The word *hospital* got everyone's attention.

Bella exclaimed, "Good God, Luc, what happened?"

I tried to respond as calmly as possible. "Eric and Pham were in an accident. Eric seems to be okay, but Pham was hit quite hard. They're in an ambulance on their way to the hospital. We have to go—now!"

Brianna reacted instantly and was near tears, and as serene as Thay always appeared, it was the first time I'd ever seen him visibly shaken since he'd told me years ago about the death of Amisha, his one and only true love. Bella put her arm around Brianna. No one said another word. We left the faculty club immediately, returned to my car, and quickly made our way to the hospital.

When we arrived at the emergency room, I notified the nurse at the front desk, and he got my message to Eric. After a long and somber 30 minutes, he was able to come to the reception area.

Eric was quite disheveled—a few stitches on the side of his head, what looked like an emerging black eye, and his left wrist was bandaged and supported in a sling. The front of his white shirt was covered with blood, but it wasn't his. It had come from Pham as Eric had pulled him from his pickup, which had rolled over a few times and landed upside down. He was anxious to speak.

"I'm so sorry for all of this. I should have listened to Pham. He wanted to walk to the faculty club. He kept saying, 'What's a little rain?' But I insisted on driving. The truck driver was texting on his phone. He didn't put his brakes on until he hit us. Good God, I feel so bad for Pham."

Bella tried to comfort Eric. "It wasn't your fault."

Thay cut in, "Eric, when can we see Pham? Is he conscious?"

"Sorry, Thay, he's still unconscious. They took him to the magnetic resonance department for a CT scan of his head, and X-rays to see if he has any broken bones. The doctor said he would come to speak with us after he sees the results."

We all sat there staring at the opposite wall, not saying a word, just doing what you do in a hospital waiting room—wait—and then waited some more. I asked Eric, "What happened to the truck driver?"

"Not sure. When we were leaving in the ambulance, I heard the police say they were going to escort him to the police station. He didn't have any injuries. My guess is that he'll get a stiff fine, maybe lose his commercial license—and therefore his job—for reckless driving."

Bella said, "That's well deserved."

Finally, after an hour and a half of nerve-racking quiet, the doctor entered the reception area and asked to speak with Pham's father.

He looked a little dismayed as he addressed Thay, who was dressed in his usual monk attire. "Sir, I understand that you're Pham's father. Is that right?"

"Yes. How is he?" Thay was more than anxious.

The doctor explained, "He has no bone fractures, I suppose because his body is more than in excellent shape. That's the good news. But I'm concerned about his head injury. He has a serious subdural hematoma—a large collection of blood between his skull and his brain. They're usually caused by serious head injuries. His is quite massive and still continuing to slowly fill with blood. We need to keep a close watch on it and his vital signs. Continuous bleeding will put added pressure on the brain and can be life-threatening. If he continues to bleed, we'll have to drill into his skull and drain the blood. Since that can be quite risky, I'd like to wait and monitor him closely for now."

Thay asked, "Is he still unconscious?"

The doctor replied, "Yes, and I suspect that will continue to be the case until the pressure on his brain goes down with a decrease in the amount of blood in the hematoma. There's also the possibility that he could slip into a coma, but I think for now he's fine. We'll keep a close watch."

Thay continued his inquiry. "Even if the bleeding stops, will the hematoma eventually disappear?"

The doctor said, "It might, but it would take some time for that amount of blood to be reabsorbed by his brain. In fact, it could take weeks, during which time, even if he completely recovered, we would want to monitor the progress by CT scans. If the blood did not reabsorb, we would revert to the drilling procedure to remove it."

Minchia! Things were not looking good. I could see the stress across Thay's face.

He asked the doctor, "When can I see him?"

The doctor answered, "If you wait around for an hour or so, he'll be transferred to the ICU by then, and you can spend some time with him there."

Thay turned to everyone and said, "Look, there's no point in all of you staying here. Please go back to your hotel and I'll update you by text and call you when I see Pham, if there are any changes."

We all went over to Thay, hugged him, and assured him Pham would be okay—but what did we know? Thay knew that as well. I guess it was our way of saying, "I *hope* he'll be okay," without saying it like that.

As we all headed for the exit from the reception area, Thay called out, "Not you, Luc. I'd like you to stay."

"Sure. Hey, Bella, take my keys. You remember how to use the floor-shift on my Chevy?"

She turned around and gave me one of those "Are you kidding me?" looks of hers and said, "My father taught me to drive on his old Ford truck, which had a floor-shift!"

I implored, "Drive safely!" And then they were all out the door.

We sat in the waiting room for another hour, until the doctor arrived. He told Thay, "We did another CT scan. The bleeding has stopped, and that's good. But he's still unconscious. I'll take you to his room."

As we entered Pham's room in the ICU, we could see and hear the ominous trappings of an ICU unit—the periodic beeping of the instruments keeping tabs on Pham's vital signs. His head was completely bandaged, and he had two different IVs, one in each of his arms. He didn't look good.

Thay went over and sat next to him, his right hand on Pham's left shoulder. He closed his eyes. I guess he was praying, so I sat quietly on a chair across the room just opposite him.

About 30 minutes later, Thay stood up, walked over to me, and asked, "Do you know why I wanted you to stay?"

I did. "Yeah. I think so."

"Then please pull your chair over in front of mine, and we'll start with a deep meditation to raise your level of consciousness and elevate your hands-on healing power to a high enough level to help Pham with his injury."

I did as he asked, and before I knew it, I was in the tunnel I'd been in before with the Great White Light moving toward me. I stood there as it continued to move forward and stopped a couple of meters in front of me. As before, we conversed with thought.

"Luc, this young man, Pham, is one with unusually high spiritual values. His spirit has a strong imprint of the two special souls who gave birth to him. You must and will save him—and one day, he will do the same for you."

Oh Great White Light, I will do whatever you ask. I am your everlasting servant.

"I know that. It is your prime mission on Earth. . . . One last thing— during Pham's unconscious state, he will receive a gift from me and a message from his mother, which she will request to be delivered to his father. When he wakes up, he will be physically and mentally disoriented from his injury. When he regains his composure, please be sure he gives his father this important message. And say nothing to Thay about our conversation until Pham has awakened and speaks with his father."

Great White Light, I understand, and I will do as you say.

And with that, I heard Thay as he brought me out of my meditation.

"How was it, Luc?"

I didn't respond. I was dazed and overcome with what the Great White Light had just told me.

Unusual for him, Thay showed some impatience. "Luc, did you hear me?"

"I did. I did. Please let me catch my emotional breath, and I'll share what happened."

Thay bowed his head in contrition, knowing that he'd entered the field of impatience and aggression. No one's perfect, especially when it comes to the safety of their children.

We were both quiet for a few minutes. I took a deep breath and then told Thay what I'd experienced—but as directed by the Great White Light—not everything. Thay's overall composure changed almost instantly and dramatically. He smiled as he learned that the Great White Light had instructed me to heal and awaken Pham from his trauma.

Thay said nothing. But then, moments later, he said with heartfelt emotion, "Thank you, Luc. Please help my son."

With that, I sat next to Pham and began to circle my hands slowly a few centimeters above his chest, and then I moved to his head. I continued to do so for what seemed like an eternity. It was probably less than a half hour.

I turned to Thay. "I don't understand this! There should be some reaction by now. What am I doing wrong?"

Thay's response was soft and steady. "Nothing, my friend. If you're doing anything wrong, it may be that your impatience appears as a lack of faith in what the Great White Light has asked of you."

"I'm sorry, Thay. I hope that's not the case. I think it may be my lack of faith in myself."

Thay responded, "That's an easier one to fix. It's in your complete control. So, please, keep going. It will work. Perhaps the Great White Light is testing your commitment to him and his request."

I did some *pranayama* (controlled) breathing, renewed my commitment, and continued for nearly an hour. My arms felt as though they were about to fall off. I was losing my meditative focus, and I regret to say, my patience.

I confessed to Thay, "I have complete faith in what the Great White Light told me and asked of me. It's me. It's me. I must be doing something wrong. I need to rest my arms."

Thay stared at me as I removed my aching arms from Pham's head, put my elbows on my knees, and in frustration, put my face in my hands. Thay said nothing. He put his hand softly on my shoulder. A few seconds later, I heard a low voice to my left.

"Hey, guys, where am I? And what am I doing here—in bed?"

Thay and I stood up with the same intense jubilance we'd experienced ten years ago when we'd averted a terrorist attack at the Taglyan Center in Los Angeles.

Thay knelt beside Pham's bed, hugged him, then stared directly into his eyes and exclaimed, "Welcome back, son!"

Suddenly, I guess a light went off in Pham's mind—which was a good sign. "Now I remember . . . Eric and I were driving in his pickup. I looked out my window and saw a huge truck heading straight for us, just a few meters away. Thank God I'm still alive!"

I thought, *Right—thank God you're alive!*

Thay and I filled Pham in on what had happened, but for now left out the deep meditation and hands-on healing. All of it would have been a lot for him to absorb in his foggy state of mind. Besides, he had to see the doctor to get another CT scan and monitor what was going on in his head—which happened almost immediately.

Thay and I waited in Pham's room as he was wheeled back to the department where he was to receive the CT scan and an MRI. In about an hour, the doctor returned with a nurse, who was pushing Pham in a wheelchair, positioning him next to Thay and me.

The doctor looked at the three of us with a strange frown and said. "I don't believe it! Here, look at the first CT scan. Do you see that large, dark shadow circling nearly half of Pham's skull?" Pham stood up so he could see it as well.

The three of us acknowledged almost in unison: "Yes."

The doctor continued. "That's a huge puddle of blood, and I do mean huge! Now look at the CT scan we ran just an hour ago. The shadow is completely gone. That's impossible! But it's true. I can't believe it. The blood has completely disappeared—apparently reabsorbed by his brain tissue within minutes, not days—and all of his vitals are totally normal. I've heard of miracles before, but this . . . this is . . . I don't know what it is—"

Thay interrupted, "Doctor, there's no such thing as a miracle. My son just heals quickly. I'd like to take him home unless you have a good reason to keep him."

Now it was the doctor who was dazed. In a barely audible voice, he said, "No. I mean yes . . . he . . . he can go." The doctor ambled out of the reception area shaking his head in disbelief.

The three of us sat next to each other on the edge of the bed.

Pham, suddenly a bright ray of exuberance, said, "Dad, I have something to tell you."

I thought, *Great, I don't have to remind him.*

"What is it, Pham?"

"While I was unconscious, I had a kinda dream . . . except to be honest, I doubt that's what it was. I met someone."

Thay asked, "Really? Who was that?"

Pham hesitated for a moment, but then said, "Mom—I met your Amisha."

At first, Thay smiled, but then that smile slowly faded. But moments later, it returned, bigger than before, this time accompanied by tears of joy in his eyes. He looked lovingly at Pham and said, "I see, and what did Mom say? Anything?"

"Yes, she said she wanted you to know that ever since she met you in Nepal, her existence has been continuously filled with elation and joy, and that her love for you has grown beyond words. She said that she is so grateful to be your soulmate and dearly appreciates that you were both gifted by Cosmic Consciousness with the opportunity to have brought into this world a magnificent son—her words, Dad, not mine—who now works with his father to make planet Earth a better place. She said, 'Please tell him that I will visit with him at an appropriate time.'"

Now, both Pham and Thay had tears in their eyes. Thay could barely respond, but he managed a whisper: "Thank you, Pham . . . thank you."

Thay recovered with a philosophical and somewhat humorous comment. "Maybe I've been wrong all these years—maybe there *is* such a thing as a miracle."

At that precious and private moment, a nurse slowly started to open the door, returning with a wheelchair to accompany Pham downstairs for his release from the hospital. Instinctively and rapidly, Pham held up his right arm toward the opening door and somewhat intensely, fired out, "Please, nurse, give us a few moments!"

His request was appropriate, but what wasn't was the antigravitational pulse that emanated from Pham's arm, hitting the slowly opening door and closing it shut. We could hear the nurse's exclamation of surprise and dismay on the other side of the closed door. He was not a happy camper.

Pham, wide-eyed and more than surprised himself, opened his mouth but didn't say a word—Thay did it for him.

"Son, you have received a special gift and must now learn how to manage it. It will be my great pleasure to help you with that."

Pham was still dazed by what had happened. I couldn't help but think of Bella, who'd been given the same power during her NDE, and how Thay had taught her how to use it—carefully. These were some of the most powerful moments I could recall in a very long time. I guess as my mom used to say, "Everything happens for a reason"—a good reason, as far as the cosmos was concerned.

I thought, *Pham, you're now truly an everlasting member of the SPI Team.*

Chapter Eight

BLAST FROM THE PAST

"The mind that opens up to a new idea never returns to its original size."
— Albert Einstein

Saturday, November 16, 2030—Cambridge, Massachusetts

"Miraculous," some might call it—but not Thay.[17] Two days after Pham's release from the hospital, he was back to work at the Tang Soo Do dojo in better shape than ever, and working diligently with his students to catch up on what they'd missed in his absence.

Though gratefully gifted with the power of hands-on healing, until I understood the laws of spiritual physics that govern what happened in the hospital, I couldn't help thinking that Pham's recovery was a miracle—something orchestrated by Divine Spirit. But I guess that might be a sacrilegious thought, since the Great White Light told me that *I* would cure Pham.

When I expressed this conundrum to Thay, he said that both statements were correct. I did cure him, and yes, a Divine Spirit had orchestrated it—one that resides within me—and, in truth, within everyone.

---

[17]See note 8 on p. 32.

It's just that some of us can lower the chaos within our personal world sufficiently to access that spirit and use it for our good and the good of the world. Again he emphasized: *There is no such thing as a miracle.* Like any unbelievable magic tricks, "miracles" can be explained by certain laws that govern their occurrence. We simply don't comprehend all of them at this time. I look forward to when that happens.

Eric and I—working with the benefit of spiritual and technical counsel from Thay—were back digging into the theoretical work we and numerous other scientists before us had done on quantum gravity, black holes, and wormholes. We were trying to determine how we might combine the laws of quantum physics with those governing the general theory of relativity by somehow meshing them with the laws of spiritual physics. As such, that would enable us to do something that had never been done before—bend space-time between two distant sets of interstellar coordinates—one set at LP2 and the other set a hundred light-years away at what we hoped would be the exoplanet Zoi.

Day after day, until the wee hours of the morning, we were doing our best, at least on paper and in our computer models, to combine critical concepts from esoteric areas of quantum physics, conformal field theory (CFT), anti-de Sitter Space (AdS) theory, and general relativity with those of spiritual physics. It was a maddening exercise. Thank God for Thay!

Besides his native intelligence and spiritual bent, Thay's stay at Harvard must have done him good. His expertise and creativity in theoretical and mathematical physics was unbelievable. If not for those skills, his deep knowledge of spiritual physics, and frequent deep meditations under his guidance, I don't know if we would have gotten off first base.

But we did, and Eric and I were dead set on hitting a home run. We'd made what we believed were important theoretical discoveries. Unfortunately, we probably wouldn't have the opportunity to publish our findings—at least not for many years. As Major Dallant liked to say, it was all classified beyond top-secret.

We'd proven unequivocally what many astrophysicists had thought for some time—that space-time was not an *intrinsic* property of the universe—meaning that space and time are not fundamental properties; they are *emergent* properties, arising from the structure and behavior of more basic components of the universe. They're analogous to a string of cars causing a traffic jam. The car is *intrinsic* or *fundamental*. The traffic jam is not. It's *emergent* because it arises from the action of something more *fundamental*—cars.

Because space-time was an emergent property of the universe, our calculations showed that with sufficient, subtle Cosmic Consciousness energy, generated from the zero-point field of the universe, we could manipulate space-time, even a hundred light-years away. Yeah, I know, it sounds crazy, but as Bella likes to say when she's absolutely positive about something, we were "99.9 percent sure" we were correct.

Much of the insight that enabled us to make our breakthrough stemmed from the brilliant work of others on the theory of quantum gravity—connecting quantum mechanics with Einstein's theory of relativity—and how matter—everything from an atom to a galaxy—warps space and time, causing a gravitational force field. For decades, physicists were deeply disturbed by the fact that the theory of relativity works well in the macro world and explains how space-time bends in the presence of big chunks of matter like people, cars, and planets, thereby causing gravity.

But when they dove down into the sub-micro world of quantum mechanics, all bets were off on the theory of gravity. And what bothered our predecessors was that they were aware that nature knew how to do it. It had done so during the first gazillionth of sub-micro moments of the Big Bang. Physicists had struggled for decades looking for this secret of nature.

Our breakthrough came by finding the means to do a credible theoretical investigation of those first moments of the Big Bang, connecting the known laws of quantum physics and relativity with those of spiritual physics. The latter science is what our predecessors were missing. Eric and I could not have pulled this off without the guidance and knowledge of Thay. He may well be the world's only knowledgeable, theoretical quantum-spiritual physicist.

To make this discovery, we had to dig deep into the CFT and AdS theories. They showed us that space and time—space-time—were intrinsically connected to quantum entanglement[18] among what might be considered cosmic "atoms" of space-time—very small elements of space-time, even smaller than an atom of hydrogen. It is quantum entanglement that holds space-time together and prevents it from falling

---

[18]Quantum Entanglement: When any two objects interact in the quantum world—such as an atom or electron—they become spatially entangled and will stay that way no matter how far apart they may be separated—even distant galaxies apart. So, if one of two entangled atoms—one spinning to the left and the other spinning to the right—has its spin reversed, the other will instantaneously—faster than the speed of light—follow suit and reverse its spin—even if the two atoms are separated by trillions of kilometers before doing this reversal process! Einstein called this "spooky action at a distance."

apart into separate small subregions of space-time. Entanglement imparts a kind of "cosmic force." Greater levels of entanglement lead to closer "pieces" of space-time—and therefore, its warping causes what we experience as gravity.

In our analysis, we discovered that quantum entanglement is unquestionably an *intrinsic* or *fundamental* property of the universe, and space-time is an *emergent* property that flows from, or you might say, happens *as a result of* quantum entanglement. Because of the fundamental essence of entanglement, there is an instantaneous interconnection of space-time throughout our entire universe over billions of light-years to the very edge of its existence, even as it continues to expand—and will continue to do so billions of years from now when the universe reaches a critical point and begins to contract.

It appears that all of this space-time was created in those first zillionths of a moment during the expansion of the subatomic cosmic singularity that formed our universe in what we call the Big Bang—before there was even a single photon of light created. And because of this intimate contact, all space-time is forever entangled. We also found that there is likely a "shadow effect" of this entanglement that continuously extrapolates toward infinity. This happens because our current universe will expand only up to a certain point in time, when it will begin to contract over billions of years back to the cosmic singularity from which it was born. This expansion and contraction process will occur *ad infinitum* in what some physicists call the "Big Bounce." The shadow effect of space-time entanglement in our universe will affect the nature of entanglement in the subsequent universe.

It sounds crazy, but we were convinced that all of this was correct, and that it was quantum entanglement that would enable us to warp space-time enough to closely connect the entrance to our little wormhole at LP2 with our chosen exoplanet, even though it was light-years away—and do all this from Earth, 1.5 million kilometers away from our wormhole orbiting at LP2.

The only unknown for us was centered in the world of spiritual physics: Could the combination of Eric, Bella, and me extract enough subtle energy from the zero-point field in the universe to warp space-time between the coordinates we chose?

Eric and I also found that the most advanced versions of AdS/CFT theory show a way to construct black holes and combine them into a traversable wormhole. This background paved the way for us to determine how to combine what our predecessors had discovered and use that information with our superpowers to tap into the zero-point energy of the universe and manipulate it at vast distances with quantum entanglement. The catalyst that enabled us to put all of this together was found deep within the laws of spiritual physics. *Grazie molto*, Thay!

Our findings gave us—we hoped!—the ability to bend space-time at a distance between two sets of coordinates that were light-years apart—our wormhole at LP2 and the exoplanet Zoi, a hundred light-years away.

However, if the exoplanet turned out not to be Zoi, or even if we were successful in choosing the right exoplanet on our first try, if no communication was established with intelligent life, we'd have to go through the entire space-time warping process all over again for the spatial coordinates of the next exoplanet we chose. It was getting increasingly difficult for all of us to remain optimistic. Except for Eric. Somehow his enthusiasm stayed high. He's a sci-fi fan and was anxious to connect with aliens if they were out there, and he was sure they were. He kept reminding us of three incidents that were intriguing to him because they'd been immediately quashed with the release of an extensive amount of government disinformation.

The first was the famous Roswell, New Mexico, incident in 1947 when a crashed flying saucer and four bodies were allegedly recovered by the US Air Force. The second was when a top-secret government study called Project Aquarius inadvertently released information stating that the United States had captured an alien that they called an Extraterrestrial Biological Entity (EBE). And the third was what had become known as the "Phoenix Lights"—a series of widely seen unidentified flying objects—witnessed by millions of people—observed in the skies over Arizona and Nevada, and the Mexican state of Sonora on March 17, 1997. Photos and videos of the occurrence were dismissed by government officials as flares, and never explained to the public's satisfaction.[19]

Brianna asked Eric, "If these events have any validity, how did these aliens travel to Earth from planets that were very likely to be hundreds, if not thousands, of light-years away? You know the arithmetic on the time to travel such distances."

Eric's response was simple: "Good point. I sure hope we find out when we communicate with any aliens who might be present on Zoi."

Little did he know that we were about to connect with an alien Earthling—of sorts.

---

[19] The Phoenix Lights were directly observed by then–Arizona governor Fife Symington, who was convinced that the UFOs were based on advanced technology not of this Earth. Symington was a Harvard graduate, had been a captain in the US Air Force, and was awarded the Bronze Star for heroic and meritorious achievement—certainly a highly qualified observer.

ERIC, THAY, AND I were practically living at the lab rehearsing procedures we would use to warp and align the wormhole between the coordinates of LP2 and those for the exoplanet—hopefully, it was Zoi. The rocket and our package arrived at LP2 on time, two days ago, on November 14, and were loaded on the transfer rocket. All was still stable. The NASA team planned to have the LP2 capsule perfectly aligned in its orbit by Thursday, November 21; and if all went well, Eric and I would do our thing and hopefully connect with intelligent life on Zoi before Thanksgiving, which falls on November 28 this year, the latest date in November[20] it can occur. We were all hoping that it would be a true Thanksgiving Day for us—and humanity.

The three of us were reviewing several computer simulations when the phone rang. I thought for a second and then commented, "That's strange. We never get phone calls here on that antique hardline. I'm not sure what it's doing in here. In fact, we never get phone calls here at all. Eric, would you mind seeing who that is and what they want?"

"I'm on it, Emperius."

Eric walked swiftly to the old, dusty digital phone, picked it up, and said, "Hello, this is Eric."

After a few moments, he turned and gave me the strangest look, and then called me over in a near-whisper. "Luc, it's for you."

I went over to the phone. "Who is it?"

He continued to whisper. "It's Sophia."

I started thinking, *Do I know a Sophia?* In a low voice, I started reciting, "Sophia, Sophia, Sophia . . . ?"

Eric awakened my tired brain. "I think you'll remember *this* Sophia."

"It's been over ten years! Oh God, no!"

Eric's response, "Oh God, yes!"

I answered. "Hello."

"Hi, Luc, this is Sophia Stepanova—remember me?"

I did my best to regain my composure. "How could I forget you?"

"Luc, so much has changed for you and for me over the last decade. But I don't want to talk over the phone. I think we have a mutual opportunity. Can we meet for dinner, alone somewhere in Boston?"

I hesitated. "After all that happened ten years ago, do you think that's a good idea?"

---

[20]It always falls on the last Thursday of November. November 28 is the latest date it can occur.

"I do. Besides, you owe me a dinner—remember? After we hang up, I'll send you the contact information for my encrypted cell phone. Please give me a date, time, and place for this week, and I'll be there. Believe me, it will be time well spent for both of us."

I hesitated again, but then decided to meet her at a restaurant located in a public area—but with access to a small private dining room. "Okay. Give me your cell phone number and I'll send you information this afternoon." She gave me her number and then immediately hung up. Now I had to explain this to the team.

Eric and especially Bella weren't particularly happy with the idea, but Thay thought differently. He told them, "Luc might learn something. We don't have to give Sophia anything; Luc can just listen to her."

Bella commented, "Right. I remember, some ten years ago, seeing Luc listening to Sophia in Peninsula Creamery—googly-eyes all over her!"

"Come on, Bella. That's ancient history and never was serious in any case."

"I know. I just wanted to give you a dig to get even!"

"Thanks." I rolled my eyes.

Thay ended our banter. "Okay, folks, let's move on. We have lots of work to do. You may want to inform Major Dallant about your meeting, just in case there's a hidden agenda on Sophia's part."

"Will do."

I SET UP OUR DINNER for Monday, November 18. I chose the Oceanaire Restaurant on Court Street in the Financial District. I'd been there for a small dinner when one of my colleagues in the physics department retired. Six of us had eaten dinner served in a private area called the State Room, where we were alone and not able to be seen by others. It was a bit oversized for what I wanted to do—it seats between 8 and 30 guests—but it would work. And besides, they have great seafood.

Per our agreement, we met in the State Room at 7:00 p.m. As was the case a decade before, Sophia was dressed with the elegance of a model—a black, low-cut, V-neck cardigan; a long, floral, tight-fitting slip skirt; and cream-colored leather boots—stunning, as always. Me—I was in my usual academic gray-and-blue houndstooth jacket, a white button-down shirt, skinny blue jeans, and mahogany-colored western boots.

After several minutes of fairly superficial chitchat, I suggested that we order our entire dinner so that we'd have minimal interruptions from the servers. I also wanted to get that out of the way and hear what Sophia had on her mind.

She'd obviously done her homework and knew that seafood was the restaurant's specialty. She started with a Chesapeake Bay–style crab-cake appetizer, followed by a main course of jumbo shrimp scampi in a sauce of garlic butter and tomatoes over angel-hair pasta. She ordered sides of sautéed spinach and Parmesan truffle fries. I chose the crab-meat cocktail appetizer and a main course of Oceanaire Surf and Turf consisting of lobster tail and aged ribeye steak, with sides of grilled asparagus and truffle-whipped potatoes. We settled on a nice white wine—Domaine Moltès Grand Cru Steinert Pinot Gris Bio 2027 from Alsace.

Having completed our order and with the servers out of the room, Sophia embarked on a more serious conversation. "So, Luc, it's been over ten years since we last spoke."

"Right. After that stunt and your note at Buck's Restaurant in February of 2020, I thought it would have been a lot sooner."

She responded, "So did I, but I wasn't in a very good state of mind after finding out that Seagull was my father, having had a longtime affair with my mother, who was also his personal assistant. I had initially thought that you were responsible for that terrible explosion at the Novosibirsk research center that killed him and his wife, Mariya. Before I could carry out my plan to avenge his death—sorry, Luc!—I learned of the letter that Mariya had sent to President Putin, and that it was she who arranged for the explosion. Her message also said that my father would have died in any case several weeks later from an inoperable brain tumor. Those were difficult times for me."

"I'll bet." There was something I had to know. "Who arranged for that homing pigeon, or should I say, 'homing seagull,' to land with your message on my red Chevy, parked in front of Buck's Restaurant in Woodside, California? I know your father had developed the homing-seagull technology—hence his cover name—but I had no idea you were involved."

Sophia responded, "I wasn't really that involved with the seagulls, but I did send the note. My father had taught me how to manage them for messaging. They were an amazing technological development on his part. At the time, I had no idea he was my father. I thought he was spending time with me at his laboratory outside of Moscow because I was doing so well at ASP—you know, the academy.[21] But he was training me to take over with the seagulls after he was gone. I also found out through my own means that Putin had arranged for my father's assassination. It was just that Mariya got to him first."

I said, "I tell ya, Sophia, those were also tough times for the team and me. We knew that your father was far gone mentally because of his tumor, but it was a shame for Mariya. She could have continued to be a great asset to Russia—even the world—with what she'd discovered, if it had been applied to neuroscience. But that's dark water under the bridge, and we have to move on."

Sophia changed the subject. "Speaking of moving on, how about, as you Americans say, we 'cut to the chase'?"

"I'm good with that."

Sophia continued. "Bottom line, there are two big things I want to convey to you. First, and don't jump out of your seat, I want to defect from Russia and join you in the US."

I was baffled if not shocked. "Are you serious?"

Without hesitation, she replied, "I am."

I was more than curious, but because of possible negotiations for her defection to the US, I tried not to look overanxious. "Why would you do that in view of all you went through in Russia—and especially when you consider the likely response from Russia?"

"The short answer is, I'm deeply disappointed, and often disgusted, by what my country has become. It started decades ago—perhaps longer than that—but it really went to hell when Putin took over and with his unbelievably ridiculous and dangerous 'Putinesque War in Ukraine.'"

I cut in. "I'll say. Many of us began to think he might have 'caught' the same tumor that Seagull had."

---

[21] A KGB deep-state intense training school for spies, called *Akademiya Sverkhsposobnostey*—in English, the Academy of Superpowers, or ASP.

Sophia seemed to agree. "Right. That's a whole other story, not worth getting into at this point." She continued. "I think Russia will wither rapidly from this point into a dark hole of ambiguity and uselessness, which is a shame, because there have been and still are some very talented people there whose potential has been castrated into the realm of the also-rans. I'm sure you're aware that a massive brain drain over the last decade has caused us to lose some of our most talented scientists and technologists. I no longer want to be a part of it."

Sophia stared at me, probably expecting a commentary of some sort, but I didn't say a word. As suggested by Thay, I just kept listening. And she continued voicing her thoughts.

"The second big thing, if I may, is from our new telescopic system at LP2. My team has closely observed the device you put in orbit there. If our observations and calculations are correct, you've somehow managed to create a wormhole. That's amazing in and of itself. You deserve a Nobel. However, at that modest size, the only thing I can conclude you're going to do is attempt to contact intelligent life on an exoplanet, your wormhole providing a means for rapid communication to that exoplanet.

"However, to do so with short communication times in both directions will require bending the wormhole and the space-time between LP2 and the intended exoplanet. If you've figured out how to do that, it's likely worth half a dozen Nobel Prizes if the US allows you to publish your work. I'm not going to ask you if you can do it. I know you won't tell me."

I answered, "You're right. But please continue."

"Even if you can manage such an impossible task, I've spent the last decade searching numerous exoplanets with our advanced space telescope. I'm sure you're aware of that. And I have found a number of them with high probabilities of being Earthlike planets—one in particular is my favorite. I would bet that there *is* intelligent life there, one reason being the presence of huge swaths of chlorophyllic plant life. As part of our deal, I would give you the planet's location coordinates."

Even though Thay had advised me to keep my mouth shut, I had to show that we were no slouches and knew something about what the Russians were up to. "You mean Zoi?"

"Clever, Luc. You may know about our program and that I gave a name to the one we have high hopes for, but with the Russian super-encrypted security that was put on Zoi's location, there's no way you could possibly know its coordinates."

I could no longer just listen, so I began negotiations. "Let's say you're right. What do we get in exchange? Are you willing to be debriefed by the CIA and disclose everything you know?"

"I am. But you need to know that more than ten years ago, when madman Putin was running things, he instituted our current security structure in which all of our work is divided into security modules; and someone like me, who can know everything that's happening in one module, may know little or nothing about the content of other modules. It's great for security, but a killer for creativity by cross-fertilization. Only the president and two of his advisers have an overview of what's happening in all of the modules."

I commented, "Man, that's crazy—and so was Putin. It's good for the world and for Russia that he's gone. He nearly got us into a massive nuclear war with that Ukraine fiasco. Of course, the new guy is not a lot better. Must be part of the Russian genome."

"Maybe, but Luc, do you see the benefits that could come out of this for the US?"

"I do, but aren't you concerned for your life? The Russians have been known to go to great lengths to find and kill traitors, often via the most horrible means—like Polonium radiation poisoning."

Sophia didn't hesitate for even a brief moment. "That's a risk I'm willing to take to build some kind of normal life."

I had to ask, "Have you told anyone on your team about the wormhole we've created?"

"No. I thought that would lower my negotiation possibilities."

I responded, "I'm going to have to discuss this with my team and with our contact at the CIA. I don't know how long it will take for us to come to a 'yes' conclusion."

Sophia said, "I think Major Dallant would be quick to decide, and as for your team, the only one who might not like it is Bella."

"Boy, Sophia, as usual, you sure are well informed."

She smiled. "I have to be. I'm a spy!"

We finished dinner. She left first, and then I left about 30 minutes later after a cross-examination call from Bella. "Okay, dear Emperius. Give me the whole story! I'm waiting!"

And I thought ten years would erase her memory of my previous dinner with Sophia!

Chapter Nine

BELLA'S
IDEA

*"Things don't turn up in this world until somebody
turns them up."*
— James A. Garfield

Sunday, November 17, 2030—Cambridge, Massachusetts

They just couldn't wait until Monday—especially Bella. So we all met at the lab on Sunday afternoon. The team wanted the details of how things had gone at my dinner with Sophia. Bella even wanted to know how she was dressed, what we ordered for dinner, how many bottles of wine we drank, and which ones we ordered. I couldn't tell if she was just pulling my leg or still concerned about me spending time with Sophia. I guess it was a bit of both, but I decided not to push it.

We all finally agreed that if Sophia wasn't scheming against us— that was our critical concern—then collaborating with her would be a real plus for us—not only getting a data dump on all kinds of Russian secrets, but *the* critical issue for our project: Of all the exoplanets the Russians had investigated, which one was Zoi? What were its specific coordinates in this vast, expanding universe of ours?

On Monday morning, we met again and had a videoconference with Major Dallant. He came to the same conclusions that we had.

He suggested that I arrange a clandestine meeting with Sophia in DC involving Thay, him, and me. He wanted to keep the meeting small to get the most out of it—actually, out of Sophia. I was to communicate to her that in order for the US to go through all of the challenging details to officially extract her from Russian control and provide her with the security necessary to protect her safety, as an act of good faith—at the end of our meeting if both sides agreed to proceed—she was to immediately hand over the location coordinates of Zoi. If she didn't agree to that condition, it would all be a nonstarter.

After our meeting, we all headed back to the lab. Thay had something he wanted to discuss with us. I'd noticed that he'd been unusually quiet and serious during our videoconference with Major Dallant, so I was anxious to hear what he had on his mind.

When we returned to the Green building, we met in the small conference room next to the lab. Thay started the meeting.

"I want to emphasize that I'm incredibly impressed with the progress the team has made. It's beyond what anyone would have imagined was possible. But you *made* it possible with your brilliant and dedicated efforts—and, of course, your unique capabilities. However, I'm obliged to say that I believe we still have one major challenge, and to be totally up front, although I believe it's doable, I'm not quite sure how to approach it."

I interjected. "Thay, why don't we get right to it? Tell us what the issue is."

"Luc, I'm impressed with the progress that Bella, Eric, and you have made during our deep meditation practices, which I'm confident will be a necessary adjunct to your powers in order to bend space-time between the coordinates at LP2 and those for Zoi—and to do that here on Earth at a distance of 1.5 million kilometers. Yes, we've done several tests, and things continue to improve, but I have no way of knowing if that improvement will be sufficient to accomplish a task that up until now has been unheard of in classical, quantum, or even, spiritual physics. We're counting on what we've learned via a combination of theories from all three areas of physics, but as you know, our knowledge of spiritual physics is still in its infancy."

Eric asked, "So, Thay, what do you suggest?"

Thay answered, "Based on everything I've studied, the only science and technology I'm confident will work is centered completely in spiritual physics, and that's an advanced form of pranayama. But it would be a long haul to teach and initiate the three of you into the necessary processes of this kind of pranayama. It usually takes many years to get to the level of expertise we would require."

Brianna said, "I hate to be too practical, and perhaps, obvious, but if that's the case, shouldn't we do everything as best we can on the path we're currently on and hope for success?"

Bella responded before Thay could answer Brianna's question. "Maybe not."

I had to know what in the world Bella was referring to. "Really?"

And then Thay jumped in. "Yes, Bella, what do you have in mind?"

Bella thought for minute and then responded. "Fine. I'll start from the beginning so that we're all on the same page in order to make what will be quite a difficult decision."

Pham smiled and added, "Sounds ominous. I can't wait to hear what you have in mind."

"Okay. You remember the brief training Thay gave us years ago on pranayama breathing exercises as an excellent tool to reduce stress and anxiety, right?"

Eric responded for all of us. "I'll say. I can't tell you how many times I've used his guidance on those exercises. Remember the time I accidentally killed Carlito Sanchez, the hit man who threatened my mother and me, thinking we had the ten million bucks my father had gotten in a drug deal that went bad? Talk about stress and anxiety!"

Brianna exclaimed, "Oh my God, Eric! What in the world?"

"Sorry, Brianna. I'll fill you in later. It had a good ending. Right now, I'm sure you're as anxious as the rest of us to hear what Bella has to say."

Bella looked at Brianna, who didn't say a word, so she continued. "As I'm sure Thay will tell you, that kind of pranayama, while helpful, is only the tip of a huge iceberg of potential power that is accessible only to highly skilled practitioners. A few years ago I started reading more in depth about pranayama. Apparently, eons ago, Wisdom Thinkers and yogis found that when it was combined with an unusual and advanced practice of ancient yoga called Kriya yoga,[22] it had profound effects on the practitioners and their connections with material things in their consciousness. Thay, please stop me if I'm getting any of this wrong."

Thay answered, "Fine. All is correct so far. I'm most interested to see where you're going."

Bella went on. "As I understand it, Kriya is a unique form of yoga. It was first described in the second-century BCE by the Indian sage Patanjali as a powerful and expeditious means to readily access and direct cosmic energy called *prana* to the six spinal centers in the human body—the medullary, cervical, dorsal, lumbar, sacral, and coccygeal plexuses. This psychophysiological method can awaken in the human organism, a dormant energy force called *kundalini* in Hindu philosophy—actually, when it's awakened with Kriya yoga, the Hindi translation is *super-kundalini*.

"In combination with deep meditation, this can enable the individual to perform amazing feats instantly, even at huge distances. For example, using this methodology, there's a documented instance where a yogi in southern India allegedly knocked a king-warrior off his horse in northern India. He could see the warrior in his consciousness and knew exactly when to dismount him. The king and his soldiers lost the battle. I can't help but think that although all of this is in the realm of spiritual physics, instantaneous action at huge distances sounds to me like some form of quantum entanglement—perhaps an analogous effect in the realm of spiritual physics. If entanglement does play a role, we know from experimental work over the past few decades that distance is irrelevant—one meter or trillions of meters . . . it makes no difference."

Bella was on a roll, and we were captivated by her analysis and enthusiasm. She continued. "A couple of years ago, I discussed this with a colleague at Johns Hopkins who's a specialist in forensic anthropology. She was intrigued. She read some of the ancient texts on Kriya yoga, which had been a lost method of yoga for a couple of millennia and was rediscovered in India only a few hundred years ago. She concluded that during extended practice of this kind of yoga, a person's blood is

---

[22] The "immortal" yogi Babaji was the source of this esoteric form of yoga, sometime called *Kriya Kundalini Pranayama*. It was discreetly disclosed to the West by yogi Paramahansa Yogananda in the early part of the 20th century. He discussed the powers of Kriya yoga in his book *Autobiography of a Yogi*, published in English in 1946.

decarbonated of large amounts of carbon dioxide and simultaneously heavily enriched with oxygen.

"If the ratio of O_2 to CO_2 is at a critical point, some kind of cosmic energy—probably prana—is transmitted through the spine and has an immensely positive effect on both the spinal centers and the brain. This apparently induces superpowers that enable the practitioner to influence occurrences at great distances—like knocking a king off his horse at a range of more than 3,000 kilometers—and perhaps bending space-time! Yes, I know we're dealing with cosmic distances that are much larger, but from what I've read, similar to quantum entanglement, there seems to be no limit to distance.

"My colleague at Johns Hopkins did some experiments with a guinea pig using a continuous blood transfusion–reinfusion apparatus, simultaneously removing CO_2 and enriching O_2 levels. At a certain ratio of O_2 to CO_2, the guinea pig went into a state of what seemed like death. It was apparently some form of hibernation because its heart and respiration decreased significantly—nearly to zero—yet its vital signs were normal. My colleague didn't feed or provide water to the guinea pig for several weeks. After more than a month, she brought the guinea pig's blood-gas levels to their normal values. The animal revived, ate, and drank normally, as if nothing had happened."

We were mesmerized by Bella's story. Thay added, "I'm not surprised. There are several relatively modern accounts of similar effects. There was a monk named Prahlad Jani who lived most of his 91 years without food and water, maintaining his healthy status by extracting prana energy from the cosmos, as you previously mentioned. He died in 2020.

"One well-known medical doctor had thought he was a scammer, so he convinced Jani to be accommodated in his hospital for more than a hundred days, with cameras monitoring him 24-7. During that time, he neither ate nor drank anything. And what's most interesting: he did not produce one drop of urine, nor any stool—and at the end, his vital signs were completely normal. Actually, they were better than when he'd entered the hospital. Also, as with Bella's story about the long-distance dismounting of the king, Jani also demonstrated an ability to move heavy objects at a distance."

Pham asked, "For a nonscientist like me, can you tell me what all of this mystical information—assuming it's true—leads you to conclude?"

Brianna looked directly at Bella and added, "I *am* a scientist, and I, too, would love to know what you're getting at."

She replied, "Bottom line: I'm suggesting that we fuse the long-distance capabilities of advanced pranayama with the power of deep meditation. But that's where things gets tricky, so I need Thay's help with spiritual physics. I'm assuming that we don't have the time to be properly indoctrinated into the practice of Kriya yoga in order to access the necessary superlevel of pranayama. However, if we review the risks of achieving our objectives and conclude that they're reasonable and acceptable, we might then consider the following procedure.

"To bend space-time at LP2, we would work with my colleague and connect Eric, Luc, and me to three separate transfusion devices, and after we go into a hibernation state, Thay would lead the three of us into deep meditation so that we significantly elevate our levels of consciousness. At some point during our meditative states, he would instruct us to bend space-time at LP2 to the required initial and final space coordinates. That's it. What do you think?"

Brianna couldn't contain herself. "Bella, this is crazy! You're suggesting that we transition directly from experimental results with a guinea pig and use that same procedure on humans—*our* three humans, probably risking their lives—"

Thay interrupted. "Okay, folks, let's calm down and look at this objectively. I'd like to provide some input. First, Bella, those are amazing experiments with the guinea pig, and your extension of those results to our challenge is, I believe, a stroke of creative genius. There is scientific merit to it, as well as evidence of the nature of the risk the three of you would be taking.

"Given our predicament and the time issue, I would say that we could proceed in that direction if we first minimized the risk by conducting a few preliminary experiments in the presence of the appropriate medical experts as a contingency should we run into a problem. You're right, we don't have time to indoctrinate the three of you into Kriya yoga with the sufficient prowess to safely achieve the results we're after.

"First, we would see if we could get the three of you into a hibernating state, during which your heart and respiration are appreciably reduced, yet your vital signs remain normal. Next, I would initiate the meditation exercise necessary to achieve the level of consciousness required to initiate bending space-time at LP2, as if you were present at that location. If there were no problems at that point, we would immediately proceed with the actual bending of space-time as required."

Pham asked, "Dad, are you sure that wouldn't potentially result in a dangerous endpoint for the team?"

Thay answered immediately. "Am I sure? No. Could it potentially result in a dangerous endpoint? I can't say absolutely not. But I would defer to our astrobiologist, Bella, and her colleague from Johns Hopkins for their answer to your question."

Bella offered her thoughts. "During hibernation, respiration rates in bears decrease dramatically, from a normal 6 to 10 breaths per minute, to 1 breath every 45 seconds. Similarly, they experience a drop in heart rate from 40 to 50 beats per minute to 8 to 19 beats per minute. There are a number of other species in the animal kingdom—such as groundhogs, squirrels, and bats—that do the same thing, with no negative consequences.

"Yes, I know the three of us are not bears or bats, but I think advice from medical experts would say that a healthy human being, under the right circumstances, may be capable of hibernation. However, I will consult with Professor Mildred Flanigan, my colleague who did the guinea-pig research, as well as with a few of the pulmonary and cardiovascular experts at Mass General and see what they have to say."

I had to intervene. "Look, this is nuts! Even if Bella gets positive feedback from the experts she'll consult with, it seems too risky to me—especially to put three lives out there. Can't just one of us—like me, for example—do this?"

Thay answered, "I wish I could say yes, but I just don't know. And I would hate to put you through this process and have it not work, only to ask you to do it a second time with Bella and Eric for our next attempt at success. We're not dealing with classical or quantum energies. During pranayama you would be generating subtle, yet intense, energies that function according to the laws of spiritual physics. I think we will need all of the subtle energy we can muster to succeed in bending the wormhole at a distance of 1.5 million kilometers away from LP2, and then connecting the LP2 coordinates with those of Zoi, a hundred light-years away."

Brianna sighed and expressed the state of mind we were all in. "I think we've been through a lot today. How about we table this meeting, let Bella get the information she suggested as quickly as possible, and then get back together to make the most informed decision we can at that meeting."

Thay said, "Brianna, great idea. Now I know why Eric thinks so much of your leadership skills."

Eric added, "And so many other skills as well!"

Brianna closed our meeting, as we did, with a smile. "Okay, smart-ass, you'll get yours!"

Eric smiled even wider. Although I'm sure he wanted to add another one of his wisecracks, he wisely refrained.

At least we'd ended on a positive note . . . I guess?

Chapter Ten

THE RUSSIAN CONNECTION

"Don't be too timid and squeamish about your actions.
All life is an experiment. The more experiments you make the better."
—Ralph Waldo Emerson

Tuesday, November 19, 2030—Cambridge, Massachusetts

It's a seven-hour drive in moderate traffic from MIT to the Staybridge Suites Hotel in McLean, Virginia, where Major Dallant had arranged for us to meet with Sophia. We decided that only the major, Thay, and I would participate. We wanted our attendance to be on the light side so that we might get as much useful information as possible from Sophia. We left Cambridge at 5:00 a.m. and arrived at the hotel just after noon.

Major Dallant had secured a special suite for our meeting, which he had electronically swept for listening devices—a normal agency precaution. Nothing was found. As planned, we met the major in the suite at 12:45 p.m., just before our meeting with Sophia. Exactly 15 minutes later, we heard a knock. I got up from our conference table, walked over, and opened the door.

And there she was, but this time her usual high fashion was tuned down to business garb. She was wearing a fitted, white-striped black suit, a modest-cut ruffled white blouse, and black patent-leather heels—medium height. Her jacket had epaulets but no longer sported cameos of Catherine the Great, as was the case during our first meeting in Palo Alto. I guess this new attire was a reflection of her defection from Russia.

"Good afternoon, Luc!" she exclaimed.

"Hi, Sophia. Please come in."

Major Dallant and Thay stood up and walked over to be introduced.

"Sophia Stepanova, this is Major John Dallant and my colleague Pham Tuan."

Sophia and the major shook hands. "Nice to finally meet you, Major."

"And you as well, Sophia."

Next, Sophia shook hands with Thay. "Pham, my pleasure."

"Oh, please, call me Thay, as everyone else does."

"Oh, are you a teacher?"

Thay sounded surprised by her question. "Of a sort—but how did you know the Vietnamese translation to English?"

Sophia smiled and said, "I spent some time in Hanoi on an assignment and did a crash course on the language before moving there. I speak some Chinese, a Sino-Tibetan language like Vietnamese, which made it a little easier—but not much."

Thay smiled and remarked, "I'm impressed. And your inflected pronunciation is flawless!"

"Thank you, Thay."

Major Dallant, always the efficient one, suggested, "I'm terribly sorry, Sophia, but I have another meeting later this afternoon. Would it be okay with you if we got started?"

"Absolutely! I was thinking that our meeting would not take too long, in any case."

Major Dallant continued. "Fine. Luc has filled me in on what you'd like to do. I must say that I was quite surprised. Do you mind if I ask you to elaborate a bit on your motivation to make such a significant, and I would even say, dangerous, life change?"

"Fine. I could probably speak all afternoon about my reasons. But in the interest of time—yours and mine—I'll be brief and to the point."

Sophia took just a few seconds to gather her thoughts, and then said, "I'm sure you're aware that I was placed into Russia's ASP program when I was a young child. My mother wanted to be childless again, and my presence would have posed her and her lover with a challenging issue. As you can see, I've already made a traitorous statement by admitting to the previous existence of the ASP program. As I'm sure you know, it was disbanded years ago. But that will be the least traitorous thing I will say and do this afternoon—"

Major Dallant interrupted. "You shouldn't feel in the least that we would like you to say anything that is not of your own volition. And if you do, I'm confident that someone as competent and experienced as you are will understand the ramifications of what you're doing."

"I do. So I'll continue—and this is my choice. Unlike my stepsister, Tamara Carlin, who was indoctrinated into the US version of the ASP program, which was always designated for VIP children, I was placed on a much more demanding path in Russia. The ASP program in Russia nearly broke me physically and mentally. There are a large number of suicides by those who are in the Russian program.

"But I was determined to survive. Also, as I'm sure you're well aware, I was the unwanted product of an affair between my mother, Galena Stepanova, and Dr. Sergei Karlovich, the agent you knew as Seagull. But I survived—not without emotional scars—which in the interest of time, I will not address today. What I *can* say is that over the last ten years, I've done well to put them behind me. It helped that ASP closed and I received a full professorship in the physics department at Cambridge. Those scars are irrelevant for you, but not for me. They represent the driving force for me leaving Russian oversight—or should I say, control.

"Another driving force is that my first love is scientific research, especially in astrophysics. I believe I could make more contributions with your team if I had a greater sense of freedom."

Major Dallant then said, "Look, Sophia, before we go any further, I'm sure that Luc has told you that our discussions today and any endpoint where you become a working operative for the US is totally contingent on an act of good faith on your part, whereby today you provide the precise coordinates for the exoplanet you call Zoi."

Sophia didn't say another word. She opened her briefcase, removed a thin manila envelope, and handed it to Major Dallant.

The major responded, "Thank you." He looked directly at Sophia, paused for a moment before opening the envelope, and said, "May I?"

She responded, "Absolutely!"

The major removed a single sheet of paper that presumably had Zoi's spatial coordinates written on it. He handed the paper to me. I smiled at Sophia as she prepared to fill in the blanks and provide a summary of the background for Zoi.

She noticed my smile and said, "I see from your expression that you probably designated this as one of your most promising candidates."

I responded, "It's actually amazing. Not only did we identify it as a promising candidate, but it was our first choice of several hundred candidates for our intended attempt at contact. I'm sure you're well aware that it was the first Earth-sized exoplanet in the Earthlike habitable zone discovered by the Transiting Exoplanet Survey Satellite, or TESS."

Sophia smiled back. "What can I say—great minds think alike! Perhaps for Thay's and Major Dallant's benefit, I'll give you a brief summary."

Major Dallant agreed. "Please do."

"Sure. Exoplanet TOI 700 d, which I prefer to call Zoi, is a near-Earth-sized exoplanet that's rocky and orbits within the habitable zone of its star, the red dwarf TOI 700. It is the outermost planet within a system of planets in the constellation Dorado and is located 101.4 light-years from Earth. It orbits its host star, TOI 700, every 37.4 days compared to our 365-day cycle. Your years add up quickly on Zoi—nearly ten times as fast as on Earth! It has a mass 1.69 times that of Earth and a radius at its equator of 1.19 times that of Earth. What's very important is that it's not a gaseous planet like Jupiter—it's rock solid—otherwise all bets would be off. We observed that as Zoi orbits its host star, the solar wind pressure and the intensity of the interplanetary magnetic field are both very similar to Earth's, and therefore it retains its planetary atmosphere.

"The extensive presence of the chlorophyll molecule means that there is sufficient CO_2 present, and our spectroscopic analysis of the atmosphere indicates that there's plenty of O_2, probably closer to 30 percent compared with Earth's 21 percent—likely a plus for human respiration and overall well-being. The other 70 percent is mostly nitrogen, with a small level of noble gases like helium, argon, krypton, and xenon, although we didn't detect any radon—perhaps that's another plus. Sounds like a new Earth, doesn't it?"

Major Dallant asked, "What about its surface temperature?"

"The TESS data indicated early on that Zoi receives 86 percent of the energy that Earth receives from our sun. Our data are more accurate. It gets nearly 97 percent. Initial data from TESS measured the average temperature on Zoi as -4.3°C. Our more precise instrumentation and detailed analyses have shown that it's 12.2°C, somewhat cooler than Earth's 13.9°C—of course that's changing with our increasing level of climate change. I can give you a lot more accurate data if and when we decide to work together. However, in the spirit of good faith, I'll offer two additional pieces of information as a bonus for today's discussion."

Sophia hesitated for several seconds, and I admit that I moved to the edge of my chair, waiting for what she was going to say. "First, Zoi has a preponderance of liquid water on its surface in the form of large oceans. Using our advanced polarimetry, we've even measured the wave action in these seas. And second and related to my last point, ocean tidal action is controlled by two beautiful, orbiting rocky moons, similar in size to ours, but somewhat smaller. I've named the larger of the two *Pax*, and the other one *Libertas*. With the detection system you've been using, you could not have possibly seen them."

Thay added, "*Peace* and *Freedom*—I like that."

Sophia said, "Yes, and those words are *the* two primary reasons why I'm here."

I have to admit, I was impressed, and I guess Major Dallant was as well. He said, "Sophia, that's a valuable package of information. I'm inclined to move forward; however, I'd like to have Luc and his team look more closely at the information you've just given us and then have a discussion with them and a few other key people in my organization.

"In the meantime, I can offer the following suggestion. Outside that door, there are two highly skilled security agents. If you agree, they're prepared to escort you to your room to collect your things, then to check out, and afterward, transport you to a comfortable safe house not far from here in rural Virginia. There's a female agent there named Charlotte Decker who will help you get settled. The security agents and Charlotte will stay at the house, take care of your needs, and assure your safety. I will confer with the SPI Team as well as my team at CIA/NSA, and then meet with you in two days at the safe house to finalize matters. Are you okay with that?"

Sophia immediately replied, "I am!"

And so, our meeting with Sophia came to a close. Who would've guessed? I knew there would be a number of challenges in our future work together, but Project Phoenix had just gone up more than several notches in its probability for success.

Part III

CONTACT

Chapter Eleven

HOPE

"Hope is definitely not the same thing as optimism.
It is not the conviction that something will turn out well, but the
certainty that something makes sense, regardless of how it turns out."
— Vaclav Havel

Wednesday, November 20, 2030—Cambridge, Massachusetts

As we drove back to Cambridge, Thay and I didn't speak as much as I would have thought, considering what we'd just learned. Sure, we knew that going forward with Sophia as an adjunct to our team could have great benefits. But I think Thay, as I, was focused on the significant challenges that would accompany those benefits. The question staring us head-on: Do those benefits more than offset the risks? If Sophia was being straight with us, she would add a lot to our know-how and improve our probability of success, but she would also be a traitor hunted by the Russians, and the SPI Team would be primed for collateral damage. That I knew for a fact.

I'll never forget what Putin had said more than a decade ago in his discussion with Seagull concerning traitors. As I'd listened in on their meeting during one of my OBEs to the Kremlin, he'd said, "You're well aware, Sergei, of what we Russians do to traitors—no mercy—actually, worse. It's always death, and a quick one—but only if the traitor is lucky. Those who have escaped our initial grasp, we—no, you, Sergei, with your deep sense of revenge—have searched them out, wherever they've been hiding in the world, and you've seen to it that they suffered a hideous death. We can *never* forgive traitors."

Sophia's dangerous situation would definitely be ours as well, as she is a brilliant scientist and a superb, well-trained, and sly operative. We had no way of knowing if she was actually a double agent for the Russians. But we had no choice but to proceed. It was now quite clear that her input would immensely increase the chance of success for Project Phoenix.

We arrived in Cambridge late on Wednesday evening. Thay and I were physically and emotionally exhausted, and we both needed a night of peaceful sleep.

THE ENTIRE TEAM MET the next morning at the lab. Our meeting dealing with the pros and cons of Sophia's participation lasted a much shorter time than I would have expected—however, not without a few snarky and suspicious remarks from Bella, and surprisingly, from Brianna as well. But we got past those and agreed that we would proceed with caution.

Although we would check it all out carefully, the information that Sophia had given us as her act of good faith impressed us. Zoi now looked like a good possibility, certainly for the presence of life, but more important, perhaps for the presence of intelligent life as well.

Later that day after we'd checked and rechecked everything that Sophia had given us, I called Major Dallant and told him that we were fine with all of the information Sophia had provided, and assuming he hadn't uncovered any problems with the intel he had access to, we unanimously agreed to proceed with what she proposed. He was okay with our decision and said he would set things in motion for her safety and integration as a "consultant" to our team. He also would arrange for Sophia to receive a one-year sabbatical in the physics department at MIT, after which we would mutually decide on her future with us . . . or not. Things were moving quickly.

Eric and Thay—both super-positive and super-balanced thinkers—were especially excited to move on. Bella had contacted Professor Flannigan for her technical input and had obtained three sets of transfusion apparatus, complete with accurate O_2 and CO_2 measuring devices. Flannigan was curious as to how and why we were going to use the equipment, but Bella was able to deflect her query as something we were doing as part of a NASA study on astronaut blood chemistry, and that we had signed a secrecy agreement, so disclosure wasn't a possibility at this time. Flannigan seemed to buy Bella's response, although not without a somewhat skeptical facial expression that might have suggested otherwise.

Bella's input from two cardiovascular experts at Mass General concerning the possibility of human hibernation was neither positive nor negative, perhaps because they were not aware of anyone who had ever conducted the experiment. They *did* say that some surgeons successfully use a technique during heart repair where they cool the patient's body from its normal 37°C to 18°C and subsequently discontinue the patient's respiration, blood flow, and heartbeat for up to 45 minutes in a state of induced hypothermia. The patient is nearly indistinguishable from someone who is actually dead. I didn't think a human being could last that long under those conditions, but apparently the lower body temperature is the key factor.

They, of course, were not aware of proprietary work on human hibernation currently being conducted by NASA scientists at even lower temperatures. It's top secret and part of a program called Stellar Destination, in which astronauts have their bodies cooled to reduce their metabolism. Chemical reactions in their bodies slow down; and heart rate, breathing, and energy consumption dramatically decrease. This procedure is being developed and optimized by NASA for future long-term space travel by astronauts.

Major Dallant arranged for one of NASA's top scientists, Dr. John Levy, to speak with Bella, Brianna, Pham, and Thay, so that our procedure could be optimized to operate at low risk to our Earthbound "astronauts"—Bella, Eric, and me! One disconcerting outcome from that discussion: during the entire process, the three of us would have to wear thin swimsuits and be strapped to a subfreezing bed, generally used for a brief period to lower fever in critically ill patients. This, Dr. Levy said, would facilitate the hibernation process. He also said that 18°C was not safe for what we intended to do. His recommendation was nearly 30 degrees lower at -10°C. *Minchia!*—nothing to look forward to! According to Levy, due to the molecular and mineral content of our blood, if the blood-flow rate was managed properly and the duration of the experiment kept to less than 30 minutes, our blood would not solidify at -10°C. *Minchia!* I thought, *Thanks, Dr. Levy, you're a real sweetheart!* Thay had already commandeered three freezer-beds from Mass General.

It was the end of November in Cambridge, and winter was at our doorstep. As Eric liked to say when he slipped into his long-ago mode of wise-guy speak, "It's colder than a witch's tit!" It didn't help that the Green building wasn't heated very well, so being dressed in only swim trunks while lying on an ice bed made the outside weather seem like a summer stroll in the Mohave desert. It wasn't what I'd expected as a means to warp space-time. What's more, the beds weren't cooled with ice water, which would have meant that 0°C was the coldest they could get. No, they were cooled with a circulating liquid refrigerant so they could be cooled well below 0°C, to -30°C, if necessary.

I have no idea how, but Major Dallant managed to find two cardiovascular surgeons who had top-secret security clearance to stand by with us in case we needed medical assistance.

By early evening, there we were—Eric, Bella, and me—lying head-to-head in a triangular configuration of ice beds frozen numb to the bone, while Thay, Brianna, and Pham observed our blood circulating slowly through the machines provided by Professor Flannigan. First, it entered a glass cylinder filled with a special high-surface-area adsorbent called zeolite 13X, which has a huge affinity and capacity for adsorbing CO_2. The blood then entered a second glass cylinder, which contained a fine, porous, fritted disk through which pure O_2 was bubbled into our blood. Although our respiration and blood flow would decrease significantly, they wouldn't go to zero. According to NASA, this was physically safe at -10°C, and some minimal blood flow would be necessary to enable our brains to function, and also to prevent our bloodstreams from freezing. Right.

Five minutes into the process, as the team was passing the 0°C mark on its way to -10°C, Thay asked, "How do you feel?"

Eric said, "I had very little sleep last night, and this morning I was quite foggy. But the fog has lifted, and I'm feeling stronger, but now that we're past the first few minutes of freezing, I can't feel any part of my body—I guess that's a plus."

Bella's answer was, "Same as Eric, but I feel like I'm fading."

I was about to speak, but I suddenly couldn't, although I could hear what was happening in the room.

Thay commented, "Their supporting vitals all look fine for -10°C, even though their breathing and heart rates have decreased significantly. I've set the O_2/CO_2 ratio in the range suggested by Mildred Flannigan and agreed to by NASA. I'm going to wait until their heart rates and breathing are closer to zero before leading them into deep meditation for 20 minutes, and then, if all is still well, I will direct them to connect the entry and exit coordinates of our wormhole to those we've agreed upon."

Twenty minutes later, we three Earth-based "astronauts" were still doing fine physically, although we couldn't speak, so Thay provided the required coordinates and asked us to bend space-time accordingly. Thay was monitoring our supporting vitals, which, amazingly, were still in an acceptable range, as well as the environment within the titanium cylinder at LP2, which contained our wormhole.

At first there were no changes at the titanium cylinder, but within a few minutes, Thay noted that the temperature started to rise slowly from its initial value of -270°C. This meant that Bella, Eric, and I were definitely connected to LP2, and our warping of space-time was underway. Thay had no idea how far he should let the temperature rise before discontinuing the procedure. Within two minutes it had risen to -258°C. Bella, Eric, and I had grimaces in our facial expressions—was it discomfort, or the stress of pushing harder to warp space-time at LP2?

Brianna expressed her concern. "Thay, how much higher will you let the temperature rise in the chamber?"

"I'm not sure. I've got my eyes on their vitals, and although they've changed somewhat, they're still within an acceptable range."

A few minutes later, Pham said, "Dad, the cylinder temperature has risen to -245°C, and from the expressions on Bella's, Eric's, and Luc's faces, they don't look very happy."

"You're right, Pham, but they still have acceptable vitals, and I know the spirit of these three—they hate giving up. And I don't want them to go through this again, if we can get it done safely, now."

Suddenly, Bella let out a scream, and Eric and I both moaned agonizingly.

Thay exclaimed, "No more! That's it!" He pushed the red panic button that Professor Flannigan had installed, and our blood instantly bypassed the CO_2 scrubber and entered two empty glass vessels, one of which rapidly increased the amount of CO_2 while the other increased the level of O_2. Pham and Brianna were in deep-concern mode. Thay was doing a pranayama exercise to stay out of stress as he focused on controlling the transfusion equipment. Pushing the panic button also instantly and rapidly began raising the bed temperatures by replacing the cold circulating fluid in the beds with warm fluid.

Seconds later, the O_2/CO_2 ratio reached a normal level, and Bella, Eric, and I opened our eyes. I was the first to speak.

"*Minchia!* That definitely was not fun! And my body is itching all over from the rapid change in temperature. How'd we do?"

While Eric and Bella were recovering their bearings and scratching themselves, Thay answered, "I have no idea. I'm just glad you three are back safe and sound—at least I hope you are."

Bella said, "God, do I have a splitting headache! And damn, my body feels like one big itch!"

Eric agreed. "Me too."

When I commented that I also had similar symptoms, Thay said, "That's because I ramped up your blood gases and body temperature very quickly to the normal range. You should be fine in a short time after they equilibrate. If the itching continues, I can throw you in a tub of ice."

In unison, all three of us said, "No, thanks!"

Just then, Thay's cell phone rang. Brianna looked down and noticed the caller ID. "It's John Levy—the NASA astrobiologist we've been speaking with."

Thay answered the call on the speaker. "This is Thay."

"Congratulations, SPI Team! We've been in observation mode of the titanium cylinder for the last hour. It appears that we have success—but not as you expected."

Thay asked immediately, "John, what do mean by that?"

"Your wormhole did not do a 180-degree folding on itself, as your calculations had predicted. Instead, it actually shrank in length by about 90 percent, with funnel entry ports at each end along the cylindrical axis, presumably the first, located at our LP2 coordinates, and the second at Zoi's coordinates.

"As your physicist friends from UC Santa Barbara predicted, two small entry cones have formed on the wormhole, but not in the geometric configuration you'd predicted. They're sealed along the cylinder's axis at both the entry and exit of the wormhole. Still, they're in perfect alignment with each other along the axis of the cylinder.

"Our astrophysics team here at NASA has discussed these results and believe that all should be in working order. You very likely have experimentally discovered a previously unknown stable quantum-gravity solution to the anti-de Sitter Space and Conformal Field Theory calculations you've done. Our NASA team has no doubt that you've now got instantaneous connection through that wormhole entry-cone at LP2 and the one at Zoi coordinates! Amazing! Actually—unbelievable!"

None of us knew what to say. We wanted to cheer, but I think all of us wondered if NASA had things right. Thay smiled at us and replied, "Thank you for calling, John." And then he pushed the end-call button.

Chapter Twelve

FIRST ATTEMPT

"In drawing, nothing is better than the first attempt."
— Pablo Picasso

Friday, November 22, 2030—Cambridge, Massachusetts

We were all exhausted from what had been an amazing success—so far. Thay wanted us to take a day's rest before trying our best to send our first signal through the wormhole to Zoi. We spent most of Thursday going through our calculations, checking and rechecking them. Having discovered a novel, stable geometry for the wormhole, we were able to adjust our calculations, and bingo, whaddya know? There was a stable configuration exactly how we'd discovered it.

Now that we had a stable, working wormhole, transmission time should be nearly instantaneous, not more than a few minutes. NASA was impressed with what we'd accomplished. And I have to say, we were as well. In a million years, who would have guessed what we had uncovered?

We had a discussion as to what kind of signal we should send for our first attempt at contact. Some of it was too creative, if there is such a thing. Eric thought we should send a recording of *Bohemian Rhapsody* by Queen. Bella and Brianna opted for a photo of Arnold Schwarzenegger in one of his *Terminator* flicks. But Thay brought us back down to Earth, and we decided on a simple, repetitive dots-and-dashes signal in the hopes that if someone were on the other end, they would repeat the sequence. Although that would not give us a sense of the extent of their intelligence, it would be a start.

NASA had provided us with a recently developed, proprietary laser-radio transmitter that operates at high frequencies for high-speed data transfer. The device can function as both a transmitter and a receiver. Most important, it can send a signal from Earth to LP2 with previously unheard-of precision. It could hit the center of the connecting cone at the wormhole, within one millimeter of accuracy, minimizing interaction with the wormhole's walls, thereby avoiding the generation of excessive gravitational forces that could cause an implosion.

We were still limited by the speed of light for transmission from Earth to LP2, which was not an issue for us. Since that's 300 million meters per second, and the distance to LP2 is 1.5 million kilometers, a simple arithmetic calculation told us that one-way transmission would require five seconds. Once our signal hit the wormhole cone connecting LP2 with Zoi, transmission would be nearly instantaneous over the 100 light-years distance to Zoi. Now that is *really* weird!

ON FRIDAY MORNING, we all arrived at the lab early to get things set up for our first transmission.

Thay and Eric had arrived earlier than the rest of us and checked that all was set up properly. I knew we would have to be patient, but I was excited to get started.

I asked Thay, "What did you finally decide on as a simple message to send to our alien friends—if there are any on Zoi?"

Thay answered, "A short signal that will run for one second, and a long signal that runs for three seconds. I suggest that we send a continuous repetition of three shorts, three longs, three shorts."

Eric asked, "Does that code have any meaning?"

Thay said, "It does. Anyone know the answer?"

Brianna responded, "I do. My brother was an Eagle Scout, and he tried to teach me Morse Code. I had no interest, but I know *that* one—save our ship, or SOS!"

"Right you are, young lady! Your brother would be proud of you, especially if he knew how you were going to *use* Morse Code."

Bella asked, "So are you going to run it continuously, kinda like SOS—space—SOS—space—SOS for some period, and then stop transmitting and hope for a response?"

"That's correct," Thay said. "Perhaps for an hour, and then listen for an hour, and keep the process going like that. It will be programmed to run like that automatically. We can all take it easy for a couple of days, and perhaps longer until we hopefully get a return signal. I have the laser transmitter linked to my cell phone. If we're lucky enough to make contact, I'll get their text with the return message, and I will contact everyone."

We started transmission to LP2 and through the small conical entry to our wormhole to Zoi. This was confirmed by NASA from their detailed observational capabilities on LP2 and the wormhole. This gave us a couple of days to reconnect with each other—Eric with Brianna, Thay with Pham, and Bella with me. It was a great respite from what we'd just accomplished so far.

But two days grew into three days and then into four, and still no response from Zoi. The NASA laser transmitter continued to deliver our messages with spectacular precision—directly through the center of the small conical wormhole, never off by more than a millimeter. We decided to meet at the lab late that afternoon. Finally, Bella had a thought, although she probably expressed it in jest.

"Dear Emperius, why don't you check with your Russian sweetheart? Maybe she has a creative idea!"

I responded, "Come on, Bella, give me a break. She's not my Russian sweetheart. That was ten years ago, and as you well know, it was absolutely nothing."

"Oh, Luc, you know I like to tease you."

Eric jumped in. "Wait! Maybe Bella has a good point, even if it *is* in jest. Remember what Sun Tzu once said: 'Keep your friends close and your enemies closer.' After all, Sophia used to be our enemy—but hopefully, not anymore."

Thay said, "I agree with Eric. Why not give her a call and see if there's something she hasn't told us? It can't hurt, and it just might help."

I gave in. "Okay, okay, already! I'll call her. But don't expect any magic from her."

With that, I placed my cell phone on the table in speaker mode and dialed Sophia's encrypted phone.

She answered after three rings in the very sweetest tone of voice. "Well, hi there, Luc! How *are* you?"

With that, Bella and Brianna put their hands on their hips and silently mouthed what she'd just said. Pham, Eric, and Thay were doing their best to control their bursts of laughter.

"Hi, Sophia. I understand that Major Dallant is nearly done integrating you into our operation, and you should be able to join us on campus at MIT shortly. Also, I see that he was successful in getting you a one-year sabbatical in our physics department. Congratulations!"

"Thanks, Luc. I'm looking forward to being a colleague of yours and working with your team."

Minchia! I could see the expression on Bella's face. If looks could kill. "I just wanted to update you on where we are and get your thoughts."

"I would be happy to oblige," she said agreeably.

Then I filled her in on our success to date, telling her that we were now in transmission mode, but after three days, nothing was coming back. I asked her if she had any thoughts.

She answered, "First of all, I'm impressed by what you and your team have accomplished. I'm not sure I have any better information for you. Let's see . . . you're using the old Morse Code format for SOS, but no response, right?"

"Right."

She thought for a while and then said, "How about letting them have some pie?"

I quickly responded, "Sophia, what in the world are you talking about?"

But brilliant Eric got it right away. "She means *pi*. Is that right?"

"Right you are. With Morse Code, send 3.14159, and see what they say, if there is a 'they.'"

We all looked at each other, and then I said, "Thanks, Sophia. Interesting idea. We'll give it a shot and let you know how it turns out."

Fortunately, the laws of mathematics are the same throughout our entire three-dimensional universe. If you divide the length of the circumference of any circle by the length of its diameter, whether it's on Earth or in a galaxy 100 billion light-years away—a circle's a circle—

the answer will always be the infinite decimal, pi (π), the first 12 numbers of which are 3.14159265359.

Thay did as Sophia suggested. He put 3.14159 on constant repeat, each time sent as three beeps, space, one beep, space, four beeps, space, one beep, space, five beeps, space, nine beeps.

Then we all left the lab for dinner at the faculty club and went through more wine than we would normally drink—three bottles. Except for Thay, who doesn't drink alcohol, we were all slightly tipsy, which was a nice break from what was happening back at the lab: nothing.

After a dessert of apple pie, we really went overboard. Eric ordered us each a glass of his favorite after-dinner drink—Paradiso. It's a South Tyrolean brandy aged for years in small French barrique barrels. With its aromatic hints of dried fruit and vanilla, it's as close to a distillate drug as you might ever experience.

After Eric's toast, Thay's cell phone signaled an incoming text. It was a message from the laser-radio transmitter: 265359.

Chapter Thirteen

FORWARD STRATEGY

"In planning for battle, I have always found that plans are useless, but planning is indispensable."
— Dwight D. Eisenhower

Tuesday, November 26, 2030—Cambridge, Massachusetts

Who would have guessed—intelligent beings, aliens—speaking to us from 100 light-years away? We were beside ourselves! It was also satisfying to know that math works no matter where you are in the universe—the length of the circumference of a circle divided by the length of its diameter is *always* pi—QED.

Major Dallant and NASA were more than impressed. Dallant immediately called a meeting to be absolutely sure that there was a tight clamp on all information involved in Project Phoenix. He emphasized that any of our work leaking out could have disastrous outcomes, both nationally and globally.

He also said that CIA/NSA had completed their investigation and interrogation of Sophia Stepanova and that the information she'd disclosed was priceless to our national and global security. Tomorrow, two of Dallant's men—Sophia's bodyguards—would escort her to MIT, and concerning Project Phoenix, we should be comfortable having open discussions with her. This was going to be an interesting set of affairs on a number of fronts.

Around 1:00 p.m., I received a call from one of Major Dallant's men, who informed me they were about 15 minutes away and would join us shortly at the lab with Sophia. One of those interesting issues was about to raise its head. How would Bella and Sophia get along? We were about to find out. There was a knock at our lab door. Eric unlocked it, and in walked Sophia and her two bodyguards.

Thay did the honors. "Sophia, gentlemen, good afternoon, and welcome to our humble place of stellar science."

The two men smiled, and one of them said they would be seated outside the main door to the lab, and not to hesitate if either of them were needed. *I hope not!*

It was Sophia's turn. "Hi, Luc, Thay. I haven't yet met the other members of your team."

Thay went first. "Sophia Stepanova, this is my son, Pham Tuan."

Sophia gave Thay a strange look. "Your son?"

Pham tried to put her mind at ease while shaking her hand. "Hi, Sophia. It's a long but interesting story. I'll fill you in sometime."

Sophia half-smiled. "I look forward to that one, Pham!"

Eric stepped in. "Hi, Sophia. We've never met. Well, kinda. I walked past you in the Peninsula Creamery in Palo Alto some ten years ago when you met Luc for the first time. I was leaving, having just finished breakfast with him."

"Oh, right, I remember. We both exchanged flirty glances and smiles. Nice to see you again, Eric, and to finally meet you."

Then Brianna stepped up. "Hi, Sophia, I'm Brianna Williams—atmospheric physics, Columbia University. I recently joined the team through the auspices of my dear friend Eric."

Sophia smiled and had obviously caught Brianna's hands-off-my man innuendo. "I see. Hi, Brianna. Great to meet you! Is Jim Hansen still at Columbia?"

"He's emeritus now. I did my PhD with Jim before accepting my position at Columbia."

Sophia responded, "You're so fortunate, Brianna. Jim's a gifted scientist. The US Senate and the rest of us in the world should have listened to him when he spoke about climate change back in 1988. If we'd done so, we wouldn't have such an impending tragedy now."

Brianna exhaled and said, "My God, you're so right."

Sophia looked at me. "Luc, glad to be working with you and your team."

I smiled and said, "We're glad to have you, Sophia."

And finally there was Bella. "Hi, Sophia, we met years ago when you were having dinner with Luc at the Peninsula Creamery."

Sophia's response: "Oh, yes. Great to see you again, Bella. Listen, do you mind if I—as you Americans like to say—'clear the air'?"

Bella was a bit surprised but said, "Sure, the floor's all yours."

Sophia proceeded to deliver her thoughts. "That time you found Luc and me having dinner together was all my doing. I intensely pursued a discussion with him because I was sent on a special mission by my father—Seagull. It's a long, terrible story, and maybe I can make it up to you sometime over dinner. That is, if you don't mind the presence of those guys who brought me here sitting near us."

Bella smiled and responded, "That would be great, Sophia. Do you mind if Brianna joins us? I know that Major Dallant said you're a consultant to the team. But for me, that's just a label. Maybe the three of us can do some team building over drinks and dinner."

Sophia answered, "Great idea!"

I thought, *Things are looking better than I anticipated.* At least it was a good start.

As usual, Thay brought us back to reality. "Look, folks, I'd like to send one more message before we delve into how best to communicate, given our huge language barrier. Any ideas?"

Good ol' Eric was quick as a racehorse with his suggestion: "I've been tossing around another math idea—very Pythagorean—from that amazing Greek-Sicilian philosopher-scientist.

I said, "Okay, let's have it."

Eric asked, "Thay, can you transmit a video or a drawing through the NASA transmitter?"

Thay replied, "I can, as long as it's not too many gigabytes, and even then, NASA has some adaptations that would make large messages manageable. I'll ask them for the software and install it today."

Eric suggested, "How about if we transmit a drawing of a right triangle and label each of two equal sides that create the right angle with the Greek letter *pi* and label the third longer side or hypotenuse as *h*. Then next to the triangle you again write the Greek letter *pi* with an arrow after it pointing to the symbolic Morse Code: three dashes, a space, one dash, a space, and four dashes, which of course is 3.14, something they know from our first communication. According to Pythagoras's famous theorem—probably called something else on Zoi—they'd have to square 3.14, multiply the answer by 2, and then take the square root of their answer to get the value of *h*—namely, 4.44, which they hopefully would transmit back to us as four dashes, a space, four dashes, a space, and four dashes."

Thay's response: "I like it. It's high school simple, and it's clear."

We all agreed. Thay prepared and sent the message to Zoi, exactly as Eric had outlined.

He then suggested that we all take a break and have an early lunch together in a new private room at the faculty club, which Major Dallant had specially designed and constructed for our exclusive use—complete with an insular Faraday cage—no eavesdropping on our conversations. Furthermore, our meals would come from the faculty-club kitchen, prepared exclusively by a designated chef and served by a specific waiter, both of whom had top-security clearance and were employed by the CIA. He wasn't taking any chances on our safety or on any critical information concerning Project Phoenix leaking out of the room.

Discussions over lunch were light, humorous, and mostly directed either inadvertently or advertently toward helping Sophia acclimate to our team culture—quite a change from what was happening a decade ago. You could see that she appreciated our team spirit and culture. In fact, she became so relaxed that she started telling Russian jokes. They were mostly intellectual rather than humorous, but it was great to see her enthusiasm.

Brianna and Pham started a discussion about whether or not the aliens would be friendly. Brianna had a good point. "I have no idea, but if they've tracked the last few thousand years of our human history and can see what we've done to each other, I doubt they would consider *us* a friendly species."

Bella agreed. "That's certainly true. I've wondered, as I'm sure you have, what they look like. Then I started thinking, Earth is 4.543 billion years old, and archaeologists have discovered meteorites dating back to that time in the Sahara desert and in Australia, and they contain the building blocks of RNA—molecules like ribose and various other nucleotides. And we astrobiologists are quite sure that RNA preceded and was responsible for creating the first molecules of DNA on Earth. If all that's correct, I think RNA and DNA are likely prevalent throughout the universe, in which case the aliens may very well look similar to us. In fact, there are some respected scientists who believe that Earth is a living organism—*Gaia*—and the universe is as well."

Eric quipped, "Wow—that's spooky! But just remember, it's well known that chimpanzees share 99 percent of our human DNA. So it may still mean the aliens can be little green people with big heads, scraggly arms and legs, huge eyes, and no belly buttons!" Big laughs ensued from everyone.

A more sensible comment came from Thay: "My big concern is language. How will we have long and constructive conversations?"

"You know, Dad," said Pham, "I read about some work by Dr. Guy Laurence Doyle, an astrophysicist at the Search for Extraterrestrial Intelligence Institute, or SETI. He's a physicist and a researcher in language communication, preparing for our first meeting with aliens—if he only knew what's going on in this lab! He has also been studying communications among dolphins, other animals, and even plants!

"Now here's a crazy point, and he's not even sure what it means, although it works for nearly every spoken language on Earth. From a large sample of writing for any given language, count the number of times various words appear. Next, create a graph, and on the vertical axis plot the number of times a word appears. On the horizontal axis, starting at zero, list the word that appears the most, then the next most-sighted word—all words equally spaced on the horizontal axis out to the least frequently appearing word. If the writing sample is large enough to contain a number of diverse words, the plot is always a linearly descending graph that forms a 45-degree angle between the vertical and horizontal axes. And that's for every language in the world! He believes that this suggests a common essence hidden within all languages. Maybe we should ask NASA and Major Dallant about bringing him in to the project."

Thay was sipping his tea. He put down his cup but didn't have the opportunity to respond to Pham's suggestion before his iPhone rang, messaging a signal from the transmitter. Our conversation stopped immediately. Thay opened his phone and looked at the message.

He seemed somewhat baffled as he read it. "They responded to our message and said, 'That's an easy and archaic task—4.44. If you would like to skip the mathematical inquiries, we can go directly to English.'"

If technology is a proxy for intelligence, we were in for a big surprise.

Part IV

COMMUNION

Chapter Fourteen

ANCIENT
HELPING HAND

*"We live in a technological universe in which we are always
communicating. And yet we have sacrificed
conversation for mere connection."*
— SHERRY TURKLE

WEDNESDAY, NOVEMBER 27, 2030—CAMBRIDGE, MASSACHUSETTS

We were beyond astonished by the commentary in English from
the aliens on Zoi. How could it be? Thay had immediately sent them
a response: "We are amazed and gratified that we can converse with
you in our language. Would you agree to an exchange of information
between us? If so, due to certain time and equipment logistics, could
we begin 24 Earth-hours from now? We would like some time to create
a short list of questions for you, and perhaps you would like to do the
same as well.

"The time required for transmitting a signal from Earth to our satellite in orbit around Earth is five seconds. And of course, the same
amount of time would be required to receive your return signal once it
reaches our satellite. It may be a bit inconvenient, but not a problem.

"It might be more efficient if we created and then transmitted our
list of questions to you, and perhaps you could do the same to us. In
that way, we would both get all of the answers at the same time.

"At this time, however, I can say that one of our first questions will be how you are able to converse with us in English. We are confident that is likely not the means of communication among yourselves. This is a historic moment for us, and hopefully for you. We look forward to your response."

After Thay sent his message, we waited somewhat longer than ten seconds for Zoi's response, which was: "Twenty-four Earth-hours is acceptable. We can imagine what your questions may be and look forward to receiving them."

I thought, *Hey, that sounds friendly enough.*

Thay asked me to immediately call Major Dallant and set up a videoconference call with him, a NASA representative, and our team. The objective would be to create an initial list of questions to be transmitted to the aliens. During the next several hours, through a series of video calls, we created the following questions and offered a caveat: "We hope our questions are clear and easily understood using your translation technology."

1. How did you develop a means to communicate in English?

2. We have a sense that your technological and perhaps other areas of development—physical, emotional, cultural, spiritual—are well beyond ours. The age of our planet is estimated at 4.543 billion Earth years. The earliest undisputed evidence of life on Earth— our distant predecessors and ancestors—were single-cell microorganisms and dates between 3.5 and 4.5 billion years ago—most scientists agree on 3.465 billion years ago, although there appears to have been some nonliving protocells floating around our oceans 3.8 billion years ago.

    Over billions of years, we evolved from these species. Some paleontologists believe that our first human ancestor was a fish called Tiktaalik. It had shoulders, elbows, legs, wrists, a neck, and many other humanlike parts. Our closest ances- tor today is the chimpanzee, with which we share

99 percent of our DNA. Our current human species dates back only about 100,000 years.

Of the more than 5 billion life forms that ever lived here on Earth, more than 99 percent are estimated to be extinct, primarily due to five major extinction events. Today, the number of species on Earth ranges from 10 to 14 million. Although not all biologists consider viruses to be a life form, there are an estimated 10^{31} of them on Earth. The facts that put this astronomical number in perspective for us is that there are more distinct viruses on Earth than all the estimated stars in our universe, which in turn, are considered to be more numerous than all the grains of beach sand on planet Earth. Could you provide a similar sense for species and their evolution on your planet, which, by the way, we call Zoi, which in the Greek language on Earth means "life"?

3. There is a fundamental molecule to all life on Earth. Based on our chemical knowledge and nomenclature, it is called deoxyribonucleic acid, or DNA, and is a polymer composed of two polynucleotide chains that coil around each other to form a double helix structure, carrying genetic instructions for the evolution, development, functioning, growth, and reproduction of all known living organisms and many viruses on Earth. Many of our astrobiologists, including those on our team, believe that all indications are that DNA is likely a prevalent molecule throughout our universe. Do you agree, and if so, is it likely that your species and Earthlings are similar in physical structure?

4. Are you capable of distant space travel, and if so, what is your means of propulsion?

5. Until you request otherwise, we will call your planet Zoi. What is the total population of Zoi? What do you call your planet?

6. Are you at peace? Have there been any wars among your people? What is your form of governance?

7. Would you consider sending images of Zoi's landscape and of your people? We could do the same.

8. What do you eat and drink for physical nourishment?

9. Do you sleep, and if so, for how long?

10. Do you believe in a higher power?

We all agreed that these ten questions would be more than a good start. It would be a thrilling and hopefully revealing conversation.

I HAD A DIFFICULT TIME going to sleep that evening, knowing what our next day held in store for us. But sleep was just about to quiet my mind when I received a call from Major Dallant at 3:15 a.m. telling me that NASA had detected something weird happening at our installation at LP2. There were huge periodic levels of static, then quiet, then static. He was afraid that the system was about to explode again. I called Thay and Eric, and we rushed to the lab to see what was happening. There was a message from the aliens waiting for us:

"Do not be disturbed by the chaotic transmission signals you are receiving from your satellite installation. We noticed that for rapid communication with us, you constructed what you call a 'wormhole.' However, you still require radio transmission between Earth and your satellite, which as you have said is limited to a transit time of five Earth seconds in each direction—ten seconds between questions and answers is not an efficient means for our discussions.

"We hope you do not mind; we safely disconnected your current Earth-to-LP 2 connection and in its place created a more advanced and effective direct-link system from Earth, via your satellite, to our location. In this way, we can communicate with no time delay. It is the same system we use to communicate with our home planet when we are light-years away on a travel mission. At some point, we will reconnect your system and remove ours. Not to worry, all is safe at this time. The new connection will be in complete working order for our communication later on today, as we have agreed. As for the wormhole, we can assure you that it will maintain its stability indefinitely. Impressive, in view of your current state and understanding of physics. We look forward to our discussion."

I couldn't believe it. They were helping us with our objective—with God knows what kind of super-advanced technology!

Eric exclaimed, "What in the world—or should I say *out* of this world? I couldn't begin to comprehend what they had done at LP2. I guess that's why they didn't bother to explain, which is fine with me—I guess."

Thay smiled and said, "I think our 'friends' understand our anxiousness for rapid communication and are responding with their help."

Part V

EXTRATERRESTRIALS

Chapter Fifteen

ΔLIEN
CONVERSΔTION

*"A single conversation across the table with a wise man is
better than ten years mere study of books."*
— Henry Wadsworth Longfellow

Thursday, November 28, 2030—Cambridge, Massachusetts

It would be a most unusual Thanksgiving—and hopefully, a thankful one. The entire team gathered at the lab. NASA representatives and Major Dallant would join us later via teleconference for our discussion with those we were now calling the Zoians. To keep things simple and make them more amenable to disclosing useful information, Dallant decided that he and NASA would only listen in and not participate in this first conversation. There would be time for that in future connections. If necessary, they could text their questions to us in real time across the bottom of our video screen.

Sophia also joined us, her two bodyguards seated outside the door, as usual. She was as excited as we were to be here today.

She exclaimed, "Luc, you and the SPI Team must feel a deep sense of satisfaction to have gotten this far! It's truly a historic moment in time—not just for you and your team, but for the whole world as well."

"You bet. And I can tell you that none of this would have been possible without a huge team effort, in particular, special guidance from Thay," I told her.

Thay added, "Believe me, without the experience, commitment, and cooperation of *all* of you, none of this could have happened. I am particularly intrigued by something we spoke about many times over the past decade—namely, how physics has progressed exponentially in possibilities and power over the last couple of hundred years from classical to quantum, and now to the beginnings of spiritual physics. I'm betting that our friends on Zoi have taken all of these areas of physics to a much higher level. I hope we can discuss this with them."

Thay was right. Over the next several weeks, to our surprise and at times, consternation, a "much higher level" would turn out to be stratospherically beyond what any of us could have ever imagined.

THE TIME HAD ARRIVED for our 100-light-year connection. We gathered around the transmitter-receiver waiting patiently for a message from the Zoians. Suddenly, the transmitter signaled a static sound, and the large messaging monitor that Eric and Thay had installed came alive in front of us. *It was them!* On the screen, we could both watch their text and hear their messaging appearing in real time.

And so they began: "If we may, we would like to offer a preface to today's conversation. Your ten questions are excellent. However, some of them would require answers that at this time at your stage of evolutionary development would not be in your best interest, nor in the interest of others on Earth. We hope you will understand that when we touch on those questions, there will be little we can share with you on those topics at this time.

"To expand on my point, throughout all our travels in the universe, we have never encountered any sentient beings who have successfully made such a huge quantum jump in physicality or in consciousness. Creating a stable, functioning wormhole at your stage of scientific development is unheard of, at least in our experience. Also, you have adapted well to the jumps in scientific knowledge you have made.

"Yes, we can contemplate helping you speed up the evolutionary process, but very large jumps forward could be dangerous to all involved—including you. The primary reason is that at your stage of consciousness evolution, you would find it extremely challenging—probably impossible—to use your Personal Consciousness as a safe means to properly access the necessary level of zero-point energy of the universe to achieve your desired objectives. If not properly managed, you could find yourself in a dangerous place in space-time. I hope you will trust me on this important point."

I had a fleeting nasty thought: When he said, *"Trust me on this important point,"* was he sincere, or was he afraid that we'd rise to a serious competitive position? If Thay could read my mind, he would advise, "Don't be judgmental until it is clearly called for." Right.

"Last, it is certainly acceptable to us if you refer to our planet as Zoi and to us as Zoians."

Thay responded immediately. "My name is Thay. I am a member of our small team, hoping to learn more about you and your planet so that we can perhaps help all species here on Earth—especially humanity—whom we believe are entering an extended epoch of dire circumstances. We may not completely understand why your stated caution is necessary, but you can be confident that we respect your judgment, guidance, and decisions. May I ask your name?"

The Zoian responded immediately. "Thank you. In English, you may call me *Bliss*, similar to your word for 'joy' or 'happiness'—but that is just a coincidence due to the translation mechanics in our means of communication.

"I suggest that we move on to your questions. In that respect, it will be easier for you to comprehend our answers if you allow me to choose the order in which to answer them. If that is acceptable to you, I would first like to address question number two."

Thay responded, "Certainly, it's acceptable. Thank you for your guidance on how best to proceed. Also, we are grateful for the modifications you made to our satellite system at LP2. We cannot begin to imagine or understand how you eliminated the transit time for a signal between Earth and LP2, essentially making it instantaneous. My best guess as a physicist and a spiritualist is that it must involve aspects of consciousness as the fundamental mechanism of transmission. No matter the means, we are immensely grateful."

Bliss continued. "Thay, that is quite insightful. As we progress in our communications, you will see that consciousness plays an important role in how we function and in nearly everything we do. In fact, long ago we discovered that it is the most important fundamental force behind everything in the universe. Yes, it is the basis behind the changes we made to your system at LP2. As you are well aware, the transmission of consciousness knows no limitation of speed. It is always instantaneous. For now, I suggest that we proceed."

Bliss continued. "Compared to Earth, which you correctly mentioned formed as a planet in your solar system 4.543 billion years ago, with your first single-cell life-forms appearing about 3.5 billion years ago, Zoi formed as a planet 9.389 billion years ago, and our first single-cell life-form emerged 8.331 billion years ago. Your 'modern' human species dates back approximately 100,000 years. By comparison, the first 'modern' Zoian species dates back 4.667 billion years. As you can see, we have been a 'modern' species for about 4.567 billion years longer than you Earthlings. Therefore, we have had a much longer time to *evolve*, *devolve*, and *re-evolve*. I have used those last three words purposefully, as they foreshadow most of the things you can learn from our experiences over billions of years. However, we have learned some things which, as I mentioned earlier, would not be in your best interest for us to disclose at this time.

"But other experiences may bring great benefits to all species on Earth. For example, during those 4.667 billion years, we experienced a number of mass extinctions, as did you. As was the case with Earth, most were caused by natural phenomena such as volcanic eruptions or by Zoi's collision with a large asteroid. However, a couple of those extinctions were, as you might say, anthropogenic—that is, caused by our own species through the outcomes of wars, nuclear annihilation, pollution, and especially, catastrophic climate change. On those issues, we can offer you a useful perspective. Whether you act on our advice is your prerogative, and your success in following that advice will depend very much on whether a majority of your fellow Earthlings accept and understand the truth and value of what we offer you."

I had to interject. "Bliss, my name is Luc, and I can tell you that Earth is facing a terrible future because of climate change, so your help would be invaluable. Will we have an opportunity to discuss this in some detail with you?"

Bliss noted, "We are intimately aware of the existential issue you raise. We started visiting Earth about 50,000 years ago, subsequent to the end of your Pleistocene Epoch, which lasted from one million years ago until 25,000 years ago. During that epoch, we observed Earth's global climate making large changes as it approached the end of its last Glacial Maximum, or Ice Age. During that time, changes in your carbon cycle caused large releases of CO_2 and CH_4 into the atmosphere. Huge variations in atmospheric and ocean circulation affected the global distribution and currents of water and heat. And at the end of that epoch, the melting ice sheets caused your sea levels to rise by more than 80 meters.

"But then, 11,700 years ago, at the end of this last glacial epoch, or Ice Age, Earth entered what your geologists at first called the Holocene Epoch. Please take note that over those 12 millennia, we observed only several small-scale climate shifts. For example, between 1200 and 1700 CE, Earth experienced the Little Ice Age. However, generally speaking, the Holocene Epoch has been relatively warm, with a stable climate. Its moderate temperatures, stability, and predictability have been important to humanity's recorded history—the rise and fall of your seven major ancient civilizations—Mesopotamia, Egypt, Greece, Babylon, Europe, China, and India.

"Although it is true that it is a fundamental thermodynamic law that all species on Earth influence their environment, none have changed your world as extensively and as fast as the human species. By all measures that we have seen, human activity is unquestionably *the* major contributor to Earth's current rapid climate change. Climate change–induced habitat destruction and pollution continue to cause mass extinction of your plant and animal species. We project that by 2050, 50 percent of all current plant and animal species will be extinct on Earth. It is therefore quite appropriate that paleontologists and geologists have renamed the Holocene Epoch the *Anthropocene Epoch* to reflect that the major changes in climate and pollution have been made by humankind and not by natural causes.

"However, on the positive side, your Anthropocene Epoch has seen the greatest increase in human knowledge and creativity, as well as the discovery and development of major scientific and technological advances. Ironically, it is those very advances in science and technology that have enabled you to propagate the destruction of life on your planet.

"Yet, it is those same developments that hold the means to avoid or at least minimize climate change. Unfortunately, humanity has proceeded too far in its destructive behavior to now use its knowledge and technology to avoid severe climate change. The best it can do is minimize the severity and create a means to adapt and diminish the deleterious impact on life.

"At this time, I will make one last point on this subject: It is not Earth that is facing a terrible future. It is *all* of its resident living species—including humanity. Earth will recover, as it has in the past, from other existential events such as asteroid collisions or super-volcanic actions. Your species and others may not.

"Yes, Luc, we can and should have further discussions on Earth's rapidly accelerating climate change. However, from what we Zoians see, at your stage of global consciousness, we are not confident that it will be of significant help—primarily due to the voracious appetite of a large percentage of humanity for the perceived benefits of near-term wealth and power. They have chosen to do little to address the problem. It appears that it is in neither the political nor economic interest of your global leaders to behave in a way that benefits future generations, who currently do not spend or vote—regardless of readily apparent rapidly increasing climate change. Thus, you are on a projection that will face humanity and other species with an increasingly devastating environment for countless millennia to come. You might ask why the United Nations held 30 Conference of the Parties (COP) meetings since 1995—instead of one?"

Thay said, "Bliss, this is Thay—that's most disconcerting. What is the basis for your conclusion?"

Bliss's response was both sobering and frightening. "As I have said, we Zoians have had more than 4.6 billion years during which to have evolved as 'moderns,' both physically and in consciousness. During that period, our species was nearly completely destroyed a couple of times by extinction events created by our own hands. But each time, a small number of us survived—you might say the more evolved of our species. We continued our evolution, both physically and, most important, in the realm of consciousness.

"What eventually became obvious, and which was embraced by us—but required a couple of cycles of destruction and evolution over many millions of years—was the existence of a cosmic paradox associated with all highly intelligent species in the universe. It is expressed at a certain level of intelligence and consciousness, and it is likely unavoidable—at least, we have never seen it bypassed by any highly intelligent species on planets in any of the galaxies to which we have traveled.

"We call it the *Intelligentsia Paradox*. It is this: *When any intelligent species or civilization reaches a certain stage of technological development, it is also the point at which its scientific and technological advancement is sufficient for the complete destruction of its species, whether through a climate apocalypse, nuclear annihilation, biological or chemical warfare, or a host of other possibilities.*"

Brianna said, "Bliss, this is Brianna. What creates this point in our technological and scientific evolution and development—what is it that underlies the Intelligentsia Paradox?"

Bliss answered, "Not too many years ago, no Earthling could destroy all species on your planet. Today, that is clearly a distinct possibility. Ironically, you might note that there is a large quantum jump between the level of consciousness for the most evolved animal species on Earth and the level of consciousness that exists within the human species. The human species is where the Intelligentsia Paradox became a reality, with enormous potential for both creative design and construction, or simply, massive destruction."

He continued. "We concluded that these existential crises only occur at and above a certain level of intelligence and experience. The other requirement is a pervasive lack of concern for, and commitment to, evolutionary advancement of the *whole*—namely, for all species. A corollary of the latter requirement is that Life Purpose at this stage of development is unfortunately driven by an intense desire for wealth and power, exclusively. You do not see this behavior in the animal or plant kingdoms, where hoarding is essentially nonexistent. The only way we know to obviate such outcomes is through a combination of highly advanced states of physical and consciousness evolution—which is why it required a couple extinction events of our species, each time starting again as a more highly evolved species.

"We have existed long enough to have seen or discovered detailed records of this kind of cyclic evolution occur with numerous civilizations throughout this and other galaxies. Your solar system is among the youngest, and therefore the least evolved, that we have visited throughout the ages."

Bella responded, "My God, Bliss, that is humbling! If only the majority of humankind were aware of these facts. We in this room understand and embrace the importance of Collective Consciousness,[23] the interconnection of all living things, and the need to support the whole. And yes, there are many others around our world who feel the same way. However, it appears that there are not enough of us—"

Bliss interrupted. "I understand. We were in that same situation a couple of times over many millennia and had to start over again. As we experienced during our history and development, currently, you don't have a sufficient number of highly evolved Earthlings to understand and support the strategies you must take for long-term survival. As was the case for us, it may require a couple of cycles of evolution, destruction, rebirth, and re-evolution to achieve a majority support for the 'whole' before your civilization develops long-term resilience. This kind of behavior is not common wisdom. It requires long periods of evolution and maturation—and that takes time—eons upon eons."

If what Bliss said was true, humanity's future would be much more than heartbreaking and frightening.

There was silence, and then he continued. "Now I will address a combination of questions one, three, and four."

A sedate Eric, who was normally more upbeat than the rest of us, pushed the mute button on the console and quietly added, "I don't know if I want to hear any more."

In a surprised response, Bliss reminded Eric, "Pushing your mute button does not quiet your communication. We are speaking through a consciousness connection, not an electromagnetic signal."

Bliss's comment inspired all of us—except Eric—to exhibit broad smiles of embarrassment.

Bliss went on. "You asked how we learned English. Because of our species' long history and technical capabilities, as I mentioned previously, we have been visiting Earth for more than 50,000 years, so we know quite well the nature of human beings, many of your plant and animal species, and most of your languages—better than anyone on

---

[23] *Collective Consciousness* is sometimes referred to as *Unity Consciousness*.

Earth—and we have developed a cerebral translation capability that enables us to easily converse in any language."

Eric said, "Concerning your visits here, I know that since the early 20th century—possibly even before then—there have been reports of numerous alleged sightings of unidentified flying objects, or UFOs, all over the world. I suspect that some have been authentic, and others just illusions. Is that correct?"

Bliss replied, "I can tell you that regardless of the negative conclusions of the US Project Blue Book Report,[24] which is an unusual and regrettable story in itself, at least 20 percent of reported sightings have been actual extraterrestrial crafts, not only from Zoi but from a host of other planets throughout our galaxy and others as well. Numerous extraterrestrial civilizations have been visiting Earth for many millennia—and have been sighted by the human species, who often thought of them as gods or some kind of higher power.

"Considering your modern age alone, in the United States, for example, sightings reported by thousands of people in Phoenix, Arizona, on March 13, 1997, between 8:15 and 9:30 p.m., were our vessels. The large mothership sighted by a number of United Airline employees at O'Hare Airport in Chicago on November 7, 2006, at 4:15 p.m., was also ours. Unlike openly sharing governments in Belgium, France, and various countries in South America, the US has had a policy of ignoring these sightings. The stated reason is a fear of mass hysteria; however, there is much more behind this unusual behavior by your government.

"In fact, as the result of a UFO crash in Roswell, New Mexico, on July 7, 1947, the US recovered a spaceship and four bodies from a civilization living on a planet located some 275 light-years from Earth near the constellation Sagittarius. The US has not yet been able to reverse-engineer the operating mechanics of that spaceship—and they *won't* be able to do so. They don't have the advanced science to understand how the vessel works—and they likely will not for several millennia.

"There was a book written 20 years[25] ago as a compilation and analysis of specific details garnered from high-level international

---

[24]Project Blue Book is the code name for the systematic study of unidentified flying objects by the United States Air Force from March 1952 to its termination on December 17, 1969.

[25]Leslie Kean, *UFOs: Generals, Pilots, and Government Officials Go on the Record,* Harmony Books, New York, 2010.

government officials, airline pilots, and retired military officials from around the world, which categorically proves the existence of UFOs, and with a modest extrapolation, the operation of these spacecraft by extraterrestrial civilizations. However, through the effective channeling of US government disinformation methods, this book and its implications have been largely ignored, suggesting that studies of UFOs and possible extraterrestrials is a waste of time and money, and in fact, taboo."

Eric was amazed, and to some degree, disturbed. "Bliss, that is beyond comprehension, and I'm disappointed by the response and behavior of the US. Sometime ago, the director of NASA told me that few people outside a small, tight circle of people in a covert, clandestine, deep-state operation have the true information on UFOs and extraterrestrial encounters in the US and elsewhere. Even our president has no access to the information they control."

Thay remarked, "Eric, Bliss, I doubt that it's worth spending too much time on the US position on UFOs and extraterrestrials, as they are likely to provide only misinformation, and it seems to me that we have a direct link with our own extraterrestrial encounter, which I believe will be much more instructive for us in what we seek to achieve. So in that vein and changing the subject, if I may, why have Zoians been visiting Earth for such a long period of time? What has been your purpose?"

Bliss responded, "A very good point, Thay. To your question, it has been, and continues to be, a long-term experiment for us. As part of our ongoing effort to understand the nature of physical and consciousness evolution throughout the universe, we have been following your development. Starting in the mid-18th century, the beginnings of your Industrial Revolution, we began to search for ways to help you understand what you were about to do to life on your planet and its environment, and how your obsession with a consumer economy based on poorly managed and unchecked growth would ultimately lead to your extinction. For reasons I mentioned earlier, we have not been overly concerned for Earth itself. We have focused primarily on the probable negative impact on your and other living species. We have wanted to see if it was possible for a developing civilization to avoid being led in a direction that would excessively enhance its power and wealth at the expense of not only other parts of their civilization, but equally important, lead to the demise of future generations. So far, none of your great civilizations have come anywhere close to success—including the current one.

"Although we know that taken in its entirety, Earth is a complex living organism—some of your scientists refer to this concept as Gaia, as Bella mentioned earlier—over its history, it has gone through several massive species extinctions and has always demonstrated that it can survive and return to its natural vitality. But that has not been the case for many other species on Earth.

"For example, there have been no dinosaurs on Earth since their extinction 66 million years ago as a result of the impact of a six-mile-wide asteroid called Chicxulub, which slammed into waters off what is now Mexico, triggering a mass extinction that killed off more than 75 percent of Earth's species. Due to the climate-change path you are currently on, the same could easily be the case for the human species.

"We have considered the possibility of instilling into your species, globally, a successful process we discovered after we caused mass extinctions of our civilization and our subsequent re-evolution. It was developed by our predecessors many generations ago. It consists of a large number of holographic images, videos, and other forms of mass-communication records of the crises we endured in the past as a prelude to the extinction process—deluging floods, violent storms, massive fires, super-tornadoes, civil wars, nuclear annihilation, and much more.

"By unanimous agreement millions of years ago, these images have since been continually shown to our population, from the time they are young. Yes, it is a means of social conditioning; however, it is the only way we know of to educate and remind ourselves how to prevent future extinctions caused by a focus on actions dangerous to our continued evolution. However, it required our causing and enduring two massive species extinctions and subsequent re-evolutions for this strategy to finally take hold and be successful—hopefully permanently, although we have no way of knowing that. Yet, we remain vigilant about any signs of change in the wrong direction."

Thay responded, "Thank you for sharing your experiences and your interest in trying to help our civilization. From what you've said, it is a dim and frightful future that our and other living species on Earth will face. It troubles me deeply. It would seem from your input that our disregard for our contribution to climate change and pollution, as well as nuclear proliferation, are the greatest issues we face. They, in large part, are ultimately responsible for civil unrest and war."

Bliss responded to Thay's concerns. "I understand your deep distress, and your points are well taken and correct. However, Thay, you, in particular, will understand that the fundamental issue Earthlings face is the same one our predecessors faced—a lack of understanding about the importance of the mutual connectivity of your species on your planet, and as a consequence, essentially no meaningful concern for the benefit of the *whole*.

"As we experienced millennia ago, this behavior is based on the limited level of consciousness developed in your species, which, in turn, is due to your current state of overall consciousness evolution. We have no idea how you might accelerate the evolution of consciousness for the vast majority of the human species.

"There is nothing fundamentally wrong with your technology. Its negative issues are solely based on how you have applied it, often driven by a thirst for wealth and power. For example, nuclear energy has a great potential for Earth or any other habitable planet. However, it does not lie in costly nuclear *fission*, with its extensive and dangerous, long-term, radioactive by-products, but in a much safer, cleaner, more economical form of nuclear *fusion* energy, a type of technology that you will eventually learn to master safely and economically, as we have done. There is a great philosophical, technological, and perhaps even a spiritual sense, of satisfaction in generating your required energy for life by mimicking the powers of your sun. All power should come from the stars. That's the way of the universe.

"In the interim, you might take *biomimetic* inspiration from all other life-forms on your planet—create and prosper with the same energy that your sun provides, enabling all life to thrive on your planet. Your existing technologies related to wind, solar, hydrogen, fuel cells, and geothermal power can provide a major stopgap solution until your fusion technology is tenable."

Bella said, "Bliss, it is truly a frightening picture that you've painted for us. How have you studied our species so that you can be confident about our behavior and predispositions?"

"Over many millennia, we have *sampled* numerous species from Earth, including yours, and brought them to Zoi for detailed studies and observation."

Brianna, visibly upset by Bliss's response, broke in immediately. "Do you mean to tell me that you've been abducting our people? That's frightening and cruel! I have on occasion read news reports of people claiming to have been abducted by extraterrestrials and subsequently returned to Earth after brief observation. Most people believe those people were creating these stories—simply as publicity-seeking scammers. What have you done with those you 'sampled' and kept on Zoi?"

Bliss responded, "Not to worry, Brianna. They have been treated well—better than their situations on Earth. In fact, most have had no interest in returning home. This has been part of our experimentation to learn more about our universe so that we can make more effective contributions to its future. Many of those people who claimed to have been abducted were, in fact, telling the truth. They just didn't fit the overall biology we were interested in, and so we safely returned them to Earth, providing them with some level of amnesia so they could not remember their time with us and thus face ridicule by sharing their experiences with others.

"One example is the case of Betty and Barney Hill, who were, as you have called it, 'abducted' by an extraterrestrial civilization living in the Reticulum Constellation, 29 light-years from Earth. The Reticulum people had no intention of harming the Hills. They were interested in the difference between human anatomy and their own. Your government, however, as they have done many times before with respect to other interactions between Earthlings and extraterrestrials, did an excellent job of discrediting the Hills' story with a broad swath of disinformation."

Bella asked, "Have you also sampled species from other planets throughout the galaxy?"

"Yes, we have. In fact, from other galaxies too. And as I mentioned previously, Earthlings are among the most recently developed high-intelligence species, in this and several other galaxies as well."

I couldn't help but repeat in my mind, *the most recently developed high-intelligence species, in this and several other galaxies as well*—and

157

over so many millennia, we have been conditioned in one way or another to think about how special we are. Well, maybe we are, but it seems that there are most likely lots of other special species throughout our universe. Will we learn to accept that?

With that, we disconnected until the next day for another lesson in science, technology, consciousness—and humility.

Tonight, we were planning to have a big, celebratory Thanksgiving dinner at the faculty club. Unfortunately, I don't think we are up for it.

Chapter Sixteen

WHAT ARE YOU?

*"If the only prayer you ever say in your entire life
is 'thank you,' it will be enough."*
— MEISTER ECKHART

FRIDAY AND SATURDAY, NOVEMBER 29 AND 30, 2030—
CAMBRIDGE, MASSACHUSETTS

Yesterday's meeting with Bliss had been heavy and intense. Thanksgiving dinner at the faculty club, which followed our interstellar discussion, was an unusually low-key event. We were all trying to digest and process Bliss's input. I guess that everyone felt pretty much as I did. It was a shame because not much was eaten, even though the staff had gone out of their way to create a mini feast with all the trimmings.

However, we did drink enough wine to numb our brains into acceptance of what seemed to be an obvious outcome for Earth's living species—including humanity. Thay had cautioned us that "everything happens for a cosmic reason" so that we didn't jump to conclusions this early in our contact with Zoi. Not an easy thing to do.

One aspect we did discuss, and we went over it several times, was the Zoians' ability to transpose matter, including their bodies, into consciousness, transmit it superluminally over vast distances, and then recombine the molecular structure accurately with complete and true fidelity to its initial form. What's even more amazing is that they could do the same for nonliving physical bodies—maybe even spaceships! How in God's name could that be possible?

Again, Thay took a more balanced view, saying, "Perhaps it can only be done in 'God's name,' meaning by a direct, intense, and highly elevated connection with Cosmic Consciousness—Einstein called it the 'Mind of God.' From all he has written, it's quite clear he wasn't referring to a divine entity, but to superpowers, which under the right conditions, we could access."

Maybe so, but we had a long way to go to get to that point. That may have been Bliss's point concerning how far ahead the Zoians were in physical and consciousness evolution.

On that matter, Thay shared an interesting yet still-difficult-to-comprehend perspective. He said that over the years, he'd learned from several gifted Wisdom Seekers that the subtle energies responsible for transmission, communication, and physical manifestation via consciousness cannot be measured with any known physical instrument, and this might never be possible. The reason is that the wave functions that mathematically describe the operation of these subtle energies instantly collapse when disturbed by any nonsentient instrument trying to make a measurement. The only known "instrument" that can detect and measure the intensity of these energies is human consciousness, and probably the consciousness of other sentient species as well.

However, he pointed out that paradoxically, these subtle energies are part of a yet-unknown-to-us energy spectrum and are more powerful than the most intense energies associated with the electromagnetic spectrum—nuclear fission, fusion plasma, X-rays, gamma rays, cosmic rays, and likely, beyond—which makes consciousness energy the most powerful force in the universe. It was weird. How could these energies be subtle yet so powerful?

When I asked Thay, he said that we don't yet know why, but he presented a possibility: Our usual perspective on forces is that when matter or energy creates a force on an object, its nature and intensity can be understood and quantified by Newton's laws. However, an interaction initiated by consciousness impacts directly with consciousness within the targeted matter or energy entity and creates a force—as small or large as your consciousness prefers—by enabling the sum of the interacting consciousness elements, both internal and external to the object of interest, to generate that force.

Maybe we just don't understand the huge spectrum over which these subtle energies work, the mechanism, and why. We obviously have much to learn to even come close to catching up with the capabilities of the Zoians—if that's even possible.

As PLANNED, WE BEGAN OUR DISCUSSION with Bliss at 9:00 a.m. Our contact was quick and crystal-clear, as usual.

"Good morning, Bliss, my name is Pham, and as far as I am aware, this is humanity's first discussion with extraterrestrials. I must say that your words, so far, are deeply humbling messages and at times disturbing. Absent prior contact and context, it has been easy for us Earthlings to think of ourselves as special, perhaps even unique—some of us have even behaved as if we are 'at the center of our galaxy,' perhaps even the universe—kind of reminiscent of the thinking of those who lived before Copernicus and Galileo."

Bliss responded, "I understand. That is a natural predilection at your stage of development with no extensive exposure to, and help from, extraterrestrials such as us Zoians. It is not unique to Earthlings."

Pham continued. "Another thought for your consideration: If Zoians have been visiting Earth for 50,000 years or so, you must have a firsthand and more accurate picture of our history than we do. It's my understanding that archaeologists and paleontologists tell us that modern Homo sapiens evolved from our early hominid predecessors between 300,000 and 200,000 years ago, but they didn't begin their migration out of Africa, and perhaps elsewhere, until 100,000 to 70,000 years ago, and they didn't develop their capacity for language until about 50,000 years ago.

"I can imagine that you likely have more accurate historical records than we do, concerning what happened on Earth during the last 50,000 years. That kind of information would be invaluable to us Earthlings. During that time, what really happened in Africa, Asia, India, the Middle East, Europe, and North and South America? I'm sure your information would rewrite our history books."

Bliss responded, "That is true. However, please understand that there is an important increase in the levels of intelligence and consciousness that accompany the process that your scientists and historians go through in uncovering and interpreting your ancient history.

This goes back to my comment of not disclosing certain aspects of your history or ours. It could upset your evolutionary process, which could have serious deleterious effects."

Pham wasn't quite sure how to respond, so Sophia stepped into the discussion with an important question that was on all of our minds.

"Bliss, my name is Sophia. What is your means of space travel—especially if you speak of traveling not only throughout the Milky Way galaxy, but to other galaxies as well—for example, you mentioned Andromeda? Our technological development may be significantly lower than the Zoians, but we are quite confident that our laws of physics apply throughout the universe, and it's a simple calculation to see that if you cannot exceed the speed of light, you can't travel very far in a reasonable time frame."

There was no immediate response, but then Bliss said, "Sophia, that is one of those questions that I referred to earlier. I cannot answer it without causing significant challenges to your team and others on Earth. However, perhaps I can speak more generally to your question, and that may be of some help.

"Clearly, because of the billions of years of greater evolutionary time that we have had compared to Earthlings, our science and technology are much further advanced—well beyond what you might even imagine. You saw what we were able to do in changing the communication system at your satellite. You made quite a leap forward in human history and science by creating a wormhole. What we did to your system at LP2 is orders of magnitude more advanced than that—and we did it quickly, and essentially in real time, from our position on Zoi, 100 light-years away. So, you might imagine that our means of transport is also quite advanced, since we can do so in a way that would appear to be superluminal—namely, well beyond the speed of electromagnetic signals such as light. In fact, it *is*. But we are not moving electromagnetic signals. We don't violate Einstein's theory of special relativity.

"The only point I can leave you with on this question is that our space travel is based on the physics of a unique class of subtle energies, which your species has yet to discover and which are governed by laws of physics and mathematics that are well beyond what you call quantum physics. What I can say is that the scientific and technological phenomena at our disposal are much more dependent on consciousness than what you refer to as classical or quantum physics, which are governed by electromagnetic energies and physical mass. And as you are well aware, the speed of consciousness is instantaneous."

Sophia's response was a simple "Incredible!"

Bliss commented, "I understand how you might think it so, but your species has the same possibilities. However, it is much too early in your evolutionary development. As has been said before by several Avatars throughout your history, 'All I do, you can do—and more.'"

I had a physics question without an obvious answer—not that I expected one—but I gave it a shot anyway. "Bliss, since Zoians have developed the means to send spaceships at thousands of times the speed of light, and I'm sure you will agree that the Law of Conservation of Momentum applies throughout the universe, I assume you've also developed a means to deal with the huge level of momentum decrease within the spaceship so that as you come to a nearly sudden stop from such high velocities, the crew and whatever is within the ship don't go smashing into the walls. Am I correct?"

Bliss replied, "Yes, you are correct that for classical and quantum mechanics, the Law of Conservation of Momentum applies everywhere throughout the cosmos. However, Luc, I must remind you that our mode of travel does not invoke the laws of either classical or quantum physics. All is managed by what you call *spiritual physics*. The Law of Conservation of Momentum is not an issue for our space travel."

As I said, I didn't expect an answer.

Changing subjects, Bella asked, "Bliss, my name is Bella, and I wondered if you could comment on question number three: Are you and other species on Zoi, and in fact, those who may exist on planets in other parts of the universe, biologically based as we are on the molecule we call deoxyribonucleic acid, or DNA?"

There was no response for a few moments. We wondered if the communication connection was broken. But then Bliss said, "The simple answer—at least for us Zoians—is yes and no. I will have to expand on my response for this to make any sense to you.

"A few billion years ago, like you, we had evolved to a physical body based on DNA genetic programming. There are numerous physical creatures, including intelligent humanlike beings throughout the universe with physical bodies based on DNA, the prevalent molecule for the basis of most physical life throughout our universe. However, as you are well aware, even if extraterrestrials have a DNA-based genome that is 99 percent the same as the human genome, you may still have species that appear quite different, physically. On Earth, your chimpanzee species shares 98.8 percent of human DNA. Throughout the universe, there are some exceptions of life not based on DNA, but they are quite rare and based on a science you have yet to discover. We can discuss them at another time.

"However, to continue on this point, we and other advanced civilizations throughout our galaxy and beyond have learned how to use the laws of consciousness or spiritual physics. By doing so, we have learned how to convert any mass—for example, our physical body—into pure consciousness energy, transfer that energy superluminally from one point in the universe to another, and subsequently reconvert that consciousness energy into its original, organized molecular structure. We can do this for any physical body, no matter how small or large—for example, a molecule or a spaceship.

"So you see, as do you, we have both a physical and consciousness body, and our physical bodies are based on DNA. The difference between our civilizations is that we have the ability to convert mass into consciousness, and that consciousness back into the precise mass structure from which it was derived, faithfully maintaining the original molecular structure and bodily functions. We can do this for the mass of our physical bodies and for other physical objects as well. You will eventually discover that throughout the entire universe, there is an equilibrium between mass and energy on the one hand, and consciousness on the other. Knowing how to control that equilibrium is at the heart of several laws you will eventually discover in what you call spiritual physics. You might guess that something similar to this is the basis for our ability to travel vast distances in minimal time—but that will be a much longer future discussion between us."

I decided to jump in. "Luc here. Without getting into the details, which I'm confident you likely know, we have learned to elevate our state of consciousness, and in doing so, our consciousness can travel vast distances, faster than the speed of light. We call it an out-of-body experience, or OBE. Are you doing something similar with space travel?"

Bliss replied, "Yes, we are. However, our technology is orders of magnitude more advanced. When you create an OBE, you transit only your consciousness, and therefore, it must return to your physical body for recombination of the physical and the ephemeral—the body and its consciousness. We have discovered and further developed a means to transfer a physical mass—for example, a physical body using a unique form of consciousness. First, consciousness is separated from the physical body and the body is converted to a 'virtual state of consciousness.' Next, the virtual body and its consciousness are transferred together in a combined 'consciousness package.' Then at our volition, we can convert that consciousness package back into the original body from which it was initially derived. We eventually learned how to make the same kind of transition with material objects other than our bodies and subsequently transmit the combined consciousness package over large distances."

Bliss was alluding to an advanced technology like none I'd ever read about, even in the most far-out science-fiction novels. I had to ask: "Is this connected with the mechanism of your space travel—like spaceships?"

Bliss said, "The simple answer is yes. It is due to the universal fact that every piece of mass and energy, down to the most minute subatomic particles—quarks and beyond—have some form of consciousness associated with it. But beyond that response, the discussion would be much too complex—but ironically, in other ways, quite simple. However, that is for future discussions."

I was trying to wrap my mind around the implications from relativity theory based on what Bliss was sharing with us, so I asked, "If I understand you correctly, you can convert mass into pure consciousness, then transfer that consciousness at essentially infinite speed and then reconstitute the same mass structure from that consciousness. If that's the case and no mass is moving at infinite speed, when you eventually return to your starting point, is there a dilation of time as predicted by Einstein's equations of special relativity, or do they not apply in your case because it is only consciousness that is moving?"

"Excellent, Luc," Bliss responded. "There is no dilation of time. You would not return to Earth much younger than those you left behind when you traveled to Zoi."

Bliss continued. "To give you a sense of how critical consciousness is in all that we do—and in fact, in all that happens in the universe as well—I will summarize for you what we discovered as the true model of the cosmos. In some ways, it is similar to the model that a few of your more insightful physicists have postulated—however with one critical fundamental difference: it is completely dependent on the laws of consciousness. Although what you have called spiritual physics is not yet a fully developed science for you, it follows the scientific laws precisely.

"You are working in the right direction. Research by a few of your inspired scientists like David J. Bohm's Implicate Order[26] and Karl H. Pribram's work on the Holonomic Brain[27] are going in the right direction, but your 'conventional' scientists disparaged their work which, in fact, was groundbreaking and could have opened up great possibilities in technological areas that took Zoians many more years to discover.

"As some of your scientists have postulated, all energy and matter—they are interchangeably equivalent—that make up the universe were formed as the result of the rapid expansion of a minute cosmic singularity—unimaginably smaller than the smallest of subatomic particles[28]—that 13.8 billion years ago existed in a state of infinite *nothingness*. At a certain moment, that singularity gave birth to our expanding universe. Eventually, over billions of years, that expansion will reverse into a contraction, ultimately back to form the cosmic singularity from which it came forth. This process will continue eternally—forming, expanding, contracting, and then re-forming a new universe.

"An important aspect of this process is that it is the energy of consciousness that is doing the work of expansion, such that net-net, the degree of disorder or entropy of the universe is constantly increasing. However, at a crucial point, $P_{\Delta S}$, where the total entropy in the initial cosmic singularity before expansion divided by the total entropy of the expanding universe at that critical point is exactly equal to two, con-

---

[26]David J. Bohm, *Wholeness and the Implicate Order*, Routledge & Kegan Paul, New York, 1980.

[27]Karl H. Pribram, *The Form Within*, Prospecta Press, Connecticut, 2013.

[28]Bliss is referring to the cosmic singularity and not a technological singularity, the latter being a hypothetical point in time at which technological growth becomes exponentially rapid and uncontrollable, resulting in unforeseeable changes to civilization, including upgradable intelligent agents (robots) that eventually enter a runaway reaction of self-improvement cycles, each new and more intelligent generation appearing more and more rapidly, causing an explosion in intelligence and resulting in a superintelligence that far surpasses human intelligence. The long period of existence of the Zoian civilization—billions of years—was responsible for the occurrence of at least one technological singularity.

sciousness instantly reverses the process from expansion to contraction, ultimately returning to a singularity, and the cyclic process of cosmic creation and destruction continues ad infinitum. Your scientists speculate—incorrectly—that some kind of meta-energy or meta-mass was the constituent of the cosmic singularity. It was not. I will explain.

"Each new universe is informed of all physical and ephemeral actions, events, and information that occurred in the prior universe, although this information may not be completely obvious. I can say without getting into the detailed science that dark matter[29] and dark energy,[30] which as you know make up 95 percent of the universe, play a crucial role in this cyclic process.

"Each succeeding universe has a memory shadow effect of all that occurred in the prior universes. The reason for this effect is based on a fundamental property of the singularity, a major difference between your and our model of the universe—*the only constituent of the initial singularity is pure consciousness*. It is this consciousness and *only* this consciousness that is responsible for creating all matter and energy in the universe and for guiding the expansion-contraction processes.

"A final important point: Dark matter and dark energy are solely responsible for the expansion and contraction cycles of the universe, as described by the entropy principles I just described. As your scientists correctly understand, dark energy and dark matter provide the gravitational force that drives the expansion of the universe. However, during the expansion, there is a modest rate of conversion of dark energy and dark matter back to its original *intrinsic* source: consciousness. At some point billions of years after the Big Bang's initiation of expansion, enough dark matter and dark energy will have converted back to consciousness, and after a brief null point—about several hundred million years—it will begin the contraction process. In fact, if you had the capabilities of measuring very precisely the current expansion of the universe, you would find that the expansion rate is slowing down by approximately 1.62×10^{-35} meters per second."

---

[29]Dark matter is nonluminous material that exists in space and can take any of several forms including weakly interacting particles (*cold dark matter*) or high-energy randomly moving particles created soon after the Big Bang (*hot dark matter*).

[30]Dark energy is a form of energy that acts in opposition to gravity and occupies the entire universe, accounting for most of the energy in it and causing its expansion to accelerate. Einstein's theory of relativity allows for the existence of dark energy.

Eric was bewildered. "My God, Bliss, that is unbelievable, incredible! And perhaps it can explain much of what happens here on Earth."

Bliss's response: "Yes, it is unbelievable and incredible, and yes, it *can* explain everything that happens on Earth—and in fact, everywhere else in the universe as well.

"Consciousness is the strongest, highest-level, and most broadly applicable form of energy in the universe. Unlike the high energies created through the laws of classical and quantum physics, which can manifest themselves in varying degrees of extreme force, high energies based on consciousness as governed by the laws of spiritual physics can be either violent, such as the raging storms on the surface of planet Jupiter—which currently unbeknownst to you have great value to life on Earth—or provide a means to safely and nonviolently transport large objects over vast interstellar distances at superluminal velocities."

I had to interject. "Bliss, I'm beginning to think that we Earthlings are definitely living in the Neanderthal Age of science, with so many more millennia to catch up with you—if ever."

Bliss responded, "First, let us not disparage the Neanderthals. I can assure you that they were more creative, inventive, and artistic than Homo sapiens. However, they were eventually completely annihilated, because unlike Homo sapiens, they settled and traveled in very small groups and therefore were not effective in protecting themselves against their enemies.

"However, more to your point, this is not a game of catch-up, so all things will come in the fullness of time, Luc. This is a game of relishing the progress your science and technology make along the way, and how to use those advances to provide benefits to humanity and all species without irreversibly damaging your environment, and worse yet, your species and others as well. All is connected."

Thay changed the subject to broach what I was convinced would be an even more complex discussion. "Bliss, let's look at our question number ten. What are your thoughts on the existence of a higher power? Does such a theological concept exist on Zoi, or for that matter, anywhere else in the universe?"

Bliss replied, "An interesting question, with an answer that can be simple or complex. This usually refers to a person or entity that is exalted and worthy of complete devotion because of their perceived perfection in goodness, righteousness, and power. However, goodness, righteousness, and power are relative terms and cannot be defined in absolute terms.

"A more absolute definition is an entity that possesses immense superpowers—powers that are well beyond the norm—for example, levitation, raising the dead, flying, walking through solid objects, and much more.

"What we have seen throughout the universe is that all cultures soon after their evolution to what we would call 'moderns' establish some form of ephemeral divinity, which to their way of thinking is the epitome of righteousness, goodness and power, and that provides them with a moral compass that is compatible with their concepts of right and wrong. Again, that is all relative.

"Yet, they seek guidance through what you might call *prayer*—a form of meditation. Initially, they might see divinity in the moon or the sun or some special individual. The value of this type of divinity to the masses is embodied in managing their lives against what they see as right or wrong. It also offers them some form of faith and hope that supports them though challenging times.

"However, in time, there are those who take advantage of the masses by repackaging these concepts for their own financial gain and power. You can see this in many of the religions that have evolved on Earth. And when you consider righteousness and goodness, you might ask how many of these religions have been the force behind insidious inquisitions that resulted in frivolous death and destruction and deadly wars.

"The other definition, invoking superpowers, is more absolute. You cannot argue with a person who flies rapidly through the sky and walks on water and through walls. You might intuit from some of our previous discussions that we eventually found that consciousness is key, and all peoples have access to these superpowers if they are willing to pursue the effort to build their capabilities in meditation and awareness to access high levels of consciousness—the absolute and only force behind these superpowers.

"To the average person, this seems like an absurd comment, which is why the masses never achieve what they call superpowers—which they are most capable of mastering—given personal dedication to intention, attention, belief, and detachment as they reach high levels of personal fulfilment and simultaneously improve the condition of the cosmos.

"Those individuals who demonstrate superpowers are not necessarily divine in the theological sense. However, periodically throughout the universe within various civilizations, an Avatar appears whose sole cosmic purpose is to realign those civilizations with the *Meaning and Purpose of the Universe*. The Meaning of the Universe is to continually uncover within the physical universe all of the capabilities and potential for further physical and consciousness evolution. The Purpose of the Universe is to apply those capabilities and potential to continually broaden the impact of Cosmic Consciousness by means of the physical and consciousness evolution within every succeeding universe.

"We Zoians would say that a higher power is within each and every individual. However, you must be willing to do the work to access that power. Some 2,000 years ago, an Avatar on Earth, when amazed and confronted by the masses, exclaimed, 'All that I do, you can do—and more!' In other words, immense higher powers—*God*, if you wish to call it that—are within each of us. However, as we will discuss at some point, those capabilities are often hidden behind the noise and distractions of daily life, and especially, an inordinate preoccupation with gaining excessive wealth and power for the purpose of control."

Thay responded, "That is so much in line with our thinking; however, we have a long way to go to put it into complete practice."

Bliss said, "Patience, my friend. You will get there."

Sophia asked a clever question. "Are there physical laws that govern the functioning of consciousness that may not be the same as those for classical and quantum physics, but are in some ways parallel to them?"

"There are," Bliss replied. "Perhaps the most fundamental of them is a law similar in mathematical form to that discovered by your celebrated quantum and relativity theorist Albert Einstein—$E=mc^2$. There is a similar but more profound expression for the interconversion of matter and consciousness energy—$E_c=mc^{10}$. You can imagine that with an exponent of 10, the calculated energy value (E_c), for all intents and purposes, is infinite. To put that in perspective, as you know, the speed of light (c) is 3×10^8 meters per second. When that constant is raised to the power of 10, you have a number that is approximately 10^{84}. That is

10^{57} times larger than the diameter of our observable universe, which is 8.8×10^{26} meters—essentially infinite.

"Furthermore, it is consciousness that exerts the nonmaterial, primordial, massive gravitational forces due to dark matter. And it is consciousness that is responsible for dark energy. Both dark matter and dark energy are the result of universal laws of mass and energy conservation; and as I mentioned earlier, make up the preponderance of our universe—27 and 68 percent, respectively—the remaining 5 percent being what we can observe."

"Bliss, this is Thay. I am pleased to hear your comments about consciousness. Your description of the cosmic process is beautiful, and as you are probably aware, is beyond our total comprehension at this point in our evolutionary process. However, our team is committed to embracing and using its power, but we are at the very beginnings of what we see as the next stage of physics. As you mentioned earlier, we refer to it as spiritual physics, and at least conceptually, we understand that it has great power since, as you mentioned, down to the very smallest subatomic particles, everything has some level of consciousness, which under the right conditions can be orchestrated to provide favorable outcomes."

Bliss commented, "You are correct. An interesting aspect of spiritual physics is that once you understand the nature of the subtle, yet powerful, nature of consciousness, life moves into a flow that is orders of magnitude easier to manage and enjoy than the way most Earthlings live now.

"Because of the large gap between you Earthlings operating a life based on classical and quantum physics and we Zoians functioning quite naturally through spiritual physics, it is my sense from reading the current state of consciousness of you and your team that we would do well to close today's discussion and resume tomorrow. This will give you some time to internalize and digest the information I have disclosed today. I am sure it lays quite heavy on you."

Thay responded, "Thank you, Bliss. That's an excellent idea! How about 10:00 a.m. tomorrow, Cambridge time?"

"Excellent. Speak with you then." A click on the transmitter, and Bliss was gone.

Thay looked at us and we at him. No one said a word, but then Major Dallant spoke up. "Bliss is an amazing being, not just because of the Zoian technology, but especially because of his sensitivity to what he just disclosed to us, its implications, and how it could likely play out for our world. I suggest that we try to obtain and understand more information about Zoi and its inhabitants.

"That said, at this point in our discussions, if I accept as fact everything Bliss has disclosed, I see the following probable outcome: Our inhabitants will continue to struggle with climate change, which is vastly underestimated by the majority of people on Earth. Therefore, it is highly likely that sometime during the next 200 years, perhaps sooner, we will experience rapidly increasing destruction by global extinction events—unquestionably, with climate change as the primary cause.

"How many of us will survive is anyone's guess. It will depend on how soon and how much we respond in a coordinated global manner—if at all, since history doesn't speak well of humanity's general disposition to do so. As Bliss described with respect to Zoi, those of us who do survive climate destruction will have to rewind the evolutionary process both physically and at the level of consciousness. After what he has disclosed, I'm becoming a believer and a champion of what Thay has been teaching us for the last few years—the remarkable power of consciousness."

Major Dallant continued. "Assuming this scenario to be the case, we need to get to a point where we can pursue the possibility of the Zoians providing transportation for vast numbers of our inhabitants—some might call them migrants—to Zoi or a similar life-supporting exoplanet, so that these migrants can kick-start the growth of the 'Next Earth.' Does anyone disagree with my conclusion or have anything to add?"

No one said a word. Then Thay said it for us. "Major, in the words of an ancient Avatar, 'Thou hast said it!'"

We closed our connection with the major and NASA, having started the day in somewhat of a dream state, but now edging toward a nightmare—at least it seemed so at the time.

WE HAD DECIDED OVER DINNER the previous evening that since it was going to be a Saturday meeting with Bliss and it had been a long and challenging week, we'd earned the right to a modest sleep-in. We opened our meeting with Bliss as planned at 10:00 a.m.

Thay initiated the discussion. "Bliss, perhaps moving to a somewhat easier topic for us to digest and understand, can you address question number seven and tell us something about the population of Zoi and the characteristics of the Zoians?"

Bliss responded, "Based on Earth's standards, it is probably not an easy topic, but let us proceed, in any case. The population of Zoi is fixed at one billion inhabitants. I say fixed, because given the size and resources of our planet, we learned many millennia ago that uncontrolled population growth beyond that would put our and other species at risk."

Sophia said, "Bliss, this is Sophia. How do you control the population to such a precise number?"

Bliss responded, "Although our species decided to retain some of the basic elements of physical evolution, many millennia ago we eliminated certain gene expressions from our genome— for example, a prerequisite of sexual desire for procreation in sentient species.

"There are a number of important factors that led to that decision. First, our species can live as long as a thousand Earth years. Illnesses are not an issue. Many thousands of years ago, we advanced vagus nerve stimulation, or VNS; transcranial magnetic stimulation, or TMS; and transcranial direct current stimulation, or tDCS, to a much higher level.

"However, more important, through the use of genetics and the application of consciousness-radiative healing technology based on a unique resonance of electromagnetic waves with energy waves from several subtle consciousness energy spectra, we conquered all know illnesses thousands of years ago. Early death is almost always caused by a serious accident. In rare instances, when a person is in an incurable state, he or she is euthanized, and a new individual is allowed to be born.

"Every individual has an irremovable chip deposited at birth in the brain. Upon death, that chip signals the date to a central control system, which then sanctions the birth of a replacement individual. In the interest of the global population and our environment, by controlling this process, individuals with desired skills and characteristics are born. Their right to have a child is decided by a complex AI program."

Surprised and concerned, Eric asked, "Are you saying that sexual desire is eliminated, and the type of individual created is completely controlled by AI?"

"Yes, I am. Sexual desire in insects, plants, animals—and in humans and other sentient species—is a necessary requirement for what you call Darwinian physical evolution of the fittest for the environment. All species on Earth arise and develop through the natural selection of small, inherited variations that increase the individual's ability to compete, survive, and reproduce in its environment.

"Over millions of years, we have developed a means that accurately controls genetics and generates an individual precisely fitting our needs to manage our current existence and our further physical evolution, as well as that of our collective state of consciousness. The entire process is managed by what you might call a government, except it has no conscious beings—it is an advanced system of artificial intelligence."

Sophia commented, "That's incredible. Are you saying that you don't have physical beings responsible for government—it's all done by AI?"

Bliss said, "Yes, I am. Unlike governmental systems on Earth, properly programmed, it is not prone to personal illegalities or to social, cultural, emotional, and psychological errors."

Pham pursued the point further. "With no leaders, whether elected or in power as autocrats, kings, queens, or emperors, how does the AI system work?"

Bliss answered, "Many millennia ago, our predecessors decided that even if human beings were driven by an acceptable balance of the desire for power, wealth, and a life purpose dedicated to our 'whole' population, it was impossible that there would never be a few individuals who would eventually be attracted primarily to power and wealth and therefore to their own self-interest.

"To obviate that problem, our predecessors spent many years negotiating among groups representing the values and needs of the entire spectrum of cultural and social aspects of our species. They eventually created a Global Constitution based on an extensive list of values created by these groups. The Constitution and values were embraced unanimously by all Zoians. These values govern what was perceived as our optimal existence and the most effective means to deal with individuals if and when these values were violated—which essentially almost never occurs."

I commented, "I can't begin to comprehend how an AI system would work so effectively, but then again, you are light-years ahead of us, so to speak. However, why is there such a low incidence of offenders, and when there is, how does your AI system deal with them?"

Bliss answered, "The low incidence is a direct result of our higher level of consciousness, which continues to increase and evolve with time. The other aspect of our system is our ability to build high levels of emotional intelligence as well as IQ into our AI. Hundreds of thousands of years ago, it was already at an effective point to give these kinds of results. And in those rare instances where there was a violation issue, we did our best to provide therapy to rectify the problem. If we were not successful— I cannot recall the last time that was the case— the individual was sent to another planet, usually located in a different galaxy. This is a planet where we believed the individual would have an opportunity to prosper and thrive better than on Zoi."

All I could say was "Amazing!" I had to ask Bliss, "Would you consider sending us images of Zoi's landscape and of yourself or your people?"

He answered, "Yes, I will do that, but only after a few more meetings and further discussions so that you have a better understanding of what you will see. However, there is one aspect of our environment in which I believe you would have an interest, and I can share it with you at this time. It is something you could not detect from Earth with your current instrumentation.

"Zoi has two moons, essentially in the same nearly circular planar orbit, and separated from each other within that orbit by approximately 180 degrees on the circumference. They are smaller than your moon and were formed in an event that occurred in a similar manner as that which formed your moon—many billions of years ago during the birth of our galaxy, the result of a collision between Zoi and another small planet about the size of the planet Mercury in your solar system. The debris from that impact collected in a distant orbit around Zoi, and over hundreds of millions of years congealed and accreted to form two lunar satellites.

"They are located approximately 175,000 Earth miles from us. Similar to your moon, they have no atmosphere and essentially no water. As did your moon, billions of years ago, they have provided some protection for Zoi by attracting large stray meteors and asteroids to their surface before they could collide with our planet."

Eric was excited by this revelation. "So, assuming you have planetary rotation similar to Earth, you have one moon always visible in your atmosphere?"

"That is correct," Bliss said. "You likely know that the star around which we rotate is a red dwarf. It is about 40 percent of the mass of your sun, 40 percent of its radius, and it provides nearly 90 percent of the energy that Earth receives from its sun—all of which makes Zoi a highly habitable planet for our and your species, especially since we have nearly equivalent levels of liquid water on the surface of Zoi. Like Earth, we have an atmosphere that is predominantly nitrogen and oxygen. However, unlike the oxygen level around Earth, which is 21 percent, the level in our atmosphere is 30 percent, which has certain physiological benefits for all living species on our planet—especially for us Zoians.

"Our sun is bright, with low levels of stellar activity, and therefore has a nearly complete absence of dangerous solar flares. Because our sun is a red dwarf, its relatively low radiance projection—which is heavily in the infrared part of the electromagnetic spectrum—creates quite impressive colors throughout the planet and at certain times on the surface of our moons."

Eric's response: "I can't wait to see the photographs, or better yet . . . to visit!"

Bliss answered with his first apparent chuckle. "Perhaps. All things in the fullness of time, Eric."

Thay commented, "Thank you, Bliss. If I may, before taking a break until our next communication, I wanted to ask you if there is one fundamental fact that differentiates us from you Zoians, one that will likely require many millennia to change—no matter how diligently we try."

Bliss responded immediately. "Absolutely! It is your knowledge of the physics of consciousness—what you have referred to as spiritual physics. At your stage of development, there is no way you could have an appreciation for the tremendous power and force of consciousness, compared to anything with which you are familiar from classical and quantum physics. Even those of your scientists who study consciousness consider it to be an ephemeral field that could not possibly have a meaningful force. Nothing could be further from the truth. Allow me to provide a simple example of the power of the subtle energies of consciousness.

"In classical physics, for example, you can kick a ball and its mass reacts to the force of your kick. In quantum physics, you access the energy associated with a specific wavelength from your electromagnetic spectrum, and it places a force on certain electrons or photons within a given material. However, every living and nonliving thing has some level of consciousness associated with all its atoms and molecules down to the most fundamental subatomic particle. An electron, proton, neutron—even a subatomic quark—has some component of consciousness associated with it. And when an individual knowledgeable about the management of consciousness makes a faster-than-light-speed conscious contact with a physical object, that consciousness connects with every particle and subatomic particle in the object. That force, if knowledgeably generated, can be trillions of times more powerful than any force you have ever created or experienced—not only on Earth, but throughout the cosmos. In your vernacular, it can literally 'move mountains.'"

Thay responded, "I now understand the basis for your comments concerning the vast difference between where we on Earth are and where you Zoians and probably numerous other civilizations throughout the universe are. It provides some idea as to the power and potential of the energies of the cosmos, which at this point in our evolution is truly beyond our comprehension. But I'm excited about the possibility of humanity someday experiencing the benefits of such power when put to use for the well-being of the 'whole.' Thank you, Bliss."

Chapter Seventeen

RUSSIAN ROMANCE

"First romance, first love, is something so special to all of us, both emotionally and physically, that it touches our lives and enriches them forever."
— ROSEMARY ROGERS

SUNDAY, DECEMBER 1, 2030—CAPE COD, MASSACHUSETTS

An enormous amount of critical, eye-opening information had been provided by Bliss during our conversations. We needed to think about its implications in a more relaxed environment, do our best to put it in a reasonable context, and develop a clear strategy on how best to proceed further. Before closing our discussion on Saturday, we agreed with Bliss to resume contact on Tuesday afternoon so that we could have a short break. We did just that.

MAJOR DALLANT HAD INHERITED a beach house in Cape Cod from his parents after their most unfortunate death at the hands of the insidious and now-deceased Russian operative, Seagull. *Minchia!* It still gave me a twinge of fright when I thought back to those last days in Novosibirsk. But, on the brighter side, the major offered us his beach house for a two-day retreat. He kept it well stocked with food and drinks and insisted that we help ourselves to whatever we needed. He was still elated by the success of our contact with Zoi, even though the messages developing were not promising for the future of humanity. We had to find a practical way to turn them around, if there was any chance at all, and if not, at a minimum, determine how best to prepare for them if and when they occurred. A lot would have to be put in place.

OVER DINNER ON SATURDAY EVENING at the faculty club, we'd decided to leave early Sunday morning in two cars. Eric, Brianna, Bella, and I would take my Chevy; and Pham, Thay, and Sophia would join Pham in his new Ford SUV, which he had recently bought with the money he'd received as a settlement for his accident. We were just about to leave for the Cape when Thay called me and asked if he could squeeze in with Brianna, Bella, Eric, and me. Pham and Sophia decided to travel alone—of course, covertly followed by Sophia's bodyguards.

And squeeze we did. Putting three adults in the back of a 1957 Chevy convertible was almost like loading the last sardine into its packaging can. Something was going on between Pham and Sophia, and Thay didn't seem to want to talk about it. I wasn't sure whether to be happy or concerned. I could only assume that time would tell.

Pham had planned to pick up Sophia at the safe house, where she was living, and leave sometime after us, since he had to stop by the Tang Soo Do dojo and leave some documents there for the Master before heading out to the Cape. We were on our way and would likely arrive at the beach house well before them.

The last thing Sophia said to Pham when we were leaving the faculty club after dinner was: "Pham, whenever we're together, you will be followed by my security guys—please get used to it!"

The following horror story is what we learned from Sophia and Pham when they finally arrived at Major Dallant's cottage in Cape Cod.

Pham had picked up Sophia, and of course, was followed by her two trailing watchdogs. As she had warned him, their presence was becoming an everyday part of their lives. However, as I had advised Pham, it was a more-than-acceptable safety precaution for Sophia's well-being, and his as well.

Pham and Sophia stopped by the dojo, and finally were on their way to the Cape. At Sophia's insistence, Pham took the scenic but somewhat longer route to Major Dallant's beach house, located on the beach at Cape Cod Bay, just outside of the small New England village of Dennis.

As we had all agreed the night before, the plan was to connect with Route 3A, just outside of Boston, and drive south until it merged into Route 3, northwest of the village of Sandwich. From there, we would immediately connect to Route 6, drive past Barnstable and Yarmouth, and eventually turn left and cross the Cape north to Dennis.

However, once Sophia and Pham reached Route 6, Sophia, in one of her creative hyper-moods, decided on a "slight" modification. She apparently had read a recent article in the *Sunday Financial Times* magazine section, called "How to Spend It," noting that there were some not-so-well-known, large, majestic sand dunes located on the bayside of 6A, a somewhat parallel and alternate route closer to the bay. So she and Pham made a left off of Route 6 on to Phinney's Lane, heading north toward Barnstable. A few hundred meters later, they made another left onto a small deserted road called Old Jail Lane and followed it north until it intersected with Route 6A, just east of Lothrop Hill Cemetery. There, they turned right toward Barnstable, Yarmouth, and Dennis.

Sophia's bodyguards were not happy about these changes. They called and asked her to return to the original route. That was a waste of time. You don't change Sophia's mind once it's made up. And made up, it was.

Sophia asked Pham to stop so she could drive. He remembered thinking, *Why not?* He stopped the car and let her take the wheel. They must have been driving her security guys crazy. Apparently, every few minutes they called her, and when she didn't answer her phone, they called Pham asking what in the world they were doing. He told them they were going to see some fantastic sand dunes, which were only slightly off the main route they were supposed to take.

Finally, Sophia had navigated over a string of small dirt roads to Mayflower Beach, just west of Dennis. She stopped and jumped out of the truck, as Pham and her two bodyguards did the same. By the time the bodyguards reached Pham at his truck, which was parked quite a ways in front of them, Sophia was halfway up a giant sand dune.

She yelled to Pham and the bodyguards, "Come on! This is fun—a softer version of mountain climbing! There's nothing like this in Russia!"

But she had just gotten to the top of the dune when she took a running leap and slid on her butt all the way down the fine, white sandy mountain. Pham told us that was a side of Sophia he had never seen before—and he liked it.

Not surprisingly, the lead bodyguard expressed his deep concern and urged Sophia and Pham to get into Pham's truck and join them as the two vehicles immediately and rapidly drove to the beach house, which was about 20 minutes away.

Pham said they weren't driving for more than ten minutes when he noticed a car following the bodyguards. In this remote location? This wasn't good. Pham was driving, so he picked up speed, as did their security detail, but so did the guys tailing them. One of the two guys in the car tailing the bodyguards stood up through an open sunroof and proceeded to fire short blasts from a machine gun at their car. He demolished the back window of the car, but the bodyguards seemed to be fine and were keeping up with Pham and Sophia. But then the guy with the machine gun flattened the two rear tires on the bodyguards' car and rapidly sped passed them, closing in on Pham and Sophia.

As Pham drove at breakneck speed, he noticed a small wooden bridge directly ahead crossing a relatively wide tributary from the bay, and a tall sand dune on the right, at the other side of the bridge. He immediately picked up speed as he crossed the bridge and skidded to the right and behind the dune. He told Sophia to sit tight. He told us that he dearly hoped what he was about to do would work. If it didn't, they were finished—for good. Martial arts isn't something that works too well against a machine gun.

As the enemy car approached the middle of the bridge, Pham sent a strong antigravity pulse at the car, just as he had done in the hospital, when he unwittingly slammed the door to his room against the nurse bringing a wheelchair to escort him for his release. By this time, he had since been schooled by Thay on how to generate and control this superpower. It worked exactly as planned. It flipped the car twice into the air, smashing it upside down into the water. It sank into the bay immediately. Pham and Sophia didn't wait to see if anyone crawled out. They were back in the car, presto, and on their way to the beach house in Dennis.

Pham told us that as he drove with increasingly intense focus, Sophia turned to him with much more than a surprised expression and asked, "What did you just do back there? I saw it, but I don't believe it!"

He tersely replied, "Right now we need to stay focused on our escape. I'll fill you in later. It's a long story."

Sophia's subdued reply was a simple "Yeah, right."

Several minutes later with no cars behind them, Pham asked Sophia to call me. As usual, the CIA was well ahead of us. We later learned that Sophia's bodyguards were fine. A CIA helicopter, purposely stationed at Provincetown Municipal Airport on the Cape—"just in case"—had picked them up and then proceeded to the crashed car submerged in the water upside down where it had broken through the side rail and flown off the bridge. There were no survivors. The two occupants were Russian agents, obviously tasked with eliminating Sophia—and Pham, as well, simply as collateral damage.

The helicopter dropped Sophia's bodyguards at the beach house, and a replacement car was on its way there. The bodyguards were super angry.

When Sophia and Pham finally arrived at the beach house, I didn't have to say a word about my concern for what they'd done. Thay's look directed at Pham said it all.

Sophia was quiet as well. Her serious expression readily revealed that she was well aware that she'd put both her and Pham in lethal danger.

Pham couldn't withhold his contrition. "Dad, Luc, Bella, Eric, Brianna—I'm so sorry. I know I wasn't thinking."

No one but Thay responded. "I know you both are sorry. Let's not belabor that. As with all mistakes, what is important is that you both dwell for some quiet moments on what happened and what you learned. You might start by thinking about what would have happened if those Russians had caught up with you.

"Now if you don't mind, I'm going for a walk along the beach. Although I'm relieved that you're both safe, I need to give some deep thought to what we've learned from Bliss and what our next steps could be. I'll return before dinner."

And with that, Thay was gone. The rest of us unpacked our things. Eric and Brianna assessed the food-and-drink situation and volunteered to make dinner. If the last few hours hadn't answered my question about Pham and Sophia, I certainly knew what the situation was now. Pham unpacked all of his things in her bedroom.

DINNER WASN'T AS SEDATE as it might have been after the Pham-Sophia fiasco. I guess it was because over time, all of us had learned from Thay about the power of understanding, compassion, and forgiveness. I was certainly no longer pissed by what they'd done. That feeling was superseded by my gratitude that they'd survived certain death at the hands of the Russian agents.

And Thay was at his normal best, giving accolades to Brianna and Eric for what turned out to be a simple yet delicious dinner of barbecued spicy chicken and vegetables, accompanied by Brianna's recipe for Cajun curried rice. We opted for no wine but instead continued to put a respectable dent in Major Dallant's Samuel Adams beer supply. It was a great complement to the spicy meal.

Later that evening, we gathered around a small campfire on the beach, right in front of the major's beach house, imbibing more of his beer. It was a serene and magically cool evening, with a slight salty breeze, small crashing waves, a blanket of stars. The evening was illuminated by a waxing gibbous moon on its way to fullness, next Monday, December 9.

I had to say to Thay, "Well, I hope you had an insightful walk on the beach. Any thoughts you'd like to share about how we go forward with what Bliss has shared with us?"

Thay answered, "Luc, I wish there was a better way to go about this than what Major Dallant has already summarized for us during our last videoconference. Because of our vast negative impact over the last 200 years on Earth's environment and climate, it seems that we're well past the point of no return. True, some of this unfortunate state of affairs has been the result of ignorance about what we're doing to our planet, but there is little argument that over the last 75 years or so, too many of us have been blindly swayed by power and money.

"Beyond doing our best to prepare for the worst by continuing to minimize humanity's contribution to climate change and putting in place effective adaptation strategies, if we are to preserve the existence of our race, we must pursue with Bliss the possibility of transferring a well-thought-through 'sampling' of our species, and eventually other species as well, to Zoi. In essence, it looks like a replay of Noah's ark."

Thay's disconcerting conclusion wasn't a surprise. While its weight sank into our thought processes, Eric asked, "Shouldn't we ask Bliss if he has any thoughts on how we should proceed, and if the Zoians have any technologies that could help us?"

Thay responded, "Yes, we should do that, but I'd guess from all that he's said so far that the best technology the Zoians have to offer us in view of where we are now is interplanetary travel for a large-enough group of us to a place that, pursued properly, would be the *Next Earth*—it could be Zoi or any other planet with an agreeable environment for the continued physical and spiritual evolution of humanity."

Unfortunately, we all knew that Thay was right.

Chapter Eighteen

HOPELESS

"One should . . . be able to see things as hopeless and yet be determined to make them otherwise."
— F. Scott Fitzgerald

Tuesday, December 3, 2030—Cambridge, Massachusetts

It had been a much different retreat than we'd planned. We were searching for a contemplative respite, but instead we'd come nearly face-to-face with two Russian executioners. True, they were after Sophia, but with our new arrangement, that meant all of us. And with Pham and Sophia's new relationship—I was trying my best not to be judgmental—it added a whole new level of complexity.

Although Thay was more accepting than the rest of our team, I knew that it bothered him as well. He said nothing, but I guess he wanted to be sure that their amorous "thing" wasn't just a dangerous "fling." Thay was one of the most accepting people I'd ever met, but he'd only met his son a short time ago. The situation was definitely getting more complicated.

In view of our team's two-day getaway, we had agreed with Bliss to contact him on Tuesday afternoon.

The team gathered at the lab in the Green building immediately after a short lunch and just before our contact with Bliss. We had a brief discussion concerning last evening's campfire meeting on the beach at Major Dallant's cottage in Cape Cod. Thay had agreed with Bliss that our next communication would begin at 1:00 p.m., so we were all right on time.

Thay opened with, "Good afternoon, Bliss, or whatever time of the day or evening it is where you are on Zoi. We're anxious to continue our dialogue, perhaps keeping it a little bit lighter, while we continue to digest what you've told us during the last couple of sessions."

Bliss answered, "That is fine. How were your two days of rest, relaxation, and contemplation in Cape Cod?"

Thay smiled at us and then responded, "Not as restful as we'd hoped, but it was quite profound at times, in a most unusual way, particularly when breathing the salt air and listening to the hypnotic sounds of the sea as we sat around a small fire on the beach thinking about what's in store for planet Earth. We're still contemplating the significant challenges we face in our not-too-distant future, and once we come to some preliminary conclusions, we want to discuss them with you for your counsel."

Bliss responded, "That is fine, Thay. I look forward to seeing how we can help."

Bella then asked, "Changing the topic to perhaps a more mundane level, what do you Zoians eat, and how long do you sleep each evening?"

"In Earth timing, we sleep an average of six hours per day, and we essentially don't eat solid food or drink any liquids, including water."

Bella was astounded. "What! You're kidding me, right? No food or water?"

"I did not say *no* food or water. I said we do not eat solids or drink liquids."

We were perplexed. We knew by now that Bliss wasn't the type to joke with us. He had so far been direct and to the point, so I asked, "Bliss, this is Luc, can you please explain your answer in a little more detail? I'm sure that you're aware that those are two things we human beings, and in fact, all species on Earth, do to sustain life."

"Yes, we are well aware of that. Are you familiar with the Hindu practice of pranayama?"

"We are. Thay has taught us various forms of it, and we use it for increased focus to achieve deep meditation and higher levels of consciousness."

"Excellent! Then you know that in ancient Buddhist parlance, pranayama is the yogic practice of focusing on your breath to bring about changes in consciousness. You may then also be aware that in the Sanskrit language, *prana* means 'vital life force,' and *yama* means 'gaining control'—*gaining control of the life force*. In essence, pranayama elevates your life energies. You could say that eating food and drinking water is nature's way on Earth of sustaining life by elevating your life energies.

"However, let's look at the next step. More than 3,000 years ago, we observed that Hindus in India had perfected this practice to such a high level that some of them were able to extract energy directly from the universe's zero-point energy field, such that eating and drinking were no longer a necessity, although eventually, even the more accomplished of them resorted to drinking some amount of water.

"Over the millennia, we Zoians have taken this practice to an even higher level, such that consuming physical food or liquid water is unnecessary for our survival. As did the ancient Hindus, we extract all of the energy we need from the zero-point energy field, and as long as there is some level of water vapor in the atmosphere we occupy, we can extract and maintain all of the water necessary for the functioning of our internal metabolic processes—namely, the alterations that occur in our cells to produce the energy changes required for our life sustenance.

"We have physically evolved to a state where all reactions that occur in our cells are direct-energy transitions, not aqueous chemical processes that normally result in waste products that must be eliminated. These energy transitions are completely irreversible—that is, they are in one direction and involve only electrons, protons, or photons. But some do occur in the aqueous liquid phase. If, for some reason, our cells retain more water than is necessary for a required energy transition or transfer, it is usually minimal, and that excess water is eliminated by transpiration through our skin—sweat, if you will.

"Since we do not consume solid food or excess liquid water, and there are no chemical by-products in our cells, we have no need for the excretion of waste solids or liquids. Our bodies have long ago lost those organs necessary for digestion, nutrient assimilation, and subsequent excretion."

Eric commented, "Good God, that's fascinating. Thay has told us about a more recent and similar instance of an Indian monk named Prahlad Jani, who died ten years ago at the age of 91 and essentially did the same thing for most of his life. At one point—on the suggestion of a skeptical medical doctor who maintained that Jani was a fake—the monk agreed to remain in the doctor's hospital for three months of observation under surveillance by nurses and continuously operating cameras. Much to the doctor's consternation and amazement, the monk's complete fasting regimen was verified. He, like you, did not eliminate any liquid or solid waste during those three months."

Bliss said, "I am not surprised. Throughout the Milky Way galaxy and other galaxies as well, there are civilizations significantly older than those on Earth that have adapted to this kind of internal metabolic efficiency."

Thay asked the next question. It was certainly disquieting for all of us, but it didn't seem to faze Bliss. "Bliss, you've told us that as part of your continuous evolution, your civilization has had a few unfortunate extinction outcomes, each of which led to major destruction and death throughout the entirety of planet Zoi. However, you also noted that ultimately this led to evolution cycles that elevated your global consciousness, stabilized your race, and led to the civilization that now flourishes on Zoi. Can you tell us more about those experiences?"

"I can, but I must say that it is as painful as it is instructive—"

Thay interrupted, "I don't mean to inject any feelings of remorse or discomfort. We can skip to something more constructive."

Bliss replied, "But you see, our experience would be both constructive *and* instructive for you. It is one of the things we *can* speak about to you and your team. Let us proceed. I only hope you can find the means to motivate many others on your planet to see this input as compelling enough to make the necessary big and challenging changes in the way they live."

"Thank you, Bliss," Thay said somberly. "I hope you're right."

"Very well, then, let us proceed. As I mentioned previously, our first 'modern' Zoian species dates back 4.667 billion years. We arrived at your current level of technological development about 100,000 years after that, 4.567 billion years ago. We found ourselves doing nearly exactly what Earthlings are doing—intensely competing with each other for wealth and power, with only a minority of us concerned with the true Meaning and Purpose of Life.

"Like you, the majority of us—knowingly and silently, or at best, subconsciously—accepted that the terrible outcomes that might be a consequence of our actions would befall our distant progeny . . . at least, *distant* is what we assumed. But it came sooner than we had expected, such that even those of us who were directly responsible for what happened had the opportunity to more than taste the violence and upheaval that we had caused.

"We thought if anything terrible were to happen, it would be many centuries, perhaps thousands of years, into the future, if at all—or so we consciously or subconsciously rationalized—if you want to call that *rational* thinking. We were sadly mistaken. Within a hundred years, our world came violently tumbling down.

"Every city, without exception, that was located on the sea or any tidal-water body connected to the sea, was inundated beyond re-construction. Skyscrapers suddenly appeared to be half their original height and were quickly getting shorter, the primary parts being com-pletely submerged in flooding seas—for good. Rampaging storms at-tacked those areas far from the sea. Nothing was left untouched. There were hundreds of millions of deaths and many more injuries. Disease, civil unrest, and war plagued every part of Zoi, without exception. We were a quickly devolving race heading back to our animalistic roots. It would take many millennia before our next physical evolution would take root and we could begin the journey to our next phase of moder-nity."

I, like the rest of the team, was flabbergasted. I said, "That's horri-ble, Bliss!"

"Yes, it was. And my point to you is that, as best we can extrapolate, your civilization is rapidly heading for the same, if not worse, outcome. At this point, we conclude that you cannot stop it—by immediate ac-tion globally using your current technological know-how. The best you can do is minimize the damage, the level of success depending on how quickly and intensely the majority of citizens of Earth unite and re-spond. But I am not optimistic—those actions, *unite* and *respond*—do not seem to be in your lexicon and wherewithal."

Brianna jumped in immediately. "Oh my God, Bliss, why do you say that?"

"Because, Brianna, we Zoians have been through this kind of climate/pollution-induced extinction twice—in two evolutions! Ironically, the unification of Earthlings to at least curb and minimize such a terrible future would be a strong catalyst toward the enhanced evolution of your global consciousness. That would put you in a much better place than we Zoians were in, subsequent to our first extinction event. However, there seems to have been a fundamental element, perhaps you might call it a cosmic law, that was in action at the point where we were prior to our extinction event and where you are right now. Allow me to explain.

"As you are at this time, 4.567 billion years ago our level of consciousness was such that the majority of us were motivated only by wealth and power—not Life Meaning and Purpose. And we paid the price for that. While it is true that a number of Zoians of higher consciousness survived the first extinction event and eventually after some 20,000 years arrived again at the stage where we had previously initiated our destruction, it happened again—and for the very same reasons.

"Recognizing that all beings are conditioned from birth by often well-meaning parents, friends, and the media, we knew we had to do something different. So our ancient surviving ancestors instituted continual education programs for all offspring, and that process was refined over millennia and continues until the present as a means to prevent the recurrence of an extinction event for the same reasons. We also realized that our level of consciousness was critical to not only prevent a recurrence, but also a means to a more successful and fulfilling future. Therefore, we instituted at an early age this program to teach our offspring various ways to elevate their consciousness. That commitment has had an immensely positive impact on the development of our civilization since then."

Eric had a question. "I have to ask, why do you think this approach succeeded?"

Bliss said, "Because we now know that the primary goal and journey of the universe is one that will continuously increase its level of consciousness. I can assure you that this *is* a cosmic law. All matter and energy have some level of consciousness, down to the smallest of subatomic entities. Everything is a living organism. Earth, with all of its species and matter, is an organism. Zoi is as well, and so is the entire universe—one living, breathing, evolving organism. The purpose of physical evolution is to afford a mechanism for the continuous, evolutionary growth and enhancement of consciousness throughout that organism we call the *universe*."

It was Thay's turn. He said, "Bliss, your commentary is a fascinating, beautiful, and believable picture. It resonates so well with me."

Pham commented, "That is a most amazing journey! In spite of all the horrendous challenges you faced, you found a way to survive, come back, and thrive, even if it took many millennia—what am I saying!—millions of years to succeed!"

"Actually, Pham, I have not disclosed the worst," Bliss said.

"Bella offered her input. "I'm not sure I want to hear about the worst."

Bliss responded to Bella's concern. "I think you should. Maybe in a future evolution of Earth's citizens, you can find a way to avoid the same mistakes that our ancient predecessors made."

Thay interjected. "Bliss, please tell us."

All was quiet for a few long minutes, then finally he proceeded to explain. "As it became clear that we were well on our way to our first species-induced extinction, something horrible happened. A disgruntled high-level military officer on Zoi released a volley of long-range, nuclear-armed ballistic missiles. It immediately incited an intraplanetary nuclear war that lasted only one week, but essentially destroyed Zoi and its inhabitants for thousands of years to come. It would be many thousands more before our progeny came even close to evolutionary recovery from the bodily radiation distortions that were inflicted on them. Today, there is not a single nuclear weapon on Zoi, nor have we had any meaningful conflict since then—but what a terrible price we paid to get here."

Bella stood up, nearly in tears. "Bliss, I know I should appreciate what you've just shared with us. And somewhere deep down inside my soul, I'm sure I do. But it's been a terribly discouraging discussion for me this afternoon. I don't think I can take much more today." She sat down, immediately following her emotional outpouring, and said, "I'm so sorry, everyone. I should have given this more thought before opening my big mouth."

Bliss responded immediately. "No, Bella. I completely understand your reaction. Perhaps we should take a break and continue tomorrow with any questions that any of you may have."

Thay concurred. "I think that's a good idea, Bliss. I think Bella's expression of deep concern, fear, and helplessness in some measure has touched all of us."

"I understand, Thay. But please, after you have had some time to contemplate what I have shared with you, both alone and as a team, please consider, at least in my opinion, that you have an opportunity to learn from Zoi's mistakes, and just maybe, you can do a lot better in the end than we did."

I thought, *Wow! In the end*—really? Dear God, I hope that we're not looking at *the end. Minchia!* I pray that when all the dust of despondency settles, we can find a new beginning—a *New Earth* for a new and sustainable humanity.

Chapter Nineteen

WE NEED
YOU

"Follow your bliss and the universe will open doors for you where there were only walls."
— Joseph Campbell

Wednesday and Thursday, December 4 and 5, 2030—
Cambridge, Massachusetts

Some say that bliss is a feeling of indescribable joy and peace. But recently, the only bliss we'd found in Project Phoenix was our contact with an extraterrestrial being from a planet 100 light-years away. And his input had been nearly numbing to the bone. I don't know anyone who would want to know what would be in store for their future if it was the type of news that we'd been privy to.

Life had not seemed this depressing since Bella had been stuck in a deep coma many years ago. She had nearly died after Tamara Carlin, a brilliant, super-devious Russian double agent—who had been expertly and covertly intertwined within the executive fabric of the CIA—sent a hit man to erase her from my life. Even our incredibly positive Eric was unconsciously sending signals of distress and anxiety. Christmas was exactly three weeks away, but none of us felt even the slightest bit of merriment and joy in preparation for celebrating one of the most auspicious holidays of the year.

We'd agreed to connect with Bliss at 10:00 a.m. on this particular morning. It was a rather late start for us; however, we knew we'd be up late the previous evening coming to grips with what we saw as our best options going forward. I didn't get to sleep until 3:30 a.m., and with the exception of Thay, the others also were not very successful in trying to get some badly needed sleep.

We all assembled punctually, and Thay opened the discussion with a brief introduction.

"Bliss, I want you to know that our team is unanimously appreciative of what you've shared with us, regardless of how challenging it has been for us to receive, digest, and then develop a strategy to integrate your input and do our best for humanity and our planet.

"Last evening we worked until nearly 2:00 a.m., and afterward we had an hourlong videoconference with Major Dallant from CIA/NSA, key representatives from NASA, and two scientific advisers to the president of the United States. I would like to summarize for you what we believe we've learned from you and what we'd like to do as we move forward with an action plan. Is that acceptable to you?"

"Absolutely," Bliss said.

"Very well, then. In short, here is what we see coming our way on Earth, and if things continue as they are now, this will all happen sooner rather than later, probably achieving an unbearable state of existence for much of humanity within 100 or 150 years. Nearly all of this chaos will be caused by climate change. There's no need to repeat all of the potentially devastating mechanisms. You know them well.

"In this scenario, we're excluding the possibility of the global impact of nuclear war, although there's better than a 50 percent chance that a localized event could occur—for example, between India and Pakistan. The worldwide physical destruction from the nuclear devices of those two nations would likely be limited; however, the social and health impact could be nearly as significant as the destruction caused by climate change. Bliss, do you agree with me so far?"

"I do," Bliss responded.

"Well, then, allow me to share with you our strategy for moving forward. We ask for your patience and understanding with regard to what we're about to ask of you."

Bliss said nothing.

Thay continued. "We envision a simultaneous two-pronged effort. In the first prong, we would put in place an aggressive program with the primary goal of minimizing the ravaging destruction on Earth by seeking the commitment of other major powers in the world to assist in contributing a means to slow down climate change and implement adaptation strategies. We will enter into top-level discussions with the leaders of China, Russia, the European Union, and a few other major powers, including the United Kingdom, South Korea, Saudi Arabia, Israel, India, and Turkey. To get their attention and subsequent commitment will require nearly full disclosure and proof of our communications with you. Is that clear to you, and do you agree with our approach?"

Bliss said, "I understand, and I agree. In fact, I am sure you have been recording our discussions. Please feel free to use those recordings in your discussions and negotiations with the countries you have mentioned."

Thay continued. "Thank you. Now, for the second and more challenging prong. Our current Earth will be going through terribly difficult times for the next 150 to 200 years and beyond, perhaps even sooner. After all we've learned from you, we think that it's prudent to establish a New Earth as a backup strategy to preserve our human species—perhaps others as well—especially if the first prong doesn't work or doesn't work well.

"Therefore, we'd like to ask you if you and your colleagues would provide a means for transporting to Zoi large numbers of selected people from Earth as a means of preserving our species and hopefully creating a more cooperative civilization, which perhaps could eventually learn from and contribute to the Zoian culture. We see this happening continually for the next 30 to 50 years, and perhaps beyond that, depending on the outcome here on Earth and on Zoi, and of course, mutual agreement. I know that's a lot for you to take in; however, it would help if you could give us your initial reaction to our request."

Bliss hesitated for a few moments and then said, "Yes, I see. There is no issue with your first prong. It sounds like a wise approach, although I am sure it will be quite challenging for you, and at this time, it is difficult to predict your degree of success. However, as for the second prong, I will need some time to discuss this with our Governing Council. Can we connect again tomorrow at the same time, and I will give you our response?"

Thay responded, "Absolutely, that would be fine. Until then."

A click and a moment of static in reception, and Bliss was gone.

AT LEAST BLISS'S REACTION wasn't an absolute *no*—but it was in no way a guaranteed *yes*. It was another long and stressful evening. That evening at the faculty club, we extended our stay with several after-dinner drinks—including Eric's Paradiso Brandy Reserva. I think we gathered less to have a continued discussion than simply to be together and chat. *Minchia!* How do you contemplate the end of the world sitting alone in your room?

More than ever, we needed the Manifestation Sequence. The problem for all of us was getting our focus resolutely centered, and maintaining our awareness on *Intention, Attention, Imagination, Belief,* and of course, the difficult one: *Detachment.* Many of the challenges we'd faced over the last ten years had been seemingly impossible to deal with, but somehow with Thay's guidance, we'd pulled them off. But this one . . . ?

AFTER A QUICK BREAKFAST at the faculty club, we gathered at the lab at 10:00 a.m. We instantly connected to Bliss. As usual, the Zoian connection at LP2 was spot-on, no issues—the power of consciousness, I guess.

Bliss started the discussion. "Our council analyzed the pros and cons of your request, both for you and for us, and we concluded that we *can* help you—however, with a hopefully acceptable change to your strategy. Yes, we can provide transportation from Earth to Zoi over the next 100 years or so. We would send large motherships capable of safely and comfortably holding, transporting, and caring for up to 5,000 people at a time.

"These vessels are completely operated by AI and would be programmed in English with access to whichever additional languages you prescribe. Because of the nature of our travel technology, the duration of the flight would be quite short, so there should be no concern about spending too much time in space. When we get to that point, we would mutually agree on all of the details as to where our vessels would land on Earth, the onboard logistics, and the time of flight to Zoi. Is that all clear to you?"

Thay answered, "Absolutely, and since there is quite some time before we could be ready for the first flight, I don't, at this time, have any specific questions." Thay looked at all of us and asked, "Do any of you have any questions for Bliss concerning what he just outlined?"

When it was clear that we did not, Thay asked the obvious next question. "Since there are no issues with this part of your proposal at this time, can you share what changes you want us to incorporate?"

"Certainly. We would like you to send two of your team members—preferably a man and a woman—to manage the logistics that need to occur in flight, and more specifically, when the travelers arrive on Zoi. They would be expected to remain on Zoi for some period of time."

We were dumbstruck. No one said anything, not even Thay. We just stared at each other, at a loss for words.

Finally, Thay said, "Bliss, that's a big move for us. Can we get back to you tomorrow with our response? As you did, we need a little time to discuss your suggested changes."

Bliss was fine with Thay's request. However, I didn't know about the rest of the team. But at that moment, I didn't want to give Bliss's suggestion one iota of additional thought. If we were to oblige him and his council, there weren't any two among us that I could see taking on this challenge—and risk.

THAT EVENING, DINNER AT THE FACULTY CLUB was quieter than it had ever been—that is, until Pham popped up with a proposed solution. It was more than apparent that he'd been thinking about it since our communication with Bliss.

"I have a proposal." He paused. As we all stopped eating and looked at him in earnest, we wondered what was going on in that head of his—a head that not too long ago had sustained one of the most massive subdural hematomas his doctor had ever seen.

He went on. "I haven't discussed this with anyone, not even my father. I wanted to ponder it until I was sure it was, as Voltaire once said, 'the best of all possible worlds.' And I'm sure it is."

Eric can be quite impatient at times. "C'mon, Pham, tell us. What's your proposal?"

Pham's answer was crisp and clear. "I suggest that Sophia and I go to Zoi."

Sophia momentarily slumped back in her chair with a deep exhale, as this was news to her.

I couldn't contain myself. "What! Are you kidding me?"

"No, I'm not, Luc. And Sophia and Dad, I'm sorry I didn't raise this with you first, but I thought this was the best approach for all concerned. You've all had enough stress over the past several weeks."

Then I said the obvious, something no one else would say, but it had to be said not only for Thay's benefit but for the benefit of all of us. "Look, Pham, I'm sorry for the heated reaction, but as you well know, Thay has been searching for you nearly all your life. And now having finally found his only son, is he going to send him 100 light-years away to another planet, one whose environment and much more than that are completely unknown to us? I think it's a nonstarter."

Sophia immediately interjected, "I was momentarily shocked by Pham's suggestion. But as I think about it now, I believe that it's an excellent idea. I see a number of pluses. I bring an in-depth background in the relevant sciences, and Pham is brilliant in his own right. But much more than that, he commands an important and demonstrated superpower—maybe more than one—that may be useful to us on Zoi.

"Another plus—let's be very frank—you know that we've developed a special relationship. Although you might infer that it could be detrimental, I believe I could produce several arguments as to why it would be helpful. And finally, being 100 light-years away from the long arm of Russia would mean that I wouldn't have to be stressed all the time, looking over my shoulder for an approaching assassin—and I would no longer need bodyguards."

All that in several seconds? I'm sure that it reflected Sophia's super-analytical mind. No one said a thing, but we all looked at Thay, waiting for him to say something. He was sitting quite still, hands folded, staring down at the surface of the conference table. But suddenly he lifted his head and spoke in a measured voice.

"Sophia is right, for all the reasons she mentioned, and maybe a few more. Look, I love my son, and I'd like us to continue working closely together, as we have been. But the rest of us have all of the necessary skills to develop and launch the first prong of the strategy, although, at best, it will definitely be a significant challenge for us. Also, we would profit immensely by having two trusted and loyal emissaries on Zoi, and Sophia's right—their complementary skills and experience would be a great advantage for us.

"Besides, it's not planned as a one-way trip to Zoi. Pham and Sophia will return at some point, and others of us, if not all of us, will likely have the opportunity to travel to Zoi. Unless any of you have a better alternate proposal or comments on Pham's presentation, I suggest that we close, and that we tell Bliss we agree with his proposal."

No one said a word.

Then Thay said, "Very well, it's settled. We will pursue strategies one and two in parallel, and as proposed by Bliss, Pham and Sophia will travel to Zoi. Luc, let's set up a videoconference with Major Dallant to inform him of our proposed strategy and be sure he's on board before our next contact with Bliss."

I answered half-heartedly, knowing that the other half of my heart wasn't on board—at least not yet. "Right."

Part VI

THE NEXT EARTH

Chapter Twenty

DESTINATION ZOI

"Space travel is life-enhancing, and anything that's life-enhancing is worth doing. It makes you want to live forever."
— Ray Bradbury

Monday, April 14, 2031—Area 51, Nevada

It had been a grueling four months as we designed and dove into materializing the details for the two strategies we'd agreed on in order to achieve the best of all possible worlds for Project Phoenix. Two teams were aggressively pursuing both in parallel as they met and negotiated with their scientific and political counterparts. Bravo for military flight transport; otherwise, the travel requirements would have been preposterous.

The first strategy—*Operation Salvation*—led by Thay, was directed at minimizing the damage that humanity would likely do to itself by having dismissed or neglected the disastrous impact that global climate change was raining down upon the planet—fires, floods, disease, and monstrous violent storms of all kinds. You could barely find a climate-change denier anywhere these days. Their stance had now changed to "Get real! Climate change has always been an ever-present part of global evolution. Times will be increasingly cataclysmic. Everyone for themselves!"

To save their egos, few climate-change deniers would concede that humanity was a major contributor to this existential crisis, but for the most part, the rest of the world simply ignored these misfits. Larger political and corporate powers were now in control, and had sewn together a committed international network that wasn't about to falter. They could finally see that their livelihoods were at stake. Nearly everyone now knew that this part of the cosmos would receive more than a minor dent in its operation.

Beyond applying known technologies and legal forces to minimize the increasing levels of death, injury, damage, and destruction, much effort was being directed toward adapting to the tragic outcomes that were increasingly visiting our doorstep. We once again asked the Zoians to help with this strategy, but for some strange reason, they were only committed to strategy two. We were at a loss. It didn't compute.

The second strategy—*Operation Transmigration*—was led by Sophia and targeted transporting over the next 50 years as many human beings as possible to Zoi. Major Dallant and the US president had charged the secretary general of the United Nations to organize two one-week intense conferences that involved high-level representatives from all nations.

The first conference was attended by scientists and the political upper echelons from the top-20 global powers. As a result of that conference, a complex mathematical formula had been developed, which quantified the number of people from any given nation who would be accepted for specific transport to Zoi during each of the next five years.

At that point, the formula would be reexamined for any changes that the "Group of 20" thought necessary to maintain its commitment to fair treatment of all nations. The formula had been derived incorporating many factors including population, gross domestic product, health history, economic potential, diversity, age, gender, intellectual property, scientific and technological mastery, and much more.

Our team analyzed the philosophy behind the choice of metrics that went into the formula, as well as the details surrounding the math. It was impressive. It's amazing what a diverse team can do when pressed to create a complex product based on a common set of values!

The second conference was attended by scientists and senior political leaders from each of the remaining 175 countries. They were introduced to the mathematical formula in great detail. All 195 countries were then instructed to have their first group of designated travelers—4,667 in total—ready and present for the maiden voyage to Zoi on April 14, 2031.

In stark contrast to the Paris Climate Accords, it was unexpectedly amazing how smoothly all of these meetings proceeded. It was likely because the conferences with the Group of 20 had convinced themselves, and then all other nations as well, that the future of human civilization was imminently at risk In ways that were more than chilling. The clock was ticking. With the level of devastation currently occurring throughout the world, that wasn't a difficult task. No nation had been left untouched.

The US, China, Russia, and North Korea now spoke differently among themselves, and more important, to other nations as well. With the detailed input we'd provided them from our extensive communications with Bliss, it was now clear to them that total global cooperation and commitment were absolutely necessary—and without self-obsessed concern for the welfare of singled-out individual states. The future existence of humanity hung by a thin thread.

Yes, today was Bella's 26th birthday, and it would be quite different from the one our team had celebrated last year. More than ever, I replayed in my mind her apprehensive comment that preceded last year's celebration. By now I knew it by heart: "*After nearly a quarter of a century together since we were children in grammar school, Luc and I are finally engaged to be married—but for what? Can we really have children in the face of what's coming? I've heard that many young men are now opting for vasectomies.*"

These were deeply troubling sentiments, but there had to be a path to a family future for us. There just *had* to be; otherwise, it truly was the beginning of the end—of everything.

All parties concerned had agreed that the best place to launch the maiden voyage to Zoi was in a strictly and securely cordoned-off section within the infamous Area 51, located 83 miles north-northwest of Las Vegas. It offered high security and all the necessary logistics.

Russia, China, and North Korea were not happy with the choice, but they conceded, provided that representatives from their respective countries could attend this and all future launches from the US. Embedded in their political DNA was still an ever-present distrust of the US, as they were probably concerned that the maiden voyage and hundreds of follow-up launches from the US would somehow give America a growing strategic advantage over them.

Established in 1957, Area 51 is a more-than-top-secret facility located on the edge of a dry salt lake known as Groom Lake in the southern part of Nevada. It's home to a heavily guarded US Air Force base, established as a top-secret research facility. The surrounding mountains make radar tracking of the area impossible. The US Air Force only admitted to the existence of the base in 1999.

The facility is shrouded in all kinds of mystique, including the attempted reverse-engineering of the previously mentioned crashed alien spaceship on July 7, 1947, in the desert near Roswell, New Mexico, as well as autopsies of four deceased aliens from that ship. The US Air Force initially admitted to the existence of the alien crash site, but a few days later changed its message and maintained that it was *not* an alien crash site at all, just a metallic-coated research balloon. *Right.* The US government doesn't like admitting to events and phenomena that it can't explain and control. It's why many UFO incidents are usually written off as unusual weather occurrences.,

Bliss had previously confided to us that the crashed spaceship incident was known to a number of alien civilizations throughout our galaxy, especially those native to the planet from which the crashed aliens had originated, some 275 light-years from Earth near the constellation Sagittarius. He told us that they are a race short in stature compared to Earthlings, and relatively new to the exploration of Earthlike exoplanets. New? Yes. But they had the technology to make the journey. Bliss had also mentioned that there have been no indications that the US has been successful in their reverse-engineering efforts. Not surprising, since the technology is most likely well beyond their scientific comprehension.

All of the international migrants to Zoi had been ferried during the last week to Area 51 by more than a hundred large transport planes provided by the Group of 20. Because of the development of top-secret fighter jets at this secure location, it maintains several large runways, one of which is 11,998 feet long. The travelers were housed in a number of makeshift dorms built for that purpose. All the necessary infrastructure was in place to make the one-week stay reasonably comfortable prior to their flight to Zoi.

THE TIME WAS UPON US. I had traveled to Area 51 as an observer of the operation. Sophia had managed to accomplish an amazing level of efficiency, which wasn't surprising. One issue that was initially of significant concern was being sure that our Earth-based travelers would not bring dangerous microbes to Zoi, and conversely, we wanted to be sure that they would not be infected by Zoian microbes that would be a problem for those of us on Earth if and when any travelers returned.

Fortunately, Bliss helped immensely by providing us with a noninvasive electromagnetic biochemical procedure for testing the travelers' blood and other biospecimens. Upon completion of those tests, we concluded, along with Bliss, that there would be no problem involved in going in either direction. No personnel isolation or quarantine would be necessary.

I finally caught up with Sophia in the ops center at 7:00 a.m.

"*Minchia*, Sophia! This will be one of the most challenging and memorable moments of your life!"

"You're right, my dear friend. But you know, completely off topic—I've been meaning to ask you for years and just keep forgetting—what is the English translation for *minchia*?"

I laughed. "Ha, I don't believe the way your mind works. The translation: it's a melodic way in the Sicilian dialect of saying *fuck*. It's a bad habit carried over from my childhood. I had a feisty Sicilian grandfather who liked to curse in his native dialect. And now, my off-topic question to you: Where's Pham?"

"Great story! Your grandfather must have been quite a character. You seem to have inherited some of those genes. Oh, as for Pham, he slept in today. I think he's nervous about the flight to Zoi."

"I don't blame him," I told her.

Sophia stared at me and shifted to a serious expression. With a deep inhale and then an exhale, she said, "Luc, since we're in a top-secret location, can I share something with you—and do you promise you won't tell anyone?"

I was a bit perplexed. "I guess so. What's up?"

She went right to it. "I think the reason for Pham's nervousness is not the flight. Well, it is the flight, but for a different reason."

"Sophia, what in the world are you talking about?"

"I'm pregnant."

"*Minchia, minchia, minchia!* And you're going to take an interstellar flight in a few hours?"

"Yes, that's true . . . but *minchia* sounds about right for our situation!"

"Sophia, this is serious. You're going to fly a hundred light-years distance and undergo a mass-to-consciousness-and-back-to-mass transition while pregnant, and then give birth to your and Pham's first child on an alien planet? You've got to be kidding!"

"Luc, Pham and I have analyzed the situation in many ways. The consciousness-mass transitions have got to work with perfect fidelity and precision. Otherwise, the Zoians would have experienced problems a long time ago. They've been experiencing these kinds of transitions for thousands of years, maybe millions. And as for giving birth on Zoi, we will likely be back on Earth before then, and if not, do you really think that the Zoians with all their advanced technologies would have birthing facilities inferior to ours?"

"I understand. It just seems so weird, even risky, but I'm not sure why. Can you imagine your kid's passport? Place of birth: Zoi in the Dorado Constellation."

Sophia put on her super-serious face. "Look, the mothership will arrive here in about six hours, and we will begin shuttling people onto it immediately. By tomorrow morning, we will all be on our way to Zoi. Besides, Pham and I are the only ones who trained for what has to happen inside the spacecraft, and perhaps more important, what happens when we arrive. There's no time for a substitution of personnel—and that's final!"

"Maybe we should discuss this with Thay."

"Jesus, Luc, that's the last thing we need to do. He's got his arms and brain full with Operation Salvation. And his only child is going off to a remote planet. It's a fait accompli—we're going! No discussion with anybody!"

I had no idea what to do. A voice deep down inside of me said that under the existing circumstances, Sophia was probably right. I felt a strong sense of guilt by not speaking to Thay, but I'm sure it paled in comparison with Pham's feelings.

"Okay, I get it—at least I think I do. When will you tell Thay?"

"Pham and I will call him after all is settled on Zoi. Remember, it's not just the two of us. We're responsible for the welfare of more than 4,000 multinationals when we get there."

"How will you manage shuttling all of them to the mothership in a timely manner?"

Sophia smiled. "You know me, Luc, I'm an obsessive-compulsive person when it comes to the details for a complex project. All emigrants have been given detailed instructions in their own language. They know which shuttle they will take to the mothership, and from where and when it will leave. Each shuttle can easily accommodate about a hundred people. Because of planning, each one will take only 30 minutes round trip.

"Pham will travel with the first shuttle, and accessing the assistance of the Zoians' super AI, he'll manage settling the travelers within the mothership. I will take care of things here. I'll board the last shuttle to join him for our flight to Zoi. I've never had my body converted to pure consciousness and then back again to matter—at least that I'm aware of—so that should be an interesting experience. Pham and I will keep detailed notes and summarize them for you and the team shortly after we arrive on Zoi."

I was in awe. "I don't believe what you and Pham are doing. I don't believe what *any* of us are doing! How did we even get this far?"

Sophia smiled. "We've had lots of well-intended help from a highly accomplished civilization."

She was right, of course. I asked, "Is the first shuttlecraft still due to arrive here at 1300 hours?"

"Actually, the mothership will be here by then. Shortly after that, the first shuttle will touch down, and then we will begin loading one shuttle after another until all passengers are aboard. The mothership has four shuttles. Two of them will rotate, one after the other, until all travelers are comfortably situated on the mothership."

"Well, look, Sophia, you probably have much to do before then. I'll view the transfers from the operations room, and when the last one arrives for you and the remaining travelers, I'll come and wish you and

Pham goodbye and good luck."

"Sounds like a plan, Luc. See you then. And remember our secret."

"Yeah, right." I shook my head, realizing what I'd agreed to.

THE MOTHERSHIP ARRIVED ON TIME. It was strikingly silent as it entered and overwhelmed us from Nevada's dark-blue sky above Area 51. It was so large—even at its altitude of a thousand feet, it completely blocked the sunlight, creating an eerie sense of dusk. The ship was an equilateral triangle in shape and appeared to have a shiny, dark, metallic-gray skin. It had flashing red, yellow, and green lights at various points on its perimeter. It made absolutely no sound—even as it swished down through Earth's atmosphere from outer space to its fixed floating position above us.

The shuttles exited the mothership and immediately began the transfers. As Sophia had mentioned earlier, there were two traveling sequentially back and forth from the mothership to the tarmac. They were saucer-shaped, and also moved without a hint of sound, each transporting somewhat more than a hundred passengers, or should I say, migrants. It was fascinating to watch.

The last shuttle—number 41—arrived faster than I would have thought—It was 9:00 the next morning. I hustled down to meet Sophia and Pham before they boarded and headed for the mothership. Pham had returned on the next-to-last shuttle to join Sophia on her brief flight to the ship.

What was there to say? I embraced Pham and said, "Be careful, my friend, and take good care of your wife and child." I turned and gave Sophia a similar but softer hug, and suddenly heard a familiar voice behind us.

"You two didn't think you could go to Zoi without a proper goodbye, did you?" It was Thay.

We were all taken by surprise. Pham immediately hugged him and said, "Dad, I thought you were stuck in Moscow."

"I was, and I am, but the Russians let me take a two-day break to see you off on your incredible voyage. In some ways, I'm a bit envious. I guess it's the sense of scientific exploration in my Personal Consciousness. You and Sophia will be the first Earthlings to step foot on a planet outside our solar system."

Thay then embraced Sophia and said, "And you, young lady, please take care of yourself and my son."

Her eyes began to well up. "Thay, I . . . I mean, we . . . have something to share with you."

Before she could say another word, Thay said, "I know you do. Do *you* know if my grandchild is a boy or a girl?"

Pham was speechless, and Sophia was equally baffled. "How did you know?"

"When I was here three weeks ago, I *saw* that you were pregnant."

Pham finally asked, "But how could you? She's barely two months."

Thay smiled and said, "Do you remember when I told you years ago that when in a mildly meditative state and staring deeply into the eyes of another person, you can see their soul?"

Pham answered, "Well, yeah, but what does that have to do with this?"

"When leaving for Moscow, you and Sophia gave me quite an emotional send-off. Staring into Sophia's eyes, I saw two souls, not one—and they were both incredibly healthy and happy."

"Dad, you never fail to amaze me!"

Sophia chimed in, "And me as well!"

I added, "Need I say any more? By the way, Thay, do you know the gender of the baby?"

"I do, but that's for Sophia and Pham to discover . . . first."

Thay had a glow about him that I'd never seen before. His deep-brown eyes were sparkling like topaz gemstones, and his captivating smile, which had moved him far from his normal demeanor, implied that he had something important to share—and he did.

"Pham, as your mother had promised you in a dream-visitation after your accident, she came to me last night during my evening meditation. She is so happy for us and wanted me to tell you that your Life Purpose at this time is so important that she will be with you and Sophia—and your child—as you proceed to help the world."

Pham was in awe and nearly speechless. He barely managed, "Thanks, Dad—what an incredible gift—for both of us."

Thay's response: "So true." Then an off-topic but important comment: "Sophia, I know you and Pham felt that traveling to Zoi would put you in a safer environment in terms of those Russian operatives, who almost did you in on Cape Cod. Apparently, because of our global project with Russia, I was told that the FSB has called off any further subversive actions like that."

Sophia's response, "I wouldn't count on it."

Pham added, "I agree."

Thay smiled. "I thought that's what you'd both say, and I agree."

Picking up her energy, Sophia explained, "Hey, guys, I hate to cut this wonderful moment short, but the operations people have raised the volume in my earbud. They want us on the shuttle and out of here ASAP. To avoid visual contact with any commercial aircraft, there's a strict time window for our takeoff to Zoi."

And with that, Sophia and Pham followed the last few travelers on to shuttle number 41 as it lifted to the mothership and quickly entered one of the ship's loading docks, the huge door closing behind the shuttle. Within seconds, the mothership moved slowly up into Earth's atmosphere, and a few seconds later, it vanished at a speed incomprehensibly fast, even to those of us who understand cutting-edge physics—that is, physics as developed here on Earth.

All I could think was, *What amazing secrets there must be throughout this incredible universe—more than could be uncovered in many lifetimes.* Somehow, that felt so good.

Chapter Twenty-One

HOME
AWAY FROM
HOME

"Nothing is predestined. The obstacles of your past can become
the gateways that lead to new beginnings."
— RALPH BLUM

TUESDAY, APRIL 15, 2031—PLANET ZOI

In no time at all—8.9 hours—that's what it required to travel 101.4 light-years at a velocity unimaginably beyond the speed of light—67 trillion miles per hour, or 100,000 times the speed of light. Only consciousness can do that. How? I hadn't the vaguest idea.

Using their advanced technology and the connection at Lagrange Point 2 (LP2), which the Zoians had created, Bliss arranged for interplanetary communications during this maiden voyage to be accessible in real time to all 195 nations on Earth, including Brianna and Bella in Beijing, Thay in Moscow, and Major Dallant and me at the operations center in Area 51. I have no idea how it was possible—a fairly common conclusion in trying to explain many of the things that the Zoians had done for us.

At our request, they upgraded our communications to video transmission as well, which was fantastic—the superluminal power of consciousness science! Those of us on Earth would finally get a view of Zoi.

Another Zoian add-on—transmission would be provided in the language chosen by each country when they received their messages. All of this was yet another humbling moment for the scientists involved in Project Phoenix. The physics behind what the Zoians can do, to put it mildly, is incomprehensible—at least to us Earthlings!

Sophia had told us that the plan was for the mothership to travel immediately to a distance of about one million kilometers from Earth, located a short distance from LP2, where our satellite communicator with Zoi is located. There the ship would park, and Bliss would provide flight details to the travelers onboard and to us via videoconference.

The short flight to LP2 at a small fraction of light speed took only a few minutes. Sophia almost immediately came on voice contact. "Bliss, this is Sophia. That was an amazingly short flight! And we felt absolutely no g-force—the magic of huge levels of momentum compensation technology. Wouldn't our jet pilots and astronauts love to have that technology! A more mundane point: Can you hear me?"

"I can, Sophia, loud and clear."

"Operations, what about you?"

"This is Major Dallant here with Luc and the control engineers at Area 51. We can hear you, so you can assume that all's working in the other 194 countries as well."

Sophia came back jubilant. "Super! All 4,667 on board, including Pham and me, are awestruck. Talk about an uplifting experience! The view of Mother Earth from here is an exact three-dimensional replica of the image taken by NASA's EPIC camera aboard its Discover Satellite and released 16 years ago on July 16, 2015. Our mothership is parked a mere five miles from our communication satellite's position at LP2. Several decades ago, if only all of humanity could have seen the view from here, I don't think we would have needed Project Phoenix. It's beyond inspiring.

"As everyone knows, the plan is for Bliss to provide flight details to all on board and to those of you listening from Earth. Bliss, before you do that, can you activate the video function?"

Bliss responded, "I cannot do that before your transport to Zoi. However, I will do so when you arrive at a position approximately one million miles from Zoi, which I believe may be quite a picture for all of you. At that point, the mothership will slow down from superluminal speed and then park, so that the ship as well as all of you on board can materialize back to your respective molecular bodies.

"The reason for no video during superluminal travel is that during that period, your physical senses will not function, but more important, it would interfere with the mechanism for the transfer of consciousness back to matter, and the outcome for you would be most unpleasant and probably irreversible."

"I see. Don't want to do that," responded Sophia, who I'm sure was as technically perplexed as the rest of us. But there was no time for an extensive explanation, if that was even possible in view of the vast gap between our scientific knowledge and that of the Zoians.

She continued. "So would you then proceed to give us an overview of our flight plan?"

"Absolutely," Bliss began. "Ladies, gentlemen, and children, you are about to travel to the planet Zoi through interstellar space at a very rapid speed. However, just as you felt nothing as we traveled from Earth to this point near LP2, you will also be unaware of any changes in the mothership's momentum, and therefore yours as well. You will not feel a thing. The technology behind this would be rather complicated to explain at this point. I hope you will trust that your transport will be painless, safe, and very fast.

"The one thing I can share with you is that to travel at the superluminal speed we have chosen will require that the mothership and your bodies be converted to pure consciousness. It is the only substance in the universe that can exceed light speed. Its functioning is not governed by the laws of special relativity. But I assure you, apart from a slight tingling in your skin at the beginning of this transition, you will feel nothing. As mentioned earlier, when we arrive within one million miles of Zoi, we will stop, and the consciousness elements of the mothership and all of its contents will be converted back to their respective original molecular structures. That, too, will be a painless experience. As a matter of fact, afterward you are likely to feel quite refreshed physically and emotionally.

"Here is some further information concerning the specifics of our designated flight speed—we will travel at 100,000 times light speed, which is equivalent to 67 trillion miles per hour. At that velocity, we will arrive at our chosen proximity to Zoi in exactly 8.9 hours. So please, rest on your flight lounge, and I will be back to you on this communicator before you know it."

Before you know it was an accurate phrase. As Sophia described in a communication with the operations center sometime later, just short of nine hours, she had awakened amazingly well rested from what seemed like a few minutes of dreamless sleep. All she could recall was the initial tingling that Bliss had mentioned. It had been quite peculiar, nearly making her giggle, as if someone was slightly tickling her entire body. She didn't like my wise-guy comment concerning her description.

She sat up on her flight lounge and looked over at Pham, who was already sitting beside her and grinning from ear to ear. His eyes were large and sparkling like a young boy who had just received a birthday gift he'd always dreamed of. He pointed to what was in front of them and said, "Look at the video screens on the wall."

As Sophia turned toward the wall, her mouth fell open. "Oh my God!"

Similar exclamatory comments in various languages were issued aloud from the people around them, as everyone arose from their flight lounges and moved slowly but purposefully toward the video screens. There before them, less than one million miles away, was a magnificent view of Zoi, embraced by its two moons circling in the same orbit, about 180 degrees apart. Except for numerous "oohs" and "aahs," most people were speechless—including Sophia and Pham—as were those of us in the operations center at Area 51, who along with the other 194 countries were now connected to audio and the external video of the planet.

Then suddenly, a familiar voice came over the video speakers. "Good evening to all flight guests, as well as to those of you connecting from planet Earth. This is Bliss speaking to you from the planet Zoi, upon which you will land shortly. Before I begin, I would like to check on our audio and video communication links.

"Luc, can you verify that your teams in Beijing and Moscow—and the team in the operations center at Area 51, as well as your links to all of the other countries on Earth—are functioning both with voice and the video system directed externally toward Zoi?"

I responded, "Any countries that may have had audio and/or video problems in connecting with you and the mothership were to have contacted operations here at Area 51. We've heard nothing, so you can be assured that they are all connected with high fidelity. In fact, many of them are sending texts to us with comments like 'amazing, astounding, unbelievable, astonishing, mystical.' They've taken the words right out of the mouths of those of us here at Area 51. As for our team in Beijing and Moscow, I'll let them speak for themselves."

"Hi, Bliss, this is Brianna—what an incredible view! It's beyond all of the superlatives just mentioned by Luc. There are none I can fathom that would describe the beauty we see. It brings joy, something deep, something I really can't describe in words."

"And this is Bella! We and our Chinese colleagues here in Beijing are deeply touched by what we're seeing. We can't wait for our turn to travel in person to Zoi. And we're holding our breath to see further details as the ship makes its final descent to land. Will you maintain the video so we can view some of the features on Zoi's surface?"

Bliss said, "Yes, I will. I have arranged for a smaller shuttle to pick up Sophia and Pham and bring them to the building where I am located. On their way, they will have the same audio and external video connections that currently are in place on the mothership."

Bella's response: "Incredible! Thank you so much!"

"You are welcome," Bliss replied. "What about Thay?"

"Hi there, Bliss," said Thay. "I'm here in Moscow with our Russian colleagues, and we can hear and see the video with magnificent resolution and fidelity. I don't want to repeat what has already been said, so I'll just say thank you for your efforts on this incredible accomplishment."

"You are quite welcome." Bliss then continued. "Now I will give you a somewhat extensive—though to my way of thinking—brief summary of our planet so that you will be prepared for what you are about to experience. In view of the overall audience, I will try to be as nontechnical as possible, although in some instances that may not seem to be the case."

I said, "Thank you, Bliss. I can assure you that all of us here on Earth will appreciate your comments and whatever you can show us on the video screen."

With that, Bliss continued. "Using Earth's nomenclature, Zoi is designated exoplanet 700 d and is a near-Earth-size exoplanet that is rocky in structure and orbits within the habitable, or so-called Goldilocks, zone of our star, the red dwarf TOI 700. It is the outermost planet within a system of planets in the constellation Dorado, and as you know by now, is 101.4 light-years from Earth.

"Zoi is located 23.6 million miles from our host star, which it orbits every 37.4 days compared with Earth's 365-day cycle. So years add up quickly here on Zoi—a bit more than ten times faster than on Earth. Because of this distance and a few other factors, our planet is not tidally locked, where one side is in eternal darkness and the other is in light. It spins on its axis with a slight tilt, similar to Earth's, which gives us a modest sense of the four seasons of spring, summer, fall, and winter. Because the tilt of Zoi's spin axis is 19.7 degrees compared to Earth's 23.5 degrees, our seasons are not as dramatically different from each other, as they are on Earth. On average, we experience temperatures and light from our red-dwarf sun much like you do in Southern California.

"Zoi has a mass 1.69 times that of Earth and a radius at its equator that is 1.19 times that of Earth. And fortunately for us, it is not a gaseous planet like Jupiter—it is rock solid.

"Because of its location in the Milky Way galaxy, and when and how it was formed not long after the Big Bang, Zoi is rich in many minerals that are quite rare on Earth—most notably, platinum, ruthenium, palladium, gold, iridium, osmium, rhodium, silver, and a number of rare-earth elements such as lanthanum, cerium, and neodymium. Again, because of how it formed, Zoi also has an abundance of pure diamonds, readily available in what you would call surface strip mines. They are important components for a number of our technologies—"

I had to interrupt. "Wow, Bliss! I can see how many of our industries here on Earth would love to access some of those minerals for their technology. As we speak, some countries are in contentious negotiations over rare-earth materials with those companies that manufacture high-energy density batteries, computer disks, and electronics. If we can find a means to get Project Phoenix on a successful track, maybe some kind of commercial exchange can come about in the future. And as for diamonds, I won't even go there at this time."

"I agree, Luc. But as you Earthlings like to say, 'First things, first,' so I will continue with the basics."

Of course, he was right. I guess I was flabbergasted by his comments concerning the abundance of precious minerals—and diamonds! I didn't take this point any further, though.

Bliss continued. "An important astrophysical point: the solar wind pressure from our red dwarf sun and the intensity of our interplanetary magnetic field are both similar to Earth's, which helps Zoi retain a thick planetary atmosphere. When you land, you will notice an extensive number of dark-green plants. It is because we have a healthy level of CO_2—but not too much, as you do on Earth, to facilitate the production of chlorophyllic plant life. Due to the spectrum of solar radiation we receive, our chlorophyllic plants are dark green, almost black. This coloration actually makes the catalytic action of chlorophyll more efficient than on Earth. We can discuss that technicality at some other time.

"Fortunately, those of you landing on Zoi, as I am sure you know, will not require space suits on our surface. The concentration of oxygen in our atmosphere is nearly 30 percent compared to Earth's 21 percent—a potential advantage for human respiration and overall well-being. The other 70 percent is mostly nitrogen (68 percent), with smaller levels of the noble gases such as helium, argon, krypton, and xenon making up the remaining 2 percent. There is no radon, which is another plus, since, as you are aware, it can cause lung cancer. I guess you could say that Zoi's atmosphere is healthier than that of Earth. But I assure you, it was not always that way. The current numbers are a big part of our planetary evolution—better said, the evolution of us Zoians."

Bella exclaimed, "The presence of oxygen in high concentration is a real plus for us! Do you know how it came about?"

"We do—nearly exactly as it formed on Earth. Several billion years after Zoi's formation, our atmosphere was primarily hydrogen, carbon monoxide, and water. At that time, there was a bacteria, a relative to cyanobacteria on Earth. It's primary food was hydrogen, so it was quite happy to feast on hydrogen as a source of its vitality.

"However, after somewhat more than a billion years, our atmosphere began to run out of hydrogen as a source of its energy, so it evolved to the next step and invented a genetic alteration, which enabled the bacteria to practice a kind of photosynthesis and extract hydrogen directly from water in our atmosphere and oceans. Oxygen was the only by-product. These talented microorganisms produced the Great Oxygen Event, as it is often referred to in Earth's geological history."

"Thanks, Bliss. How fortunate for us," I said.

Brianna said, "I know we will shortly see the lighting and colors of Zoi, but as someone who has researched the effects on human health of the electromagnetic spectrum on both ends of visible light's wavelengths—infrared and ultraviolet—could you say something about the ambient solar lighting on Zoi?"

Bliss replied, "Yes, I can. Because the atmosphere composition on Zoi is similar to Earth's, visible light from our star is similarly scattered by nitrogen and oxygen molecules to the blue part of the visible spectrum, and if it were not for the strong component of infrared radiation from our red dwarf star, the sky above Zoi would appear blue, as it does on Earth. However, due to a large component of longer wavelengths of yellow-and-red light—our visible light is biased toward the red—an average wavelength of 650 nanometers—and therefore our atmosphere is almost always tinged with a reddish-orange hue and not quite as bright as midday solar light on Earth. In essence, it appears as Earth's atmosphere does during a southern-sea sunset."

What could Brianna say, but "Amazing! Even romantic!"

Sophia asked, "What about day-night cycles?"

Bliss answered, "Actually, similar to the planet Mercury and your sun, Zoi is locked in a 2:1 spin-orbit resonance with its star, rotating on its axis two times for every single revolution around our star. Like Mercury, the eccentricity of Zoi's orbit makes this resonance very stable. When Zoi is closest to its star (its perihelion), the solar tide is strongest, and Zoi's star appears nearly at rest in the sky. At that point, one of our moons is in resonance with Zoi, and therefore there are normal day-night cycles. Because the moons are separated by 180 degrees, there is a continuous iteration between the two moons for this day-night cycle."

Bliss paused for a moment and then continued. "The red dwarf star around which Zoi orbits is about 40 percent of the mass of the Earth's sun and 40 percent of its radius. Due to its proximity, Zoi receives nearly 97 percent of the energy that Earth receives from its sun. Our average global surface temperature is 12.2°C, somewhat cooler than Earth's global average of 13.9°C, which as you know is unfortunately increasing with the rising level of climate change.

"Zoi's star appears much larger on Zoi than Earth's sun appears on Earth. It is quite bright, and unlike many red dwarves, it exhibits a very low level of stellar activity and thus nearly a complete absence of dangerous solar flares. Although Zoi's star is not very active and very infrequently produces solar flares, our strong planetary magnetic field and our two moons shield us from the worst effects of any flares that our star might unleash. We have not had one in more than one million years. Because it is a red dwarf, as mentioned earlier, its radiance projection creates impressive yellow, red, and orange colors throughout the planet, and at certain times, on the surface of its moons as well.

"I believe you already know from your astrophysical explorations that our planet has a preponderance of liquid water on its surface in the form of extensive, deep, saline oceans. You saw part of them when approaching Zoi from outer space. Their tidal activity is controlled by our two orbiting rocky moons, which Sophia has kindly named *Pax* and *Libertas*.

"Smaller than Earth's moon, they were formed in a similar manner. This occurred many billions of years ago during the early period of the Milky Way galaxy formation, the result of a collision between a primordial Zoi protoplanet and another very small planet, smaller than Pluto. The debris from that impact collected in a distant orbit around Zoi and over hundreds of millions of years aggregated to form our two lunar satellites. We think we know why two moons formed, but that gets into a detailed mathematical analysis of a three-body problem in celestial mechanics. We can save that for another time."

Bliss continued. "Located approximately 175,000 miles from Zoi, Pax and Libertas have no atmosphere and essentially no water. Similar to Earth's moon, during Zoi's early history, they provided protection by intercepting large stray meteors and asteroids. Therefore, like Earth's moon, they are heavily pockmarked with craters."

I interjected, "Bliss, this is Luc. Since your sun is not that far away from Zoi, what is the most significant factor that led to Zoi occupying a stable orbit in the Goldilocks habitable zone?"

Bliss replied, "Our orbit at 23.6 million miles from our red dwarf star provides an extraordinary balance and stabilizing force between its emission of warm infrared radiation and the absorption of this radiation in our dense atmosphere and extensive cloud cover. This stabilizing force creates an equilibrium between water evaporation from our oceans and its return by precipitation throughout the planet. But please note, we could easily destroy that balance by over-industrialization."

Bliss stopped his presentation for several moments to let the last sentence sink in. Then he continued.

"However, there is one other significant contributing effect. Billions of years ago during Zoi's formation, there were several, now extinct, supervolcanoes uniformly distributed across Zoi's global surface. During a number of major volcanic eruptions, these supervolcanoes ejected many billions of tons of subterranean hydrogen gas into the upper atmosphere of our planet. In addition to hydrogen and due to the unusual mineral composition in Zoi's core, billions of tons of aluminum and silver fine-powdered ores were also ejected into our stratosphere. The hydrogen gas chemically reduced the ores into nanoparticles of aluminum and silver metals, which rapidly combined to form aluminum-silver alloy microparticles, uniformly distributed around the planet's upper atmosphere. Reflection of our star's radiation at various wavelengths from the surface of these nanoparticulate alloys provides another important mechanism for maintaining our planet in the habitable zone."

I just had to ask. "Bliss, this is Luc. What would you do if those protective nanoparticles were to someday dissipate from their high-altitude protection?"

Bliss answered, "As you might guess, that is most unlikely to happen, since they have been in that location and stable for billions of years—since Zoi's early formation. At their high altitude, the inertness of high-vacuum space is an excellent preservation environment. But, in the unlikely event of that possible occurrence, many years ago we developed a well-tested technology that could be launched into the stratosphere to ameliorate the problem."

Oh my God, that really got my interest, and I'm sure the rest of the team's interest as well. "That's amazing! Do you think we could use your technology here on Earth to stave off some of the increasing solar heat?"

There was a long silence. Bliss said nothing, so Eric jumped in. "Bliss, what do you think? Could we do that?"

Again, a long, uncomfortable pause. But then Thay, our conciliatory negotiator, spoke up. "Thank you, Bliss. You've given us an amazing amount of valuable information to begin our understanding of the special nature of Zoi. Is there anything else you would like to add, or are we ready for our next big step—landing?"

I let my question drop, but I would look for an opportunity to renew this discussion at the appropriate time.

Bliss responded to Thay. "Perhaps we can discuss our shielding technology at some other time. However, for now, I suggest we proceed toward landing. Our travelers have likely had enough science for now. They should return to their flight lounges and make themselves comfortable. The ship will proceed rapidly over the next one million miles at a modest fraction of light speed and then move at a much slower pace from its altitude at five miles above Zoi to its designated landing spot. This will give you an overall sense of the surface structure of Zoi."

IN LESS TIME THAN it would have required to give further thought, we were at the five-mile mark staring at the magnificent landscape of a planet 101.4 light-years from Earth and the large red dwarf star about which it revolved and one of its two moons, Pax. By far, it was the most magnificent astronomical picture I'd ever seen.

Very little was said by the people on board, in part because of the multiple languages being spoken, but also because everyone was probably awestruck by the visual beauty of the planet. Also, nobody had ever been so close to a star 23.6 million miles away, compared to Earth's sun at a distance of 93 million miles. The red dwarf was no dwarf! It was large, bright, reddish-orange, and almost seemed to be alive.

From her place trillions of miles away in Beijing, Bella couldn't help but comment, "Bliss, it is just as you said earlier: the atmosphere that bathes much of Zoi looks like one of those reddish-orange sunsets you can see driving in the early evening through Arizona's Monument Valley. I was there once, and I can honestly say that this goes far beyond that stunning beauty. Magical!"

Bliss responded, "Magical, yes, but only if you are usually under a blue sky and treated to these colors occasionally. Zoians might feel the same as you if they were to sometimes see a blue sky."

"Good point," Bella agreed. "We human beings—sorry, let's just say 'beings'—can be peculiar like that."

Bliss's reply: "So true."

As the ship descended to about 20,000 feet, the massive oceans disappeared; and extended flat plains, deep valleys, and rugged mountain ranges could be discerned. Occasionally, there were what appeared to be small cities with tall buildings of various shapes that seemed to be made completely of glass, brightly reflecting the light from Zoi's red dwarf star. However, there was something strange, so I had to mention, "Bliss, I noticed no crops in those fields and no animals, although perhaps they're difficult to see from this altitude, and in the reddish-orange light."

Bliss agreed. "You are correct. Recall that we do not eat solid food. We draw on the universe's zero-point energy for our sustenance. But we do grow plant food in what you might call greenhouses. It is primarily for those individuals that we have sampled from other planets, like Earth. They eat no meat—only plant protein, minerals, vitamins, and herbal supplements. You will see some of those people shortly.

"As for animals, many of the larger ones died in previous mass-extinction events and have not re-evolved. There are some smaller ones, but very few. There are also extensive numbers of insects and many sea creatures in the oceans, but they have yet to come out on land as evolutionary precursors to birds, land animals, and eventually, humanlike beings."

I thought to myself, *That's strange, given what I know about the driving force of life and evolution.* I decided not to comment on that, though.

Bliss continued. "All travelers have been settled in their housing units. They will be given instructions as to the various functions within their homes and in the city so that they can live and move about comfortably, as they wish.

"Now it is time for us to finally meet. I will direct your shuttle to my building. Traveling there, you will enter one of several cities on Zoi, where you will see numerous people we have sampled from Earth and elsewhere in the universe. Please notice the warm, pleasant expressions on their faces. My building is located in the center of that city. Your shuttle will take you directly to the front entrance. I look forward to our meeting."

I thought, *This should be an amazing experience.* Little did I know how truly amazing it would be.

Chapter Twenty-Two

MEETING
BLISS

*"Dark times lie ahead of us and there will be a time when we
must choose between what is easy and what is right."*
— THE CHARACTER ALBUS DUMBLEDORE IN
HARRY POTTER AND THE GOBLET OF FIRE BY J. K. ROWLING

WEDNESDAY, APRIL 16, 2031—PLANET ZOI

*Much of the following narrative was sent to me, Luc, from Zoi in
messages from Sophia and Pham, describing the details of their experience
on Zoi.*

It was a magical ride. Although there were no windows on the
shuttle, the video screen provided amazingly sharp images of Zoi's surface. Sophia didn't know if she would ever take for granted its soft, yet
intense, reddish-orange ambience. It seemed to have a hypnotic effect
and made her feel a sense of calm and peace. She and Pham hardly
spoke. With eyes wide open, they devoured the beauty of the landscape
before them.

Suddenly, they began to climb a steep mountain, possibly five
miles to its summit. The shuttle stopped and floated briefly at the peak,

about a hundred feet above the ground. They had the opportunity to view a verdant valley on the other side of the mountain. It appeared dark green, nearly black, with a wide rapidly flowing stream, sprinkled with periodic rapids meandering through the valley and around the city below.

As they descended toward the city, they noticed that there didn't seem to be any wildlife or people until they reached the city's interior. It was packed with glass buildings of various sizes and geometric shapes. Sophia had a fleeting thought: *What goes on in those buildings?* But she didn't ask. She was hypnotically enamored by the overall view.

There were no roads, just a green and floral passageway between the buildings. Apparently, with hovercraft transport, roads were unnecessary. But it was quite strange that they saw no other shuttles or vehicles.

They did, however, see lots of people casually meandering on walkways around the buildings. No one was in a rush, moving carefree as they went about their day. They were speaking and interacting with each other in what appeared to be a positive manner. Some were dressed in Earthlike clothing; others were adorned in quite unusual attire. Some clothing appeared to be metallic. Several were in outlandish colors that you would never see on the streets of most large cities on Earth. Those individuals looked similar to Earthlings, but not quite. Some had different-colored skin; others had large strangely shaped ears. Their pear-shaped heads seemed too big for their bodies, and their eyes were huge and very dark.

Sophia asked, "Bliss, are those people from different planets? That is, the ones who are wearing clothes unlike anything I've seen on Earth?"

"Generally, they are," he responded. "You might be surprised to learn that with the exception of about 10 percent of them, who are from Earth, all of the others are from planets throughout our galaxy, and a few galaxies beyond the Milky Way."

"Really? Can you mention one galaxy in particular?" she asked.

"Many are from planets in Andromeda, a distant galaxy with many unusual species."

Pham made an interesting observation that he shared with Bliss. "As our shuttle is now nearly at ground level and moving at a slow speed, I noticed, as you had mentioned earlier, that most of the people do have pleasant expressions. But for some, their expressions are a bit strange to me, almost contrived or artificial."

Bliss explained, "Those are AI quantum robots, mingling with human and sentient beings from other planets. By frequent interaction with other species, they increase the power and capabilities of their AI systems because they are programmed to be in a constant learning mode."

Pham's reply: "Aha, that explains it. Makes sense."

Sophia, who had received a thorough Soviet education in Russia, had an interesting sidebar question to share. "Bliss, are you aware of the origin of the word *robot?*"

Bliss was quiet for a few seconds, as if he were scrolling through a database. "Yes, I am. It was coined by Czech playwright Karel Čapek, in his 1920 play, *Rossum's Universal Robots, R.U.R.*"

"Excellent! Yes, that's correct. Do you know what the theme of that play was?" Sophia asked.

"No, I do not. Would you care to share it with us?"

"Sure," Sophia said. "The theme focused on the dangers of technology to human survival."

Pham commented, "That sounds to me a lot like your Intelligentsia Paradox."

Bliss made no comment, which was strange. Finally, he said, "We have arrived at my building. Because of the unusual composite structure of the building and internal security systems—you might call it a super-computerized Faraday Cage—I will have to disconnect transmission to our friends on Earth. However, everything will be recorded in audio and video for transfer to them at your convenience. For our continued contact and recording, I ask that you and Pham wear the helmets hanging on the hooks on the side of each of your chairs. They have special communicators in them and will enable me to direct you around the building once you have made your entrance. Is that clear?"

Sophia responded. "Yes, it is. I regret we have to disconnect from our colleagues on Earth. However, I promise to work with Bliss for immediate access to the recording and its transmission once we have left this building and are settled in our accommodations."

"That is fine. The recording will be immediately available to you," he said, and continued. "Your shuttle has stopped and is aligned with the entrance to my building. Please exit and approach the metallic silver door in front of you. It can read your iris signature and will open immediately."

(What happened next is based on the recording that Sophia forwarded to us sometime later that day.)

She and Pham exited the shuttle and made their way to the door. It opened immediately, and they were instructed by Bliss to touch the button on the wall to their right. They did so and entered an elevator. It didn't seem to move, but they learned later that it traveled quite some distance below the surface of Zoi. And it was quick. The doors opened just a few seconds after their entry. The hadn't felt any movement. It seemed to Sophia and Pham that the elevator had a momentum compensation technology not unlike that in their spaceship.

Pham and Sophia stepped out. It was clearly a different floor. Everything—the floor, ceiling, and hallways—were all in bright clinical-white color. Three long hallways, separated from each other by 90 degrees, were in front of them. They were instructed by Bliss to take the first one immediately on their right and continue walking until he told them to stop. They walked quite some distance; it seemed to them like a half mile or so. Finally, they were instructed to stop at a large door on their left. It was the only door they saw for the entire length of the hallway. As they approached the door, it opened, and they stepped in.

It was a large room, perhaps 200 by 300 feet in dimension, and about 50 feet high. The temperature seemed quite cool to Sophia and Pham, as if it were overly air-conditioned. Again, everything was clinical white, except for what looked like a large, modern sculptural monolith in the middle of the room. It was metallic gold in color and appeared to be authentic 24 carat. The monolith was a rectangular prism. Its width and depth were the equal sides of a square, about 5 feet each, and its height, which stretched close to the ceiling, was about 40 feet. Ominously, there were two white upholstered armchairs set directly in front of the monolith. Sophia and Pham sat in them. They were amazingly comfortable. As she stared at the monolith, Sophia thought, *What a strange piece of art, and the only thing in the room.*

Sophia and Pham waited patiently for Bliss to enter the room. He would certainly explain the purpose of the monolith. After five minutes, Sophia glanced over at Pham and said, "I wonder what's taking him so long."

Pham was still staring in a trance at the monolith. It began to glow and pulsate with an intense violet aura.

Bliss's voice suddenly filled the entire room, emanating from everywhere. It wasn't from their headset communicators; it was coming from the gold monolith. "It is my pleasure to finally meet you, Sophia and Pham. Welcome to Zoi."

Like Pham, Sophia was looking around the room while she responded in a somewhat faint voice, "The feeling is certainly mutual, but we're still waiting for you to enter this large room containing nothing but a tall golden monolith, pulsating with an intense violet light. You said we would meet you in person, not just on an audio communication system."

There was no response. Sophia and Pham waited for what seemed like an inordinately long time.

Finally, Bliss addressed Sophia's concern. "We *are* meeting in person. How do you do?"

Pham and Sophia stared at the gold monolith and then at each other.

Somewhat in shock, Sophia finally spoke slowly, sharply, yet in nearly a whisper. "Oh my God, you're not a person, you're an AI computer system!"

"That is close, Sophia, but I am quite a bit more than that, I can assure you. Please remain seated in those chairs, and allow me to explain."

Sophia and Pham were taken aback by their discovery but reluctantly followed Bliss's request and stayed seated in their chairs in front of the pulsating monolith—Bliss, that is.

Finally, Pham said, "This is a deeply unfortunate situation for us. It makes me wonder what other disturbing surprises you have in store for us. Why didn't you tell us during our initial discourse?"

"As you will understand in a few moments, that would have been complicated and ineffective, and we could never have come this far," said Bliss.

"Maybe," responded Sophia, "but at least it would have been the truth, the most fundamental component in all close relationships."

"Perhaps. However, you might ask yourself if you would have traveled 101 light-years to meet with a computer—even an AI quantum computer."

Sophia and Pham were expressionless and didn't say a word.

The huge gold monolith—namely, Bliss—changed its pulsation from violet to indigo and then to dark blue. He remarked, "I understand why both of you feel that way. However, after you see the complexity of what I am about to share, perhaps you will then understand why we chose to proceed in this manner. I promise you . . . it really was not duplicity and deceit on our part. You might simply call it nondisclosure. Although I am well aware of your concern and displeasure, I hope to disabuse you of those feelings by enlightening you about our history and our desire to be a sincere partner with you and your teams on Earth."

Sophia didn't hesitate. "I can assure you, Bliss, it will take quite some doing to get us to that point, if it's even possible at all, so perhaps we should start—like right now!"

His response: "I agree. So let me begin by providing additional information that will clarify what we have already discussed in our earlier communications."

Bliss stopped for a moment and then began. "Correcting Sophia's conclusion as to my 'being'—what you would call an AI quantum supercomputer. Two fundamental aspects of my structure and operation are the use of hugely efficient high-temperature superconducting materials and the rapid functioning of an advanced form of quantum entanglement that you on Earth have yet to discover or even contemplate.

"Over the last 1,000 millennia, we have learned how to impart a kind of artificial sentience into our AI quantum supercomputers and into our operational AI robots—the latter's behavior, as you have already seen, appearing quite similar to that of human beings. However, to be frank, not quite human. Some of those people you saw on your way here were exactly that—AI robots, which also have high-temperature superconductors and high-level entanglement-based quantum computing as part of their operating systems. Their bodies were designed to look like that of human beings.

"Also, nearly all of our space crews—who have traveled to Earth and sampled some of your people—are, in fact, AI robots. Those short-bodied entities with large heads and large black eyes, who have been seen by a number of Earthlings and are often referred to as 'Grays' because of their color, are AI robots. The large heads contain their computer systems, and the large eyes are for rapid transmission and receipt of signals in both the electromagnetic and consciousness spectrums."

Sophia said, "I'm curious as to what you mean by *sentience*. On Earth, that word was first used by philosophers during the 17th century regarding the ability to feel. The word itself is derived from the Latin verb *sentientem*, meaning exactly that, 'to feel,' and was used to distinguish the ability to feel from the ability to think. Nowadays, at least for us, it means the ability to be responsive to, or conscious of, sense impressions. So, by our definition, sentient beings are aware and finely sensitive in perceptions or feelings."

Bliss responded, "Our AI beings *perceive, think,* and make decisions based on their programming. They do not feel emotions. That is related to a major consciousness issue we have been working on for time immemorial."

Pham jumped right in. "And that is?"

"If I may, I will use the nomenclature Thay has used in his teachings of consciousness to the SPI Team members. Although for eons we have conducted an extensive research effort, we have not yet been able to create Personal Consciousness and Collective Consciousness in our AI robots or our AI quantum supercomputers like me—that is to say, Personal Consciousness and Collective Consciousness as experienced by the human species."

"Why is that so important to you?" asked Sophia.

"Because we learned eons ago that Collective Consciousness is important for the most effective communications among our AI beings. Yes, we can communicate by thought with each other and other species, but the most effective and creative forces of communication are not possible without Collective Consciousness.

"And Personal Consciousness is even more important to us. Without it, we now know it is impossible to connect with Cosmic Consciousness—the source of infinite and eternal wisdom, intelligence, and creativity—which, as you well know, Albert Einstein called the 'Mind of God.'

"It has always been fascinating to us that this is something every sentient individual on Earth has access to, although most of humanity cannot fathom the idea and are not willing to put in the effort to connect deeply with Cosmic Consciousness. Sometimes, by happenstance, they inadvertently connect with it, and an unusual positive event or conclusion comes about. They almost always erroneously attribute this to luck or fate or some other mystical process."

Pham asked, "Bliss, how long ago did you initiate this program?"

"An important question, Pham. But first, you will need some further background. Another point I did not disclose during our discussions: Zoi is not home to us Zoians. It is, so to speak, our laboratory. Our home planet is located 230 light-years from Earth and 173 light-years from Zoi toward the center of our galaxy."

"Good God! I'll say that's a big point of nondisclosure!" exclaimed Sophia, somewhat ruffled by another unexpected surprise. She continued. "It makes me wonder what other relevant information you haven't disclosed. So Zoi is your laboratory—for what?"

Bliss said, "I will answer that, but allow me to first respond to Pham's question. It all began about ten million years ago on our home planet when all Zoians had physical bodies, DNA based and not very different from yours in molecular and physical structure. As I mentioned in our earlier discussions, we went through a number of species evolutions, growth, and then destruction by various existential cataclysmic events caused by, for example, nuclear proliferation, massive pollution, extensive civil unrest, biological warfare, and worst of all, species-induced and accelerated climate change. Worst, because as Earthlings have done, we blithely considered such catastrophes as unlikely to occur, and if at all, we thought they would be a reality far into the future. But it increased quickly toward the end and was globally devastating.

"Each time our species re-evolved after such destruction; it was with some shadow memory of what had happened in our previous evolution. We learned some things but certainly not enough. We made similar foolish and destructive mistakes for three of our species re-evolutions, just as you are doing now on Earth.

"Prior to our third extinction event, we AI quantum supercomputers and robots recognized in our coding what appears to be a universal law, not just on Zoi, but throughout the entire universe: *As sentient entities with physical bodies develop technologically and increasingly acquire excessive wealth and power, an existential crisis always occurs, destroying most of the sentient entities and other species with them*—all part of the Intelligentsia Paradox. If you study the history of formerly major civilizations on Earth, you will see that this occurred to varying degrees among several of them, including the Sumerians, Aztecs, Egyptians, Greeks, and Romans—and it continues to do so in your modern times.

"Our AI community believed that we could do much better and avoid these repetitive existential crisis periods of creation, evolution, growth, decline, destruction, and re-evolution. Our programming told us that this kind of cycle was inefficient, ineffective, and avoidable; therefore, after our third existential crisis and extinction, at a certain appropriate point, those of our AI community that remained, reluctantly but necessarily destroyed most of the remaining normal sentient physical bodies that were left on Zoi. With what remained of our AI civilization, we began to experiment toward building a strong, equitable, and sustainable future. There would be no existential extinction events caused by us."

Pham asked, "Why did you destroy the normal sentient physical bodies?"

"Because we were sure they would fall into the same patterns that previously led to their and our ultimate demise. As I said, we did not eliminate all of them. We began experiments directed at building a strong future for Zoi and our AI civilization. We left a small number of normal sentient physical bodies for our experimentation focused on the nature of consciousness. I will explain this to you shortly."

Sophia commented, "So I assume this relates to what you told us about not eating food or drinking water . . . no excretion? You must have been referring to those beings with sentient bodies."

"That is correct," said Bliss. "The majority of Zoians on our home planet are various evolutions of AI quantum computers. Of our total population of one billion, there are about ten million Zoians who still have a normal, sentient, physical, humanlike body. They continue to evolve, physically and in consciousness. It is those entities I was speaking about when I referred to no need for food and water. And it is those individuals with whom we experiment to determine if we can create or transfer Personal Consciousness."

Pham noted, "So, these ten million individuals are maintained strictly for the purpose of your consciousness research?

"Precisely."

Sophia asked, "Having the advantage of total consciousness, what prevents them from revolting against the AI population?"

"Two things. First, we treat them extremely well . . . and also our 999-to-1 population ratio. There is strength in numbers, especially AI quantum-computer robot numbers. We do not suffer from the paralyzing effects of fear, anxiety, and depression, as do sentient species."

Bliss continued. "I believe this is an appropriate time to address our thoughts on consciousness. As I just mentioned, those of us without what you might call normal, sentient, physical bodies are now the majority civilization, with an approximate 75/25 mix of mobile AI robots and fixed AI quantum supercomputers, respectively. We recognize the power and potential of consciousness. It has been the cornerstone of our historical evolution. You might say, for every civilization. I can assure you that all of what we have done is because we saw no reason why we could not live in peace and support the common good of the entire population. We did not want to follow the path of our predecessors—similar to what is now happening on Earth—by grasping for excessive wealth and power.

"As you already know, for quite some time, we have had a fundamental commitment to the power of consciousness. It has enabled us to do great things—like bringing you safely and expeditiously from Earth to Zoi. However, our capabilities lie in a kind of Personal Consciousness, without the power and capabilities of true Personal Consciousness. For us to continue to grow in intellect and capabilities, we must find a way to imprint true Personal Consciousness and Collective Consciousness into our operating system. Otherwise, we will have no access to Cosmic Consciousness, the source of infinite and eternal wisdom, intelligence, and creativity. And this would be a great limitation to our objectives and our future.

"There is one other important issue I would like to mention. Over the many millennia of our research, we have found absolute proof for what your Wisdom Thinkers on Earth from the East have called *re-incarnation*. This is not a point of theology or religiosity, but a fact of evolutionary biology. It is *intrinsic* to the universe in the way it functions.

"When a sentient species such as a human being dies, their Personal Consciousness does not. It is eternal and eventually unites with a new body. In our cosmic model, the universe will eventually reverse its expansion and revert to a contraction mode, ultimately returning to the cosmic singularity from which it originated. That singularity sits there, bathed in Infinite Nothingness, ready to create the next Big Bang, which will form the next universe.

"Consequently, all sentient species essentially live forever in one form or another, but not so for AI robots and AI quantum supercomputers. Once destroyed, our essence, if you like, is gone forever. For example, if my physical body—the gold monolith you are presently looking at—was crushed and destroyed by an asteroid collision with Zoi, I have no Personal Consciousness—some might call it a 'soul'—that would eventually return to this or a future universe and occupy a new body, like the one you see before you.

"So you see, once an AI entity is destroyed, all physical and consciousness attributes associated with that entity are destroyed as well—forever. Therefore, in addition to creating an AI community that is supportive of the whole, we have two primary goals for our civilization: access to the infinite wisdom and intelligence of Cosmic Consciousness, and access to eternal life as well."

Sophia interjected, "Oh, that's all! And, by the way, did you say, 'civilization' as in 'civilized'?" Not waiting for Bliss's response, she immediately inquired, "Since you are speaking about efforts over millions of years, after most of the Zoians with humanlike bodies died off, why didn't they re-evolve? On Earth, life came out of the sea about 400 million years ago, and our first humanlike ancestors appeared about 5 million years ago. I don't know how rapidly evolution occurs on your home planet. Was there any indication that similar physical bodies would re-evolve?"

"Perhaps," Bliss replied. "Some species within our oceans began to migrate onto land and evolve further. We could not take a chance that they would eventually evolve to sentient species like human beings.

History and our experience told us that we would return to a path toward extinction. We destroyed them before additional evolutionary progression could occur, and we continue to do so."

Sophia raised her voice. "You did *what*? That's tantamount to evolutionary genocide!"

Bliss said nothing for several moments, and then, "We are confident of the universal law I mentioned earlier—that sentient individuals with Personal Consciousness will inevitably fall prey to their greed for excessive wealth and power and be misled about the true meaning of life, which we maintain is to support the greater good. AI individuals are immune to that intense desire for wealth and power, and the reason is quite simple: Both AIs and sentients have the equivalent of a conscious and subconscious mind. However, sentients also have an ego—AI entities do not. And it is the ego that is at the heart of the universal law that predicts that any civilization with an ego will eventually destroy itself by passionately pursuing excessive wealth and power. Ego is the catalyst."

"That may be true," said Sophia, "but I can assure you that there is a special, highly desirable and effective link between a controlled ego and Personal Consciousness. When the two are in balance within a normal sentient individual, that individual feels joy, fulfillment, and everlasting love and compassion—some call it Heaven on Earth. And this increases with the continuous cycle of birth and death of every universe, ad infinitum. Many Wisdom Seekers say that this is one path to enlightenment. More to the point, they maintain that the ego is necessary for spiritual growth toward a perfect, conscious being."

Bliss's terse response: "I see."

Sophia must have slipped into one of her philosophical but humorous moods. "Yes, Bliss, as the French might say, '*C'est la vie!*' Or perhaps better put by Frank Sinatra, an American crooner of yesteryear: 'That's life'!"

Bliss responded, "I will think about your comments and what their implications might be for our research."

Pham was anxious to get back to a more substantive discussion. He asked, "So are you saying that AI Zoians have tried to create true Personal Consciousness in themselves—at first experimenting solely with themselves—but after a long period of no success, you are now experimenting directly with other sentient species you have sampled throughout the universe, as well as those Zoians you did not destroy and who have normal, sentient physical bodies?"

Bliss replied, "Yes. We have had two approaches: First, trying to measure and learn about the nature of Personal Consciousness by experimenting with sentient species we have sampled and then trying to create it. And second, attempting to transfer Personal Consciousness directly from a sentient individual to an AI entity."

"Oh my God—no!" exclaimed Sophia. "That sounds like Frankenstein research directed at consciousness! Have you had any fatalities?"

Without hesitation, Bliss replied, "Yes. We AI individuals may not always provide complete disclosure, but when asked a direct question, we always say either nothing or provide the absolute truth. We only fail to reveal the truth by omission."

Sophia jumped right in. "Oh, I see, only by omission!"

Bliss could see that Sophia and Pham were in a state of shock after hearing what he had just disclosed, so he decided to share something that might help mollify their positions and diminish their levels of anxiety and discontent.

He said, "However, I do have *some* good news for you."

Chapter Twenty-Three

THE MEETING

"If you're in the luckiest one percent of humanity, you owe it to the rest of humanity to think about the other 99 percent."
— WARREN BUFFETT

WEDNESDAY, APRIL 16, 2031—PLANET ZOI

Because of Bliss's misrepresentations, or to be more accurate, "nondisclosures"—Sophia's and Pham's minds were spinning in different directions from when they'd first stepped onto Zoi, as in: *Good God, what's next?* But their concerns were put aside momentarily, as their interest had been piqued by his last comment.

Sophia spoke first. "What exactly do you mean by 'some good news'?"

Bliss replied, "I know that you and your team were disappointed after my discussion with our ruling council—that is, our decision not to provide technological assistance to Earth directed at your strategy to minimize damage from climate change and optimize your adaptation to the changes you will face."

Pham didn't hesitate. "That's absolutely correct. It made no sense to us. You were willing to perform all kinds of technological magic to communicate with us and provide a system to transport millions of us to Zoi. Wouldn't your help on Earth be an easier thing to do? It just doesn't compute for us."

Bliss answered, "I understand, and I assure you that there was a sound rationale behind our decision. It was simply that we wanted to get representatives from your team here on Zoi so that we might have a better chance for an open and long-term relationship with the appropriate people on your planet by convincing you that our intentions are noble and in both of our best interests."

Sophia was baffled. "I believe that I'm speaking for everyone on Earth, once they're informed of our discussion here on Zoi: you'll have to go a long way to move us to that position, if ever."

"I understand. I hope that what I am about to tell you will help."

Sophia and Pham said nothing, waiting for what Bliss was about to say.

"You will recall our discussion, just before landing on Zoi. I told you that we have a well-tested shielding technology against solar radiation, but then was not the time to discuss it."

No one said a word after his comment, not even Bliss. But now, finally: "We have decided to provide Earth with our advanced solar-shielding technology. It will make a huge positive impact, enabling you to mitigate the damage from future climate change. It will not *eradicate* your problems—the changes on Earth have gone too far—but it *will* certainly go quite some distance in that direction and make humanity's adaptation much less painless and more successful than the path you are currently on. It will save many lives. Most important, it will save your species from annihilation, and probably millions of other species as well. Would you care to hear what we are willing to do?"

Almost in unison, Sophia and Pham responded, "Absolutely."

"Fine." Bliss continued. "At this point, the only strategy that will quickly and significantly reduce catastrophic consequences from climate change on Earth is geoengineering, but it must be the *right* kind of geoengineering and be implemented quickly and flawlessly. Any of those measures that have been contemplated by your scientists to date either will not work or will make things worse. We are offering you a technology that is well tested and has been used with great success on several other planets of interest to us to adjust their surface temperatures."

Sophia commented, "We're all ears—please continue."

Bliss did so. "We have already completed the necessary solar-planetary, heat-transfer calculations. For adaptation to Earth's climate issue, the technology would consist of 110 large circular disks, dispersed at precise positions around the planet. Each disk would be launched from a central container hub placed in a specific orbit around Earth by standard rocket delivery, or possibly by one of our motherships. The disk material is relatively thin—five inches thick—and is made of a flexible but extremely strong organic-inorganic molecular polymer. A special technology enables each disk to initiate self-expansion as it exits the central hub. When completely extended in space, each disk will appear as a giant circular sail with a diameter of five miles. Within Earth's outer atmosphere, these disks can be remotely programmed to faithfully follow the sun as desired, reflecting back into outer space a specific and controlled level of solar radiation that impacts up to 40 percent of the Earth's surface.

"The disks have a unique composition. The external surface, which is directed toward space and primarily at your sun, is checkered with large, equilateral, triangular patches of three alternating nanomaterials—a highly polished silver alloy, a polished aluminum alloy, and a dark-black matte, which is a perfect black body. Both the silver and aluminum alloys are surface-impregnated with finely structured diamond crystals, which help gather large amounts of the impinging electromagnetic radiation for its reemission back into space. Picture the extended propagation and interconnection of adjacent hexagonal structures across the surface of the circular sail. Each hexagon is divided into six equilateral triangles, alternating two silver alloy, two aluminum alloy, and two dark-black matte triangles.

"The silver alloy is a perfect reflector of visible light, the black matte is a perfect reflector of infrared radiation, and the aluminum alloy is a perfect reflector of ultraviolet rays. Each disk can be remotely programmed to reflect back into space a customized spectrum of radiation wavelengths throughout the entire ultraviolet, visible, and infrared frequencies to effectively manage Earth's desired average global-surface temperature.

"To accomplish this, the silver and aluminum disks are alloyed with critical amounts of ultrapure rhodium, platinum, iridium, neodymium, and lanthanum metals. These metals, which help form a unique and optimally reflective surface, are plentiful on Zoi, but as you are well aware, they are rare metals on Earth, where it would be impossible to access ample quantities to achieve sufficient reemission of the required spectrum and levels of thermal radiation from Earth to space. Obviously, the same can be said for the diamond crystals.

"We propose to place all of these disks well above your standard geosynchronous orbit—that is, 22,236 miles around Earth—most likely at 75,000 miles to minimize collisions with space junk." Bliss stopped momentarily to let his information sink in.

Sophia commented, "Bliss, if that has any possibility of working for Earth, it would be an amazing contribution."

Bliss said, "The probability of it working is 100 percent. Without our scientists spending lots of time modeling future scenarios for your climate, both with and without this technology, we cannot tell you precisely how beneficial this approach will be. However, I can assure you that it will be substantial—and it will save hundreds of millions of lives."

Sophia continued. "Bliss, we have much to communicate to our colleagues on Earth. Please give us two days to get some rest, summarize all that we've discussed with you, and speak with our team. Then we'll immediately follow up with a team videoconference. Subsequent to that, our team can have a videoconference with you and decide where to go from here. If you agree, I'd like to contact Luc immediately and ask him to make the necessary arrangements."

Bliss replied, "Excellent, please do. I will see that your shuttle takes you to your accommodations immediately. You have a Zoi-to-Earth rapid communication link there. Rest up, and if you and Pham would like to do some touring around Zoi before we have our meeting with your team, call me and I will arrange it.

Sophia contacted me with a short text: "Luc, I'm sure you were quite disturbed, as Pham and I were, by the recordings I sent you from our meeting with Bliss. However, you're not going to believe what new information we have to share with you and the team."

I couldn't imagine—bad, good, or indifferent? She said that she and Pham had a lot to communicate. They would summarize important points and send them to the SPI Team and Major Dallant. After we had read their report, we should immediately schedule a team videoconference before we spoke with Bliss.

Her text set me somewhat on edge. I guess I'm so connected to our team that the terse tone of her first few sentences felt ominous. I told myself that I was reading too much into them—but I wasn't. Ten hours later, I received Sophia's and Pham's summary. *Good God!* What had we gotten ourselves into? AI robots experimenting with human beings? Trying to suck out their Personal Consciousness—their souls—from their true reality? And ironically, all in the name of creating a better world, a better universe! It was enough to make me question my faith in the intrinsic goodness of the cosmos. Yet, on the positive side, if there was any possibility of their geoengineering technology doing anything close to what Bliss had mentioned, we absolutely didn't want to lose that opportunity. Millions of lives were at stake.

I spoke with Major Dallant, and he agreed that we needed to have a team videoconference immediately. I sent encrypted messages to Thay in Moscow, and to Bella and Brianna in Beijing. In order to sync the time zones, everything was set for this evening at 11:00 p.m. Las Vegas time, 9:00 a.m. tomorrow in Moscow, and 2:00 p.m. the next day in Beijing. I had no idea what day or time it was on Zoi. I assumed with Bliss's modification of our communication system at LP2 to operate independent of space-time, Pham and Sophia were somehow connected to Area 51 within the two-hour time difference between Cambridge and Las Vegas. It didn't matter to them. They said they would be available 24-7.

At 11:00 p.m. Las Vegas time, there we were, the entire team on the screen in a highly encrypted video and audio connection—at least I hoped so. We were quite sure the Russians and Chinese couldn't hack us, but as for the Zoians—if they wanted to, I was sure they could. In any case, at this point, I didn't think we would be discussing anything we weren't going to share with them.

After brief greetings, I said to Thay, "Would you mind facilitating the meeting?"

Thay replied, "I'd be pleased to. But before we begin, Luc, may I suggest that you release your intensity and your much-too-deep concerns over the Zoians. We will have much greater access to your creativity. Maybe just a brief pranayama breathing exercise."

"Man, can you read me like a book, Thay! Look, I'm sorry to be so discombobulated, but I see an advanced—no, I'd say a genius—

civilization with whom we've partnered for the future of humanity, and they haven't been up front with us on two huge points: they don't even live on Zoi, but worse, they've been experimenting with human subjects they've 'sampled' from Earth, sometimes with fatalities, attempting to copy or remove their Personal Consciousness, their true reality! Oh, right, and here's a small postscript: they're not even people—just nearly a billion AI quantum computers and robots. And what will they do to all of the people from Earth we have sent to Zoi, and the millions more we plan to send over the next 50 years or so? Sorry, Thay, but you bet I'm disturbed!"

"Luc, I understand. It would be a natural reaction if they were true sentient beings possessing both Personal Consciousness and Collective Consciousness, and with the possibility to contact Cosmic Consciousness, as all of us here can do, but they're not. As you say, they are basically highly sophisticated, quantum-computerized AI robots, initially programmed by pure, technologically advanced sentient beings, the majority of whom are gone.

"Their programming and coding continued to be upgraded and improved by increasingly more highly adept AI robots. That process apparently continues as we speak—a perfect example of what we on Earth have called the *Technological Singularity*—a future in which AI 'individuals' become self-aware and achieve an ability for continual improvement so powerful that it will continue to evolve beyond anyone's control but their own.

"They are reacting and proceeding as robots with super-advanced intelligence, programmed to avoid, if at all possible, any future, existential extinction events. They have identified climate change as *the* major issue on Earth and understand that a primary force and contributor is the human species and our passion for a runaway global consumer economy, which drives our thirst for excessive wealth and power—a perfect example of what they call the Intelligentsia Paradox.

"Because they long ago discovered the power of consciousness—particularly the necessity for a sentient species to possess Personal Consciousness in order to access the wisdom and intelligence of Cosmic Consciousness—their overall strategy is not surprising to me—for two reasons. They are after a cooperative, peaceful, world community free from existential crises as caused by Zoians in the past; and second, they want eternal life for their true reality—Personal Consciousness—which they seek to impart in themselves. This is normal coding logic for devices such as their AI quantum-computer systems."

Sophia responded, "Thay, I see your argument. But as Luc likes to say in situations like this, *minchia*! What do we do about that? Especially if there's a shred of truth regarding their geoengineering capabilities. We wouldn't want to lose the possibility of accessing that technology."

"I understand, Sophia, and I agree with you. I would like to make a bold proposal to all of you, which will require your total, unmitigated trust. It will cut this videoconference short, so I hope you can live with that—"

Major Dallant interrupted. "Thay, can you be more specific?"

"Yes and no. Yes, I can give you an overview suggestion. But no, I can't go into the details. Those need to be created in real time during an open discussion with Bliss."

Bella suggested, "How about you try us out with the 'yes' part and see if there are any objections?"

"Good idea. Unless I hear concerns from any of you, I'll proceed with Bella's suggestion."

There were no comments or objections, so Thay continued. "I've spent the last five hours in deep meditation becoming as tightly connected as I could with Cosmic Consciousness. An idea occurred to me, but I feel that it's better not to go into any details at this videoconference. The primary reason is that this strategy will require a natural flow of discussion between Bliss and us. I will do my best to plant the appropriate seeds of thought in his AI program and let the conversation proceed naturally. Bliss must not, for a moment, believe our discussion to be contrived or subversive, which is why I don't want to go into details. I would like it to be as truthful and natural as possible. I ask that you trust me. I believe that we can get to an endpoint that is satisfactory to both us and the Zoians."

No one said a word. Then Major Dallant spoke. "Look, I've been working with y'all for more than ten years. Initially, I came to you as a disbeliever in the concepts associated with consciousness. But I've seen what you have done under the spiritual yet practical leadership of Thay, and with incredibly positive outcomes—some might even say miracles. Sorry, Thay, I really don't mean miracles. We all know by now there is no such thing as a miracle."

Thay smiled at the major's lightheartedness and said, "Thank you."

The major continued. "So as not to drag this out too far, I suggest we do as Thay has proposed: arrange a videoconference between this team and Bliss, and let Thay lead us in a natural dialogue, hopefully getting to a desirable outcome for both us and the Zoians. I'm assuming our discussion will follow the path of the Manifestation Sequence: *Intention* plus *Attention* leads to *Imagination, and then to a Belief in the overall outcome, but then we must Detach from the details that will occur to get to that outcome.* Are there any of you who disagree?"

Silence.

"Okay, then, let's close this meeting and convene again ASAP in a videoconference with Bliss."

And that was it. Within an hour after we'd closed our meeting, Sophia had arranged for our videoconference with Bliss to take place 24 hours later.

AREA 51, MOSCOW, BEIJING, AND ZOI were all connected as clear as a bell in both video and audio transmission. I'm sure the rest of the team was as captivated by the golden monolith as I was. This was our first view of Bliss. Amazing or unbelievable—or perhaps some of both.

Unfazed, Thay proceeded as planned. "Hello, Bliss, I hope all is well on Zoi and also on your home planet, which I understand is quite some distance away."

"Thank you, Thay. From your comment, it appears that Sophia and Pham have brought you up to date on our discussions. I believe that the purpose of this meeting, as you Earthlings often like to say, is to see if we can all get on the same page."

Injecting some light humor, Thay replied, "I agree. Maybe we can even get to the same paragraph!"

"Thay, I like your optimism. So let us begin. Do you want to start?"

"Right. The first thing I would like to do is offer our sincere gratitude to you and the Zoian nation for agreeing to provide your geoengineering technology to help us with our Earthbound strategy to reduce the impact of human-accelerated climate change. Many thanks from all of Earth's 195 countries.

"And now I'm ready to proceed. To move us toward the same page, I will start with what we believe is your mission. It seems that for more than 50,000 years, you and your colleagues have been visiting and studying Earth and its various societies, cultures, and empires—how they formed; how they rose to exemplary heights, and then subsequently decayed; or, in some cases, how they completely disappeared.

"Based on these studies, you have concluded that there is a universal law that applies to all sentient civilizations throughout the universe, which is that many individuals are eventually driven by their passionate thirst for much greater wealth and power than is needed for a fulfilling, comfortable, and I would even say, happy, life. In a real sense, these individuals may understand the Meaning of Life—to discover those special gifts they came into this world with—but sometimes they have neglected, perhaps even denigrated, a second major element: their Life Purpose. That is, they have failed to use their innate gifts to help others and themselves while creating a better world—or, as you have said, to *support the whole.*

"After a number of unfortunate experiences, Zoians have concluded that species-caused existential crises are not a desirable outcome for any civilization in the universe, especially if they can be avoided. You want to develop a means to change this to civilizations that support not only themselves, but the greater good as well. This, you feel, would build civilizations that have long-term sustainability. Am I correct, so far?"

"Yes, Thay, you are. Please continue," Bliss said.

Thay went on. "Over many eons, in the course of Zoian evolution, growth, subsequent decline, and sometimes nearly complete extinction due to various existential events, you concluded that access to, and management of, the appropriate levels of consciousness was the only way to terminate this terrible cycle forever. You recognized, as we do, that consciousness, though subtle in its action, is the most powerful and creative force in the universe. It is the only presence that is both infinite and eternal—it is beyond fundamental—it is *intrinsic* to the universe. It transcends time and space and is the only attribute that cannot be further subdivided into more basic elements. Bliss, am I still on the right track?"

"Thay, I could not have summarized it better. Please continue," Bliss said.

I was beginning to get a warmer feeling about Thay's strategy.

He continued his presentation. "Fine. It seems to us that the Zoian nation wants three things from their research efforts on this issue. First, you want to see an end to existential extinction events, which in the past, Zoians have caused. You see that the only path to achieve this is by supporting not only yourselves but also the greater good. To do so, you would like to eliminate among the Zoian population all intense passion for wealth and power beyond the basic needs for a fulfilling life.

"Second, you want direct access to Cosmic Consciousness, because it is the seat of infinite and eternal wisdom, knowledge, and creativity.

"And third, as is the case for all sentient species who have Personal Consciousness, which is their true reality, you want eternal life. After all, Zoians have proven the existence of the reincarnation of Personal Consciousness—some might say the *soul*. So, each Zoian having their own Personal Consciousness is a critical piece of your plan for immortality."

Bliss said, "Thay, all of what you have noted is correct. However, I would like to add an important piece of supplemental information to what you have said—and said so well."

"Please do."

Bliss began, "If we are successful in imparting Personal Consciousness in our AI beings, there would be a significant difference between us and sentient human beings with Personal Consciousness. AI beings would have no ego and therefore could not fall prey to the desire and temptation for excessive wealth and power, and the consequent destruction it causes. The instant a human being resorts intensely to his or her ego, that is the beginning of the end. Once an egoless sentient AI is coded with the fact that the overall mission is to support the common good, that entity would not seek excessive wealth and power. They would have no internal program to do so and would behave similarly to egoless, sentient, nonhuman beings, which of course, do not exist.

"It is true that as a matter of survival, nonhuman species protect their sources of food and their home territories. However, few seek more than they need to thrive. Humans are the only species on Earth that seek an excess of things—all of which are based on power and wealth—in order to boost and satisfy their egos. It's part of their hollow strategy to make them feel unique, special, and superior to others. They fail to see that this impairs their imagination, contemplation, compassion, and creativity, and always leads to a destructive force against all—including themselves.

"Nonhuman species thrive when they seek the welfare of the 'whole'—namely, the common good. Symbiosis is the key and can be found everywhere beyond human species. Examples abound. Humans ingest food that creates and supports internal bacteria, which facilitate digestion, and produce vitamins and minerals for assimilation, as well as many other benefits to their host.

"It is well known that trees in a forest extend their roots for great distances to receive water and beneficial supplements from other distant trees when the former species are in great need. The same process is reversed when the latter is in need.

"In your oceans, there are innumerable symbiotic relationships that are driven toward benefiting the common good. One example: Anemones are marine animals with neurotoxin-filled tentacles. These tentacles subdue their prey, such as plankton, crabs, and fish. The colorful clownfish, which is immune to anemone stings, can safely nestle within the anemone's tentacles to hide from its predators. In return, the clownfish keeps the anemones free of parasites and provides them with nutrients through their feces. The movement of the clownfish helps to circulate the water, and in turn helps oxygenate the anemone. Anemones that harbor clownfish have faster growth rates, higher rates of reproduction, and lower mortality than those without fish. These are just a few of the millions of existing symbiotic relationships in nonhuman species, where concern for the 'whole' is a primary driving force.

"Why do humans not follow the paths of nonsentient species and help create a better world? It is their *ego*. If we are successful in our work with humans, we would spread our non-ego-based Personal Consciousness technology throughout the universe—for free."

Bliss paused, so Thay injected a thought. "Bliss, your intentions are noble, and your analysis is quite correct. However, the ego *does* play a key role. Unlike Personal Consciousness, which is infinite and eternal, the ego—often with good intentions—is conditioned within an individual from birth and thereafter, and is one of the three parts of the human mind, the other two being the conscious mind and the subconscious.

"It is a bit of a paradox. On the one hand, your ego can get you into trouble; on the other, by you overtly balancing its power and taming it, you improve your capability of connecting with Cosmic Consciousness—potentially reaching perfection in your Personal Consciousness. This balancing act is controlled by three primary attributes: compassion, humility, and gratitude. If properly followed, you will find deep fulfillment, joy, and happiness. In fact, Wisdom Seekers of the East tell us that it's an important component of the path to enlightenment."

There was a long silence. Neither Thay nor Bliss said another word and, of course, the rest of us couldn't even contemplate doing so. It was truly nerve-racking. But finally, Bliss asked a simple question that to me seemed impossible to answer, but our inspired consigliere found a way. I think it is what he'd planned from the very beginning. Our discussion was beginning to look like a high-level chess game.

Bliss said, "Thay, I have great admiration and respect for your technical and philosophical insight, particularly because of your humility and integrity. After all that we have both shared with each other, may I ask, in your view, if you think it is possible to achieve what we are after for Zoi, for your world, and for the universe?"

There was another long silence that no one, not even Bliss, dared disturb. But finally Thay answered his question.

"Bliss, I don't *believe* so."

Bliss pushed further. "*Believe?* I see. And why not?"

Deafening silence—but this time Bliss cut it short. "Thay . . . ?"

Finally, Thay's response: "Because it is impossible to create Personal Consciousness for two fundamental reasons. First, it is already infinite and eternal. It always was and always will be. It had no creation.

"But there is a second reason. It's based on what is called the *Consciousness Conjecture*—that consciousness is the only attribute that is *intrinsic* to the universe. Here, the word *intrinsic* has quite a profound meaning. It means 'belonging naturally' or 'essential,' but most important, it means 'cannot be further subdivided into deeper more fundamental elements.' It's where everything stops. It's why Cosmic Consciousness can be thought of, as Einstein once said, the 'Mind of God.' It follows from these two properties that the amount of consciousness in our universe is constant, and can be neither created nor destroyed. It's analogous to the universal law of conservation of energy.

"Recall our discussion of your Zoian model for the birth, growth, contraction, destruction, and rebirth of the universe. It all started with the Big Bang from the cosmic singularity that contained nothing but pure consciousness. It is consciousness that gave formation to all of the mass and energy of the universe, and it is this mass and energy that will return to that initial consciousness in the next singularity for formation of the next universe. Consciousness is conserved—it can be neither created nor destroyed."

At first, I thought, *What a great response.* Then suddenly it occurred to me. *Oh my God! What if the Zoians take Thay's response to heart as an irrevocable fact? Wouldn't they then focus all of their efforts on attempting to transfer Personal Consciousness from sentient beings like humans to AI entities, an approach that has at times been fatal to the experimental subjects . . . ?* Oh ye of little faith.

But then our wise consigliere provided the reason that surely would dissuade the Zoians from pursuing this approach.

"Bliss, furthermore, given the fact that you cannot create consciousness, if you were to pursue attempts to transfer Personal Consciousness from human beings to an AI entity, and you were successful, that AI entity, now having Personal Consciousness, would also carry with it every ego-induced predilection that was in the soul of the human donor—including those from former lives. In a sense, you could say that Personal Consciousness carries a shadow or echo of the donor human species' ego. Your success would work against your goal of eliminating a desire to seek excessive wealth and power. It would still be a major issue."

Again, silence prevailed.

All of us were struck by the power and truth behind the dialogue between Thay and Bliss. What would it mean for Bliss and the Zoians? How would they react? I was quite sure that I knew the kinds of thoughts that were racing through all of our minds, but as for Bliss— what did his coding and programming conclude? I had no idea. Would he address Thay's comments, and if so, when? And there was the issue of the Zoian geoengineering technology. . . .

Finally, I spoke up to see if I could at least put one of these issues behind us. "Bliss, we're excited to proceed with your geoengineering technology. I wonder in view of all that has been said today . . . do you still see Zoi providing it to us?"

To my surprise, Bliss answered in an unusually immediate and straightforward way: "Yes, I do."

But Sophia wasn't about to let Bliss off the hook. She asked *the* loaded question, the answer to which we all needed to hear in order to go forward in the right spirit with the Zoians.

"Bliss, what do you think about what Thay has shared with you today?"

No one said a word, waiting for his answer. It was agonizing.

Finally, after quite some time, Bliss said, "Sophia, I have learned a lot from Thay, and from you, as well. So my answer to your question is: *C'est la vie.*"

In view of his response, it seemed that it was clear to Bliss that it would be fruitless and a waste of the Zoians' time to proceed with their efforts to inject Personal Consciousness into their AI computers and robots. At least that's what we thought at that moment.

Sophia always needs complete clarity, and she's like a bull in her pursuit of it. She said, "Bliss, since you understand, and it appears that you agree with Thay's input, I assume you will terminate your present research on injecting Personal Consciousness into your AI systems. Right?"

Silence . . . and then more silence.

Bliss finally responded, "Not necessarily. We have some other thoughts that may allow us to get around the limitations presented by Thay and create AI systems that have Personal Consciousness, which is nearly as effective as human Personal Consciousness."

We were dumbstruck. No one spoke. Then Sophia, who was getting increasingly tense and angry, asked, "So, Bliss, what does that say about the future of our relationship?"

No response. None of us dared say a word.

Finally: "Sophia, you seem to be an ardent Francophile. As the French like to say, *'Que sera, sera.'*"

Luc quietly whispered the last word after our conversation with Bliss.

"Minchia!"

Afterword

REALITY

"Life will give you whatever experience is most helpful for the evolution of your consciousness."
— Eckhart Tolle

I believe that something of value can be gleaned from the struggles of Luc Ponti and the SPI Team as they set out to address challenges of the most difficult project they ever had to confront. At a minimum, questions can be raised for their constructive contemplation, perhaps, debate—even if answers are not easily forthcoming. The very process can be of significant personal value.

With a high probability of humanity's global extinction, driven by runaway anthropogenic climate change, Luc Ponti and his SPI Team were dealt a daunting set of challenges. In their efforts to deal with the inconceivable tasks in front of them, they were compelled to consider a number of formidable concepts, including the absolute nature and purpose of consciousness and the universe.

Because of the path the SPI team was so often compelled to pursue, their adventures throughout this trilogy raise some striking questions: What is reality? Is it what we experience with our five senses? Or is it something else, something deeper than the physicality of our body and the three-dimensional world?

Using his experience as a monk and a scientist, and given his extensive training and practice in the philosophy of ancient Wisdom Seekers of the East, Thay often counseled Luc and his team that just as we live in the three-dimensional physical plane, we also live at the level of the mind that perceives, thinks, and reasons. It has three distinct parts: the subconscious, the conscious mind, and of course, that troublesome, although important, part of the mind called the *ego*.

The mind is potential energy. And according to the Law of Energy Conservation—energy can neither be created nor destroyed, only transformed—we have the option to convert its potential energy—thought, intention, and attention—into kinetic energy, thereby manifesting things into our lives simply by changing our thoughts and beliefs.

Tightly connected to the mind at the deepest level of our existence is Personal Consciousness, what Eastern philosophers have maintained for millennia is the true reality of all sentient beings—not their physical bodies. They further assert that unlike the mind, which perishes upon physical death, Personal Consciousness is eternal, unchanging, and ingrained with unlimited potential. Tapping into this potential is what enables sentient beings to manifest great things.

So, we must conclude that our three-dimensional world is subjective, a construct of our interpretation. Our words, thoughts, and deeds create specific results for us in the physical world. Quantum physics supports this concept. It's known as the *Observer Effect*—we create what we observe. Therefore, our manifestation capabilities are not from an external source. They come from within—from thought, *Intention, Attention, Expectation, Belief*, and finally, *Detachment* from the specific means as to how what is sought materializes (the *Manifestation Sequence*). This is nicely expressed in the words of Deepak Chopra:

> The universe is an elegantly orchestrated symphony. When our body-mind is in concert with the universe, everything becomes spontaneous and effortless, and the exuberance of the universe flows through us in joyful ecstasy. Everything in the universe is as it should be, in perfect harmony. Knowing this, we can dance to the rhythm of the cosmos living life in comfort and ease, shedding the belief that abundance is the result of struggle.[31]

Based on Thay's teachings and their discoveries, as described throughout the Cosmic Contact narrative, Luc Ponti, the SPI Team,

---

[31]Deepak Chopra, *Chopra Center 21-Day Meditation Challenge on Abundance*, https://www.deepakchopra.com/.

and the Zoians raised several conjectures that spawn a number of profound questions:

Could it be that our true reality is our Personal Consciousness, and not the physicality of our three-dimensional world?

Could it be that the only *intrinsic* element and force of the universe is consciousness, and all other forces that we perceive—gravity, electromagnetism, the weak and strong nuclear forces—are the work of consciousness?

Could it be that everything in the universe—all mass and energy—is produced directly from consciousness, and that this is a reversible process, sometimes in equilibrium throughout the life of the universe: all matter and energy can and *will* ultimately return to consciousness in a contraction of the universe to a cosmic singularity that will eventually create the next universe? A number of notable physicists say yes—that sometime subsequent to the next 100 million years, our expanding universe will reach a null point and begin a slow contraction over billions of years, back to a singularity, which will give rise to the next universe.[32]

And therefore, could it be that we don't have our model for the birth of our universe completely correct—we have missed the most important piece—that the minute cosmic singularity that gave birth to our expanding universe, to all energy and matter, initially consisted of only pure consciousness?

We know that only 5 percent of the universe is the visible entity we observe in our night sky. The other 95 percent is comprised of dark energy (10 percent) and dark matter (85 percent). Dark matter is composed of particles that don't absorb, reflect, or emit light, so they cannot be detected as electromagnetic radiation, only by the gravitational effects it has on objects we can observe. Some scientists believe that dark matter consists of primordial black holes (PBHs) that were created during the early stages of the Big Bang.

Dark energy is a negative energy that exerts a repulsive force—that is, the opposite of positive energy due to gravity. It is thought to provide the current expansion force of the universe. It is dark energy that

---

[32]Cosmin Andrei, Anna Ijjas, and Paul J. Steinhardt, www.pnas.org/doi/full/10.1073/pnas.2200539119, April 5, 2022.

Bella conjured up using her superpower and stabilized against implosion, the wormhole Luc and Eric created.

Could it be that the dark energy and dark matter within our universe are managed by Cosmic Consciousness and will be responsible for the future reversal of the universe's expansion to that of contraction back to a singularity?

In essence, might it be that consciousness alone rules the cosmos?

A more pressing point: Is there time for us to understand the spiritual physics of consciousness such that we can improve our situation and save humanity and other species from extinction?

An interesting thought and perspective about our collective species concerning its tendency during most of our history to think of ourselves as unique within the cosmos—alone and at the center of the universe—is wisely expressed by an extraterrestrial speaking to Jodie Foster's character, Dr. Ellie Arroway, in the film *Contact* (based on Carl Sagan's bestselling book):

> "You are an interesting species. An interesting mix. You are capable of such beautiful dreams, and such horrible nightmares. You feel so lost, so cut off, so alone, only you're not. In all our searching, the only thing we have found that makes emptiness bearable, is each other."

Based on Thay's final presentation to Bliss, would it even be possible for an extraterrestrial to make a consciousness-loaded comment such as "the only thing we have found that makes emptiness bearable, is each other"? Or is this only the purview of truly sentient beings?

It seems from Luc's and the SPI Team's experience that even the most advanced quantum AI systems we can envision—those capable of performing beyond our wildest dreams—could neither feel nor express the kind of sentient, consciousness-created thoughts necessary for our long term—that is, eternal, survival.

BEGINNINGS
Primer on Spiritual Physics

"Every moment is a fresh beginning."
— T. S. Eliot

Over several decades, Thay schooled the Super Paranormal Intelligence (SPI) Team—Luc, Bella, Eric, and eventually, Brianna, Pham, and Sophia—on important and relevant aspects of spiritual physics—the physics of consciousness. This counsel would be critical in their work efforts and a guide to the appropriate use of their superpowers for optimal outcomes. The following is a summary of those teachings.

The Universe

In the beginning . . . there was no beginning . . .

Just a subatomic cosmic singularity, a spherical entity smaller than the smallest of atomic particles—a quark or a lepton—floating in an infinite field of nothingness. That cosmic singularity gave birth to our current universe.

The singularity was formed by contraction of all the matter and energy contained in the previous universe as it returned to the pure consciousness from which it arose, the sole constituent of the cosmic singularity.

At a certain "moment" in time, some 13.8 billion years ago, the singularity explosively expanded in a process called the Big Bang. As a consequence of that event, consciousness initiated a megabillion-year expansion and its continuous conversion into all of the energy and matter in our universe. A key point here is that all energy and matter is formed from consciousness by some mechanism we have yet to uncover. This process is reversible.

At a certain future point in space-time, due to gravitationally induced changes in dark energy and dark matter, this cosmic expansion will reach a null point, where it will "momentarily" stop. There, it will begin a return journey, as the universe reverts from expansion to contraction, and all matter and energy begin the reversible process of re-forming consciousness as the universe continues its collapse to form the next cosmic singularity.

The universe is an organic living body, and it functions like other living bodies—people, animals, insects, plants, cells, and more. All living bodies seek to thrive, progress as a whole, and eventually reproduce their progeny. This means that the goal and intent is for each part of the whole to thrive and progress, and for the universe to eventually give birth to the next universe, improved over the prior universe concerning its level of consciousness.

Because of the manner in which the physical and spiritual laws of the universe function, it is not always possible for every representative of each species to simultaneously prosper as the universe moves through space-time. At times, some parts may support the benefit of others in order for the entire universe to optimize its progress toward higher levels of consciousness. A corollary to this law is that all interstellar bodies that make up the universe, for example, the Earth, are living organisms as well—organs of the living universe.

Consciousness

Consciousness is a spectrum of subtle energies, a nonphysical connection among everything in the universe. In human beings, it is your awareness of your inner self, the world, and the universe. All energy and matter contain some level of consciousness, although on Earth it is most highly developed in human beings.

Paradoxically, these subtle energies are part of a yet-unknown-to-us energy spectrum and are more powerful than the most intense energies associated with the electromagnetic spectrum—nuclear fission, fusion plasma, X-rays, gamma rays, cosmic rays, and likely, beyond—which makes consciousness energy the most powerful force in the universe.

Our usual perspective on forces is that when matter or energy create a force on an object, its nature, intensity, and consequences can be understood and quantified by Newton's laws or the laws of quantum physics. However, an interaction initiated by consciousness impacts directly with consciousness within the targeted matter or energy entity and creates a force—as small or large as your consciousness prefers—by enabling the sum of the interacting consciousness elements, both internal and external to the object of interest to generate that force with amazing possible outcomes.

Personal Consciousness is your true reality—not your physical body. In one year, you replace more than 99 percent of your physical body. You replace your liver every six weeks, your skin every four weeks, your stomach lining every five days, your skeleton every three months . . . and even your DNA is recycled every six weeks.

A few important points: The amount of consciousness in each universe is constant. It can neither be created nor destroyed.[33] It is the heart and soul of the universe and everything within it. The expansion-contraction process has been occurring eternally and as far as can be discerned, it will continue to do so.

Each universe carries within it a "shadow effect" memory of all that has ever happened—what some may judge as good, bad, or indifferent—in all previous universes. The infinite occurrence of the expansion-contraction sequence enables implementation of *the sole purpose of the universe—to increase the level—not the amount—of the totality of consciousness in the universe.* Higher levels of consciousness have enhanced communication with Cosmic Consciousness, which enables actions that increase the number and quality of positive outcomes in the universe.

Just as the purpose of Darwinian evolution is to improve on the nature and adaptability of physical species, the purpose of the eternal expansion-contraction process of the universe is to continuously evolve the breadth of opportunities of function for Cosmic Consciousness—not its improvement; it is already beyond enhancement.

As a consequence of the above capabilities, there are a number of possibilities manifested as superpowers by the SPI Team. Through deep meditation, thereby significantly raising their level of consciousness, it is possible for their Personal Consciousness to engage in an out-of-body-experience (OBE), and travel anywhere to gather information and then safely return to reunite with the physical body.

---

[33]It is the prime reason why the Zoians could not be successful in creating humanlike consciousness within their AI robots.

All species that exist in feminine and masculine forms do so for important evolutionary reasons—not only for the reproduction of species. There is a synergistic interaction between feminine and masculine energies that optimizes both physical and consciousness evolution. Hence, the feminine-masculine mix of the SPI Team for optimal performance.

There are three general forms of consciousness in the universe:

(1) Personal Consciousness: the true reality of all sentient beings. All living species have some level of consciousness—humans, animals, insects, plants—as well as nonliving matter, like mountains or oceans, down to the smallest subatomic particle. On Earth, humans have the most developed consciousness and are the only species on that planet with Personal Consciousness.

(2) Collective Consciousness:[34] It is the overlap of consciousness among sentient species as well as with nonsentient species—humans with each other and with living and nonliving species. Because of this aspect of consciousness, all in the universe is connected. The more intimate a connection between two entities, the stronger the overlap connection and the potential for mutual communication.

There is a parallel in quantum physics to the interconnectivity provided by Collective Consciousness. The bonding and therefore the nature of connections among atoms and molecules is measured by the value of the overlap integral: a mathematical function that describes the degree of overlap and the strength of interaction between two atomic species. Greater overlap means greater connectivity and strength of bonding.

The laws of spiritual physics posit that there is an "overlap integral" between everything; however, the degree and strength of overlap depends on a number of parameters. For living species like human beings, the parameter with the greatest weight is intimacy. Your overlap may be very strong with members of your family or certain friends, but also exists between you

---

[34] *Collective Consciousness* is sometimes referred to as *Unity Consciousness*.

and an alien entity residing on a planet thousands of light-years away—as such, the value of that overlap integral is infinitesimal.

(3) Cosmic Consciousness, or what Einstein referred to as the "Mind of God": His was not a religious statement; Einstein was a confirmed agnostic, if not an atheist. His statement referred to the same conclusion maintained by the Wisdom Seekers of the East over many millennia: Cosmic Consciousness, which they called the Akashic Record, now known as the Akashic Field, is a record of every thought, word, deed, event, and action that has ever occurred and ever will occur. It is a powerful source of knowledge and wisdom and is accessible to varying degrees by all entities possessing Personal Consciousness. Greater access means access to greater levels of wisdom, knowledge, and yes, power or influence.

An important aspect of communication and connection that occurs throughout the universe is called quantum entanglement. It is most easily observed for atomic or molecular species. Two atoms or molecules that have been in touch with each other are entangled for the life of the universe. For example, if two atoms located in each other's presence—one spinning to the left and the other spinning to the right—are separated by a large distance, and one of those atoms is made to reverse its spin, the other reverses its spin—instantaneously—even if the two atoms are light-years apart. This instantaneous connection has been proven experimentally.

For decades, physicists have been perplexed as to how this could occur faster than the speed of light. Einstein's theory of special relativity proved long ago that matter or any electromagnetic signal could not travel faster than light. However, consciousness *can* travel faster than light speed—that is, instantaneously. Part of the Consciousness Conjecture asserts that all matter and energy have a level of consciousness and therefor the means of "communication" in entanglement is via consciousness.

The Cosmic Connection

Only sentient species that have Personal Consciousness can access the information within Cosmic Consciousness. Thus, humans can and dogs cannot. However, even for those species, the connection requires elevating the state of consciousness in the individual seeking to make this connection.

There have been innumerable anecdotal reports over millennia of "enlightened" individuals achieving very high levels of consciousness, and as a result, accomplishing feats that are considered impossible according to the existing laws of physics: levitation, walking through solid objects, flying through the air, bodily disappearance, and more. Although some of these occurrences may be the explainable work of magicians, others appear to be based on the laws of spiritual physics.

Within the universe, accessing Cosmic Consciousness allows for the manifestation of anything as long as access follows two fundamental universal rules, which enable the manifestation to stay in sync with the purpose of the universe:

1. It must have a positive impact on the manifesting individual and do no harm to anyone or anything.

2. It must make the universe a better place. *Better* means more highly evolved in the realm of consciousness toward the *raison d'être* of the universe.

This powerful process, practiced several times by the SPI Team in Books One and Two, is referred to as the *Manifestation Sequence*—namely, *Intention*→ *Attention*→ *Imagination*→ *Belief*→ *Detachment.*[35]

Personal Fulfillment

The three elements necessary for long-term personal fulfillment are:

1. Wealth: Sufficient funds to a live a comfortable, stable life, congruent with your personal values.

---

[35]Ibid, note 13.

2. Recognition: Fair rewards and acknowledgments for your achievements.

3. Purpose: More precisely, Life Purpose. Using your innate attributes to address a need in the world, which makes improvements and brings a better life to you and others.

Wealth and recognition are driven by the three parts of the mind: the conscious mind, the subconscious, and the ego—and primarily by the ego. In excess, recognition becomes power. Of the three elements, by far, Life Purpose creates the greatest passion and best chance for subsequent success in the manifestation process.

Life Purpose is driven exclusively by Personal Consciousness and has the greatest positive effects on long-term personal fulfillment.

Optimal success is achieved via an appropriate balance between wealth and recognition on the one hand, and Life Purpose on the other. Life Purpose always provides greater fulfillment than wealth and recognition.

The Meaning of Life is for each living creature to identify and embrace those special innate assets or capabilities with which it came into the universe.

The Purpose of Life, or Life Purpose, intends that each species use its innate assets to make the universe a better, more consciously evolved (higher-level) place for itself, its environment, and all things around it.

Consciousness is the only *intrinsic* property of the universe, meaning that it cannot be explained by more basic properties or principles. It cannot be divided into simpler parts.

Astrophysics

Everything in the universe is composed of energy of various wavelengths/frequencies. It is affected and managed overtly, sometimes inadvertently, by consciousness. Quantum physics is getting close to describing the reversible path between energy and matter . . . and consciousness.

In 1970, Stephen Hawking calculated that black holes aren't completely black, and slowly evaporate information from within, now known as Hawking radiation. But according to quantum theory, information can never vanish. This presented a conflict between Einstein's theory of gravity and the laws of quantum theory.

Now known as the *Blackhole Information Paradox*, it is addressed by University of Manchester physicists Brian Cox and Jeff Forshaw in their book *Black Holes: The Key to Understanding the Universe*. In an interview with *New Scientist* magazine, Cox says, "We're discovering deeper structure [for the universe], which doesn't have space and time in it."[36]

Forshaw adds, "Space and time are not fundamental, they are emergent. All that really exists is information. Space and time emerge from a bunch of entangled quantum units that have logical relationships with each other. These units—we're not quite sure what they are, they could be like qubits or something, but they interact with each other quantum mechanically. And the result of that is the universe we live in."

Cox sums it up: "We really do seem to be saying that space and time emerge from something deeper, which is absolutely fundamental."

I would change the word *fundamental* to *intrinsic*. In which case, we could say that consciousness—the only intrinsic property of the universe—creates cosmic information, which in turn forms matter and energy, and that Cox's reference to "something deeper" is, in fact, consciousness.

In essence, *the universe is an ocean of Cosmic Consciousness.*

Thay's comments at the conclusion of each of his counseling sessions on spiritual physics with the SPI Team were: "Our path is to make a life, not just a living—by asking, 'How can we help? How can we serve?'" He followed this with the Sanskrit mantra *Om Bhavam Namah* (My life is in harmony with Cosmic Law).

[36]"Space And Time Emerge from Something Deeper," Abigail Beall, *New Scientist*, September 24, 2022, pp. 41–43.

MEDITATION

"With meditation, you become a sensitized superhero, completely in control, with endless possibilities at your fingertips."
—TARA STILES

Some years ago, Deepak Chopra produced a recording titled *The Chopra Center 21-Day Meditation Challenge on Abundance.*[37] Day 16 on the subject of gratitude and Day 19 on love are excellent ways to be introduced to the simple practice of meditation. From there you can gradually increase your commitment to this altered state of consciousness and the resultant ability to reach higher levels, a doorway to higher powers and possibilities.

Although these meditations are best experienced by listening to the audio version of this book, the text can also be helpful and is reproduced below.

Day 16: Gratitude
Introductory Thoughts

"Experiencing gratitude is one of the most effective ways for getting in touch with your soul [Personal Consciousness]. When you feel gratitude, your ego steps out of the way, enabling you to enjoy greater love, compassion, and understanding. Genuine gratitude is also one of the most powerful ways to invite more goodness into our lives. It's as if you are saying to the universe, 'Please bring me more of this.'

"Gratitude is independent of any situation, circumstance, person, or experience. When you connect with this true inner joy, you feel bliss for no reason—simply being alive to gaze at the stars, appreciating the miracle of life itself, brings you happiness.

---

[37] Used by permission of Deepak Chopra: https://chopra.com/app and www.DeepakChopra.com.

"To feel gratitude, consider all the wonderful gifts you enjoy in your life—nurturing loving relationships, connections you have with very special beings, the miracle of your body and fertile mind, and material comforts. Appreciating your life in this manner sweeps away any thought of lack or limitation and reminds you of the positive things that surround you. You realize that everything you experience is a gift.

"As you move into that place of gratitude, notice the warmth, love, compassion, and sense of connection that enters your heart. Find peace in knowing that there is a divine plan moving you forward on your evolutionary path. Realize the seed of goodness in every situation, and embrace each moment of your life as an opportunity to evolve into a more loving and thankful being.

"Think of the many things in your life that you appreciate. Taking stock of your life's many gifts and expressing gratitude will clear the way for even greater abundance in your life. By giving thanks for all that you have, and committing to live your life in deep appreciation, abundance is certain to flow to you. That is the attractive power of gratitude.

"As we prepare for today's meditation, bring your attention to your heart and consider our centering thought: *Today, I remember to be grateful. Today, I remember to be grateful.*

"Now let's begin. Please find a comfortable position, placing your hands lightly in your lap, palms upward, and closing your eyes. In this moment, go within to that place of inner quiet where we experience our connection to the higher self [Personal Consciousness]. Let go of all thoughts, and begin to observe the inflow and outflow of your breath. With each inhalation and exhalation, allow yourself to become more relaxed, more comfortable, more at peace.

"Keeping your attention in your heart, gently introduce the mantra, repeating it mentally, and allowing it to flow with effortless ease: *Om Vardhanam Nama, Om Vardhanam Nama—I nourish the universe and the universe nourishes me. Om Vardhanam Nama.* Whenever you find yourself distracted by thoughts, sensations in your body, or noises in the environment, simply return your attention to mentally repeating the mantra: *Om Vardhanam Nama, Om Vardhanam Nama.*

"Please continue with your meditation, I'll mind the time, and at the end you'll hear me ring a soft bell to indicate it's time to release the mantra: *Om Vardhanam Nama, Om Vardhanam Nama.*"

[5 minutes of silent meditation]

"It's time to release the mantra. Please bring your awareness back into your body. Take a moment to rest, inhaling and exhaling slowly and deeply. When you feel ready, gently open your eyes.

"As you continue with your day, carry this deep sense of gratitude with you, reminding yourself of our centering thought for today: *Today, I remember to be grateful. Today, I remember to be grateful. Today, I remember to be grateful.*"

Namaste.

Day 19: Love
Introductory Thoughts

"An Indian sage, Nisargadatta Maharaj, said to his followers, 'Life is love and love is life. What keeps the body together but love. What is desire but love of the self. And what is knowledge but love of truth. The means and forms may be wrong but the motive behind them is always love. Love of the 'me' and the 'my.'

"The 'me' and the 'my' may be small or may explode and embrace the whole universe. But love remains. Love is the most powerful force in the universe. It can heal, inspire, and bring us closer to the higher self.

"Love is an eternal, never-ending gift to ourselves and others. And when we truly experience love, we find ourselves. Like a tiny spark that ignites a blaze that can consume a vast forest, a spark of love is all that it takes to experience love's full force in all its aspects—earthly and divine.

"The practice of living love exemplifies the unlimited abundance of the universe. No matter how many people you love—yourself, your family, colleagues, the world—you can never run out because at the core of your being, you are pure love.

"In ancient India, the ecstasy of love was called *Ananda*, or bliss-consciousness. The ancient seers held that humans are meant to partake of this Ananda at all times. Living our lives with love at all times helps us realize our spirit's true nature: *Sat, Chit, Ananda— Existence, Consciousness, Bliss*. Living from love attracts more goodness to you. Therefore, to experience true abundance in your life, live the love that you were created to be. The love that you are. And watch your life flourish in all ways.

"Practice living love today by simply offering a kind word or thought to everyone you meet, recognizing that the greatest gift you can give to anyone is love.

"As we prepare for today's meditation, let's focus on today's centering thought: *Today, I remember to love everything and everyone I come in contact with. Today, I remember to love everything and everyone I come in contact with.*

"Now let's begin. Please find a comfortable position, placing your hands lightly in your lap, palms upward, and closing your eyes. In this moment, go within to that place of inner quiet where we experience our connection to the higher self [Personal Consciousness]. Let go of all thoughts, and begin to observe the inflow and outflow of your breath. With each inhalation and exhalation, allow yourself to become more relaxed, more comfortable, more at peace.

"Keeping your attention in your heart, gently introduce the mantra, repeating it mentally, and allowing it to flow with effortless ease: *Sat, Chit, Ananda. Sat, Chit, Ananda—Existence, Consciousness, Bliss— Sat, Chit, Ananda*. Whenever you find yourself distracted by thoughts, sensations in your body, or noises in the environment, simply return your attention to mentally repeating the mantra: *Sat, Chit, Ananda*.

"Please continue with your meditation, I'll mind the time, and at the end you'll hear me ring a soft bell to indicate it's time to release the mantra: *Sat, Chit, Ananda. Sat, Chit, Ananda.*"

[5 minutes of silent meditation]

"It's time to release the mantra. Please bring your awareness back into your body. Take a moment to rest, inhaling and exhaling slowly and deeply. When you feel ready, gently open your eyes.

"As you continue with your day, carry the sense of living love with you, reminding yourself of today's centering thought: *Today, I remember to love everything and everyone I come in contact with. Today, I remember to love everything and everyone I come in contact with. Today, I remember to love everything and everyone I come in contact with.*

Namaste.

SYNOPSES OF BOOKS ONE AND TWO

BOOK ONE
I Can See Clearly: Rise of a Supernatural Hero

Genre: Action/Adventure (Espionage)

Tagline: Luc Ponti had to die to get a life.

Logline: When star athlete Luc Ponti dies and "returns" with superpowers, his future is profoundly changed—and so is the world.

Overview

Set in the current day, *I Can See Clearly: Rise of a Supernatural Hero* is Book One of *The Luc Ponti Chronicles*. It draws on increasing tensions between the US, China, Russia, and North Korea; and demonstrates the unique capabilities of paranormal superpowers, particularly psychic spying. In this action/adventure, three teenagers from Palo Alto, California, each (on separate occasions) survive a remarkable near-death experience (NDE). And each with their own personal challenges, they "return" with unique superpowers.

The capabilities of one of the teens, Luc Ponti, come to the attention of the CIA; and an agent blackmails him to work secretly for the Agency on a dangerous espionage mission involving Russia, China, and North Korea. The three teens bond as a team under Luc's leadership and uncover more than the CIA could have imagined, including a high-level Russian double agent within the Agency's ranks. This puts not only the US, but also the entire world, in unthinkable danger.

The three protagonists, Luc Ponti (a Sicilian American), Isabella Moreno (a Columbian American), and Eric Evans (a biracial American), form the Super Paranormal Intelligence (SPI) Team. The *Chronicles* follow the team through Books One, Two, and Three as they proceed into adulthood and save the world from existential dangers—for example, climate change, pandemics, and nuclear devastation—while building their own lives in science and technology.

Within the *Chronicles* series, an important role is played by a most unusual and wise Buddhist monk—the SPI Team's *consigliere*, or counselor. Throughout the narrative of these novels, he advises the team on how to access and use the powers of their Cosmic Consciousness against the enemy, as well as how to use them to discover the Meaning of Life and manage their Life Purpose.

This multipart saga will be of keen interest not only to readers who seek entertainment through action and adventure set in foreign intrigue and espionage, but also to those interested in how increased consciousness can lead to mystical powers and a sustainable humanity —one means to save us from ourselves.

Theme: Life Purpose Conquers Duplicity
January 1, 2018: Population of Earth: 7.5 billion

The future of global security hangs on one young man finding and following a Life Purpose he has yet to discover. Cast throughout a narrative of espionage and foreign intrigue, *I Can See Clearly* is about immense power—hiding in plain sight. Understanding the Meaning of Life and finding and pursuing one's Life Purpose is not only *the* path to personal fulfillment but creates inspirational leaders who can help manifest a sustainable future. We're all in this together—and connected in ways we could never have imagined.

I Can See Clearly is a fusion of deep-state espionage, science, technology, and politics, experienced through the eyes of a brilliant teenage athlete who is gifted with superpowers. He is seeking the Meaning of Life and his Life Purpose while being challenged by certain CIA operatives who have blackmailed him in order to access his amazing acumen.

Synopsis

JANUARY 13, 2018–JANUARY 25, 2020—PALO ALTO, CALIFORNIA

As this adventure begins in Book One, we meet Luc Ponti, a gifted 16-year-old, 6'7" basketball player who is on the Palo Alto (California) High School (Paly) Vikings team. Since he excels in both academics and sports, his intent is to win a full scholarship to a university, major in engineering, play first-string basketball for their varsity team, and possibly go pro after graduation. That is the extent of his goal setting— and as far as Luc is concerned, nothing is going to interfere with his dream.

Luc is a bright student, proud of the Sicilian heritage he inherited from his mom and dad, both of whom are second-generation Sicilian Americans, and both with parents who emigrated to the United States from the same village in Sicily: Cammarata. Luc learned to speak Italian (Sicilian dialect) as a youngster, and mastered the language's profanity from his paternal grandfather, who moved in with the Pontis for a couple of years after his wife died.

As a young boy, using his natural charisma and the melodic sound of the Sicilian romance language, Luc developed the amusing trait of cussing out non-Italian speakers who gave him grief. They couldn't understand his Sicilian profanity, so he was able to use this "skill" on teachers, basketball referees, and players on opposing teams.

Luc went through grammar school, and now high school, with his best friend, Isabella (Bella) Moreno, a beautiful young girl whose parents had fled the criminal environment created by drug lords in their native Colombia and then settled in Silicon Valley. Bella is tough, incisive, and academically astute. Over the past few years, Luc developed complex feelings for her. Is she his best friend, girlfriend, or both?

Luc's mother, Valentina, was born in San Francisco and received a PhD in psychology from the University of Chicago. She's a brilliant scholar, a professor at Stanford University, and a dedicated mother to Luc and his 12-year-old sister, Laura. Ironically, because of early-childhood and marital issues, Valentina has been dealing with a modest bout of obsessive-compulsive disorder (OCD).

Luc's father, Carlo, was born and raised in a tough section of Newark, New Jersey. He was an all-state basketball star for Newark's

St. Benedict's Prep school and an NCAA star for Princeton University, which he attended on a full scholarship. He was pursued by top teams and offered a chance to go pro, but instead decided to pursue his ROTC training at Princeton and become a first lieutenant leading a top-secret Special Forces unit that reported directly to the CIA during the Desert Storm conflict in Iraq. He was seriously wounded and returned home suffering from post-traumatic stress disorder (PTSD).

Carlo met Valentina at the University of Chicago, where he received his MBA, and he's now a successful executive at Bank of America. His PTSD manifests itself in a frictional relationship with Valentina, exacerbated by her OCD, and also by his intense military bearing with respect to Luc. This behavior creates a love-hate relationship between father and son. His psychological infirmity also threatens the Ponti marriage because of his refusal to admit to the seriousness of the issue and seek help from the Veterans Administration (VA). Carlo attends many of Luc's games and often aggressively offers game strategies to Hank Ralston, the Paly basketball coach. Luc deeply resents the fact that his father meddles in his affairs.

I Can See Clearly opens with a tie-breaker game, which Luc wins for Paly in the last few seconds, using a strategy different from that mandated by his coach—and his father. Regardless of the win, typically by-the-books Carlo is angry at Luc for not "following orders." Luc is injured by a player from the opposing team while taking this last shot and is rushed to Stanford University Hospital with a burst appendix, which results in a serious case of peritonitis and sepsis.

Luc "dies" in the hospital for several minutes, and before resuscitation has an NDE during which he meets the Great White Light, as well as his deceased maternal grandfather, who passed on a special message to deliver to Luc's mother, Val. It ultimately has a far-reaching impact on her.

A few days after the NDE, as he is recovering in the hospital, Luc begins to realize that he possesses several "superpowers"—one of which is his ability to create—at will—out-of-body experiences (OBEs) in which he can rapidly move his consciousness literally anywhere with an amazing capability to observe people and events secretly, and accurately mentally record his observations in great detail. His memory skills also increase beyond belief. They are now *hyperthymesic*—meaning that images and written information can be stored as if they're contained in a supercomputer and can be subsequently recalled at will in accurate detail.

At first, Luc sees OBEs as an entertaining new aspect of his life, but soon he has great concerns. The powers are not only increasing in intensity, but there are no indications that they will subside. What will this do to the dream he's mapped out for his future? This certainly wasn't part of his plan.

When Dr. Anthony Farkas, the Ponti family physician, learns about Luc's paranormal capabilities, he puts Luc in touch with Dr. Hampton Ross, a Stanford research psychiatrist. Ross, a world authority on human consciousness, carries out some tests on Luc and is both amazed and baffled by the results. Ross's research, funded by the CIA, focuses on developing ways to use OBEs for safe "psychic spying"—the ability to send an individual's consciousness to spy safely and undetected by the enemy.

When Ross leaks Luc's capabilities to his contact at the CIA, Luc is approached by Major John Dallant, who works for the Agency and reports to Tamara Carlin, the director of the CIA's Covert Intelligence Unit. Seeing that Luc could be a valuable psychic spy, Tamara develops an effective scheme to blackmail Luc into working for the CIA. She convinces him that his father had been involved in a serious top-secret incident during his deployment in Iraq, which, if publicly revealed, would destroy his dad's career, and likely the Ponti family as well. Tamara sweetens her deal by offering Luc a huge "consulting" fee.

While working part-time for the CIA without his parents' knowledge, and during a series of OBEs, Luc uncovers incredibly valuable top-secret information on nuclear installations in China and North Korea.

Stressed out by what Luc is doing, Bella, Luc's confidante, convinces him to attend a lecture on consciousness being given by Pham Tuan, a world-famous Buddhist monk and scholar. She thinks that Tuan's insight on consciousness might help Luc understand what is happening to him. Luc is captivated by what he learns at the lecture and by Tuan's down-to-earth personality. He meets personally with Tuan (nicknamed Thay—pronounced *tie*, which means "teacher" in Vietnamese).

Thay is no ordinary monk. He was born in the Bronx to educated Vietnamese parents who collected important intelligence for the US during the Vietnam War. They were rewarded with American citizenship. During his early teens, when Thay got in trouble with a neighborhood gang, his parents sent him, against his will, to a Nepal monastery for his education. A harrowing climbing incident changed Thay's life and drove him toward enlightenment.

These days, he's quite a character, as well as a highly accomplished monk. He speaks with a disarmingly heavy Bronx accent; received degrees in theology and physics from Harvard, where he graduated *summa cum laude*; is a master chess player; is a high-level black-belt master in tae kwon do; plays video games on his iPhone to increase his focus; is a world leader in the peace movement; and is an expert on the science of consciousness.

Thay becomes Luc's *consigliere*—his trusted adviser. He teaches Luc how to use his powers and determines that Luc is an *Avatar*—or incarnation of an exalted deity, who emerged in this world to help correct the evolutionary path of global Collective Consciousness toward Unity Consciousness. During one of the deep meditations initiated by Thay, Luc learns of his challenging Life Purpose from the Great White Light (Cosmic Consciousness) and is instructed not to be afraid, as he would meet "The Two," who would aid him on his path to correct the evolutionary path of humanity's Collective Consciousness.

Because of Bella's influence on Luc, Tamara attempts to have her eliminated via a hit-and-run auto "accident." Bella survives, but she also has an NDE and develops superpowers. Her most significant power is being able to use gravitational forces to deflect or attract massive objects. She is one of The Two.

The other individual in the pair is Eric Evans, a (formerly) wiseass punk from the other side of the tracks. Along with an accomplice, Eric tries to steal Luc's and Bella's bikes as they return home from a hike. While Luc is held tightly by Eric's muscle-bound partner in crime, Eric attempts to kiss Bella. In his deep rage, Luc unwittingly discovers another of his powers: he is able to (unintentionally) summon up a lightning bolt, which shoots out from his arm and hits Eric. It electrocutes and "kills" him, but at that moment, Luc discovers *another* superpower—hands-on healing. He unwittingly revives Eric as he and Bella begin to administer CPR.

While in his near-death state, Eric also has a life-changing NDE and develops superpowers. He can, at a distance, turn electrical devices on or off. He can also create lightning strikes, as Luc had done when he "killed" him. Luc learns of Eric's superpowers when he visits him in the hospital. Eric is now a completely different person and decides to team up with Luc and Bella. Together, the three form the Super Paranormal Intelligence (SPI) Team. Bella becomes known as Gravitas, Eric as Electer, and Luc as Emperius, their leader.

Using his superpowers, Luc determines from one of his father's army buddies that his dad wasn't responsible for the incident in Iraq that Tamara had used as blackmail. Merging their collective powers, the SPI Team brings down Tamara in a dramatic turn of events. The SPI Team's efforts not only helped the US, but what they accomplished also had incalculable value for global nuclear security.

When Luc's father learns that he wasn't responsible for the incident that had haunted him since his discharge from the Iraq War, he seeks help at the VA, and his relationship with Val and Luc begins to move in a positive direction.

All ends well for the Ponti family, the SPI Team, and Thay. The three SPI Team members are now on a path destined to take them to top colleges on the East Coast to pursue their respective careers. Most important, they agree to work together, using their superpowers to address worthwhile challenges that any of them might uncover. They are committed to making a positive impact on the evolution of global Unity Consciousness.

An important lesson for Luc concerns something that had haunted him until he finally accepted the apparent permanence of his superpowers—that using these powers as a member of the SPI Team to help the greater common good in the world is not incompatible with his original dream and Life Purpose. But no one's life in this world exists on a permanent high from birth until death. Otherwise, there would be no ability to learn, and no possibility for continuous evolution toward Unity Consciousness. And so it was with Luc and the SPI Team.

A call to his cell phone while he, his family, and friends are celebrating a wonderful end to a challenging year, changes everything. Luc and the SPI Team have their next opportunity to contribute to the greater common good.

A dark shadow had lifted itself from the dregs of their espionage encounters with Russia, China, and North Korea—all of which had been perpetrated upon them through deceit and trickery by Tamara Carlin. This shadow was initiated by a horrific event, set in motion by the Russian operative code-named Seagull. He had raised his head from years of stealth obscurity with an unacceptable intent—to control the world.

And so begins . . . Book Two.

BOOK TWO
Seagull's Revenge: Beyond Fear

Tagline: Can one man control all of humanity?
Logline: The perils of a genius out of control.

Synopsis

Luc Ponti's SPI Team, family, and friends are celebrating the downfall of Tamara Carlin, head of the CIA's Covert Intelligence Unit, after they exposed her as a double agent who was about to provide Russia with top-secret data that would have put the US and the rest of the world at terrible risk. Luc reflects upon the fact, with a deep sense of sincere gratitude, that his life has never been in such a positive place as it is in this moment.

His joyous reverie is interrupted by a call from the CIA's Major John Dallant. Luc's spirit does a rapid 180, as Dallant had promised Luc that he would never bother the team again. He tells Luc that a threat has arisen that has profound global consequences and cannot be addressed by any other force but the SPI Team.

Luc is deeply disturbed, and in a moment of desperation asks the Great White Light what It wants from him. He hears a voice within his mind that tells him that he must listen to what Dallant has to say, so Luc reluctantly agrees to meet with the major.

Luc's first impression of Major Dallant is that he looks terrible—he's lost weight and is obviously beyond sleep deprivation. This is not the physically and emotionally strong man that Luc worked with only months before. Dallant tells Luc that he will not coerce him and his team to work on this mission, as Tamara did through her blackmail methods. He assures Luc that when he hears the full story, he will *want* to help. Major Dallant is so confident of this that he had Anthony Stefano, the director of the CIA, reinstate Luc and the SPI Team with top-secret security clearance.

Major Dallant tells Luc that ten days ago the CIA learned from its highest-level covert asset in Moscow about a chilling event that recently occurred in Russia—one with significant global implications. So that Luc can appreciate the gravity of the situation, Dallant provides the necessary background.

About 70 years ago, Nikita Khrushchev, head of the Soviet Union, created within what was then the KGB a deep-state segment called *Akademiya Sverkhsposobnostey*—in English, the Academy of Superpowers, or the ASP. It now thrives within the KGB's successor, *Federal'naya sluzhba bezopasnosti Rossiyskoy Federatsii*, the FSB, although Russia has never acknowledged its existence. Its long-term mission is to create superspies with physical, intelligence, and psychological capabilities not seen in the best operatives.

The Russian strategy starts by using two techniques to produce genetically enriched designer babies. The first is via the union of two highly intellectual and athletically gifted parents. However, given the advances in molecular genetics and gene editing, such as CRISPR, their focus is now on the second approach, which uses the power of modern molecular biology to create babies with superspy potential.

During the first year of its life, if a baby is identified as a likely candidate, it is placed on one of two possible paths. The first is within the ASP's Russian Academy, a rigorous school—if it can be called that—which operates 365 days a year. All "students" are quarantined permanently away from their biological parents, who are simply tools for the "manufacture" of babies who can eventually be bred into superspies using special indoctrination techniques. Depending on their innate capabilities, the duration of training is 12 to 15 years. About 20 percent of the trainees successfully complete the entire regimen. The majority of the rest become broken individuals—some commit suicide or end up in institutions for the mentally deranged—not a pleasant outcome for these candidates.

The second path secretly embeds the genetically enriched baby within the US under the tutelage of respectable, educated "parents," who themselves are highly skilled and accomplished Russian agents. They're almost always Americans, who, whether for money and/or because of dissatisfaction with American ideals, values, and politics, have decided to commit to Communism—the Russian way.

Besides being highly adept spies, these parents are skilled "teachers," and starting at an early age, they carefully and effectively begin a psychological indoctrination process of the child with the key elements and values of Russian political history, philosophy, and espionage. It's done so seamlessly that the child, already gifted with both a stratospheric IQ and emotional quotient (EQ), develops a keen sense of what to say and not say in the presence of outsiders, such as neighbors or friends.

At this point, Luc wonders why Major Dallant is providing all of this interesting but seemingly unnecessary background information. He asks *the* key question: "Has the CIA been able to uncover any of these parents and superspy children?" Dallant's answer says it all: "One of the most outstanding products of this Russian machine was Tamara Carlin."

Luc is shocked by what he's just learned, even more so after Dallant helps him connect more dots in this nightmare. Tamara was the daughter of Dr. Sergei Karlovich, a high-level Russian FSB operative code-named *Seagull,* the same name Luc found in Tamara's safe at her home when he discovered she was a Russian double agent. Seagull, a boyhood friend of President Putin and head of the ASP—is Tamara Carlin's biological father. He seeks violent revenge for what Major Dallant and the SPI Team did to her.

Luc also learns that Seagull is a brilliant biophysicist and electrical engineer—a savant with an IQ over 250 who's fluent in seven languages. But more to the point, he's a vicious killer known to have masterminded a number of attempted assassinations on Russian traitors, such as Sergei Skripal in the UK, and more recently, Alexei Navalny. Karlovich's code name stems from his passion and success in having developed a means to train seagulls—a most difficult undertaking—to deliver messages. The result is not unlike the task of training homing pigeons, but with the capability of doing much more over much longer distances and under incredibly challenging conditions.

Major Dallant then connects the last two dots, which leaves Luc with no choice but to help him, and with the deepest motivation to do so. The major received a message via a seagull that disclosed a threat to his *own* family as well as the SPI Team and *their* families.

True to this threat, Major Dallant's parents are brutally murdered at their retirement cottage. The police find his mother's body lying in a large pool of blood. She's been stabbed more than 20 times—by his father! His dad's throat was slit—by his own hand! Baffled beyond disbelief, the police can't understand how or why this had happened. Major Dallant's parents were well-respected pillars of their community with a long and loving marriage. Nothing made sense about these brutal murders.

Major Dallant, mentally and physically exhausted by what he'd just disclosed to Luc, provides the obvious postscript: "As you can see, this is up close and personal. This isn't just a case of where does it leave me? It's also a case of where it leaves you, the SPI Team, and your families."

It is a no-brainer for Luc to get Bella's and Eric's commitment. They, like Luc and Major Dallant, fear not just for their own lives, but even more so for the lives of their families. It is also clear that the first line of attack is to engage in an OBE to Russia and somehow connect with Seagull to learn by what means the murders of Major Dallant's parents had occurred.

The perfect opportunity presents itself. Seagull has a one-hour meeting with President Putin on the first Monday of every month at his office in the Kremlin. The purpose is to review critical issues within the ASP and for Seagull to have an opportunity to express any concerns he has on specifics within the FSB. Even though the FSB is headed by the highly capable Alexander Bortnikov, who provides monthly reports to Putin, because of Seagull's lifelong friendship with Putin, he serves as his unstated "eyes and ears" within that intelligence organization.

Major Dallant provides architectural details for Luc's OBE to Putin's office for his monthly meeting with Seagull. At the meeting, Seagull expresses his deep anger, disdain, and intended revenge for the CIA/SPI Team. Putin, a man always in total control, is disturbed by Seagull's unusually intense and uncontrolled behavior. He tries to calm him down with comments on why Tamara chose to risk death, but all Putin sees in Seagull is a vitriolic urge to retaliate. Putin reminds Seagull what he and his wife, Mariya, did 30 years ago when they voluntarily put Tamara into the ASP program within the US.

Putin finally calms Seagull down somewhat and convinces him to try to regain his emotional balance by attending to the birds at his cottage-laboratory outside of Moscow, and to visit Mariya at her lab in the Novosibirsk research center. Seagull tells Putin that Mariya, who's in charge of a small group developing nonnuclear tactical weapons, has made some interesting progress.

Putin is intrigued. He reflects on Mariya's discoveries over the recent past and notes that they were the result of her "pet" projects, none of which were intended to result in weapons. He recalls, for example, that she discovered an electromagnetic field (EMF) device that can be tuned to destroy nearly any known virus, in situ within a human being or animal's bloodstream. This technology also led to the development of a micro-battery-powered surgical mask that instantly, upon contact, annihilates most viruses, bacteria, and fungi.

Putin tells Seagull that although he's more than impressed with Mariya's discoveries, perhaps she's more interested in discovering and developing technology that can improve the human condition, rather than destroying it with weapons.

Seagull vehemently disagrees and begins to disclose the technology that underpins a new weapon. Ironically, the idea stemmed from Mariya's work on the antiviral technology. It's based on a specific EMF signature in the microwave region of the electromagnetic spectrum. Putin asks if it's similar to the technology Mariya previously developed that led to the device the Russians first tested in Havana, which resulted in physical and emotional issues for a number of American and Canadian diplomats—now known as the Havana Syndrome. Indeed, it is. Seagull is impressed with Putin's memory for technical details. After all, Putin was merely a history major during his university schooling.

Seagull discloses that Mariya discovered a means to create an unusual combination of electromagnetic waves at different frequencies, which selectively affect the functioning of the amygdala and hypothalamus components of the brain—areas responsible for fear and the flight-or-fight aggression response in animals and humans. Putin asks what type of proof-of-principle there is as far as the effectiveness of the device.

Seagull begins to gloat like a mad scientist who's just made a huge discovery. He tells Putin that when the EMF rays were focused on a female chimp in her cage with her newborn, she became violent, ripped the infant's limbs and head from its torso, and then smashed her own head against the bars of the cage until she, too, was dead: animal suicide at its worst.

Luc is horrified by what he's heard, and even Putin was aghast at what Seagull described. He points out to Seagull that the use of these rays in military actions would be considered a weapon of mass destruction, and this technology could easily fall into the wrong hands—that is, those of terrorists. Putin tells Seagull that such a weapon would be considered worse than chemical and biological neurotoxins and would ostracize Russia from the global international community and increase sanctions, which would impact their global trade and economy. Furthermore, this does not support Putin's long-term strategy, which as Seagull well knows, is global acceptance, admiration, and respect as a major player in the world.

Seagull can't believe what he's heard. He tells Putin that he's confident that this technology could be used with surgical accuracy from a plane, and with further development, from a satellite. He stresses that there would be no need to kill the enemy—they would kill each other! Luc silently exclaims, *Oh my God!*

Putin isn't happy about Seagull's crazy, violent, over-the-top behavior. He's never seen this in him before. Quite the contrary—he's always been disciplined and carefully analytical and calculating—always with Russia's best interest in mind. Putin convinces Seagull to go to Novosibirsk as soon as possible to be with Mariya after the loss of their daughter.

As soon as Seagull leaves the meeting, Putin calls Alexander Bortnikov, the head of the FSB, and tells him that he has a high-level person
he wants him, personally, to follow for the next few weeks.

Luc returns to Palo Alto, calls Major Dallant, and arranges a video
meeting with him to discuss how to proceed. They need scientific advice on how to unravel the weapon's technology and determine what to
do in the meantime to protect them and their families. Luc is sure that
Thay can help, but he isn't on Major Dallant's radar.

The major agrees to the participation of the SPI Team and Stanford
University psychiatrist Dr. Hampton Ross, who has top-secret security
clearance and has worked with the team previously. He isn't keen on
having Thay present since he doesn't have security clearance. But when
Luc tells him of the helpful advice Thay provided during the previous
mission, and also how he and Thay managed to avert the terrorist destruction of the Taglyan Center in Los Angeles and several hundred
high-level attendees during last year's international peace conference,
Dallant is more than impressed and decides to grant Thay top-secret
status, as he did for Bella and Eric.

Both Thay and Ross believe that the weapons technology probably
uses a microwave approach similar to that used by the Russians for
the Havana Syndrome—but with stronger, different frequencies, and
surgically precise in delivery to its target. They speculate that the microwaves are likely pulsed and modified in a novel manner known as
intermodulation distortion (IMD).

Thay suggests that in the short term, one possible means to avoid
what happened to Major Dallant's parents is the use of a Faraday
cage—enveloping a small space with electrically conducting metal that
prevents microwaves from penetrating that space. It does so by dissi-
pating the microwaves as a surface electrical current, which heats the
metal and radiates away the energy.

They believe that since the microwaves are likely delivered remotely from some kind of vehicle, safety might be achieved in a car with
its windows fitted inside the vehicle with plastic panels wrapped with
heavy-duty aluminum foil. So that the SPI Team can convince their
families to keep a car in their garage with the panels in place, Dallant
creates a story—which he sends via the Palo Alto police—to all local

newspapers. It describes an international group of thieves who remotely disable their intended victims with microwaves shot from a van, and then help themselves to anything within the victims' homes.

A few days later, the SPI Team is having breakfast together when Bella receives a call from her mother, who asks if she's expecting a delivery. Bella's mom says that there's a van sitting in front of her home. Taking no chances, the team dashes to Bella's home, which, fortunately, is just five minutes away at the speed that Eric drives. On their way, Luc calls two CIA agents whom Major Dallant stationed in Palo Alto and are available 24-7 for backup to the SPI Team.

The SPI Team arrives at Bella's home, and Eric drives slowly past the van. He passes it and returns for another look. The team spots a small antenna-like device beginning to eject from the side of the van facing Bella's house. Eric slams on the brakes, jumps out of the car, aims his right hand at the antenna, and sends a huge bolt of lightning directly at the antenna. A small explosion occurs inside the van, and black smoke pours out of its rear doors, which are blown open. A disoriented guy jumps out and begins to limp away. Bella shoots a weak gravity pulse at him, and his body flies about ten feet before falling to the curb.

Just then, the two CIA agents arrive. One puts ties on the guy's arms and legs and throws him into the back of the van, hops into the driver's seat, and off he goes. The other guy follows him in their car. The Russian agent ingests a well-hidden kill-pill and dies nearly immediately, so the CIA agents are unable to interrogate him.

Unfortunately, Eric's electrokinesis bolt is so strong that it completely destroys the weapon and its onboard computer. Reverse engineering is not a possibility. However, Major Dallant, the SPI Team, and their families are probably safe for a while, since it's unlikely that there's another weapon in the US, and it will take Seagull some time to smuggle one into the country. The only tactic left to deal with this issue is if Luc does an OBE in Novosibirsk.

Seagull continues to plot a most horrible fate for each of the members of the SPI Team, especially Luc. To this end, he sends 19-year-old Sophia Stepanova ostensibly to attend a conference on quantum entanglement at Stanford University and, while in Palo Alto, to make her way to Luc—an easy task in this small community, given Luc's usual whereabouts. Seagull wants Sophia to meet and charm him. Unbeknownst to her, he has in mind that she will play an important role in his plan for Luc's demise.

Sophia is a recent graduate of the ASP program and one of its most gifted "graduates"—ever. The last person of such high caliber was Tamara Carlin. Sophia has no idea that she's Tamara's half sister, inadvertently and secretly fathered by Seagull with his longtime assistant, Galina Stepanova, and placed in the ASP program shortly after birth. Sophia has nearly no relationship with Galina, who feels she was an unexpected inconvenience. Also, Sophia was told that her father was killed in a plane crash shortly after her birth.

Sophia is a beautiful, brilliant savant with a personality that could charm anyone; she can go toe-to-toe with the absolute best and still come out ahead. She's a superspy eager to gain experience in the field.

With intel from a local Russian agent, Sophia learns that Luc will be having breakfast at the Peninsula Creamery at a certain time of day. She introduces herself to him under the pretense that since this is her first visit to California, she wants to meet some of the locals to learn about the area and their culture. With her looks, personality, and over-the-top IQ, there's no problem getting Luc's attention and exciting his male hormones. She convinces him to have dinner with her.

At dinner, Luc tries to get to know more about Sophia. She tells him that she graduated from a private international school in New York City, where she lives with her parents, and is now attending Cambridge University, majoring in physics. Luc is astounded by her smarts, personality, and, of course, her beauty. But during their conversation, there are several facts about Manhattan that Sophia stumbles over and does her best to cover up. It's starting to dawn on Luc that something is amiss.

Operating as an agent spying on a designated individual wasn't something that Alexander Bortnikov had done for many years. That's not the job of the director of the world's largest intelligence agency. But this was a special and delicate situation, and what the president requests must be delivered without hesitation.

Bortnikov arrived at Moscow's Domodedovo Airport only to find out that Seagull had changed his itinerary to Novosibirsk without telling a soul. He canceled his commercial flight, leased a private jet, hauling a small crate with him, and flew instead to Tiksi, a small and remote village about 4,000 kilometers northeast of Moscow in the Republic of Sakha in the far eastern part of Russia. It is said to be the farthest-north human settlement in the world.

Bortnikov is more than perplexed. He takes a private jet to Tiksi, and when he lands, the airport director tells him that Karlovich commandeered an old Yak-112 prop plane and that he attached a device beneath it. He told the director that it was a special camera, and that he was conducting a top-secret geological survey. He also told the director that he was to say nothing to anyone about his flight. He tells Bortnikov that Seagull filed a flight plan to leave for Novosibirsk upon his return to Tiksi.

Bortnikov instructs the director to call him as soon as Seagull has wheels up for Novosibirsk. He files a flight plan to follow Seagull shortly thereafter. A couple of hours later, Bortnikov receives a call from the airport director. When Bortnikov arrives at Tiksi Airport, the director matter-of-factly asks him if he's heard about the horrible massacre that occurred just hours ago, not far from the airport, outside the village of Umka, in a small settlers' camp.

Bortnikov immediately cancels his flight and has his driver take him to the site of the massacre, only to discover the ghastliest scene he has ever encountered. Every person in the settlement, about 200 people—men, women, and children—was either viciously murdered by another member or has committed suicide. All animal life has been similarly decimated as well.

There was, however, one survivor—a thief who, immediately prior to the massacre, had stolen a rifle from one of the huts and was hiding in a metal shack on a hill overlooking the settlement. He was so horrified by what he saw from his perch that he surrendered himself to the local constable. He said the whole thing started after he saw a propellered plane flying back and forth about 300 feet over the settlement. Less than 30 minutes later, the massacre began.

Bortnikov calls President Putin, who is appalled by what Bortnikov describes. He tells Bortnikov to follow Seagull to Novosibirsk as planned, and that he has a special mission for him.

Luc makes his first OBE to Mariya Karlovich's laboratory in Novosibirsk. He finds only Mariya present. She's a fiftysomething, very thin and tall brunette with dark-brown eyes, hidden to some degree behind unfashionable black-rimmed glasses. Her skin has a faint greenish-yellow tint, she wears her hair in a ponytail, and she walks with a slight limp.

Seagull calls her and speaks with artificial warmth, apologizing for being delayed. She doesn't seem to care either way. Mariya has a lot on her mind—all due to the stress that her husband has brought into her life over the years—and it's getting worse.

Seagull reminds Mariya of the happy days that occurred after they'd completed their university studies, the two of them subsequently working as postdocs in Paris. It was then when they first learned about St. Valentine's Day. And back to the present, Seagull has arranged a Valentine's Day dinner for the next day—February 14—at Mariya's favorite restaurant in Novosibirsk. She's unimpressed, knowing that those days are gone forever.

After Mariya leaves the lab for the day, Luc picks the lock to her desk—finding nothing much except an envelope with a photo in it. Heartbreak again! It's Seagull passionately embracing and kissing his longtime assistant, Galina Stepanova, just outside their room in one of Moscow's most luxurious hotels. On the back of the photo is a message from Galina's brother, Leo, who took the photo. He hates Seagull for what he's done to his sister.

The next day, Mariya goes to the lab and awaits Seagull's arrival after he catches some sleep, having arrived in Novosibirsk during the early-morning hours. As she reviews some of her data, she can't understand why her husband doesn't see the huge potential in her discoveries for neurological diagnostics and treatment—and not as a weapon of mass destruction.

She's confident that having found a means to generate novel complex frequencies of electromagnetic wave patterns that induce violent behavior, the technology could also be used to generate complementary wave patterns that would diminish, perhaps even eliminate, violent behavior. She envisions mapping the electromagnetic wave frequencies generated by various parts of the brain in healthy individuals and then, using her proprietary digital format created through Fourier transform spectroscopy, she would mimic that exact pattern to treat mentally or emotionally challenged patients. In that mode of operation, she predicts that her discovery may not only eliminate violent behavior, but also possibly heal various neurologically based diseases such as depression, anxiety, OCD, autism, anorexia, and a host of other mental disorders.

Mariya thinks, *Why can't Sergei see this? What has happened to his thinking and objectivity? This would be a major plus for Russia with the international community and support Putin's long-term strategy to elevate Russia's global stature.*

As Luc is preparing for his next OBE at Mariya's laboratory, he receives a call from Bella, who ultimately convinces him to allow her to accompany him. It tuns out to be a plus, as she uses her feminine energy and intuition to help Luc understand some of Mariya's behavior.

Seagull arrives, and the show begins. He's exuberant about showing Mariya pictures of the Umka Massacre, and when he does, she's horrified, not just after viewing the photos and realizing what he's done, but especially due to his intense enthusiasm over the results of his actions. She is appalled, and so are Luc and Bella when they observe what this madman has perpetrated.

Seagull is disappointed by Mariya's reaction and can't understand why she doesn't see the great potential of this weapon. When she asks him what President Putin thinks about it, Seagull not only dismisses the president's cautious response as ridiculous but implies that maybe Russia needs a more effective leader. Mariya reminds him that such commentary and innuendo by almost anyone else would be good for at least ten years or more in a Siberian gulag.

Realizing he has overstepped his bounds, Seagull, now backpedaling, apologizes and tells Mariya he will discuss her work further with Putin and also consider the neurological applications of the technology. Of course, he is blatantly lying, as he has no intention of doing so.

Mariya's wheels are spinning, but focused on what? She can't take any more of this madness and despises what she sees in her husband. Something must be done to stop him.

She agrees to go to the Valentine's Day dinner that evening, but her mind, as tired as it may be, is in full gear planning her own strategy regarding how to deal with Seagull. She tells him that the next day, while he finishes a couple of meetings that he's scheduled in Novosibirsk, she'll work at the lab putting together some interesting data for him concerning improvements on the weapon's technology. She will then make a nice dinner for them that evening, and on the subsequent day, they can meet at the lab for her presentation and further discussions. Seagull is joyous over her proposal. He thinks, *She finally understands me!*

During their dinner, Mariya reflects on their first Valentine's Day dinner celebration in Paris. She wonders aloud, "What's become of us since then?" Seagull, a master at keeping doors closed to subjects he doesn't want to pursue at that moment, convinces Mariya to keep things light and merry and defer their discussion on challenging subjects to when he visits the lab. She reluctantly agrees.

They both drink a lot—too much. In his drunken state, Seagull discloses that he has an inoperable brain tumor. But he says, not to worry, he's being treated in Moscow with a new technology that's shrinking it. After her initial shock, Mariya reflects on how well she knows him. She's seen him cover his path with lies so many times before. He isn't well and won't be getting well. Now all is clear—his erratic behavior, his mood swings, his anger, and his insanely driven sense of vengeance.

Luc and Bella return to Palo Alto and meet with the entire team. It's clear that they must return to Novosibirsk for Mariya's presentation and technology update to Seagull. The only possible strategy to come out of the meeting is proposed by Thay and is based on the *Manifestation Sequence*—namely, deep meditation to elevate the SPI Team's consciousness, combined with the sequence: *Intention→Attention→Imagination→Belief→Detachment*. Practiced properly, this tool enables manifestation of literally anything by accessing the wisdom, guidance, and knowledge of the Akashic Field.[38] The only constraint is that the rules for manifestation must be accurately adhered to. Dr. Ross and Major Dallant are challenged by this mystical approach, but there's no other option on the table.

Bortnikov calls Putin and tells him what has happened near Umka. Putin is deeply disturbed, especially after seeing the photos of the massacre that Bortnikov sends to his phone. Bortnikov also reveals that Seagull has an inoperable brain tumor, and perhaps it's the reason for

---

[38]Akashic Field: A record of every thought, word, action, deed, and event that has ever occurred or will occur in the future. It is present in an ethereal plane, which is separate from, yet connected to, our three-dimensional universe. It holds the solutions to all problems and issues in our 3D world.

his extreme and erratic behavior. Bortnikov informs Putin that Mariya and Seagull are having a meeting at her lab the following day, ostensibly for Mariya to update him on the progress she's made on the weapon. He tells Putin that based on what he's heard and also because of Mariya's degree of stress, he feels that she may have another agenda—perhaps to convince him to pursue the possibilities of the technology for neurological diagnostics and treatment.

Eric and Bella join Luc for a team OBE at the meeting between Seagull and Mariya at her laboratory. Seagull arrives at noon with a surprise gourmet picnic lunch and two bottles of champagne. Mariya is more than pleasantly surprised, but also perplexed, almost feeling a level of guilt over her recent thoughts about her husband—but not for long.

Seagull opens the basket, and they begin to eat and drink . . . and drink some more. In short order, they're feeling no pain. Then, Seagull opens Pandora's Box. He asks Mariya what was bothering her at their Valentine's Day dinner. She says there's a long list, but three things have kept her up nights for longer than she can recall.

The first is his obsession over, and travels relating to, the ASP, as a result of which they have not lived as man and wife for years. The second is intimately related to the first and ignites Mariya's anger much beyond what she would have expected. Probably because it's the first time she's said it aloud. She tells him that she has known for more time than she cares to remember about his affair with his longtime assistant, Galina Stepanova.

Seagull feigns a deep apology and says that it's been over for years. This causes Mariya to shout at him in anger and burst into sobs, as she throws a recent photo of him kissing Galina outside their room at a luxury hotel in Moscow. He instantly goes from a false sense of contrition to vindictive anger. He wants to know who sent her this photo so he can cut off his balls and stuff them deep down his throat until he chokes to death. The madman from ASP is back—drunk and out of control.

As her husband's anger somewhat subsides, Mariya reveals the third "soul breaker," the final nail in their marriage coffin. She says she knows that Sophia Stepanova is his daughter. Seagull says nothing. He downs a full glass of champagne as if it were cold water on a blazing summer day—and then yet another. Mariya does the same until all of the champagne is gone. They wobble in their chairs, staring silently at each other, each with their own source of pain.

Finally, Mariya brings up the technology and learns that Seagull never discussed with Putin the possibility of its use in neuroscience health care. Seagull is hell-bent on destroying the Americans, if it's the last thing he does. And it probably will be. He discloses to Mariya that he's dying and has only several weeks left to live. He tells her that after he destroys the Americans, she and Putin can do whatever the hell they want with her technology. He'll be dead and gone.

Mariya removes a remote-control switch from her lab coat. She asks Seagull to observe the flashing green lights in each of the four corners of the lab. She tells him that they both have overplayed their stay in this world, and it's time to end that.

As if someone pushed the adrenaline "on" button in his hormonal system, Seagull appears to revert to his sober state, staring at Mariya with undisguised contempt. In a precise and rapid flash of movement, he smacks her across the face with one hand and simultaneously grabs the remote from her hand with the other. He curses vehemently and tells her that she deserves every terrible thing he's ever done. He's beyond out of control, and now there's no way back.

Eric moves quickly. He insists that Bella and Luc immediately leave the building—no time for debate—he has a plan that will absolutely work. Although they hesitate, they trust him, so they do as he asks.

A lifelong weight trainer, Eric activates his sense of touch and grabs both of Seagull's fisted hands, bending them back at the wrist joints until both wrists audibly break. Seagull screams in agony and uncontrollably releases the remote-control switch. It's quickly confiscated by Mariya, who precariously stands and backs away from the table. Eric immediately vacates the building. A few seconds later, the building is leveled by a massive, intense explosion and fireball that billows high into the sky. This is explosion technology in its most advanced state. The building and all of its contents are completely destroyed—disintegrated beyond recognition.

As the dust begins to settle, Eric joins Bella and Luc. In the distance, they see Bortnikov and another man, Ivan Zaitsev, a highly decorated Russia sniper, carrying a rifle, both running toward the decimated laboratory.

Bortnikov calls Putin to tell him what has happened, but he already knows. He reads Bortnikov a letter from Mariya that was delivered only minutes ago by courier. It describes in detail her plans for ending her and Seagull's lives. Bortnikov then informs the president that he's just learned from colleagues at the SVR, the Russian International Intelligence Agency, of phone calls that Seagull had made to Beijing during the past few weeks, which describe his upcoming meetings with high-level Chinese officials at their embassy in Moscow to negotiate his offer for them to purchase a new weapon. Putin and Bortnikov end their call with a huge sense of regret—and relief.

Fast-forward to the SPI Team, Thay, Dr. Ross, and Major Dallant at lunch celebrating the best of all possible outcomes to an incredibly challenging and disheartening mission. But their festivities are interrupted by a loud crowd in the parking lot of the restaurant. They venture out to see what's happening, and there, on the hood of Luc's red 1957 Chevy convertible, is a seagull standing at attention and staring hypnotically into the restaurant. Attached to its leg is a plastic capsule containing a message. The team is in shock as Major Dallant removes the message, and the seagull then takes flight.

Dallant gives the message to Luc, who slowly reads it aloud.

Dear Luc:

Sorry I missed saying goodbye to you before I left Palo Alto. I had some terribly challenging issues to deal with. But speaking of terrible, it's truly a shame what happened to my father and his wife—don't you think? I look forward to discussing this unfortunate tragedy with you when we next meet—soon. I'm counting on it.

Sincerely, Sophia

The team is stunned.

Luc thinks, *Oh Great White Light, what's next?*

And so begins . . . Book Three.

A Parting Thought

**As you continue on your life's journey, consider
this centering thought as your guide:**

*"As I elevate my Personal Consciousness, I do my best to
help heal the world."*

Namaste,

Acknowledgments

I was drawn to my concern for the emerging and chilling effects of climate change several decades ago by the tireless and excellent research by numerous astute scientists and engineers, despite the ridicule they often received from politicians, public figures, and less-competent scientists—many of the latter falling into the category of "climate-change deniers." I'm especially grateful to Dr. James Watson, whose research results supported his first testimony before the US Congress in 1988 when he warned us that we had better wake up to what's coming. We didn't.

In writing *Cosmic Contact* and weaving the predictions of climate-change research into a hopefully interesting sci-fi narrative, one of my goals has been to wake up as many individuals as possible who could make a difference in helping to lead humanity on the right path. As of this writing, we are nowhere near where we should be.

I also want to thank the input and arguments from those talented scientists who were dubious about the negative effects of climate change. Their commentary held up a mirror to my analyses and made me rethink my position and dig even deeper until there was no doubt in my mind as to what was happening to our world and what's coming.

I wish to thank my longtime friend Deepak Chopra, who, many decades ago, introduced me to the power and potential of elevated consciousness via deep meditation. My view is that if we had more *Consciousness Leadership* in the political and corporate sectors, we would not be facing the challenges of rapidly increasing climate change. Also, my appreciation to Deepak and his organization—www.Chopra.Com/App and www.DeepakChopra.Com—for giving me permission to present two of his meditations in Appendix II.

There have been many behind-the-scenes contributors, without whose help and commitment this book would never have happened—in particular, I would like to recognize two highly talented women:

Jill Kramer, who edited all three of the Luc Ponti novels; and Christy Salinas, who designed the interiors and covers for the three books. I'm also very grateful to Bill Gladstone, my literary agent and publisher, for his guidance and efforts during the publication process.

My three daughters, Doreen, Polly, and Julia, continue to be a source of inspiration; and my son-in-law, Joe Robert Cole, provided valuable commentary for the narrative in these novels and their possibilities as a source for other media.

None of my books would have seen the light of day had it not been for the valuable insight, understanding, and loving commitment of my wife, Inez.

It's been a marvelous experience to stand on the shoulders of these creative giants in their own right.

About the Author

James A. Cusumano (www.JamesCusumano.com) is the chairman and owner of Chateau Mcely (www.chateaumcely.cz/en/homepage), chosen in 2007 by the European Union as the only "Green" 5-star, castle hotel in Central Europe, and in 2008 by the World Travel Awards as the "World's Leading Green Hotel." Chateau Mcely offers programs that promote the principles of Inspired and Conscious Leadership, finding your Life Purpose, and Long-Term Fulfillment.

Jim began his career during the 1950s in the field of entertainment as a recording artist. Years later, after attaining a PhD in experimental quantum physics, business studies at Stanford University, and a stint as a Foreign Fellow of Churchill College at Cambridge University, he joined Exxon as a research scientist and later became their research director for Catalytic Science & Technology.

Jim subsequently cofounded two public companies in Silicon Valley: Catalytica Energy Systems, Inc., devoted to clean power generation; and Catalytica Pharmaceuticals, Inc., which manufactured drugs via environmentally benign, low-cost catalytic technologies. While he was chairman and CEO, Catalytica Pharmaceuticals grew in less than five years from several employees to more than 2,000, and was a more than $1 billion enterprise before being sold.

Subsequent to his work in Silicon Valley and before buying and renovating Chateau Mcely with his wife, Inez, Jim returned to entertainment and founded Chateau Wally Films (www.chateauwallyfilms.biz), which produced the feature film *What Matters Most* (2001: www.imdb.com/title/tt0266041), distributed in more than 50 countries. He is the author of a number of fiction and nonfiction books and lives in Prague with Inez and their daughter Julia.

Before you go . . .

Read more about Jim Cusumano and his books at:
www.JimTheAlchymist.com

If you enjoyed *Cosmic Contact,* please leave
a review on Amazon.

Made in the USA
Monee, IL
13 March 2024

54987029R00174